ROOTS OF CORRUPTION

ALSO BY LAURA LAAKSO

Fallible Justice

Echo Murder

ROOTS OF CORRUPTION

Laura Laakso

Wilde Investigations 3

2020
Louise Walters Books

Roots of Corruption
by Laura Laakso

Copyright © Laura Laakso 2020

A catalogue card for this book is available from the British Library.

Produced and published in 2020
by Louise Walters Books

ISBN 9781999630515
eISBN 9781999630522

Typeset in PTSerif 11pt by Blot Publishing

Printed and bound in Great Britain by Clays Ltd, Elcograf S.p.A.

louisewaltersbooks.co.uk

info@louisewaltersbooks.co.uk

Louise Walters Books
PO Box 755, Banbury, OX16 6PJ

In loving memory of my father and grandmother.
Every day, I hope to make you proud.

CONTENTS

Saturday

GLOSSARY

Roots of Corruption glossary and pronunciation guide

Aes Sídhe [eːsˠ ˈʃiːə] EES-FEE-E – Fey, literally People of the Mound

Bearn [bæɡrn] BAIRN – child

Blæstbearn [ˈblæːstbæɡrn] BLYERST-BAIRN – Flame Child, a type of minor fire Fey

Bradán [bˠɾˠəˈd̪ˠaːn̪ˠ] BRAY-DAWN – Proper name, meaning salmon

Cat Sìth [kʰaʰt̪ ˈʃiː] CAT-FEE – Fey cat

Cù-Sìth [kʰuː ˈʃiː] KOO-FEE; plural Coin-Sìth [kʰɔɲ ˈʃiː] KOO-IN-FEE – Fey hound

Cwēn [kweːn] KU-VAIN – queen

Cyning [ˈkyniŋ] KOON-ING – king

Deaþ [dæːɑθ] DETH – death

Grund [gʁʊnt] GRUNT – earth

Hærfest [hærvest] HAY-ER-VEST – autumn

Helm [helm] HELM – lord

Hus [huːs] HOOS – house

Magick [madʒɪk] MAD-JIK – magic

Mennisc [men.niʃ] MENN-ISH – human (adj.)

Miht [miçt] MITE – power

Modor [moːdor] MOR-DOR – mother

Samhain [saʊ.wɛn] SHAW-WIN - Gaelic festival marking the end of the harvest and the beginning of the new year, celebrated from 31 October to 1 November.

Shade Magus [ʃeɪd] [meɪgəs] SHADE MAY-GAS – Shadow Mage

Síd [sʲiːð] SEETHE – Fey Mound

Wæter [ˈwæter] WHY-AIR-TER – water

Wiga [wiɣa] WEE-GAR – warrior, champion

Wilde [wilde] wild

Folc [fəʊk] folk

Ythlaf [yːðlɑːf] YOOTH-LAAS – Water Relic, a type of minor aquatic Fey

WEDNESDAY

1

THE FIRST HINT OF ROT

Lady Bergamon walked barefoot. The grass was wet, the moss soft as velvet. A full moon cast swathes of light through the canopy, not that she needed it to guide her steps. Here in her garden, she knew each tree, each blossom, each twist of the path as well as she knew the contours of her own body.

Under the trees, the air was cooler, full of moisture. The wet chill of it swirled around her feet, stroking her calves, soft as marigold petals. Beads of dew painted the lace at the hem of her dress grey. She felt like a creature of water, and the thought made her smile.

No man-made sounds could be heard in the garden. Here, the night's orchestra consisted of nocturnal mammals, owls and a faint breeze rustling the leaves. Her passing was silent, and yet the inhabitants of the garden turned to watch her walk by. She, the creator of this place, was universally loved and respected by all who lived within its boundaries.

Her unhurried steps took her through orchards, meadows and woods until she arrived at a spring that fed a forest stream. There she paused, toes on the edge of the grassy bank. She could feel eyes on her, staring at her from the shadows on the opposite side of the pond. Her patience was infinite, and it was rewarded when a horse stepped out into the open.

The stallion was the colour of the moon, quicksilver, shadows cast on fresh snow, and his skin was stretched tight over his muscular frame. Sea kelp and mermaid's hair were woven through his long mane and flowing tail. His dark unshod hooves marked him separate from ordinary horses, for they pointed backwards. Red eyes glowed in the dark, casting faint shadows on his cheeks.

Their eyes met, and her smile widened.

Long, slender fingers crept to the top button of her dress, and the small pearl slipped through the buttonhole. The sides of the dress remained closed until the final button. Only then did she straighten her shoulders and let the dress open. As the light material slipped down her body, so did the years fall away. Her white hair darkened until it was close to black, the lines on her weathered skin faded until her face was smooth once more. A body shaped by a lifetime of manual labour straightened, the aches and pains of age giving way to the vitality of youth.

The only part of her that remained unchanged was her eyes. They carried the wisdom of a long life, of lessons learned and of experiences gathered.

She stood, naked, and they stared at each other. The quirk of a thin eyebrow broke the spell, and she crouched on the bank before slipping into the deep pool. Her hair fanned out, blending with the dark water until they merged and became indistinguishable. She angled her chin up, head tilted in invitation.

Only then was it his turn to move. As the stallion's backward front hoof touched the edge of the water, it contorted and split into five fingers. The grey fur receded into skin so pale it was translucent, while the mane contracted into a head of hair. He reared up, tail disappearing, knees twisting to allow bipedal movement and back hooves becoming toes. The last to change was the face, which turned into the handsome features of a young

4

man. His grey hair flowed down his bare back, still tangled with seaweed, and his red eyes remained fixed upon the woman in the pool.

As he waded closer, swimming the final yards, she reached a hand out to him.

'Samhain blessings to you, my love,' she said.

'And to you. Another year begins tonight, and may it be as blessed as those that have come before.'

'Every year we spend together is a blessing.'

'You look enchanting,' he said and pressed a kiss on her knuckles.

Her response was a smile as he pulled her into his arms. The warmth of his skin was a shock after the coolness of the water, and she savoured that contrast as she breathed in the scents of sea salt, spring water and rain. While he nuzzled her neck, his strong arms braced her against the pool's edge, and she tangled her legs with his.

Their lips hovered millimetres apart, and her eyes closed in anticipation. He was about to close the gap when his nostrils flared and his head twisted to the side. A growl disturbed the night's melody, and her eyes snapped open. It was not a sound she often heard from her lover, and she felt the first hint of disquiet.

'What is it?' she whispered, lips close to his pointed ear.

He turned to look at her, eyes blazing red like lava, like freshly spilled blood. 'There is an intruder in our domain.'

Casting her senses out, she searched for anything that might alert her to the presence of an outsider. After a tense moment, she realised she was looking for the wrong signs. There was no loud, destructive presence, nobody forcing their way into the garden with brute force. Instead, she found the barest hint of standing water turning stagnant, moisture rotting roots and fertile soil turning into sticky mire. With her attention drawn

5

to the right place, she detected the first tentative roots of corruption.

A strange consciousness touched hers. Encircled in the arms of her lover, in what should have been the safest place in the world for her, Lady Bergamon grew terrified for the first time in centuries.

THURSDAY

2
A CALL FOR HELP

The crack of a log in the fireplace startles me awake from dreams filled with hunt, chase and fresh blood. My eyes fly open, but even before my surroundings register, I become aware of a presence. Adrenaline courses through me, heralding a familiar fear, but it subsides when I catch the soothing scent of wood smoke. Blinking in the restless light of the fire, I find Wishearth crouched on the hearth stones. The tail of his coat rests on a burning log, but does not catch fire. His face is a landscape of deep shadows and orange highlights.

'Lady Bergamon needs you,' he says, none of the usual lightness present in his voice. 'She needs you now.'

A yawn forces my eyes closed, and when I open them again, he is gone. All that remains of his visit is a patch of warmth on the hearth stones.

I reach for my phone to check the time: half past one. Sleep beckons me, but I resist the temptation. Wishearth would not have woken me in the middle of the night if it was not important. My growing concern banishes the fatigue weighing down my limbs.

Fumbling in the dark, I get dressed and head for the stairs, still rubbing sleep from my eyes. My mouth tastes like brandy and fur balls, but splashing cold water on my face helps dispel some of the fogginess from my mind. In my office, I stumble over a box by the door and mutter a curse. Karrion and I spent last night in New London providing food for the homeless, and I had forgotten I'd left the supplies in my office when I got back. As I rub my sore shin, I wish I had taken the time to put everything away.

The night air is cold and damp, and I zip up my jacket as I take the stairs two at a time. In the yellow glow of streetlights, the dark houses have an eerie feel to them and I glance around to find I am the only one awake. My car – recently repaired after the crash – is parked in an alley next to the terraced houses.

When I round the corner, a figure moves by my car and I jump back, calling upon the claws of a bear to defend myself with. Even as my fingers contort, I recognise him.

'Are you always this jumpy?' Wishearth asks and steps into the pallid light.

'Only when walking around in the middle of the night,' I say as I let go of the power.

'You shouldn't do that. It's not safe.' Sparks flare from his eyes; each a firefly that brings brief relief from the darkness.

'Who knows what sort of suspicious characters lurk in the shadows, right?'

'Is this the thanks I get for choosing to be your backup?'

Wishearth slides into the seat next to mine and fastens his seatbelt. The seat is most of the way back to accommodate Karrion's long legs, and Wishearth stretches back as he does at his table in the Open Hearth. I am surprised to notice how much taller Karrion is than him.

I start the car and ease onto the road. 'If I thought I needed backup, I'd call Karrion. What else are apprentices for?'

'To fetch tea and do the photocopying? What good is a Bird Shaman in a fight?'

'You'd be surprised,' I say, thinking back to how Karrion saved the day less than a fortnight ago. 'And I could ask the same question of you. What are you going to do, throw a pint of Guinness at your opponents?'

Wishearth crosses his arms. 'Funja won't let me take my pints out of the pub.'

'I want to ask why, but I'm a little afraid of the answer. But when did you start obeying rules set by others?'

'The hospitality of a pub landlord is not to be disrespected.' Wishearth's tone ends the discussion.

No matter how much time I spend with Wishearth and how many questions I ask, my curiosity is never satisfied. Such is the interchangeable nature of him, but I never know where the boundaries lie or what he wants from me. At this time of night, I have no energy for trying to puzzle out his every word.

'I take it we're going to Lady Bergamon's.'

'Yes.'

'How urgent is this?'

'I'm not certain.'

'You don't know?'

'I know something's wrong. That's enough.'

More questions spring to mind, but Wishearth's expression discourages further talk. We lapse into silence, but from the corner of my eye, I see the frown he is trying to hide as he stares out of the passenger window.

The far end of Ivy Street is darker than the beginning, and I realise it is because the street lights are not working. We park under one of them, and I see that the bulb has exploded. I point this out to Wishearth, and his expression darkens. He has never shown such concern before, and I find it contagious. What has happened to Lady Bergamon that would cause Wishearth to be afraid?

Wishearth strides past the wrought iron gate and along the narrow path leading to the front door. In the darkness, the plant pots occupying every inch of the front garden are indistinct shapes. The smell of soil and rotting plant matter rises from them; pungent even to my human nose. Something feels off about the pots, as if the weave of wild power has been cut and reshaped. I frown, intending to sharpen my sight for a closer look, but Wishearth draws my attention away when he beckons me to the door.

'Wait here.'

Wishearth vanishes, leaving behind only a lingering scent of wood smoke. I stand on the threshold, looking along the street to see if anyone is awake and watching. The last thing I need is someone calling the Paladins of Justice about a burglar. Now the broken streetlights work to our advantage.

The sound of a lock disengaging has me turning back to the door just as Wishearth opens it and motions me in.

'Let me guess: you went in through the fireplace,' I say, and close the door behind me.

'That would be telling.'

'You'd make a fine thief.'

Wishearth shakes his head. 'Mortals own nothing I desire.'

'Still, you seem to be doing a lot of disappearing and reappearing.'

'Tonight, I can do a great many things.'

'Why is that?'

'It's Samhain. The hearth fires are doused and rekindled. Even those who no longer follow the old ways still observe the rituals of Samhain and the protection of the new flames.'

I nod. Earlier, after I cleared my fireplace of ashes, I scrubbed the inside with juniper and sage not just to cleanse the physical space, but also to provide a new beginning for the fresh fire I built. The dedication I spoke to my Hearth Spirit was no different from any other day, but it stands to reason that Wishearth would have gained more power from the added elements of the ritual.

'If you're so powerful tonight, why do you need my help?'

'Spirits aren't supposed to meddle in the affairs of the mortals.'

'It's never stopped you before.' I crane my neck to look upstairs.

The house is silent, and I sense a stillness that has not been present before. Tantalising aromas of food and herbs tempt me towards further exploration, but I resist their call. Every time I have visited Lady Bergamon's house, we have spent our time in her garden domain. While I am curious about her home, Wishearth's concern tempers my instinct to look around.

'This is beyond my capability,' Wishearth says and leads me down the long hallway and into the kitchen.

'Are you going to tell me what happened?'

The back door is ajar. Lady Bergamon must be in her garden. It is strange that she should be out in the middle of the night, but there are plenty of explanations that jump to mind. None of them explains why Wishearth woke me up.

'I don't know what happened. All I know is that Lady Bergamon is in trouble and she needs your help.'

On the windowsill, a vase of rowan branches is on its side and I lift it upright. When my finger touches a bunch of berries, they fall off and leave a smear on my skin. I frown.

'Come on,' Wishearth says, and pushes open the back door.

13

When I step over the threshold, I expect a familiar sensation of the world going blurry. Instead, I feel as though I have gone off a ledge, but before I fall into the void, I find my balance. My vision clears, although out in Lady Bergamon's garden, the darkness is absolute. Large drops of rain splatter against my face and shoulders as I move away from the back door. My clothes are quickly soaked through.

I call upon the sight of an owl, and the darkness before me fades into shades of grey. There is crockery on the patio table, and dodging around the large plant pots, I walk to take a closer look. A bowl, a plate and a cup, all made of clay and painted black. They have been smashed, and between shards of the plate, I see the mushy remnants of a dark bread. Sharpening my sense of smell, I also detect traces of wine and milk. They have a sour undertone, like they were spoiled before the rain ruined them.

'What is this?' I ask as Wishearth comes to stand next to me, tugging the collar of his mariner's pea coat closer around his angular face.

'Mortals these days call it a Feast of Hecate. It's an offering of food to the spirits and the Fey. Looks like someone didn't appreciate it.'

'Did Lady Bergamon set this up?'

'Who else?'

'Then who could have smashed it?'

'We'll have to ask her.'

'Where is she?'

The rain grows heavier as I look out towards the garden. There is no sign of her, and I cannot see why she would be out here in the dark while it's raining.

'She's somewhere in the garden.'

'If that's the case, how do you expect us to find her? I've only explored a fraction of the nearby lands and I don't know how far her domain extends.'

14

'Further than you can imagine,' Wishearth says.

'That's not helping.'

Wishearth shrugs. 'It's the truth. But if it makes you feel better, I don't think she's trying to hide from us.'

'It's a start.'

We step off the patio and leave behind the confines of a normal Old London garden. As soon as we walked out of Lady Bergamon's house, we entered a different era of the city's history. Lady Bergamon has never revealed how far back this version of Old London is set, but given that the skyline is clear of buildings, the air is devoid of pollution, and there are no sounds of cars and humans, it must be far in the past. It reinforces my feeling that Lady Bergamon herself is far older than she looks, but she has told me hardly anything about who she is. The one thing I know for certain is that she is the only Plant Shaman in Old London.

Being the only one of our kind in the city is something we have in common, and in Lady Bergamon, I have found a friend who understands my struggle to adapt to an unforgiving environment.

A vegetable patch and an orchard dominate the first part of the garden. When we duck under the low hanging branches of an apple tree, I can just make out the well ahead of us. On the ground in front of it lies a black cloth. Laid out on one side of it is a scythe and on the other side a human skull on a bed of dry leaves. Red candles hold down the corners of the cloth, and at the centre is a basket of apples.

Movement at the corner of my eye has me whirling around. A wicker man is hanging from a plum tree, turning slowly in the breeze. The featureless face sends a shiver down my spine.

A warm hand on my shoulder halts the uncoiling of fear within me. 'We need to keep going. This is not why we're here.'

I follow Wishearth away from the altar and towards the woods. As we step under the relative shelter of the trees, I become aware of the silence around us. The susurrus of life – birdsong, insects and rustles of leaves – has ceased, and the only sounds I can hear are the drum of raindrops and our movements.

'Listen,' I say, pausing under an oak tree.

'I can't hear anything,' Wishearth replies after a while.

'Exactly. I've never known the garden to be this devoid of life.'

'It's the middle of the night. Could everything be asleep?'

'A forest is never silent. Something else is going on here.'

Even as I say the words, I focus on the forest. Since the first time Lady Bergamon invited me into her garden, I have considered it a haven. Our power comes from a different source, but the unspoilt landscape of her domain reminds me of the Wild Folk conclave where I grew up. Here, the wilderness recharges my magic and lends me power far beyond anything available to me in the rest of Old London. But now, some of that power is out of my reach. It feels as though I am looking at the forest through a pane of glass.

We continue along a game trail that snakes through the forest. At the far end, it opens to a meadow I recognise from my first visit. A circular stone lies at the centre of the clearing. Runes decorate its edges and a short pillar stands in the middle. This is where Lady Bergamon works plant magic that allows her to find people. I watched her once, and the memory is still fresh in my mind.

Wishearth moves to continue across the meadow, but my eyes are drawn to the right, where creeping roses form an arch over another game trail. The path leads to a deep pool, where I sensed hostility before. From Lady

Bergamon's warning about avoiding bodies of water, I know her garden is not altogether benign. There is much I do not understand about it, including the lone horse I have caught glimpses of while I have been running through the woods.

Now, my instinct guides me away from Wishearth. When calling my name elicits no reaction, he follows me.

As I reach the arch, I see something white. I hurry forward, sharpening my sight further. When I see the white object is a dress in a heap, my fear overrides the fatigue and the feeling of water running down my spine, and I come to an abrupt halt.

Lady Bergamon is lying on the ground, naked and motionless. At first I fear she is dead, but then I see the faint rise and fall of her breasts. Her white hair is spread out in an uneven halo around her head, wet strands clinging to her forehead and cheeks. Crouched over her is a man whose red eyes blaze with rage. The man is also naked, though the mane of grey hair entwined with seaweed offers him a degree of modesty. His hands dig into the soil on both sides of Lady Bergamon's torso, but I notice that one of his feet is dangling in the pool behind them.

Wishearth collides with my shoulder. When he looks past me, a noise of surprise escapes his lips.

'See, I told you she wasn't hiding,' he says, but the lightness in his tone sounds forced.

Upon hearing Wishearth's words, the man on the ground bares teeth that are too sharp for a human.

'You. Spirit. Why are you here?'

'Lady Bergamon is in trouble. We came to help.'

'We need none of your help, Spirit.'

Wishearth's scent takes on the acrid tones of fresh branches on fire. 'No? I see you're doing a great job making sure she doesn't die from exposure.'

17

'We all want the same thing,' I say and step forward, arms raised. 'The wellbeing of Lady Bergamon is the priority.'

'What place have you here, Wild Woman?'

When he turns the full force of his hatred on me, I feel age stealing strength from my bones, illness wasting away my muscles and a lifetime of loss breaking my spirit. I sway, only the shreds of my will keeping me from collapsing to the ground. The rain chills me to the core, and I recall how tired and sore I am. This is not a place for me, nor have I anything to offer. It is best I leave before the despair crushes me and my body rots in the unforgiving rain.

A warm hand closing around my numb fingers returns a spark of life to my chest. It is my turn to glare at the man.

'Lady Bergamon has extended me every hospitality. I am here because she willed it so.'

The man growls. The sound is unlike a wolf, a bear or a lynx; it speaks of an older time, when monsters still roamed the untamed lands. Drawn by curiosity, I call upon my magic and inhale. At first, all I detect are the rich smells of the wet forest, and they tempt me with a promise of exploration and discovery away from this clearing where the hostility makes my skin itch. Beneath the temptation, I smell seaweed, tidal flats, the purest spring water and a hint of horse hair. His scent confirms what his red eyes have already told me: he is not human, but something far older and far more dangerous.

'Please,' I say. I inch forward. 'Let us help her.'

From the tensing of his shoulders, I expect him to launch himself at my throat, but the man eases back until he is crouching over Lady Bergamon's feet. As he does so, his hair shifts and I catch a glimpse of a pointed ear. The seaweed tangled in his hair is mermaid's hair and sea kelp, and I wonder where he might have found either. Could these lands extend all the way to the sea?

Lady Bergamon's dress is soaked through and feels heavier than I expected. It will offer her no protection, and I hand it to Wishearth. My coat has not fared much better, but I shrug it off and drape it across Lady Bergamon's torso. Despite my cold fingers, her cheek feels icy, and she remains unresponsive when I call her name and shake her gently. Her breathing is shallow, and a frown has drawn a roadmap of lines across her brow.

'What happened to her?' I ask.

'Something entered our domain. My lady reached through her plants to identify the intruder, cried out and fell into a deep stupor.'

I notice for the first time the lilt of his words. It is not quite Irish, not quite Welsh, but the cadence speaks of older times. A name is forming in my mind for what he might be, but I am not certain.

'What was it?'

'I know not. It passed through this land with the speed of an autumn storm and left decay in its wake.'

My thoughts are drawn back to the Feast of Hecate and the shattered crockery. If the offerings were for the spirits and the Fey, the intruder must be something different. A ghost, perhaps? But how could a ghost gain access to Lady Bergamon's garden?

Water dripping down my nose draws my attention back to Lady Bergamon. Her chest is barely moving now, and no matter how strong the sap in her veins and how potent her magic is, she will not survive long out here.

'We need to move her inside,' I say to Wishearth.

'No.' The man leans forward, and I smell rain, spring water and sea salt in his breath. 'She stays upon this spot where I can ward her.'

Frustration brings out my reckless side. 'Unless you can provide shelter and heat, you'll soon be protecting her corpse.'

The speed of his attack catches me by surprise, and I am flung away from Lady Bergamon. My back collides with a tree, and the force of the blow causes me to bite my tongue. I slump to the ground. Black spots swim across my vision, and my mouth is filled with the rich warmth of blood. When I blink my eyes into focus, I find a huge grey horse standing over me, eyes alight with rage. Now I know for certain: he is a Kelpie.

'You will utter no such words regarding my lady,' he says, specks of sea foam landing on my face.

My temper flares, but a hoof coming to rest on my sternum causes me to reconsider an angry retort.

'I'm sorry,' I say. 'It wasn't my intention to offend. Lady Bergamon needs help, and fast.'

He steps back, but his expression remains vicious. 'She must not leave our domain.'

'She's visited me in the past and her garden has been fine.'

'The more time she spends away from here, the harder it is for her to keep it hidden from prying eyes. But we were not under attack then. Decay has infected the web of power running through these lands. One frayed thread can undo the entirety.'

'Her house forms part of the weave, doesn't it?'

'Yes.'

'We'll take her there and no further.'

The horse backs away. 'Very well.'

When I stand up, the world spins and I have to lean on the sycamore trunk while I find my balance. The bleeding has slowed to a trickle, but my back aches and my mouth feels coated with blood. I resist the temptation to spit it out. My knowledge of blood magic is hazy, but I have no desire to find out what a Fey could do with a sample of my blood.

Lady Bergamon is heavier than I expected, and my knees ache when I lift her into my arms. I pull her as close as I can, though, in truth, I am almost as cold as she. Still, any warmth I can offer her I give freely.

The sound of an enraged gasp has me turning around, the weight of Lady Bergamon throwing me off balance. Wishearth is standing in front of the horse, a finger raised. On the horse's forehead is an oval area of singed hair. The acrid smell of burnt hair and flesh causes me to sneeze.

'Next time, think before you attack,' Wishearth says.

I close my eyes. The last thing I need is the two of them starting a fight.

'You've made your point. Come on.'

Wishearth mutters something, but joins me at the beginning of the game trail. I am almost at the arch of roses when I turn.

'How will I find you again?'

The man's words carry even though he has not moved. 'Touch any water in the garden and call my name. I will come.'

'And your name is?'

'Bradán.'

'Thank you.'

Wishearth leads the way towards the main path. When I glance back, the Kelpie remains by the pool, face contorted in anger and concern.

21

3

POWER OF OLD

Lady Bergamon is heavy in my arms as we walk through
the wet forest. I recall the deer I shot at the conclave and
how Dearon lowered the carcass onto my shoulders. It
would be an easier way to carry Lady Bergamon, but she
deserves more dignity than that. Instead, I draw power
from the forest and grit my teeth. Despite the exertion,
cold is taking hold within me, flaring up countless aches
and pains.

A warm hand pressed against the back of my neck
startles me. Wishearth sends heat deep into my bones. It
provides relief from the pain, and I draw Lady Bergamon
closer to my wet hoodie to share the warmth with her.

'Trust you to start an argument with a horse.'

'He's not a horse,' I say, adjusting my grip.

'Of course not. When did you last see one that could
talk?'

'I'm surprised he could still speak in his horse form.'

'The Fey talk in mysterious ways.'

I glare at Wishearth; his face is a picture of innocence.

'And spirits could talk a little less.'

'That's racist.' He cocks his head. 'Or speciesist. Or
beingist. I'm not sure what, but it's something.'

'You'll live.'

The forest seems to go on forever, and I am relieved
when we finally reach the edge of the lawn. My body is

shaking from exhaustion and pain, and I suspect that without Wishearth's help, the journey would have taken twice as long. But I alone have carried Lady Bergamon and I find it strange.

'You could offer to help,' I say as I stagger past the well.

In our absence, the altar has been ruined by rain and the breeze that is picking up. Who was the altar for? What kind of gods does an ancient Plant Shaman honour?

'I did help.'

'I meant with the carrying.'

Wishearth is quiet long enough for me to think that he will not reply.

'It's one thing carrying a pint to my table, quite another to bear the weight of a mortal.'

His words catch me by surprise. Wishearth never speaks of his powers and what he can do, preferring to drop cryptic hints when it suits him best. Such admission of weakness feels intimate, and I am left speechless. He does not seem to mind and he keeps his hand on my neck until we reach the back door.

Light is spilling out from the kitchen, and I notice thin branches scattered on the steps.

'What are those?'

Wishearth picks one up and holds it near my face. I recognise the smell, then the long, narrow leaves.

'Rosemary.'

'Why would Lady Bergamon scatter rosemary on the steps?' I ask.

'I don't think she did. The front door. Didn't you notice the rosemary wreath hanging on it?'

I think back to our arrival, but cannot recall anything specific about the door.

'No. I was too busy worrying about the neighbours calling the Paladins.'

'Rosemary is a plant for protection. Lady Bergamon hung wreaths of it at both doors to keep something out.'

Bending down, Wishearth finds a length of twine among the branches. The knot in it remains, and it's been cut in the middle.

'What could she possibly have to fear in the garden of her own making?'

'On a night of Samhain,' Wishearth holds the door open for me, 'a great many things.'

'What do you mean?'

'Think back to the stories of old. How often do beings cross between worlds on Samhain? And didn't you insist to Dearon when you were young that you heard the Fey ride by on this night?'

He is right, on both counts. In my concern for Lady Bergamon, I had forgotten how adrift the laws of magic and power are on this night. Anything is possible. Fear shudders through me, chasing away my astonishment at Wishearth knowing and recalling something I said to Dearon years ago.

While many more questions spring to mind, the ache of my arms discourages lingering on the threshold. Once inside, I kick off my shoes. My socks are soaked through, but there is little I can do about that. If I set Lady Bergamon down on the floor, I doubt I will be able to lift her again.

'Upstairs, the second door along,' Wishearth says and closes the door behind us.

I climb the stairs, gritting my teeth as the pain in my knees intensifies. The door Wishearth indicated is open, and I stumble into a large double bedroom. A sudden brightness blinds me, and I turn to see him in the doorway, hand on the light switch.

'Set her on the sofa.' He points to a small two-seater.

'Why not the bed?'

'Because you need to move it to the middle of the floor first.'

'Why?'

To spare my arms, I do as he asks and lay Lady Bergamon on the sofa. The burgundy fabric turns darker around her where water seeps into it. I groan as blood rushes into my arms.

'Something came through her gardens and left her like this. Who's to say the being won't return and attack her again while she's defenceless?'

'What can we do? We don't even know what attacked her. Shouldn't we figure that out first? And we need to get her warm and dry.'

'There are dry clothes in the wardrobe. I'll go and put the kettle on.'

Feeling like an intruder, I open the doors of the large oak wardrobe. The scents of lavender, rosemary and mint greet me. On the left, dresses hang on coat hangers. On the right, clothes are neatly folded on shelves. I pick out a long nightgown, knitted socks and a shawl. Balancing on my tiptoes, I reach for two blankets on the top shelf and add them to my pile.

Working quickly, I dress Lady Bergamon. I am beginning to shake from cold and fatigue and I peel off my hoodie and socks. The bathroom is the next door along, and I drop my wet clothes and Lady Bergamon's dress in the bathtub.

'Here.' Wishearth has returned and offers me a thick robe. 'You need to change out of those clothes, or you'll catch a cold.'

I wait for him to leave, but he merely stands there, looking expectant. A flush creeps across my cheeks as I take the robe and retreat to the bathroom. Undressing before the fireplace in my home is intimate enough, but it is quite different doing so with him watching for certain.

When I return to the bedroom, I find a second pair of Lady Bergamon's woollen socks waiting for me by the door. Wishearth is perched on the edge of the sofa, holding both of Lady Bergamon's hands in his. Their heads are close together, and he appears to be whispering to her. I am tempted to sharpen my hearing so I might know what he is saying, but already I feel like an intruder. They have known each other for a long time, and the deep affection they share is evident whenever they speak of one another.

Wishearth rises and brushes past me. 'You should build a fire and make an offering. I think the kettle is boiling.'

'Is it too weird being in the same room when I'm making an offering to you?' I ask after him, but receive no response. I cannot help wondering if I have offended him somehow.

The log basket next to the fireplace is full of thick branches and kindling. I build a fire and stay as close to it as I dare to let the flames warm me. A wooden box on the mantelpiece contains short twigs of different tree species, as well as dried lavender and rosemary. There are vases of rowan branches on both windowsills and that prompts me to twine together a length of rowan and rosemary.

'Hearth Spirit, accept our offering. We ask for warmth to keep away the chill of death, and protection from those who wish us harm. Guard these flames through the hours of the Samhain night.'

The offering burns with a crackle and releases an aromatic scent that eases the nagging worry within me.

'You can be poetic when left to your own devices.'

I jump, and my exhausted muscles cannot maintain my balance on the hearth stones. Curling my back, I land on the carpet. My dignity suffers the worst damage, and Wishearth's chuckle does nothing to help. He sets down the mug, bottle and spoon he is carrying and offers me his hand. The sash of my robe loosens while I struggle up, and I clutch the lapels with my free hand.

'What's in the bottle?' I ask.

'Lady Bergamon's tonic. You must give two spoonfuls of it to her every morning and evening.'

'What's in it?'

Wishearth shrugs. I pick up the bottle and unstop it. Betony and mistletoe dominate the smell, but there are hints of other herbs: fern, perhaps, and something else. The Elders at the conclave regularly drink betony tea for a number of ailments and claim that fern root oil prolongs their life.

Could this tonic explain why Lady Bergamon is far older than she looks?

'If she doesn't wake up by mid-morning, she's going to need more than a couple of spoonfuls of tonic to sustain her.'

'No.' Wishearth shakes his head. 'Plants are her kin. They survive through drought only to bloom when the rains come.'

I want to argue, but I am out of my depth, as I have been all night. 'Fine.'

Tilting Lady Bergamon's head, I feed her two spoonfuls of the brown liquid. Some spills from the corner of her mouth, but she swallows most of it. I replace the cork.

'The pain-relieving tea is for you,' Wishearth says. 'You'll need your strength for the next part.'

It comes as no surprise that Wishearth has prepared the tea exactly as Lady Bergamon does, even down to the amount of honey in the mug. I savour the warmth settling in my belly and long for the effect of ginger, willow bark and feverfew to take effect. Not bringing any of my pain medication with me was foolish.

I glance at my watch. It is ten past three.

27

'What's next?'

'Drag the bed to the centre of the room.'

Lady Bergamon's bed has a solid oak frame, and I have to swivel it one end at a time to move it away from the wall. When Wishearth gives his approval, I push aside the covers and carry Lady Bergamon to the bed. Wishearth brings the extra blankets I found in the cupboard, and I drape them over her.

'Do you want me to call a Mage contact?' I ask.

'Why?'

'You said we need to protect her from the intruder. The best way to do that is to ward this room. We need a Mage for that.'

'And do you think a Mage can set up a ward that will keep out mortals, spirits, ghosts and the Fey?'

'I have no idea. You seem to know what's going on better than I do. So you tell me.'

'You need to cast a circle.'

I laugh; the sound too loud in the bedroom. 'A circle. You think New Age Wiccan stuff will keep Lady Bergamon safe?'

The darkening of Wishearth's expression dispels my amusement, and I catch a glimpse of the power smouldering within him.

'Circles were cast long before Mages learned about warding. Druids used them, and it was ancient lore already back then. Only a few people retain the old knowledge and even fewer still cast circles that have true power, but they are no less potent than in the days of the Druids.'

Lady Bergamon once told me that Wishearth had spent time as a djinn in Arabia, but now I wonder if he was not also one of the ancient demigods of Britain.

'That's great, but I'm one of the Wild Folk. I can't cast a circle.'

'Did you learn nothing from Melissa?'

28

I frown. Melissa could cast unique illusions because she carried two different types of magical blood. But her ability was fuelled by psychosis.

'She used her life force to fuel the illusions after the power in her blood ran out,' Wishearth says.

'Are you suggesting that I burn myself to cast the circle?'

'No. I'm trying to tell you that beneath the neat categories of spell casters, it all comes down to the power in your blood. You can use that power, if you're careful, and channel it in ways you may not appreciate.'

A thousand questions jump to my mind, but the pain and exhaustion are getting worse by the minute.

'Fine. What do you want me to do?'

'We need a few items. I believe Lady Bergamon keeps her tools downstairs.'

The prospect of exploring Lady Bergamon's home energises me. On the way down, I notice that a vase of rowan branches on the windowsill by the door has been knocked over. I reach for the vase, feeling a sense of déjà vu, but it comes apart in my hand.

'That's the second one.'

'Sorry?'

'It's a puzzle for another time,' I say and leave the pieces on the windowsill.

The lounge doubles as a dining room. At the end closest to us, a table is set for six people. The crockery is black, matching the broken pieces outside. Both the tablecloth and the fabric shrouding the chairs are also black. From the casserole dish in the middle, smells of venison and root vegetables tantalise me. My mouth waters. Only one of the plates has been used. On the others, a serving of stew and a slice of bread remain untouched. A small copper cauldron sits next to each of them. I inhale. They contain burnt paper.

'What is this?' I ask.

'A feast to venerate the ancestors. Lady Bergamon begins each year by remembering her family.'

'Isn't she a couple of months early?'

'Tonight marks the changing of the year for her people.'

I want to ask more, but Wishearth turns away, arms crossed.

'We should at least put away the food before it spoils.'

'Wait.' Wishearth points to the side of the table. 'Look.'

A heart copper symbol glints on the floor. I spot three others around the table. They are evenly spaced.

'The table is warded?'

'No. It's protected by a circle.'

'How did you know?'

'All of Lady Bergamon's other precautions aside, I can feel it.'

'I didn't know you could do that.'

'You can, too.'

'No. I can sense other people's auras and the spells they cast, but not active magic.'

'Have you tried?'

'It's an instinct, not something I can control.'

'Have you tried?'

Instead of arguing with him, I step closer to the nearest symbol. I feel no press against my aura, no whisper of power. Whatever Wishearth can sense, I cannot.

'It's not your magic, it's you.'

Frustration fuels my confusion as I cast my senses wide, dipping into the magic within me. A grandfather clock ticking in the corner sounds like thunder. The creases on the tablecloth are deep as ravines. My wet bra straps chafe my shoulders. The air tastes like dust, ash and candle wax. Wishearth's familiar scent all but overwhelms my nose.

30

But I cannot feel the circle.

I am turning to Wishearth when a soft caress passes over the hairs on my wrist. Drawing back the sleeve of the robe, I move my arm away from me and the caress becomes steady pressure. When I look down, a shimmer in the corner of my eye gives me a fleeting sense of vertigo. There is nothing in front of me, but when I turn to the side, I can see light refracting on thin air. I breathe through my mouth. All at once, I taste apple blossom honey and wild strawberries, and smell juniper branches. Bringing my ear closer, I hear the circle making a sound akin to aspen leaves shivering in the evening breeze.

When at last I look at Wishearth, he nods. 'Now you know.'

'I didn't think it was possible.'

'It is the night of Samhain. A great many things are possible tonight. Perhaps the wisdom gained during the hours of darkness may be retained once the dawn breaks.'

Wishearth walks to a sideboard and opens the doors. He beckons me closer and points to a large wooden box decorated with a carving of an oak tree wreathed in mistletoe. It is heavy.

'Bring it upstairs,' he says, and picks up a black candle.

In Lady Bergamon's bedroom, I set the box on the dressing table and open it. Inside are three smaller boxes decorated with a carving of an elder, hawthorn or birch tree. Next to them, on a blue cloth, lie a sickle and the obsidian blade I have seen Lady Bergamon use before.

'You need the elder box and the blade.'

The smaller box is lighter, and I feel something moving inside. When I lift the lid, I find it contains cold iron discs the size of a pound coin. Each bears a different rune, and although the meanings are unknown to me, I recognise the style from the stone circle in the garden.

'Place one of those symbols at the four points of the compass, starting with the north.'

'Right.' My hand trembles as I count out the symbols, and my skin crawls at the touch of cold iron, the magical metal weakening my threads of power. As much as Wild Folk share the Feykins' aversion to cold iron, so do Shamans react to heart copper and Mages and Paladins to true silver. We all have a weakness to a metal of power, even if many of us choose to work with them.

I ignore the queasy sensation. 'Wait, which way is north?'

'And you call yourself Wild?'

'Karrion's the one related to pigeons. Being in the city confuses my sense of direction.'

'North is that way,' Wishearth says and points behind me.

I follow his instructions and lay the symbols on the carpet. When I turn back to Wishearth, he offers me the lit candle.

'What do I do with the blade? Does the circle require blood?'

'No. Once you've cast the circle, no one can step in and out without disrupting it. To avoid having to cast it again every time you check up on Lady Bergamon, you cut a doorway into the circle. It will allow you through, and you can do the same to leave.'

'Right. But how do I raise a circle?'

'Walk clockwise from one symbol to the next, starting with the north, and use the power in your blood.'

'Wait. I'm not a Mage. I don't know the ritual words or invocations.'

'It doesn't matter. The power is within you. Use it. Any words can complete the ritual as long as they are a conduit to your magic.'

Plenty of arguments spring to my mind, but there is

32

no laughter in Wishearth's eyes as he regards me. He is serious, and therefore, so must I be. But I have never cast a circle, or even considered doing so. How am I supposed to find the right words for a ritual? I look around the room for inspiration, and then shake my head. Why? Like Wishearth said, the magic is within me. It comes from nature.

I step up to the first symbol and imagine moonlight marking the boundaries of the circle. The floor begins to glow, and I hesitate, glancing over my shoulder at Wishearth for reassurance. He nods, and I clear my throat.

'North Wind, strong and proud, raise the circle and guard it with your power.'

A wind rises behind me, tugging at my hair, but leaving the candle untouched. I move along to the second symbol.

'East Wind, old and wise, give the circle your alertness and the prudence to perceive our foes.'

A second wind joins the first, and within its howling, I hear snippets from songs and stories of old. My concentration falters, but a drop of wax sliding across my fingers brings my attention back to the circle.

'South Wind, the bearer of rain and rejuvenation, lend your love to preserve the life within this circle.'

The scent of rain swirls around me, and I can taste moisture in the air. The candle sputters, but remains alight.

'West Wind, soft and subtle, lend this circle your cunning so that it may remain ever hidden from its enemies.'

The four winds howl around me as I return to the first symbol, and they build the wall around Lady Bergamon. I see the sun deflecting spells and attacks, keeping the bed hidden behind its brilliance, and clouds gather to hide the room from view. Crouching by the first symbol, I set the candle down. The flame flares and the heat caresses my cheek as I gather my magic. I send power into the boundary and the circle shimmers into existence. When I back away, I can no longer see the power, but I feel it as static energy along my skin.

'There, it is done,' Wishearth says.

'I had no idea I could do that.' There is a void in my magic, and I long for the restoring effect of Lady Bergamon's garden.

'Your power comes from the Wild, but it also comes from here.' Wishearth places his palm over my sternum, sending heat deep within my chest.

As Wishearth's pupils are engulfed by flames, I am mesmerised by their beauty. The scents of wood smoke, ash and dry branches envelop me. We stand there, connected by his touch, and my pulse picks up speed. He must sense it too, and sparks fly from his eyes. One grazes my cheek and I feel the fleeting kiss of fire. I lick my lips, and his eyes track the movement. He shifts a little closer and then frowns.

'You should rest.'

A yawn halts my argument. Wishearth is right. Yet I feel as though he has just cheated me out of something I dare not define.

'I'll sleep on the sofa. That way I can keep an eye on Lady Bergamon.'

'It's too small for you.'

'Then what do you suggest?' I ask.

'You should find a blanket and a pillow in the spare bedroom. And for tomorrow, I'll put a spare key under the flower pot by the front door.'

Frustrated by his lack of explanation, I leave the room. When I return, he has moved the cushions off the sofa and laid them in front of the fire to mirror my sleeping arrangement at home. He is right. I will need the heat of the fire if I am to sleep.

Neither of us speaks while I lie down and drape the blanket over me. My first instinct is to face away from the fire so the heat reaches my back, but Wishearth shakes his head. I understand why when I feel a dip in the cushions behind me. He need not touch me to send wave after wave of warmth over me. It penetrates the chill from the wet forest and the pain of physical exertion to drag me into awaiting darkness.

4
GROWING FEAR

Sunlight in my eyes wakes me up, and I roll onto my back with a groan. The blanket is tangled between my legs and I kick it aside. In the fireplace, the embers are still glowing. When I push myself up, Wishearth is gone and Lady Bergamon remains unconscious. I search around for my phone and remember that I never took it out of my coat pocket. I also forgot about the wet clothes in the bathtub.

I climb to my feet and hang onto the mantelpiece while the room spins and settles. Countless aches make themselves known. Moving carefully, I test my legs and stagger to the bathroom.

Wishearth has been busy. Instead of a bathtub full of wet clothes, I find a stack of dry ones on the floor, neatly folded. The smell of wood smoke envelops me as I get dressed and return Lady Bergamon's robe to the wardrobe.

My phone has suffered no damage from the rain, nor the drying, and I see that it is gone ten o'clock. I call Karrion and ask him to meet me here with coffee. Already my head is aching from lack of caffeine and sleep.

The sight of Lady Bergamon's still body reminds me of Wishearth's instructions about administering the tonic, but the bottle is no longer on the dressing table. I find it in the fridge. The obsidian blade is on top of the wooden box, and I test its weight while I regard the circle's perimeter. Can the blade really cut a doorway into the magic?

There is only one way to find out, and I step close enough that I can feel the thrum of magic as pressure against my body. It is unpleasant, but not painful. Starting to the right of the north-facing symbol, I cut a doorway large enough to accommodate me. The pressure against me eases. I run my hand past where I think the border of the doorway is and the change in the feel of the circle is noticeable. Slipping the handle of the blade into my back pocket, I step through.

I experience a sensation akin to walking through a waterfall, but the thrum of power remains unchanged. The perimeter feels no different inside the circle, and the entrance I cut into it closes behind me, like tide flowing in to flood the beach. Lady Bergamon's skin is warm, but nothing I do rouses her. I feed her two spoonfuls of the tonic and reach for the blade. My finger connects with the edge, and my skin parts. The pain follows, and I yank my hand back. A crimson droplet lands on the headboard. I wipe it away. Blood runs down my finger, and I lick at the red trail; the taste is salt and hunger and wildness. It soothes my sore finger and awakens memories of fresh blood on my lips, a warm heart within my reach and the smell of crushed heather beneath my paws.

Shaking my head, I distance myself from the sensations. They were not my memories, but rather a recollection of past Wild Folk generations. We dream their dreams, learn their ways and remember what came before us. It has always been thus, and it will be so while we still roam the remaining wild places. But here in Old London, a disconnect has been growing with me. I do not know what befalls a Wild Folk tamed by a city, but I fear I will soon find out.

The ache of the wound prompts me to cut another doorway through the circle and rummage around Lady Bergamon's bathroom for a plaster. I expect she treats most wounds with plantain leaves and dried puffballs, but luck is on my side and I find a faded box of plasters. The adhesive smells old, but it sticks to my finger.

Having taken the bottle back to the kitchen, I glance out of the window by the front door. There is no sign of Karrion yet. While I wait, I take a better look around Lady Bergamon's bedroom. The furniture is all made of oak, and harks back to an older era. The carpet is newer; worn but clean. On the wall, above where the bed was, hangs a tapestry. I walk closer, careful not to disturb the circle. The tapestry depicts people in blue robes dancing in a forest clearing. The full moon casts light upon the revellers, and I see that in the middle of the clearing is a circular stone. If the figures are to scale, the stone is far larger than the one in Lady Bergamon's garden. Runes fill the edges of the stone, each only a couple of stitches in height, and I wish I knew their meaning.

On the opposite wall, the decorations are no less intriguing. Resting on brackets are a sword and two spear-heads. The metal has dulled to black with age and the spears end in the sockets that would have attached to a shaft, while the sword is missing its guard and grip. All three remind me of weapons I saw in the British Museum when I first moved to London over a year ago.

Why would Lady Bergamon decorate her bedroom walls with Iron Age weapons?

The second bedroom upstairs appears to be a guest room. There is a large table filled with plant pots by the window, and the walls are decorated with pressed flowers. In all my exploration of the upstairs, I find no evidence of the cat that I have seen in the garden during previous visits. Perhaps it only lives outside.

I draw the line at rifling through Lady Bergamon's drawers, and head downstairs. There is one more room I have not yet seen, and I open the door to a library. Heavy leather-bound volumes line the walls, and a glance through the titles shows that all the ones in English relate to plants. I pull out a few of the others and find pages written in Latin and Greek with beautiful plant illustrations. Some of the books are recent, while others look so old I dare not touch them.

A hum of electricity draws me to a large cupboard. Opening the doors, I find that two thirds of the space is taken up by a climate controlled glass casing that houses dozens of scrolls. On the shelf above, thin boxes are stacked; their sides containing only numbers. I pull out one of them and ease open the lid. Inside, protected by layers of linen, is a lead sheet stamped with familiar runes. The edges of the sheet are uneven, but the writing is clear.

The doorbell rings, and I jump. After returning the box to the cupboard, I hurry to the door. Karrion is standing on the steps, his back to me, and the sunlight gilds the blue in his hair into a pale halo. When he turns towards me, I see he is frowning.

'What happened to the front garden?'

His greeting catches me by surprise, and I leave the door open while I retrieve my shoes from the kitchen. Even they are dry, and I make a mental note to thank Wishearth tonight.

'What's wrong?' I ask.

'Take a look at the plants.'

Karrion is right. The potted plants have withered and died. All that remains in the pots are brown leaves and a few stalks. Last time I visited Lady Bergamon, the front garden was teeming with life and the plants were flourishing.

'It's like winter happened overnight.'

39

I think back to the silence of the garden last night and the relentless rain. Karrion may be closer to the mark than he realises. But seasons in Lady Bergamon's garden do not follow the typical pattern. Instead, seasonal plants all flourish at once, and even in late autumn, the sunny days rival those of early summer.

'It's one more mystery to add to the list,' I say.

'What do you mean?'

'Lady Bergamon's in trouble.'

Karrion hands me a takeaway cup of coffee. 'You better start from the beginning.'

We sit in the kitchen while I bring him up to speed. When my stomach growls part of the way through my story, Karrion opens his bag and hands me a Spiderman lunch box full of tuna sandwiches. By the time I have eaten, I have finished telling him almost everything. The only things I leave out are what I learned about Wishearth's powers and that he was still here when I fell asleep.

Karrion's expression has darkened from wonder to concern. 'What do we do, Yan?'

'I want to take another look at the patio. There may be something Wishearth and I missed in the dark.'

Karrion's teeth worry his lip piercing. 'I would have helped if you'd called me.'

'I know. But I had no inkling what we were dealing with until we'd already found Lady Bergamon. By the time she was warm and safe within a circle, it was so late all I wanted to do was sleep for a couple of hours. Besides, I figured you'd be a fresh pair of eyes this morning.'

'That I can definitely be.'

When I open the back door, I see that it is still raining. Rain has never concerned me before, but the steady drum of raindrops hitting the patio sounds menacing. The steel grey clouds block much of the light, giving the mid-morning vista an air of dawn. All my instincts tell me to stay in the dry safety of the house. It is puzzling, for the outdoors is where I belong. Does Bradán share my trepidation, or are Fey immune to fear?

Clearing my throat, I say, 'I hope your coat is waterproof.'

Karrion tugs at the lapels of his black trench coat. 'Leather is stylish and practical. And my mum thought being a goth was just a phase.'

'You've certainly proved her wrong.'

'I'm also prepared for your lack of practicality,' he says, and presents me with an umbrella.

'I'm one of the Wild Folk. Practical is what we do.'

'Which is why you're about to step into pouring rain in a soft shell jacket.'

'It's not raining in the rest of Old London. How was I supposed to know Lady Bergamon's garden would be trying to recreate the great flood?'

Despite my defensive tone, I take the umbrella. It is decorated with skulls in neon colours.

'I bet you didn't pack any painkillers either. You should really think about keeping some in your car.'

To avoid telling him that he is right, I open the umbrella outside the back door and step across the threshold. Like last night, I experience a sensation of falling, but this time I know to expect it. When Karrion stumbles, I reach for his arm.

'That was weird.'

'I told you the garden feels different.'

Karrion bends to pick up rosemary branches while I walk past rows of plant pots to the patio table. Here, too, the plants have died and decayed. It was too dark last night to notice it, but my guess is they were already dead then. This level of rot takes more than a few hours, and yet all the plants appear to have died at the same time.

41

Lady Bergamon could will the plants dead, I have no doubt, but why would she? Or have the plants died because she has fallen unconscious?

The broken dishes are on the table where I left them, but all traces of the food and drink have been washed away. I stack the shards in a pile, but leave them on the table while I look out into the garden. All the trees have dropped their leaves, and they cover the grass in a carpet of uniform brown. Even maple and cherry trees, which usually offer a beautiful display of colour, seem to have none left. When I sharpen my sight, I can see the movement of the wicker man at the far end of the orchard. The cold fingers of fear caress my spine.

Looking around the patio, I find no food bowl for a cat. Should I put out food? I decide against it. The rain would ruin it in a matter of minutes. There is plenty out here for a cat to eat.

'Come take a look at this.'

I return to Karrion, who points to the back door lock.

'See that?'

Where the lock should be, only a jagged hole remains. I push my finger inside and feel sharp edges. When I withdraw it, my finger is covered in a rusty powder that smells metallic.

'What do you think?'

'I think something caused the lock to rust away,' I say, and dip my finger into a barrel collecting water from the guttering.

'Could it be natural?'

'If it was, I'd expect the whole lock to be gone. But the edges look pristine.'

'Are you saying someone did this on purpose?'

'Yes. But why? If Lady Bergamon was in the garden, there's no reason for her to lock the door. There was no one else out here, Bradán excepted, and the back door is a little snug for a Kelpie.'

'You know that,' Karrion says, his words slow. 'But would someone else?'

'What are you getting at?'

'If something did cross over like Bradán said and if they didn't know Lady Bergamon's habits, they probably expected the back door to be locked. Rather than check, they rusted the lock. Personally, I would have tried the door handle first.'

'But what was it? How did they cross to the garden and why?'

I shiver. The garden no longer feels safe. Rain continues to pound against the umbrella and my trainers are soaked through again. While my pulse picks up speed, instinct tells me to go back inside and cast a circle to protect Karrion and me. But that will not help Lady Bergamon.

'You okay, Yan?' Karrion's hair is plastered onto his forehead and water drips from the row of hoops in his left ear.

'Say someone did break in. They would have found an empty house. I haven't noticed anything that looks out of place, which is strange. There's food inside, weapons and items needed for spells. Why was nothing taken? The only things that looked out of place were the two vases of rowan branches that had been knocked over.'

'What's the significance of rowan?'

'Greoff, one of the Elders at the conclave, once told me that spirits disliked rowan trees and that the wood could be used to protect a home against malevolent entities. If I'm not mistaken, each of the cabins at the conclave has rowan in the walls. Then again, Greoff has told a great many tall tales over the years.'

'But what if he's right and Lady Bergamon was using the branches for a similar purpose?'

43

I nudge the remains of the rosemary wreath with my foot. Water squelches between my toes. 'That was also for protection. Was she warding her home against a known enemy, or was she just being cautious?'

'Either way, I don't think it worked. The wreath is in pieces and two of the vases inside were knocked over.'

'Yes, but there are further vases in the other rooms that were left untouched.'

'Why?'

We return inside and close the door. A puddle forms on the tiled floor around us. I find a cloth in the cupboard under the sink and use it to wipe away the water. Standing in the middle of the narrow kitchen, I look back and forth between the two vases.

'Let's say I'm the intruder. The wreath outside couldn't stop me and now I've gained entry to the house. I look around and I... see the vase on the windowsill.'

'It's another symbol of protection.'

'But it holds no power over me and I knock it over. Perhaps I'm showing off.'

I move to the kitchen doorway. 'To my right is the lounge. There's food there, but perhaps I can sense the circle protecting the table. The next room is the library, but I don't go in there. Why?'

'There's nothing I need in there,' Karrion says. He rests a hand on my shoulder and points along the corridor. 'Look, you can see the vase from here.'

'Yes. It's right by the door.' I turn to Karrion. 'That's it. All I'm interested in is the door.'

'Was the lock forced?' he asks.

'No, but you don't need a key to open it from this side.'

'So they came to the house because it provides access to the outside world. That would explain the plants in the front garden.'

44

I nod. 'Whatever came through killed the plants on the patio and in the front garden. It could also explain why the streetlights at this end of Ivy Street weren't working last night.'

'Right. But who and why?'

'What concerns me is it may not be Lady Bergamon alone who's in danger. And it's a big city out there.'

'How do you want to proceed, boss?'

'The advantage we have is that we have allies.' I smile.

Leaning against the kitchen doorframe, I scroll through the contacts on my phone and dial Jamie's number. When he answers, I can hear voices in the background. It is not the steady murmur of New Scotland Yard, but he is somewhere indoors. I attempt to start with pleasantries, but he cuts me off mid-sentence.

'Is this urgent?'

'I think so,' I say, taken aback by the shortness of his tone.

'Fine. But keep it brief. I've been working since the early hours of the morning. What can I do for you, Yannia?'

'Did anything weird happen last night?'

Jamie barks a laugh. 'This is Old London we're talking about. Define weird.'

'Anything out of the ordinary. Anything criminal.'

'Let's see, the usual suspects probably don't interest you. Two men died of natural causes. And when I say natural, I mean nature killed them.'

'How do you know for sure?'

'A length of ivy strangled one of them, and another had a belladonna plant in his mouth.'

'Was magic involved?'

'No question about it.'

I offer no reply as a chill settles in my bones. Jamie gets impatient and jumps to a conclusion.

'You were expecting this.'

'I was expecting... something.'

'Are you going to tell me I have a third body on my hands?'

My thoughts are drawn to the still form of Lady Bergamon upstairs, and I realise how cold I am. 'No, no third body.'

'Then what are you up to?'

'Helping a friend.'

'And your friend is connected with the murders?'

'I don't know. But it seems too much of a coincidence.'

'Right. What's going on?'

'As soon as I know, you'll know,' I say. 'But this is a perfect opportunity to test the consultancy arrangement your superiors agreed to. Let us help with the murders.'

While Jamie considers my proposal, I hear someone ask him a question about extending the perimeter. He is at a crime scene. I expect it is a crime scene we, too, wish to visit.

'Alright, but I need to clear it with the top of the food chain.'

'Can you do that while we drive to wherever you are?'

At my words, Karrion tugs at a lock of hair that has come loose from my braid. I have not spared a glance in the mirror today, but it is likely I look like I spent the night under a bridge. A change of clothes would not be a bad idea, especially given that my trainers are soaked.

Jamie agrees and gives me an address. I promise to meet him there in an hour, and we end the call. When I turn to Karrion, I grin.

'Done. Wilde Investigations is going to assist the Metropolitan Police with the case.'

5

THE MAN WHO FEARED

The address Jamie gave me is near the Thames and the Brotherhood of Justice. A shower and a second cup of coffee have refreshed me, and I am ready to tackle another case.

Jamie is waiting for us by the front gates. The lines around his eyes and mouth are deeper than usual, betraying fatigue and concern, and his suit is creased, as if he has not gone home since yesterday morning. He offers us a wan smile as we look up at the well-appointed house. The grey and white facade gleams with the aid of spells, and the plants in the front garden appear manicured within an inch of their lives. From the size of the house alone, it is clear that we are dealing with members of Old London's aristocracy, most likely Mages.

After brief greetings, Jamie hands me a thin folder and two laminated badges. 'Here's some background information on the victim. You'll need it later. And I also asked someone to bring your consultants' badges. You'll need them at crime scenes if I'm not with you.'

'Can you give us a summary of the victim?'

'His name is Natheniel Laene and he was a South Mage in his early fifties. His wife, Halen, discovered the body earlier this morning, when she returned home. Laene died late last night.'

'Had she been away for the night?' I ask.

47

'Yes. Apparently, Laene sent her away every Samhain.'

'Why?' asks Karrion as he puts the folder in his backpack. A pigeon lands on the fence near him, and he nudges it away with his magic. When he turns back to us, he is scowling.

'Laene was convinced that his first wife was haunting him and that one Samhain she'd return from the dead to murder him.'

Karrion and I look at each other, lost for words. His eyes are shining, but he keeps his expression sombre. There are dozens of questions I want to ask, but I cannot decide which one to pick first.

'This is why I gave you the folder,' Jamie says. 'What I've just told you gives you a flavour of what's waiting inside.'

'Are we okay to go in, or are the SOCO team still working?'

'Doesn't matter now, does it? You're consultants for New Scotland Yard and therefore allowed at a crime scene while it's being processed.'

While Jamie leads us to the front door, Karrion leans closer.

'For the record, our job just became a hundred times more awesome,' he whispers.

'And it's all thanks to you and your negotiating skills.'

'All I did was make a suggestion.'

'From where I was sitting, it sounded more like a demand. But that could have been the brandy talking.'

Next to the front door stands a white crime scene tent. Inside are tables covered in crime scene suits. Jamie shows us how to put on the white barrier suits, boot covers, face masks and two sets of gloves. The extra layer of rustling material over my clothes leaves me feeling clumsy and the smell of the gloves clogs my nose, but I push aside the discomfort. This will be the first time I have visited an active crime scene. From what little I see of his expression, Karrion shares my excitement.

A Paladin wearing armour and carrying a bejewelled sword admits us into the house. Jamie takes us through the marble entrance hall and past a corridor of sombre portraits into a kitchen of chrome and granite. A plain white door reveals stairs leading down. The click of a camera shutter and the murmur of many voices float up to greet us.

'He was murdered in the basement?' I ask as we descend the stairs.

'Yes. Why?'

'I just think it's odd. If I was afraid of ghosts, I wouldn't go anywhere near the basement or the loft on Samhain.'

The basement is lined with shelves on three sides and there is another door beneath the stairs. In the middle of the open space, a man is lying across a camp bed, his legs dangling towards us and his head hidden on the far side. Surrounding him are turnips that have been carved into grotesque faces. Each of them looks outward, and their twisted features awaken the disquiet that took root within me last night. Smells of decomposition, turnips and soot tickle my nose.

Three people dressed in similar white crime scene suits to ours are moving around the room. One is taking photographs, one is dictating notes that the third person is taking. A second Paladin is stationed at the bottom of the stairs, her scabbard hanging outside the barrier suit, and next to her, another woman is staring at the crime scene with unfocused eyes. Her aura extends outwards, assessing. That alone tells me that she is one of the Mages employed by New Scotland Yard to identify spells at crime scenes. When her aura touches mine, the Mage's eyes flicker towards the stairs, but the focus of her spell remains unbroken.

'Anything, Mery?' Jamie asks.

'There's a fuck ton of magic in this room, sir. I haven't the foggiest what relates to the murder and what doesn't.'

'And that's your official opinion?'

'Yes, but I'll use posher words in my report.'

'Is there anything you can tell us unofficially?'

When the Mage turns to us, I notice she has one green and one blue eye, their colours luminous. Her blonde hair has black highlights and her fringe is arranged in such a way that it almost hides the green eye. The edge of a tattoo is just visible under the collar of her overalls. I estimate her to be in her late thirties.

'The owner must have been any magic shop owner's wet dream. Our fashion icons over there found a box of artefacts and a spell book on protection magic. Rumour has it, Laene even tried to purchase a sword from the Paladins. Not that he looks like he should be swinging anything bigger than a pen. Unless he and his wife were into that shit.'

'How do you know about the sword?' I ask.

Mery nods to the Paladin next to us. 'Paladins aren't always above a good gossip.'

The Paladin flushes and clears her throat. 'I judged relaying the information was pertinent to the situation,' she says to Jamie.

'I would say so. Thank you.' Jamie returns his attention to Mery. 'Anything else?'

'For someone so concerned with protection, Laene wasn't into wards. He has the usual stuff around the perimeter, but not in this room. What's the point of locking yourself in a room if you don't ward the damn thing?'

'The victim was locked in?' I ask Jamie.

Before he has a chance to reply, Mery coughs. 'If that's all, I'm going for a fag. Someone has to maintain the upstanding public image of the Yard.'

Once Mery is out of earshot, Karrion leans in to whisper, 'I wish all Mages were like that.'

'Imagine what that would do to the political structure of Old London.'

'She'd be a better leader than the stuck-up grump running the Council.'

'Next time we have a meeting with him, be sure to tell Lord Ellensthorne how you really feel about him.'

'I'm pretty sure he already knows,' Karrion says, distaste pulling down the corners of his mouth.

'Do you mind if we take a closer look at the body?' I ask Jamie.

'Go ahead.'

I pick up the nearest turnip lantern and examine it. Beneath my fingers, the flesh feels slimy and smells of rot. The carving is crude and the tea light inside has burnt itself out. I have never seen lanterns like these for sale anywhere in Old London, though this is only my second Samhain in the city. Did Laene carve them himself? Why?

Moving around the camp bed, I crouch by the body. Familiar hunger rises within me, whispering that meat is on offer. This time I am expecting it, and the instinct to feed does not override my self-control. Still, the hunger remains gnawing at my belly, and I check my watch, wondering when we will stop for lunch.

Laene's face is black. At first, I think it is due to the strangulation, but I see a change in colour along his jaw line. When I touch his forehead, the glove turns black from the transfer. The substance smells like soot. There is no fireplace in the basement, but there could be one elsewhere in the building.

51

Laene's hand is resting against the concrete floor and I lift it. His nail beds are caked with black and the fingertips are green. He must have struggled with the ivy wrapped around his neck.

'Am I allowed to ask questions as well?' I ask Jamie.

'Of course.'

'Has a sample been collected from under the fingernails?'

The SOCO team member with the clipboard nods. 'Yes. And we've swabbed the substance covering the victim's face.'

I draw upon the nose of a nearby mouse and inhale. Laene is a South Mage, just like Jamie said. Having discovered a Leech masquerading as a Mage at the top of Old London's social and political hierarchy, I need to be sure. This close to the body, the smell of decay is strong enough to almost overpower everything else. But accompanying the dust, noonday heat and sun-baked salt identifying him as a South Mage are the sharp tang of dried sweat and the acrid scent of adrenalin. Laene was afraid and rightly so.

'Make sure you check his shirt. He's been sweating a great deal.'

'How do you know that?' asks another member of the SOCO team.

'I can smell it.'

'And who are you again?'

'They're with me,' Jamie says. 'Consultants for the case.'

'Where does that lead?' Karrion asks, pointing to the door beneath the stairs.

'The wine cellar.'

'Is that the only way in?'

'Yes.'

Karrion bends to pick up a wooden bowl from underneath the stairs and shows it to me. It contains three keys, which look identical.

'If Laene locked himself in here and the door we came through is the only way out, how did his wife discover the body? The door wasn't forced.'

'She had the only other key,' says Jamie. 'The three in that bowl came from members of staff. Laene confiscated them all last night and sent everyone out of the house. Apparently, he does so every Samhain.'

'And with everyone out of the house, he locked himself in the basement,' I say. 'What was he so afraid of?'

'I told you. Laene was convinced a ghost was after him.'

Karrion sets the bowl down. 'There's a simple explanation for his death. The wife came back after the staff had left and murdered him.'

'I have people checking her alibi,' Jamie says.

I rise to ease the ache in my knees. 'I'd like to speak to her.'

'As soon as we're done here. She's upstairs, waiting for someone to take her statement.'

Karrion joins me by the body, and I lean in to touch his elbow with mine. He replies to the tacit question with a nod and looks at the body. I kneel on the floor to inspect the ivy. Coils of it cover half of Laene's neck and purple folds of skin in between show how tight they remain. Both ends of the vine are lying on the floor. The leaves are crushed near the neck, but remain intact along the rest of the vine.

'That's odd,' I say.

'What's that?'

'If I were to strangle someone with a length of ivy, there's no way I'd be able to do so without damaging the vine. In fact, I'd probably wrap it around my hands for a better grip. The leaves wouldn't survive that.'

'Could it be done with a telekinesis spell?'

53

'Possibly. We'd have to ask Mery whether the spell would use a grip like a human hand would. As it is, it looks like the ivy wrapped itself around Laene's neck and strangled him on its own accord.'

'What sort of a spell caster could do that?'

'I'm not sure.' While I do have an idea, I dismiss it as impossible. 'Another thing to ask Mery once she's finished tarring her lungs.'

'Where do you think the ivy came from?' Karrion asks. 'There are no plants down here.'

'The garden, perhaps? Or maybe the killer brought it with him. Or her.'

'Murder is an equal opportunities sort of business.'

A camera flash reflects off something underneath Laene, but I cannot see what it is.

'Has the SOCO team finished with the body?' I ask Jamie. 'Can I move it?'

'Sure. Did you notice something?'

'Maybe.'

With Karrion's help, I lift Laene's torso and reach under his neck. My hand closes around a circular necklace connected to a silver chain. The links of the chain are broken. Once we have eased Laene back to the floor, I take a closer look at the necklace. It is an oval piece of amber and roughly the length of my palm. Within the amber is a scarab beetle with an iridescent blue carapace. The beetle is broken in two, and although the amber has kept the halves touching, the edges are crushed and jagged.

'What is it?' Karrion asks, looking at the necklace over my shoulder.

'Probably a protective amulet. It didn't do Laene much good. Can you take a photo of it? Maybe Tinker Thaylor can tell us more.'

Karrion snaps a photo, and I show the amulet to Jamie. He passes it to the SOCO team, who in turn photograph it and bag it as evidence. We look around the room, but there is little else that catches our eye. Laene had enough food and drink to see him through the night, but he seemed unconcerned about making himself comfortable. The camp bed does not have a pillow or a blanket. A broken clock on the floor shows the time as quarter to twelve. I assume the clock was broken when Laene struggled with the killer.

'Ready to meet the widow?' Jamie asks.

After a final look at the body, I nod. At least this time, we are not the bearers of the bad news.

6

THE GRIEVING WIDOW

When we emerge in the kitchen, Mery returns from her break. Taking advantage of the degree of privacy, I stop her.

'Did you see the ivy around the victim's neck?'

'Yes, though I can't say I ogled it. I don't get my kicks from strangled Mages.'

'Could a telekinesis spell have strangled Laene without damaging the leaves?'

'In theory, but not without wrecking the vine.'

Karrion glances at me, puzzled. 'What do you mean?'

Mery raises her hand and makes a fist. I notice her red nail polish is chipped and scuffed.

'Your natural grip is this, yeah?'

We nod.

'Right. But if you wanted to be precise, you'd go for something else,' she says, and opens her hand to pinch her thumb and index finger together.

'And you can do that with a telekinesis spell.'

The corners of Mery's mouth twist down and she huffs. 'Yes. Obviously. But you're missing the point. Either kind of grip is possible with a spell, but to strangle someone, they must exert the same amount of force. Or thereabouts anyway.'

Karrion begins to speak, but I silence him.

'So what you're saying is that a more precise grip

would apply the same amount of force on a smaller area?'

'I see you're not just a pretty face.' Mery laughs, but it soon changes to a wet chesty cough.

'I don't understand,' Karrion says.

'Applying a great deal of force to the area between the leaves would leave them intact, but would crush the vine,' I say. 'And the ends of the ivy were pristine.'

'Telekinesis is off the table, boys and girls.' Mery gets out a packet of cigarettes and counts them. 'Not that it was ever on the table.'

'What other kind of magic could be responsible for Laene's death?' I ask.

'Some sort of plant control would explain the vine. But the answer may be far simpler.'

Karrion shifts his weight from foot to foot. 'How so?'

'There's nothing to say Laene was killed by the ivy. It looks that way, but anyone with half a brain cell and a few dubious dating experiences will tell you that looks can be deceiving.'

I think I see where she is going with this.

'Just because there is ivy around his neck doesn't mean he was strangled with it,' I say.

'Exactly. Until the corpse doctors remove the vine and take a peek at Laene's neck, who knows what killed him?'

'So the vine is a red herring,' says Karrion.

'Red herring, green herring, green ivy, there's no telling at this stage. But keep an open mind, mate.'

Karrion flushes. 'I thought I was.'

'Not open enough. Anything else?'

I shake my head and thank Mery. She waves her fingers over her shoulder and descends into the basement. Jamie, who has paced to the window and back during the conversation, stares after her.

'She's bloody good at her job, but I try to avoid letting her speak to people.'

'Isn't diversity good for New Scotland Yard?' I ask with a grin.

'Yes, but too much honesty isn't.'

We remove the gloves and face masks, and Jamie leads us down an oak-panelled corridor to a lounge decorated with antique furniture and oriental rugs. Laene's widow is on a sofa, holding a lace handkerchief. A white standard poodle sits next to the sofa, its head on the armrest. In between drying her cheeks, Halen Laene lets her hand rest on the dog's neck.

Halen has shoulder-length white hair and pale skin. My first thought is that she lacks pigment, but when she glances up, I see her eyes are pale blue. Between her appearance and her silvery grey skirt and jacket, it looks like the sun has bleached all the colours out of her. Only her jewellery adds a splash of brightness. She wears a bead necklace that is a mixture of pearls, onyx and lapis lazuli. A topaz bracelet sits around her left wrist.

My attention is drawn to the windows on the shorter side of the room. They are shuttered and barred with planks nailed across them. Heavy curtains frame them, drawn so the windows are partially hidden. To our left, more windows afford a view of the front garden and the road.

Jamie performs introductions, and Halen rises to greet us. Her thin face and slender limbs give her an air of frailty, but her grip is strong. The scents of noonday heat, dust and sun-baked salt tickle my nose. She, too, is a South Mage.

At her request, we sit down on the sofa opposite hers.

'I know you already told me some of this, but would you mind talking us through your whereabouts and what happened?' Jamie asks. 'Start from last night.'

'My husband sent the staff away around five, and I left shortly after. It has become a tradition of sorts for a small group of my old school friends to meet on Samhain. We had dinner at a sushi restaurant, caught a show, had a few drinks at a cocktail bar in Covent Garden and went dancing. I arrived at my hotel about half past one. Natheniel had ordered me a breakfast in bed and a massage. I checked out shortly after nine and came home.'

'Did you notice anything strange about the house?' I ask. 'Anything out of place?'

'Nothing stranger than Natheniel's usual Samhain traditions,' Halen says, her tone weary.

'What do you mean by that?'

'Samhain was a great source of distress for my husband. He was extremely superstitious, and Samhain was always the hardest night of the year for him. He went to great lengths to keep us safe, or at least to give himself an illusion of safety.'

'Do you know why he did all that?' Karrion asks.

'Natheniel was convinced that his first wife was haunting him.'

We know that already, of course, but hearing her casual tone startles us. Halen notices this.

'It sounds mad, doesn't it? Even here in Old London, ghosts don't exactly wander through houses and disrupt people's lives. But Natheniel swore that Marea had been haunting him for years.'

Jamie shifts on the sofa. 'How did these hauntings manifest? Or did they?'

'Items were misplaced, there were strange smells in the house, that sort of thing.' Halen looks down, her hands twisting the handkerchief. 'But I never saw any evidence of it.'

'What about the staff?' I ask. 'Did they witness anything?'

'One of the maids claims she did, but I've always considered her to be a little silly. She'd say anything to gain our approval.'

I ask for the maid's name, and jot it down.

'Was your husband's behaviour unusual last night? More so than on other Samhains?'

'He was agitated and irritable, but I'd come to expect that.'

'Why did he send you away for the night?' Karrion asks.

'He was concerned for my safety. If Marea was going to attack him, he didn't want me to be caught in the middle.'

Fresh tears well in Halen's eyes, and she wipes them away. Her mascara has left black smudges on her cheeks.

'And did he send the staff away for the same reason?'

'Yes.'

My eyes are drawn back to the barricaded windows. Halen notices and offers me an embarrassed smile.

'One of my husband's quirks.'

'Did he barricade all the windows?' I ask.

'Only the ones facing west.'

From their puzzled expressions, Karrion and Jamie do not understand the statement any more than I do.

'Did your husband have any enemies?' Jamie asks.

'No. He was a good man and well-respected by his colleagues and friends.'

'Have you noticed any changes in your husband's behaviour recently? Did he seem distracted or anxious about anything other than last night?'

'No, he's been fine.'

'How about any trouble at work? Do you know of any financial difficulties?'

'He's been busy with a new project, but he was more enthusiastic than stressed.'

60

'What did he do?'

'He runs a property development company. Originally, he worked exclusively in Old London, but in recent years, they have expanded to New London.'

'Any unhappy clients you're aware of?'

'You'd have to ask someone at the company.'

Both Jamie and I make a note of the company name and the best person to contact there.

'When you came home this morning, did you notice anything out of place?' I ask. 'Anything you weren't expecting, bearing in mind your husband's Samhain precautions.'

'There were branches on the front steps.'

I frown, thinking back to our arrival. As far as I can recall, the steps were clear.

'What sort of branches?'

'I don't know. I can't say I paid much attention to them.'

'Anything else out of place?'

'Nothing. The staff had not yet returned, but Natheniel usually gave them the morning off, so I was expecting the house to be empty. But I was also expecting Natheniel to be back to his usual self, if a little tired. When he didn't respond to my greeting and I couldn't find him upstairs, I went to the basement.'

'You knew he'd be there?'

Halen nods. 'That's where he hid himself every Samhain.'

'Did you sense anything unusual when you opened the door? Any spell residue or a ward breaking, perhaps?'

'Natheniel didn't believe wards could keep ghosts out. He never warded the basement. And no, I didn't notice anything else either, but by then, I was worried about him.'

At my instructions, Karrion finds the photo of Laene's amulet on his phone.

'Do you know what the purpose of this amulet was?' I ask, and show Halen the photo.

As her eyes fix on the screen, Halen's face grows even paler. A moan escapes from her lips, startling the dog, and she throws herself against the backrest of the sofa.

'Oh, God. He was right. She did it.'

I wave Karrion to put the phone away, but the panicked look on Halen's face does not change.

'Who did it?'

'Marea.' The name is a wail on Halen's lips. 'Marea killed Natheniel.'

'Didn't you say you never saw any evidence of a ghost?' Jamie asks.

'That,' Halen waves towards Karrion's hands, seemingly unaware that he is no longer holding a phone, 'that's all the evidence you need.'

Jamie, Karrion and I exchange another look, while Halen sobs into the handkerchief.

'I'm afraid we don't understand, Mrs Laene,' Jamie says.

The dog lays its head on Halen's lap, but when that elicits no reaction, it lifts its front paws onto the sofa and licks Halen's cheek. She wraps her arms around its neck. It takes several minutes for her to regain some of her composure. When she does, she attempts to smile. Her cheeks are blotchy from crying and her nose has turned red.

Looking around, Jamie spots a drinks trolley and fetches a tumbler of brandy. Halen's hands shake when she takes the glass, and she downs the brandy in one swallow. Jamie offers her more, but she shakes her head.

'That amulet was Natheniel's last line of defence,' Halen says, her voice unsteady. 'It was supposed to warn him against evil spirits, and it did.'

'What makes you think Marea was responsible for your husband's death?' I ask.

'Because the amulet only worked against ghosts. For the scarab to have broken within the amber, Marea must have manifested with the intent to kill Natheniel.'

'Do you know why your husband thought Marea was haunting him and wished him harm?' Jamie asks.

'Because she hated her life with him. Natheniel agreed the marriage with Marea's father, and she had little say in the matter. She had the money, but her family needed Natheniel's impeccable breeding. They were miserable together, and before long, Natheniel and I fell in love. He told me more than once that she had promised she'd never let him be happy with anyone else.'

'Is there anyone who could have taken revenge on Natheniel after Marea's death?' I ask. 'A brother, perhaps, or her father?'

'No. Marea was an only child and her father died shortly after her marriage to Natheniel. Given that Marea and Natheniel never had children, the bloodline died with her.'

There is nothing any of us can say in response. Karrion rubs at a worn patch on his jeans and Jamie takes Halen's glass back to the drinks trolley. When he returns to the sofas, he clears his throat.

'Are you sure there was no one else who might have wanted your husband dead?'

'No. And the amulet proves that.'

'Would you mind terribly if we looked around the rest of the house and the grounds?' I ask. Most of the property will have been searched as part of the investigation, but two extra pairs of eyes cannot hurt.

'Of course. You can go anywhere you wish. But why?'

'Perhaps we'll spot evidence of the ghost elsewhere in the house.'

Halen stands and looks at us with the poise of an aristocrat.

'I know what I said sounds crazy and I don't expect you to believe me. Nevertheless, Marea killed my husband. That is a fact.'

Jamie thanks Halen for her time and hands her one of his cards. We murmur our condolences and head for the door. We have only gone a few metres before Halen calls out after us. When we turn, she is standing by the sofa, leaning on the dog for support.

'You don't know what it was like living with a constant shadow hanging over this house. Natheniel was not mad, he was frightened. The thing he feared the most killed him.'

I want to say that I know something about living under a shadow, but the words get stuck in my throat. Halen does not want my understanding any more than she wants us to believe her. Her husband is dead. What else is there to say?

The thought threatens to take me back to Dearon and the conclave, and I shake my head. I have bought myself a reprieve in Old London, and now is the time to make the most of it.

7

ECHOES OF A HOME

Jamie goes to check on the SOCO team's progress, while Karrion and I don fresh sets of gloves and take the main stairs up. Thick carpet muffles our footsteps, and an eerie silence permeates the house. Perhaps it is the lack of staff that makes the house feel lifeless, or perhaps this is how it has always been.

The first four doors we open lead to bedrooms. They look ready to accommodate guests, and each has been decorated with a different colour scheme. In one of the rooms, I draw my finger along the mantelpiece and it comes back clean. Yet, I cannot help wondering when the rooms were last used.

Further along a corridor decorated with family portraits, we find the master bedroom. A queen-sized four-poster dominates the space. To our left, a door opens to an en suite appointed in black and white marble, and to our right, further doors lead to walk-in wardrobes for the victim and his wife. Large bay windows afford a view of the garden, and a leather dog bed beneath them indicates that their pet sleeps with its masters.

'I wonder if the dog saw anything,' I say, as I take in the room.

'Find a Dog Shaman and invite them to interview Fido.'

65

'Not Fifi?'

'Despite the embarrassing show trim, definitely Fido.'

Holding back a grin, I say, 'You know, I once heard on the radio about a study in which they proved that when most men meet someone new, their eyes tend to gravitate to the genitals, regardless of the species.'

Karrion pretends to gag, and looks in the bathroom.

'There's nothing out of the ordinary here,' he says.

'Or anywhere else for that matter.'

I walk to look at the photos on the dressing table. Most of them show the victim and Halen smiling at the camera. They look happy together. In two of the photos, Halen is with the poodle at a dog show. Judging by the size of the rosettes Halen is holding, they must have won something important.

'I don't get it,' I say. 'This whole place looks like they're expecting to feature in a magazine. How do people live like this? How can anyone ever relax in a house filled with antique furniture and cream carpets? What if they spill their tea? Or the dog comes in with muddy paws?'

'I don't think the Mage aristocrats are physically capable of spilling tea. Such faults will have been bred out of them centuries ago. And the dog probably has a body suit for going out.'

'Still, it's nuts,' I say.

'Haven't you ever been curious about how the other half lives?'

'No.'

It is true. Growing up in the Wild Folk conclave, I was well aware that there were other magic users living elsewhere in England, just as there were countless humans. But how they lived was never a concern of mine. While I heard plenty of talk of Mage aristocrats, I did not appreciate that class impacted every aspect of people's lives until I moved to Old London. Perhaps others at the conclave were more aware of life outside our borders, but it never interested me.

By the same token, I rarely spared a thought for my future. When Dearon and I discussed it as teenagers, it was to imagine an endless series of warm spring days, clear summer skies, thrilling autumn hunts and waking up to a blanket of snow. What we never discussed was that my father had chosen a different future for me, one in which I had no say. Dearon knew all along, and now, years later, I still blame him for keeping the Elderman's secret.

Karrion nudging me with his shoulder draws me away from the bitterness that threatens to overwhelm me. His lips smile, but I see concern in his eyes.

'Maybe it's just me, but I think it would be nice to have someone do the cleaning for once, instead of Mum having to clean other people's houses.'

'And clear up after you.'

I laugh at his outrage.

'I'm not that bad.'

'No, but you're an easy mark. And who knows, if you keep painting and become a famous artist, one day you and Aderyn can sit back while servants answer your every beck and call.'

'That would be weird,' Karrion says with a grimace. 'I'd settle for having enough money that Mum never needs to worry about feeding and clothing the brood, and Robin, Wren and Jay can choose whatever education they want.'

'You know, you'd reach that point quicker if you didn't spend your wages on black hair dye and pigeon repellent,' I say, laughing, and dodging the playful poke aimed at my shoulder.

'I'll have you know,' he points at his hair, 'this is my natural colour.'

'Not with the blue tint, it isn't.'

'Who's to say my dad wasn't part magpie?'

'Your mum. She's said more than once that he was probably a pigeon. It would certainly explain why pigeons love you so much.'

Karrion's shoulders hunch as he tugs at his lip piercing.

'We're all kin to ravens and crows.'

'But if the feathers fit—'

With a huff, Karrion stalks out of the bedroom. I laugh and, after a final glance around, follow him.

The final door to our right is Laene's study. Mahogany bookcases line the walls, leaving space only for a wide fireplace and a portrait of a man who must be Laene's father or a close relative. Looking at the dark furniture and burgundy rug, I cannot help wondering whether all aristocratic Mage houses have a room like this. Perhaps it is one of the requirements for joining the elitist club.

While Karrion picks up a bronze statue of a peregrine falcon, I circle around the desk. Papers are stacked in neat piles on both sides. Otherwise, a lamp and a gilded pen holder are the only items on the desk.

'There's nothing here,' Karrion says. 'And how are we even supposed to know if anything is out of place?'

'You're right,' I say, flicking through the papers on the desk. 'Let's find—'

A name on one of the sheets silences me, and I thumb through the papers until I find the correct page. My initial confusion turns to dread.

'Did you find something?' Karrion asks, stopping on the opposite side of the desk.

'Yes. Nothing to do with the murder, but this is bad news.'

'What is it?'

'Laene's plans for some new work he's hoping to win. They've called it the Ivy Street Project.'

'Ivy Street? But that's where—'

'Lady Bergamon lives, yes. According to this, Laene and his business partners want to buy all the houses along the street, demolish them and erect new tower blocks on both sides of the road. He's dressing it up as meeting Old London's affordable housing quota.'

'Do you think Lady Bergamon knows?'

'I don't know. It depends on how far along the project is.'

'What happens if the residents don't want to sell their homes?'

'This doesn't say anything about that, it's just a draft press release. I imagine this sort of project would need approval from the High Council of Mages and the Elders of the Circle of Shamans. At least, I hope it does.'

'Let's hope they'll dismiss it without a second thought.'

Nodding my assent, I return the page to its place in the stack and we leave the study.

We search the rest of the upstairs rooms, but find nothing incongruous. Had it not been for the extent of Laene's precautions, I might have thought him simply paranoid. Even now, I am not altogether convinced a ghost was haunting him, but it's clear he feared something. But did that something kill him?

Downstairs yields no further clues and we meet Jamie in the entrance hall. He tells us that the SOCO team is wrapping up their investigation downstairs, and proposes we have lunch before heading to the next crime scene. I remind him that we wanted to look around the gardens, and he holds the front door open for us.

As I walk through the door, I spot a heap of branches by the steps. I recognise both rowan and rosemary.

'What's that?'

'They were on the front steps when we arrived. SOCO took a few photos and moved them aside in case we need them later. Why?'

They must be what Halen was referring to. Crouching by the branches, I spot a piece of green string. The knot is still intact. I touch a bunch of berries and they burst, emitting a faint smell of rot and smearing juice on my fingers.

'If I'm not mistaken, this was a wreath designed to protect the house from spirits.'

'The killer entered through the front door,' Karrion says.

'Are you sure?' Jamie asks.

I wipe my fingers on the grass and stand. 'Yes. We've seen this before.'

'Care to share?'

'All in good time. Let's look around first.'

I check the front door lock, but it is intact. It strikes me as strange, but I push the thought aside. We discard our crime scene suits in a biohazard bag inside the white tent and continue our exploration.

The front lawn is neatly trimmed and decorated with small Japanese maple trees. The multi-coloured leaves lie in a thick carpet under the trees, and at first glance, the scene looks picturesque. But something about it jars, and as soon as I glance towards the gardens on either side, I know why: the trees elsewhere still carry their leaves. Laene's garden is the only one where not a single leaf clings to the branches.

Stepping off the paved path, I pick up a handful of leaves. They feel dry and brittle, as if they had been on the ground for several days, possibly a week. Yet, the lawn underneath has been trimmed recently. They cannot be a gardener's oversight. Something else is going on.

I sense a rat nearby and borrow its nose. Beneath the decay of the leaves, the smell of rotting meat is unmistakable. It leads me to a spot between the nearest trees, and when I move the leaves aside, I see that the ground has been disturbed recently. Whoever did it removed a section of turf and then replaced it. Digging my fingers under the edge, I find that the grass has not yet reattached its roots. I peel it back, and the smell of meat and soil tantalises me. My stomach growls, but I ignore it and dig through the earth until my hand finds bones.

'What is that?' Jamie asks, stepping closer with Karrion.

'Beef ribs,' I say, pulling bones out of the hole, 'lamb shanks, pig shins, chicken wings.'

'Why would anyone want to bury Sunday lunch in their front garden?' Karrion asks.

'You assume it was someone living in the house, which may not be the case. But either way, I don't know.'

The meat on the bones is rotting, indicating that they have been in the ground for days. But the turf suggests otherwise. My head begins to ache as I weigh the contradictions.

Drawing upon the rat's nose again, I lift my chin and sample the air. The rot in front of me all but overpowers everything else, but I catch a similar smell elsewhere. When I follow it, I discover two further spots where meat and bones have been buried.

Jamie opens a side gate, and we walk around the house. The landscaped garden is meticulous and I find it hard to believe that the Laenes have a dog. Perhaps it is too refined to bury bones in the flower beds or dig up the lawn.

With my enhanced sense of smell, I find four more spots where meat has been buried. Here it smells fresh. Taken together with the ones in the front garden, the spots appear to form a circle around the house. But to what purpose? Was it to attract something or to repel?

At the back, the trees look no different from those in the neighbours' gardens and I point this out to the others. Karrion has been staring at the house, and he draws my attention to it with a hand on my shoulder.

'Check that out.'

Hanging from the back door is another wreath of rowan and rosemary. This one is intact. I walk up to it and touch the berries, but they remain firm under my fingers. The scent of fresh rosemary sprigs cleanses my nose of the smell of rot, and some of the hunger nagging in my belly eases.

'Why does everything out here seem normal? What's different?'

Karrion opens his mouth, but with a glance at Jamie, he hesitates.

'What is it, Karrion?' I ask.

'Right. The killer came and went through the front door.'

'What's that got to do with anything?' Jamie asks.

'That's why everything here looks fine,' I say. 'The killer was never in the back garden.'

'That'd be my guess,' Karrion says.

Brushing loose soil from my hands, I turn my back to the house.

'Whatever happened here last night, it goes further than a murderous ghost going after her husband.'

8

A WORKING LUNCH

When we walk around the house and head for the road, Mery is waiting for us next to Jamie's car. She has also discarded the barrier clothing and is dressed in a black trouser suit. Her cheeks are hollowed, as if she is attempting to inhale her entire cigarette in a single drag. I dodge around the acrid smoke clinging to her arms.

'If there's nothing else you need, I'm off,' she says. 'First Hailfax, then this place. No wonder I'm knackered.'

'Get something to eat. But don't forget your reports. Those posh words don't write themselves.'

'If only they would, I'd spin you quite a yarn, boss.'

Mery inspects her cigarette package, crumples it and drops it on the pavement. With a wave in our general direction, she walks to a dented mint-green VW Golf and drives off. Once the car has turned a corner, I pick up the cigarette package and drop it in a nearby bin.

'Where are we going for lunch?' Karrion asks.

'There's a pub not far from here called the Magician's Head,' Jamie says. 'How about there?'

Karrion shrugs. 'Fine by me, though they're not winning any prizes for originality.'

We walk to the pub in silence. I keep turning the pieces of the puzzle in my mind. Try as I might, I cannot help thinking the attack on Lady Bergamon is connected to Natheniel Laene's murder. Or were the wreaths a mere coincidence? And what of the press release regarding the Ivy Street Project?

It would help if I knew what time Lady Bergamon was attacked. But she could have been unconscious for hours before Wishearth woke me up. I doubt Bradán carries a watch in his equine form.

The Magician's Head is close enough to New London to cater for tourists coming to Old London in search of magic. The lights are dim, the decor dark, and the walls are covered in photos of celebrities wearing pointy wizard hats. Behind the counter, a man dressed in glittery robes and yet another pointy hat is pulling pints and casting a spell in pigeon Latin to entertain a group of young women. I notice that each table has either a lava lamp or a crystal volcano puffing out rose-scented smoke.

Crossing my arms, I turn to Jamie.

'This place is only missing broomsticks and cauldrons for hire.'

'You might not want to look behind the bar.'

I stare at Jamie in silence, and he runs a hand through his hair.

'I know this place is a giant cliché, but they serve great fish finger sandwiches and it was close by.'

'As silly as this place is, I'm all for fish finger sandwiches,' Karrion says.

'Fine. But the menu better not contain eyes of newt and dried salamanders.'

'Why don't I order for you?' Jamie says. 'You can find us a quiet table.'

'I'll help Jamie with the drinks,' Karrion offers and reaches for the menu, eyes shining.

I choose a booth in the far corner and sit down. The air smells of Turkish Delight, and I fumble under the table until I find an off switch for the pink volcano. Straightening in the cracked leather seat, I watch Karrion take a photo of the menu, his face alight with glee. His good cheer is contagious, and I find myself smiling as I watch him.

Karrion reaches the table first, carrying three pints of cola. Jamie follows soon after, holding a leaflet. Before he stuffs it in his pocket, I catch the title: Unlock the magical potential in your blood. Jamie's eyes meet mine, and he looks away, a hint of pink creeping up his neck.

'I ordered you toad tails and taters,' Karrion says.

'Toads don't have tails.'

'I know. Isn't this place cool?'

Karrion grins and takes a long sip from his glass.

'Where do you want to start?' Jamie asks.

'With Natheniel Laene's first wife.'

'Marea Laene died twelve years ago. Back then, I was a probationary constable and my involvement in the investigation was limited to guarding the door. But I heard enough talk back at the station to remember the case when I received the call this morning. I asked a colleague to put together a summary, which is in the folder I gave you.'

'How did Marea Laene die?' I ask.

'She drowned in a bathtub.'

My thoughts return to Laene's master bedroom and the large tub I caught a glimpse of through the open door. Is it the same one, or did Laene renovate after his first wife's death?

'Was she murdered?' Karrion asks. He has taken a notebook out and is writing things down in his terrible scrawl.

'The coroner's inquest returned an open verdict; they were unable to determine whether the death was accidental or an unlawful killing. Marea had some bruising on her arms that could have come from someone holding her under water, or could have been a sign of domestic violence. There were rumours going around that Natheniel had quite a temper and Marea had one to match.'

'Did you have any suspects?' I ask.

'Unofficially, we all thought Laene did it. He had motive and a shoddy alibi. But we couldn't find any evidence to prove his guilt, and the Crown Prosecution Service felt there was no justification to put Laene before a Herald. It was at a time when the Paladins were getting fed up with the Met not investigating cases thoroughly enough and getting the Heralds to do their job for them. After enough rapped knuckles, we learned the lesson. Laene had motive, but that wasn't enough. But what we all found unusual was that Laene was convinced Marea was murdered and he was pushing us to keep digging long after the case had gone cold.'

'Strange behaviour for a guilty man,' Karrion says. 'Unless it was a double bluff.'

'That's what we thought. But we were never able to prove whether she was murdered and who did it.'

'Did Laene think Marea was haunting him because he murdered her, or because he couldn't figure out who the killer was?' I ask, turning my glass on a coaster advertising "bewitching beers" brewed at the pub. 'What was his alibi?'

'He was meeting with one of the company directors in his office. No one else could verify Laene's movements, and employees make for unconvincing alibis.'

'What motive did he have for murdering Marea?'

'His company was in financial difficulties. They'd made some bad purchases and were facing liquidation. You see, Laene is from an old bloodline, but Marea was the one with the money. They had no children, so he inherited it all. It saved the company and made Laene a wealthy man.'

'Was there anything else that pointed to his guilt?'

'Several of my colleagues felt that he was a little too nervous and not upset enough about his wife's death, but people deal with grief in different ways. What I find the most suspicious is that six months after Marea's death, he married Halen. She's the only daughter of a baron, and I half expected her to turn up dead shortly after the marriage.'

'That would have been pretty obvious,' Karrion says.

'I agree. In any case, they remained married until last night and all rumours of loud fights in the Laene residence stopped.'

'Perhaps Laene didn't kill Marea for her money, but because he was in love with someone else,' I say. 'That might also be a reason for Laene to believe Marea was haunting him. If her spirit lingered in the house, she may have resented him not just for his part in her death, but because he'd found happiness elsewhere.'

Jamie shrugs. 'It's possible.'

'I'd like to talk to someone who's an expert in ghosts and hauntings,' I say. 'Can either of you recommend anyone?'

'Maybe,' Karrion says and reaches for his phone. 'Our neighbour was convinced her flat was haunted, and eventually, she hired a ghost tracker. I'll text Mum and ask her to find out the contact details from Mrs Barneby.'

Our food arrives. What the menu described as toad tails and taters turns out to be breaded scampi and chips. Jamie and Karrion's fish finger sandwiches look no more exciting than my food, and I experience a flash of disappointment.

Karrion finishes sending the text and puts his phone away. He passes me a pot of tartar sauce off his plate, while I reach for the ketchup.

Karrion picks up his sandwich. 'This is perfect crime-solving fuel.'

'I don't know,' I say, dipping a piece of scampi in the tartar sauce. 'What sort of carrion crow eats its fish breaded and in a sandwich?'

'The kind that knows what happiness is all about.'

'So, are you going to explain how you could tell from a bunch of twigs which door the killer used?' asks Jamie.

'Actually, I was thinking the next item on the agenda would be the second victim. Is his death connected with Laene's?'

I am reluctant to tell Jamie about Lady Bergamon. If I reveal that she was attacked and something entered Old London through her house, I will have to tell him about her domain. The secret of her garden is not mine to reveal. I am also conscious that Bradán said Lady Bergamon had to remain close to the source of her power. But when did blindly trusting a Fey become a good idea?

'We're looking into a connection. There was nothing obvious we could see this morning, but it had been a long night and it's possible we missed something.'

'Who was the victim?' Karrion asks.

'Hynryk Hailfax. He was a North Mage.'

'Who found the body?'

'Technically, the Paladins did. The victim was on the phone when he was attacked. The person he was speaking to called the Paladins.'

'Was Hailfax concerned about anyone haunting him?'

'I don't know. We haven't been able to interview his father yet.'

'Why not?' I ask.

'He was unconscious when the Paladins arrived and he was rushed to the hospital. From the last update I heard, the doctors were still trying to stabilise his condition and figure out what was wrong with him.'

Karrion steals a piece of my scampi. I pretend not to notice, but when he takes a sip of his cola, I grab a forkful of his salad.

'Could he be another victim?' I ask.

'Possibly, though the Paladins couldn't see any obvious way he'd been attacked. With Hynryk, it was clear he'd been targeted.'

'You said on the phone that he had belladonna in his mouth. Was he poisoned?'

'The plant wasn't just in his mouth. It looked like someone had pushed an entire plant down his throat, only no one was able to remove it. Maybe the branches are stuck, I'm not sure. We'll know more once the autopsy has been completed. The same with the cause of death.'

I straighten my legs under the table, food and caffeine chasing away the fatigue from my disrupted night. Bits of information swirl around my mind, and I am struggling to keep them in order.

'Can we see the crime scene? It would help paint a picture of what happened.'

'We'll head over there as soon as we're finished.'

Karrion stuffs the last corner of his sandwich into his mouth and finishes his drink. He wipes his mouth with the back of his hand.

'I'm done,' he says.

'Me too.'

I set my fork down next to the last few chips. When Jamie rises and gets his wallet out, I ask how much my and Karrion's share is. He waves away my money and goes to the bar to pay.

'How were your toad tails?' Karrion asks.

'Lacking a certain amphibian flavour.'

We join Jamie by the bar. The barkeeper raises his hat to us.

'If you ever need to hire a broomstick, be sure to come back!'

I get as far as rolling my eyes before Jamie ushers us out.

9

THE MAN WHO CARED

When we reach our cars, Jamie gives me the address and promises to meet us at the crime scene. I'm turning to slide into the driver's seat when I spot Karrion looking at the back of my car, a finger idly flicking at the row of hoops in his ear.

'I was thinking, maybe your car needs a bumper sticker. For advertising the business.'

'Saying what? "We're wild and we investigate stuff"?'

'I was more thinking something like: "Private Investigators do it discreetly".'

I glance over to see Karrion trying to keep a straight face, his eyes dancing with the enjoyment of his own joke.

'Just get in the car.'

He does so, but laughter bubbles out of him and I cannot help joining in.

Hynryk Hailfax lived in a block of flats overlooking the Thames. I recognise the area, and my eyes are drawn to another building a little further along. Reaoul Pearson lived there before his arrest and subsequent death. It has only been a few weeks, but I expect his wife will have moved on already.

Karrion follows the direction of my gaze, and the last vestiges of laughter slip from his face. Does he recall

Eolande's beauty, or have his thoughts turned to the memory of light pouring in through the windows and my leaping over the sofa, ready to tear open Reaoul's throat? I was protecting those I care about. That is the simple explanation. But there is more to it than merely helping Karrion and Jamie; the wildness of my very nature has little regard for chains and Heralds. I understand a different form of judgement and execution.

A uniformed police officer at the door greets Jamie by name and lets us into the building. We take the lift to the third floor. Another officer is guarding the door of the flat. Here too barrier suits are stacked on a folding table, and we dress with little more ease than this morning.

Inside, the rooms are spacious and light. A short corridor leads to an open-plan kitchen and dining area. From there, doors open on both sides to further rooms. The decor is modern, but simple, and I like the understated elegance.

Jamie steers us to the left and through the door closest to the tall windows. The view across the river is striking, and a ray of sunlight gilds the brown surface.

The room we enter – Hailfax's office – looks as though a gang of criminals has ransacked it. A drawing table is lying on its side, a row of awards has been swept off the mantelpiece and there are books scattered across the floor. When I step over the threshold, broken glass crunches under my feet. I notice drops of blood across the window.

'I'm not going to ask about signs of struggle,' I say, as I take in the chaos of the room. 'Do we know how many intruders there were?'

'That's the weird part. I'm not sure there were any.'

Both Karrion and I turn to Jamie.

'What are you talking about? This place is trashed.'

'As I told you before, Hailfax was on the phone when

he was attacked. The person on the other end,' Jamie gets out his notebook and flips through the pages, 'Lord Wellaim Ellensthorne, said that the victim complained about a stomach ache, but never mentioned anything about intruders.'

'Lord Ellensthorne?' I ask.

'Yes. Didn't you come across him during the Marsh case?'

'We did.'

What I leave unsaid is that Lord Ellensthorne is also a client. Over the past couple of weeks, Karrion and I have been vetting the High Council of Mages and the Circle of Shamans for him. So far, we have found no Leeches hiding in plain sight, but our work is by no means finished. The premium fees we are charging Lord Ellensthorne mean that the balance on the business account is healthy and I have been able to pay Karrion a generous salary.

'Since you already know him, do you want to pay him a visit? He may have heard something else, or Hailfax may have said something to explain what happened here.'

Karrion's expression darkens, and I shake my head before he says anything.

'Sounds good. We'll head over there as soon as we've finished here.'

When Karrion opens his mouth, I send a warning glance his way and step further into the room.

The office has a floor to ceiling window and the blinds are pushed to one side. When the lights are on, anyone can see in from the road or the river. Perhaps the location on the third floor affords a degree of privacy, but did someone walk past the building last night and catch a glimpse of Hailfax dying?

On the wall by the door is a photograph of two men standing outside a building. I recognise it as the Museum of Magic that was completed last year. The men both have the same pointed nose and long chin, but the younger man has a narrower face and his hair is lighter. Still, there is no question about them being related.

Does Dearon resemble his father?

I dismiss the thought with a flash of irritation, and focus on the photo. Jamie comes to stand next to me.

'That's Hynryk and his father. He designed the building.'

'Do you know if the flat was warded?' I ask.

'Mery said she detected all the usual stuff: protection against spells and remote viewing, an alarm ward, and something for privacy.'

'Were any of them breached?'

'Not according to her. Whoever the killer was, Hailfax must have let them in.'

'Is the privacy ward for the windows?' Karrion asks.

'Yes. Mery explained it to me earlier. The ward is like a magical set of net curtains, except that it works even when there are lights on inside. You can see out just fine, but people can't see into the flat.'

'Sounds handy. And expensive,' Karrion says.

'Hailfax was a well-known architect. From our preliminary findings, we know he had no financial problems.'

'Does his father live here too?'

'Yes. He moved in when he was diagnosed with cancer. I understand he is now in remission. Hynryk cut down his workload to look after his father.'

I walk around the room, looking for anything out of place. There are no Samhain decorations here, no sign the Hailfaxes followed the old ways or were superstitious. At first glance there is nothing to connect this crime scene with Laene's death, and yet I find it strange that two men died in nature-related ways during the same night.

'What time did Lord Ellensthorne call the Paladins?' I ask.

'It was shortly after midnight.'

Someone could have murdered Laene and then driven here in time to kill Hailfax. But why? And who?

A broken mug on the floor catches my attention. I pick up the largest shard. It contains dried liquid, and I bring the fragment close to my nose. All I can smell is coffee. Borrowing the nose of a dog asleep in the flat below, I try again. Coffee still dominates, but underneath I detect something else. The smell does not seem to come from the liquid itself, but rather from the rim of the mug. I inhale for the third time and catch the bittersweet smell of deadly nightshade.

'There's belladonna on the rim of the mug, but not in the coffee.'

Jamie jots down a note.

'So someone painted the rim with belladonna? Perhaps Hailfax was poisoned and the plant was just a distraction?'

'Are you sure it was a belladonna plant?' Karrion asks.

'The Paladins sounded certain. I wouldn't recognise one even if someone was shoving it down my throat.'

'But why use deadly nightshade?' I ask. 'There are easier ways to poison someone.'

'Maybe the killer is a gardener,' Karrion says. 'Or a rambler. A really, really deranged rambler, who hates architects. Or he's vegan and wants to kill with vegan poison? I don't know.'

'It takes hours for the poison to take effect and it's not usually lethal.' I glance at Jamie. 'Has someone tested all the food and drink in the flat?'

'The SOCO team took samples of everything. And the doorman said that Hailfax came home shortly after lunch and didn't go out again. He must have ingested the poison here.'

'If we find the source, we're one step closer to figuring out who killed him.'

'No chance it was a suicide?' Karrion asks.

'Again, there are easier ways to commit suicide. Besides, it looks like he continued working until he died. It's odd behaviour for someone looking to end their life. And there was no note.'

'I think we can assume this wasn't a suicide,' I say, and continue looking around the room.

A large sheet of paper has come loose from the drawing table and lies crumpled by a table leg. I straighten it to see what Hailfax was working on, but the neat writing in the top corner sends a shudder through me and I lose my grip on the paper. It lands on the floor with a rustle.

'Everything all right, Yan?' Karrion asks.

'The deaths are connected.'

'What?'

Jamie strides over to me. I show him and Karrion the incomplete plans for a tower block. The top corner identifies it as part three of the Ivy Street Project plans. Karrion's eyes widen.

'We saw a draft press release in Laene's office relating to this same project. I thought nothing of it at the time, but now it seems significant.'

'Couldn't it be a coincidence?' Jamie asks.

'It could, but what are the odds of two people working on the same project being murdered within an hour of each other?'

'I guess it depends on how big the project is.'

'Are we sure Laene and Hailfax were the only two to be murdered?' Karrion asks. 'If it took the killer an hour to murder the two of them, who's to say there weren't others?'

'I've received no reports of other murders in Old London since last night, but I'll check,' Jamie says, and gets his phone out.

While he is making the call, Karrion sidles up to me.

'Are you thinking what I'm thinking?'

'That depends. Are you thinking about how great pigeons are?'

He nudges me with his shoulder. 'Something broke out of Lady Bergamon's garden and it has killed two Mages.'

Eyes on Jamie, I shush Karrion to lower his voice.

'We don't know that for certain,' I whisper.

'No, but it does look like Lady Bergamon is connected somehow.'

'I don't want to tell Jamie yet, not until we have proof. Or at least a better idea of what we're dealing with.'

Karrion shifts, but he nods. He wanders to the window, while Jamie finishes his call.

'It looks like Laene and Hailfax were the only two victims.'

For now.

I keep the thought to myself, concern churning in my stomach. Or perhaps the toad tails are not sitting well with me.

'That's good,' I say, and force a smile. 'Two deaths are quite enough for our first consultancy case.'

A low cabinet stands next to the drawing table. Rifling through Hailfax's possessions makes me feel like an intruder, even if I am doing so to catch his killer. It appears the cabinet contains mostly stationery supplies, but I spot a thin folder in the bottom drawer. I open it and find news articles and letters stapled together. After I've scanned the first two pages, I wave the folder at Jamie.

'Did you know about this?'

'What's that?' Jamie reaches for the folder.

'It says here that a tower block was declared unsafe after the walls cracked. Lots of people were displaced and there was a public uproar because the residents were all low income or on benefits. It cost the High Council a great deal of money to find new homes for everyone.'

'I remember that,' Karrion says. 'It happened two, maybe three years ago. That tower block had been built specifically to provide more housing for those on benefits. People had lived there for four years at the most before they were evacuated almost overnight. Lots of Old London residents were saying that the rehousing process took a lot longer because the Council didn't care about what happened to poor people, especially those who aren't Mages. I think Braeman sorted it out in the end, but it stained the Mages' reputation for a while.'

Jamie nods. 'The police were involved briefly, but it wasn't a case for my department. No criminal negligence was found.'

'It says here that Hailfax designed the building.'

'Was it his fault?' Karrion asks. 'Because that could be a motive for murder.'

I leaf through the papers a second time. 'I think the Council tried to go after him first, but he was able to show that the construction company had cut corners.'

'That must have made the company mad. Or perhaps not everyone believed he was innocent?'

Jamie looks up from his notebook. 'But why take revenge now and not when the problems with the building were all over the news?'

'I'm not sure.' I return the folder to the bottom drawer. 'But that answers my question about whether Hailfax had any enemies.'

'I'll find out which construction company was involved,' Jamie says. 'Professional dispute sounds like a more plausible reason for murdering someone than an angry ghost.'

We look around a bit longer, but discover nothing else. Given that a SOCO team has already gone through everything with a fine-toothed comb, they may have found something we have missed. I will ask for a copy of their report later.

'Can I see the father's room?' I ask.

'Of course. This way.'

Jamie takes us to a bedroom next to the office. Everything is neat and decorated in the same style as the other rooms. A smell of sickness lingers in the air, almost disguised by a sandalwood air freshener. The bed is unmade, the covers thrown back. It makes sense, if the Paladins found Hailfax's father unconscious and rushed him to the hospital.

Could his malady be connected to that afflicting Lady Bergamon?

I search the room, but find no Samhain decorations or anything out of place. The whole flat has a lifeless quality to it, and it takes me a while to realise that there are no plants anywhere. It's as though Hynryk Hailfax and his father lived in a glass box; able to see the world and yet removed from it.

While I look around, I am aware of Jamie's phone ringing and him exchanging a few words with the caller. I am crouching by the bed, looking under it, when Jamie appears in the doorway.

'Fancy a trip to the hospital? Denniel Hailfax just woke up.'

10

THE RAVAGES OF TIME

The hospital ward is busy. The rush of people and the smells of disinfectant and illness have me reaching for my left arm. It has been long enough since I was stabbed that the row of stitches has turned into a raised red scar. I have been getting a lot of those recently.

A doctor directs us to a room with four beds. A nurse is checking the vitals of a patient by the door when we enter, but when Jamie introduces himself, she leaves. I glance around the room, trying to spot Denniel Hailfax. It takes me several moments to realise that it was him the nurse was visiting.

In the photo we saw, Denniel's hair was dark brown and I estimated his age to be around the mid-fifties. But the man lying in the hospital bed is a decade older, maybe more. His hair is white and deep lines give his face a severe feel. No matter how taxing the cancer treatment may have been, I cannot believe it could have effected such a profound change.

Denniel turns his head when Jamie introduces us, but his half-lidded eyes speak of fatigue. I pause at the foot of the bed and call upon my magic. Beneath the smell of disinfectant, plastic and people, I catch hints of moss, frost and autumn leaves. He is a North Mage.

'The doctor said my son was attacked,' Denniel says, his voice reedy. 'Is he also here?'

89

Jamie's lips tighten. He was not expecting to have to break the news. I am struck by the sudden urge to hug him, though we are not friendly enough for such sentiments and I am not certain he would appreciate it. The muscles in Jamie's neck tighten as he meets Denniel's gaze.

'I'm afraid your son died.'

A tear rolls from the corner of Denniel's eye and lands on the pillow. When he raises his hand to wipe his face, it trembles violently. His limbs are skeletal, with skin hanging loose on the bones.

'I don't understand. Who would want to hurt Hynryk?'

'That's what we're trying to find out. Did you hear Hynryk having an argument with anyone, or any sounds of a struggle last night?'

'No, I didn't hear anything at all. I went to bed early, had nightmares about a dark creature chasing me, and woke up here.'

'How did your son seem yesterday?' I ask. 'Was he stressed or agitated at all?'

'He was excited about a new project. Anxious about it too. But I wasn't left with the impression he was worried about anyone, or that he was afraid.'

'Did you spend much time with him last night?'

'We had a light supper together. Afterwards, I went for a walk along the river and then retired to my room. Hynryk was working when I wished him a good night. He always worked too hard.'

'At supper, did you eat the same food?' Jamie asks.

'Yes,' Denniel says. 'Why?'

'There is a possibility that someone poisoned your son.'

'Poisoned and attacked? Who would do something like that to him?'

'We are still in the early stages of the investigation and we are pursuing different avenues. As soon as we know something definitive, I will let you know. In the

90

meantime, can you think of anyone who may have wanted to hurt him?'

'No, he had no enemies. This doesn't make any sense. There's no reason for anyone to target my son.'

'What about that tower block that became uninhabitable a couple of years ago?' I ask.

'It was terrible.' Denniel twists the corner of his blanket between his hands. 'Hynryk received death threats and awful letters, but none of it was his fault. It was the construction company, not Hynryk. He stopped sleeping and barely ate, and he vowed he'd never work with those people again. Even after he had shown that he had nothing to do with the defective construction, it took his reputation a long time to recover.'

'How long did the threats continue?'

'Months. But eventually, people moved on to other things. Since then, he's made sure to work only with the most reputable of companies. No one should have done this to Hynryk. Not my boy, not after everything we've been through.'

Denniel has grown agitated and a nurse arrives. She checks the monitors and asks that we allow the patient to rest. After offering Denniel our condolences – a seemingly hollow sentiment – we leave. I glance back at the door and see that Denniel has turned towards the window. Tears are streaming down his face, and he does not seem to hear what the nurse is saying to him.

Out in the corridor, Jamie stops another nurse and asks to speak to the doctor looking after Denniel Hailfax. A short, plump woman in a white coat soon approaches us and introduces herself as Doctor Gupta. She takes us to a tiny room, where the walls are covered with British Heart Foundation posters and leaflet racks.

'Have you been able to figure out what was wrong with Denniel Hailfax?' Jamie asks.

'Nothing I'd be willing to write down.'

I shift, about to ask her what she means, but Jamie beats me to it.

'How about unofficially?'

'Unofficially,' Doctor Gupta perches on the edge of the desk and picks up a small plastic clock, 'unofficially I'd say he's suffering from old age. Except that he's fifty-seven, and I spoke to his oncologist, who swore Mr Hailfax was fine at his last check up three weeks ago.'

'What do you think happened to him?' I ask.

'I don't know. None of us has ever seen anything comparable. It's like he aged ten years in a single night. The unconsciousness was most likely his body's way of coping with the shock.'

'Could a spell do that?'

Doctor Gupta shakes her head. 'I asked our Mage, but she was none the wiser. We don't know how this was done. All we know for certain is that magic was involved.'

'Is there anything else?' Jamie asks. 'Anything that will help us catch whoever did this to Mr Hailfax and his son?'

'I'm sorry,' Doctor Gupta stands, 'there's nothing more I can tell you.'

We thank her and head for the lifts. They are crowded, and it is not until we are descending from the ground floor to the underground car park that the three of us have the lift to ourselves. Karrion leans against the wall, hands behind his back and with a frown creasing his brow.

'Do you think they were both targeted?' he asks.

'Or Hynryk was the real target and his father was collateral damage,' I say.

'What sort of collateral damage ages a man ten years?'

'I don't know. We're all in the dark here, and it's not a good place to be. Especially if there's any chance that the killer isn't finished.'

I nudge a bit of gravel on the floor, so lost in my thoughts that Karrion lays his hand on my shoulder to show that we have reached the car park.

'You okay, Yan?'

Karrion's voice echoes between concrete pillars and rows of cars, and I lower my voice.

'I was just thinking how unusual that ageing effect is and how I've never seen anything similar. But I'm not sure that's true.'

'What do you mean?' Jamie asks.

'That meat buried around the Laene house. It smelled like it had been in the ground at least a week. But the turf on top of it hadn't reattached its roots.'

'What are you saying?'

'I think the holes were dug yesterday, but the meat aged a week overnight.'

'I don't know,' Jamie says, scratching his ear. 'There's a big difference between a week and ten years.'

'Maybe the effect is dependent on the target. The same spell ages a person, who is longer-lived, more than meat, which has a relatively short shelf life.'

I think back to the broken crockery in Lady Bergamon's garden and the smell of decay from the offerings within it. Is that, too, connected to the deaths? What has a ghost escaping from Lady Bergamon's garden got to do with two Mages? If that is what came through to Old London. My ghost theory fits in with Laene's murder up to a point, but not with Hynryk Hailfax's death. Could Denniel Hailfax's premature ageing be caused by a ghost? Perhaps it was caused by intense fear. But should he not have been awake to be frightened?

At length, I realise that I have been staring at a fire extinguisher and that neither Karrion nor Jamie are saying anything.

'Sorry?' I say, uncertain whether I missed a question. 'I was wondering how we could stop a spell that ages its victims,' Jamie says.

'The same way we stop any other spells: by knowing what we're up against, by using the right sort of protection and by taking out the spell caster before he has a chance to cast anything.'

'Are we sure it was a spell?' Karrion asks. 'Mery didn't seem to pick up anything distinctive at the Laene crime scene.'

Jamie gets his car keys out of his pocket and turns them in his hand. 'What else could it be?'

'At the moment, we don't know,' I say. 'Ghost remains a possibility, but I want to speak to an expert.'

Karrion checks his phone. 'Speaking of which, Mum replied. She texted me the contact details for a ghost dude. Or dudette. It's not clear.'

'Good. Give them a call and ask if we can drop by a little later. I have too many questions to ask over the phone.'

'Will do, as soon as we're out of the car park. I don't have enough signal down here.'

'Before you do that,' Jamie says, 'would you mind going over to take Lord Ellensthorne's statement? He's expecting someone from the Met to interview him, and his secretary indicated that he would be home all afternoon.'

Karrion's good cheer evaporates, but he turns to me instead of objecting.

'Shouldn't a police officer do that?' I ask.

'We're a bit short-staffed at the moment, which is why I've been up half the night dealing with these two murders. There's official paperwork you'll need to deal with afterwards, but it would be helpful if you could start the ball rolling. As consultants for the Met, you can't arrest someone, but you can take a witness statement.'

'Of course.'

'I'm needed back at the Yard. I'll see if the autopsies have been performed and if any of the evidence has been processed already.'

'You'll keep us in the loop, won't you?' I ask.

'Of course. I can swing by later and we can go through the autopsy findings. I'll also bring copies of any reports that might have been uploaded by then.'

'Sounds great,' I say, and then I recall Lady Bergamon. 'But we're actually house sitting for a friend tonight. Can you meet us at her place instead?'

'Sure. I'll text you before I leave so you know to expect me.'

'I'll order us food. We can eat while going through the papers.'

'Yeah, cos there's nothing better for the appetite than looking at autopsy photos,' Karrion says, but his face is shining with excitement.

Jamie shrugs. 'You'll soon get used to these things.'

When he heads for his car, I stop him.

'Wait, you need to know where you're coming later.'

'Right, sorry.' He takes out his notebook. 'What's the address?'

I give Jamie Lady Bergamon's number on Ivy Street, keeping a careful eye on his reaction. Little escapes his notice, and as expected, he frowns.

'Ivy Street? But that's where the building project is taking place. Or at least, where they're planning it. That's quite the coincidence.'

Careful to keep my expression neutral, I meet his gaze head on. 'I know.'

11

LORD OF ALL SHADOWS

Karrion turns on his seat to face me. 'You didn't tell Jamie about the intruder in Lady B's garden.'

'I know,' I say, navigating through the sparse afternoon traffic.

'Why?'

'I told you before, we have no proof as yet. I don't want to bring Lady Bergamon into this investigation until we know for sure that what happened in her garden has something to do with these murders. If the two turn out to be unrelated, then the garden remains a secret.'

'Why is it so important that we don't tell anyone about Lady B or her domain?'

'Remember the first time we went to visit her? I had a feeling that we only found her house because she had willed it so, or because Wishearth told me to visit her. I don't think she wants everyone and their dog knowing who she is and where she lives. Ilana spoke of Lady Bergamon as an urban myth, not a real person. And Bradán told me Lady Bergamon actively tries to keep her garden hidden. That to me suggests I need to respect her privacy.'

'And yet you told Jamie to meet us at Lady B's place.'

'He doesn't know whose house it is, or that anything bad happened there.'

'Don't you trust Jamie?'

'I do, but these are not my secrets to tell. If I could ask Lady Bergamon's permission, things would be different.'

'But what happens if by not telling Jamie, we end up harming the investigation? Isn't this our chance to prove to him that we are a valuable asset to the Met?'

'By that same token, what happens if Jamie insists on taking Lady Bergamon to hospital and that destroys her domain and kills Bradán?'

'Point taken. But lying to Jamie doesn't seem right.'

'We're not lying to him, we've just not told him everything yet.'

'Fine. I trust you know best.'

I flash him a smile and brake to allow a cyclist to turn right. 'Did you want to ring your mum's ghost contact?'

Karrion gets his phone out. I half listen to the conversation while I drive along the wider streets of the most affluent part of Old London. Luck is on my side, and I find a parking spot opposite Lord Ellensthorne's townhouse, next to a walled garden. I can feel the threads of power teasing on the edge of my aura, tempting me to scale the wrought iron fence to explore the few dozen square feet of nature.

'Jessi said we can stop by once we're done here,' Karrion says, and glares at the house. 'Assuming the pompous arse won't spend all day prattling on about how wonderful he is and how all of Old London will bow down before him and his elitist policies.'

'Given that I accused him of murder and he still wanted to hire us, how bad can this interview be?'

'See, you jinxed it now. He's going to find a new way to insult us.'

'I'm pretty sure he was going to do that anyway. Come on.'

Karrion follows me across the road, grumbling under his breath. I stride up the steps and press the intercom button. Since I have already taken the measure of Lord Ellensthorne and his wealth, the heavy black door and the stark interior beyond it no longer intimidate me. I announce us, and after a few minutes, a butler I recognise from our previous visits invites us in.

'Lord Ellensthorne will see you in his study.'

We know the way, but the butler insists on escorting us past the portraits of Ellensthorne men with haughty sneers. Upstairs, he knocks on the study door and lets us in.

Lord Ellensthorne is pouring himself a drink when we enter. Straight away, my attention slips from him. He has replaced his desk and chair with a set carved by a Feykin carpenter. The wood gleams black in the sunlight streaming in past heavy velvet curtains. Along the edges of the desk, a Sídhe hunt is in progress. Fey on horseback mingle with huge hounds, each figure carved in exquisite detail. That is the gift of Feykin carpenters: they tease figures out of wood with magic, not tools.

The chair is part of a set. Armrests made of serpents in mid-flight reach away from the two elfin archers with bows at the ready. Above them, a giant raven has spread its wings.

It is a befitting throne for the First among the Shadow Mages and the Speaker for the High Council of Mages.

Without thinking, I ignore Lord Ellensthorne and step forward to touch the carvings on the nearest corner of the desk. The baying of hounds and the rumble of hooves fill my ears. I can feel the grass under my paws and my blood pounding with the frenzy of the hunt. The night air tastes wet on my heated tongue, but only fresh blood can quench the terrible thirst tormenting my throat. The mournful tone of a horn sounds behind me just as I catch the scent of our prey: a human.

I recoil away from the desk. The sensations linger within me, and I have to swallow twice to rid myself of the lump in my throat. Whatever I witnessed, it was not a figment of my imagination. The carvings are more than just decorations; they are a vision, a memory, perhaps a dream.

'How do you find my new desk, Ms Wilde?'

Cunning eyes study me from behind purple glasses and lanky locks of hair. Lord Ellensthorne has an ability to read people that has left me at a disadvantage in all our dealings. But that does not mean I am willing to roll over and admit defeat without a fight.

'Actually, I was wondering if you picked up the idea from your predecessor at the Council.'

As sudden as a spring shower, consternation flashes in Lord Ellensthorne's eyes. Antagonising a witness is foolish, I know, but I cannot help myself.

'I commissioned mine long before Braeman purchased his,' Lord Ellensthorne says.

'Planning for the future,' I say and nod.

'The only possible outcome. I was always going to win.'

'I remember.'

Lord Ellensthorne's lips curl into a sneer, and he walks past us. Now that I know what he is, the tell-tale scent of velvet darkness that identifies him as Shadow Mage is obvious.

'Have you come to give me an update?' he asks and sits down. 'I told you to deal with Mr Whyte.'

'No. We're here on Metropolitan Police business.'

Glancing at Karrion, Lord Ellensthorne tuts. 'The police standards must be slipping. It seems they let just about anyone join these days.'

'We haven't joined them,' I say before Karrion can think of an angry retort. 'We're assisting the police with an investigation.'

'How enterprising of you, Ms Wilde. For a creature of the wildest forests, such as still exist, you possess a surprising amount of business acumen.'

'Or, perhaps you underestimated me.'

'I wouldn't go that far.'

Lord Ellensthorne steeples his fingers and leans forward. He is perfectly positioned to make it look like the raven is swooping over his head to attack us. I wonder how long he has practised the pose.

'As entertaining as our verbal sparring has been, perhaps you could get to the point? I'm a busy man.'

'We're here to take your statement regarding your phone call with Hynryk Hailfax last night.'

'I see.'

He leans back in his chair, his left hand absently caressing the head of the serpent. I focus on the movement and experience a sensation akin to fingers running over my scaly body. Suppressing a shiver, I fix my eyes on Lord Ellensthorne's nose.

'I gather he died.'

'He did. What can you tell me about the phone call?'

'Hynryk called me to discuss business. We spoke for ten minutes, fifteen at the most, before he began complaining about stomach pains. At first, he thought he had eaten something that didn't agree with him, but then he started coughing and choking. Before it got worse, he mumbled something about a dark figure with flaming eyes that set his flesh on fire. I tried to question him about it, to no avail. He spoke no more, and I heard things breaking in the background, as well as his continued gagging. When the line went dead, I called the Paladins.'

'Isn't midnight an odd time to be making business calls?' Karrion asks.

Lord Ellensthorne tilts his head up. 'I'm something of a night owl, though not the powerless kind. It would be madness to while away the hours of darkness in bed when that is when I'm at my strongest. Strike iron when it's hot and cast Shadow Magic when it's dark. It's not rocket science, boy.'

'What business did you have with Hailfax?' Karrion's voice betrays his anger.

'That's between me and him.'

'Not if it's relevant to our murder investigation,' I say.

Lord Ellensthorne dips his chin at me.

'Hynryk was a talented young man, even if he wasn't fortunate enough to be born a Shadow Mage. I had taken him under my wing, and he often sought my advice on both matters of magic and in relation to the buildings he was designing.'

'Did he mention the project he was working on?'

'Yes. It was to come before the Council sooner or later, and he wanted my opinion. Unofficially, of course.'

'Did you notice anything unusual before his stomach pains began? Did he mention hearing anything unusual, or did you catch any sounds in the background?'

'Nothing. Everything seemed normal. Perhaps if I'd been there, I might have detected a breath of calm before the death began, but doing so over the phone is beyond even my capabilities.'

I am not certain whether he is describing a Shadow Mage ability or something metaphysical. Without showing ignorance, I cannot ask and I realise there is much I do not know about the capabilities of other magic users. When I was growing up, my main contact outside the Wild Folk conclave was with Shamans. Most of what I know about Mages, Paladins and Feykin, I have picked up in the past year.

'What about Hynryk himself? Did he sound distracted or concerned about anything? Did you get the impression he was afraid?'

'He was preoccupied with his work, but that was typical of him.'

'Is there anything else you can think of that may be connected to his death?' I ask.

'Nothing springs to mind. Though it occurs to me that you are dealing with a skilled killer. Until he began his struggles, Hynryk never once indicated that someone else was present in his study. Nor am I certain the figure he mentioned was truly there.'

Karrion frowns. 'How do you know he died in his study?'

'He was working on a building design when he called me,' Lord Ellensthorne says with a smirk. 'And before you ask how I can be certain, he told me so at the beginning of the conversation.'

'What makes you think the dark figure wasn't there?' I ask.

'Was he burnt to death?'

'Not to our knowledge. We think he was poisoned.'

'If there had been someone there who set him on fire, the police and the Paladins would have found evidence of that. Besides, what I heard over the phone sounded like choking, not someone screaming because they were burning.'

'Thank you for your time,' I say.

'I'd be careful if I were you, Ms Wilde,' he replies. 'It seems to me that you are way out of your league here. A killer like this is a far cry from a broken human.'

A memory of Melissa sobbing in a grimy alley resurfaces, and it brings with it a flash of anger. Not at her, but at Lord Ellensthorne for so easily dismissing the trauma Melissa had experienced and the profound impact it had on her.

'She isn't human, but one of us.'

'I'd hardly call someone with a bit of magical blood one of us.'

102

'Is that another one of your new policies for Old London? Are you going to start choosing who belongs here and who doesn't?'

'This country has been divided by social status for thousands of years. Why should a division based on power be any more abhorrent? The city should be run by those who have the greatest capacity to wield magic, and therefore the greatest scope for accepting responsibility for others. Is it not the same with Great Britain as a country? Our Queen has been bred to rule. So it should be with Old London.'

'Who's going to be the judge of that and on what grounds?'

Lord Ellensthorne straightens in his chair. 'Someone who understands how power works and can achieve the greatest things with it.'

I disguise my snort with a cough. 'Someone like you?'

'As the Speaker for the High Council and the First among the Shadow Mages, I do seem to be uniquely qualified,' he says with a thin smile.

'And once you've declared Mages better than the rest of us,' Karrion crosses his arms, 'then what? Are we to be moved into a separate area and kept away from you powerful lot? Or maybe you're already firing up the gas chambers?'

'Don't be absurd, boy. Our kind died alongside humans in the concentration camps. No one in Old London wishes to see that repeated.'

'Oh.' Karrion's cheeks heat, but I see that he is not yet ready to drop the subject. 'Then what are you planning?'

'Not that it's any of your concern, but I can imagine education and welfare being allocated based on an individual's potential. For instance, why waste higher education on someone who will never amount to much? But more than that, the urgent point to address is our relative weakness compared to the human masses. We must seek to strengthen our kind if we are to survive, and indeed, thrive, despite the lesser race. To do so, we must allocate our resources wisely.'

'That's a stupid way of doing it,' Karrion says and stands up. 'You're forcing people into a life you want for them, instead of letting people choose for themselves.'

'It's hardly a fault of mine that some among Old London's residents are more capable of seeing the bigger picture than others.'

'I think the whole thing is idiotic.'

'How eloquently put,' Lord Ellensthorne says, and I see that he considers this a personal victory.

I stand. 'Time to go, Karrion.'

'Indeed. You mustn't waste the taxpayers' money.'

'Don't worry, we don't charge the Met by the hour,' I say with just enough self-control to hide a grin.

'I see. Speaking of value for money, I assume you are maintaining sensible priorities. The task I gave you is time sensitive.'

'I haven't forgotten, though I would have expected Mr Whyte to share my interim report.'

'He did, along with your hefty invoice. I'm merely concerned that upon receipt of payment, your investigation will lose momentum.'

'I'm as eager to flush out any Leeches within the Council and the Circle as you are.'

Lord Ellensthorne nods. 'Your experience makes you uniquely motivated.'

'Or, when I take a job, I see it to its conclusion.'

'Either way, I suggest you hurry up.'

Several angry retorts spring to my mind, but I voice none of them. I have nothing to gain from antagonising Lord Ellensthorne, and plenty to lose. Nudging Karrion towards the door, I thank Lord Ellensthorne a second time. He remains seated behind his desk, and my eyes are drawn to the hounds. Hunger for blood clouds my mind, sharpening my canines and elongating my nails. I shudder and turn away, suppressing my magic. It is just the enchantment in the desk. It must be.

12

A GHOST HUNTER

Jessi's address takes us to grey tower blocks near the City
Thameslink station. Karrion lives only a short walk away
on Bride Lane. This area feels like the other extreme after
the wealth of Lord Ellensthorne's part of Old London.

A group of teenagers stands outside the building we
are heading for, practising light spells. They seem to be
egging each other on to produce brighter and more
colourful lights, until a spell flares in the face of a
bespectacled boy, who falls back with a yelp.

'That brings back memories,' Karrion says in a low
voice as we step through the front door. 'My friend Benny
and I used to argue which would land us in more trouble,
luring away the Queen's corgis or the ravens from the
Tower.'

'I'm guessing Benny is a Dog Shaman?'

'Yes. He was no braver than I was, and we never put
any of our wild plans into action.'

'Just as well. I don't think prison would have suited
you.' I call down the lift. 'Were all your friends Shamans
when you were growing up?'

'No, I hung out with Mages and Paladin kids too.
There was even a boy who claimed to be Feykin, but the
only evidence we ever saw of his Fey heritage was a foul
temper. But with the others, I ended up in all sorts of
trouble.'

'I can well imagine. Your poor mother still hasn't recovered.'

'And now she's got the brood to worry about.'

'At least you developed some sense along the way. I know what a big help you are at home.'

The lift arrives with a ping. Karrion rubs his neck and indicates that I should enter first.

'Well, we're family. What else would I do? We're not related to cuckoos.'

I smile, but say nothing further.

The lift creaks and rattles, but it gets us to the fifth floor in one piece. On the walls, brown paint is peeling and there are damp stains on the ceiling, but the worn floor has been swept clean. Smells of curried lamb, coffee, coconut and dust permeate the hallway, and I tilt my chin to identify the source of each scent. What would it be like to live among such homely smells? I can hear the sound of a television through one of the doors, and children laughing.

'This is it,' Karrion says and points to a door opposite the lift, bearing the number 502.

'Good.'

Karrion stares at the door and stuffs his hands in his pockets. 'I was expecting a plaque at least, maybe a cool sign with a marshmallow man.'

'Have I mentioned lately that you watch too much TV?'

'I'm just saying, shouldn't a real-life Ghostbuster be a bit more bustery?'

Karrion rings the doorbell. With my sharp hearing, I detect music being turned down inside the flat, but no footsteps approach. The door opening catches me by surprise, and with my eyes drawn down, I see why: the woman on the threshold is in a wheelchair. Grey eyes peer at us from behind an untidy fringe. She is already smiling.

107

'You must be the folks from Wilde Investigations.'

Karrion and I share an astonished glance.

'How did you know that?' he asks.

'My spirit guide has been following you since you rang.'

I see laughter dancing in her eyes, but before I have a chance to say anything, a man walks down the hall and rests a large hand on her narrow shoulder.

'She looked you up online,' he says with a grin that reveals perfect white teeth.

'How am I supposed to maintain an air of mystery if you rat me out?'

The woman crosses her arms, but the brightness of her smile has not lessened.

'At least this time you didn't drape a sheet over yourself.'

'I swear those humans stared at me more after I took the sheet off than before.'

'With that first impression, can you blame them?' He squeezes her shoulder, a gold ring glinting against his dark skin, and nods to us.

'Sorry, forgot my manners again.' She holds out her hand. 'I'm Jessi and this is my husband, Obeajulu.'

Karrion performs introductions. As I step forward to greet them, I inhale. Jessi smells of catnip, soft fur and paws dipped in a saucer of cream. She is a Cat Shaman. Karrion responds to an unseen recognition of an enemy with a flare of his magic, but Jessi appears not to notice. When I shake hands with Obeajulu, the scents of wet fur, bones and the sweetness of puppies drifts to my nose.

'Cat Shaman and Dog Shaman living together is unusual.'

Obeajulu laughs. 'We should be fighting like cat and dog, but instead we love like them; I'm affectionate, she's aloof, and somehow we make it work.'

'Don't listen to a word he says.' Jessie reverses away from the doorway. 'Come on in.'

Jessi leads us into a small lounge and reverses into a spot between a worn sofa and a coffee table. Obeajulu stands behind her. Although he is smiling, there is wariness in his dark eyes. We are nothing but strangers.

Karrion has been staring at Jessi, and she notices. Meeting his eyes, she spreads her arms.

'Go on, out with it. I may be a Cat Shaman, but I won't bite.'

'You're not what I expected,' Karrion says, tugging at his lip piercing.

'It's the boobs. They told me at Spooks Academy that boobs would get in the way when I fight ghosts, but I was pretty attached to mine by then.'

Karrion's eyes light up. 'There's a Spooks Academy?'

'Sure. An old haunted castle in the Scottish Highlands, where the students sleep in the dungeons and wrestle with hellhounds,' Obeajulu says. 'Of course not. To paraphrase her from earlier, don't listen to a word she says.'

'Spoilsport.'

'Someone has to be. I'll make coffee.'

'There's coconut and rum cake in the tin,' Jessi says.

'I remember.' Obeajulu winks. 'When she's not playing with poltergeists or wheeling over my toes, Jessi bakes.'

'We all need a hobby and there's only so much your toes can take. Now bugger off.'

Obeajulu leaves, his laughter lingering in his wake.

'I understand you have a ghost problem,' Jessi says.

'Possibly.' I briefly explain our arrangement with New Scotland Yard. 'We're investigating a murder which may have been committed by a ghost.'

Jessi makes a discordant noise and shakes her head. 'Unlikely, but tell me more.'

'The victim was strangled with a length of vine without anyone gripping it. He was convinced his first wife was haunting him. His widow was sceptical until we showed her a photo of a broken protection amulet the victim was wearing, at which point she became insistent on a ghost being responsible.'

While I have been speaking, Jessi has been tracing the outside seam of her jeans, her nails scratching on the rough surface. She appears unaware of the movement, or how her hand flexes in a rhythmic pattern. All she is lacking are claws.

'Can I see the photo?' she asks.

I hesitate, but cannot see any harm in showing her the amulet. When she looks at Karrion's phone, her lips purse and her hand stills.

'I've seen that amulet before.' She tilts her head back to stare at the ceiling. 'It belongs to Natheniel Laene.'

'Your memory is impressive,' Karrion says.

After the initial ruffling of his feathers, his magic has settled down. He is less threatened by Jessi than Fria. Is it because Jessi is in a wheelchair, or because she is married? Or perhaps his hostility with Fria was a reaction to her subtle assertion of power.

'It's not that,' Jessi replies. 'Aside from that being the most powerful protection amulet I've encountered, Natheniel was a frequent visitor.'

'Why?' I ask.

'You said it yourself: he was convinced his first wife was haunting him.'

'Was she?'

'I never sensed the presence of a ghost in the house. There was something off about his aura, though. I suggested he spoke to a Paladin in case he was cursed.'

'Did he?'

'I don't know. He never referred to it, and I just assumed

110

it wasn't a curse. He could have had an undiagnosed mental illness, but that's not my area of expertise either.'

'Yet, he was afraid, wasn't he?'

Jessi nods. 'I've never come across anyone so fixated on the notion that he was haunted.'

'Could it have been guilt?' Karrion asks. 'The police thought he may have murdered his first wife, though they had no proof.'

'As I said, that's not my speciality. I didn't think a ghost was after him, but that didn't mean that I refused to help him protect both himself and his wife, Halen.'

'Was his fear always worse around Samhain?' I ask.

From my vantage point at the far end of the sofa, I can see down the corridor and into the kitchen. Obeajulu is preparing a tray of drinks, humming a tune I can't quite catch, but every so often, he glances towards us. He catches my eye, but before I can decide whether to smile or look away, he focuses on pouring coffee.

'Yes. He was hysterical and the worrying exhausted him for weeks. The last couple of years, Halen booked them a holiday right after Samhain to let him rest.'

'Why didn't they just go away on Samhain?' Karrion asks.

'It isn't just in England that the veil between the worlds is at its thinnest on that night. Natheniel didn't think anywhere was safe for them.'

'Did you help him with the protection he had in place for Samhain?'

Obeajulu returns with the tray and passes coffee and cake to us, before sitting in the armchair next to Jessi. I can smell the rum, together with the delicate aroma of coconut. The moist sponge melts in my mouth, leaving behind the burn of alcohol.

'Yes,' Jessi says, stirring her coffee. 'I advised him on what was effective against spirits and I expected him to

111

pick a few things he liked best. Instead, he used them all. And my knowledge wasn't enough for him.'

'He wanted Vodun,' Obeajulu nods, 'lots of it.'

'Are you a Vodun priest?' Karrion asks, his expression brightening into delight.

Obeajulu laughs. 'No. My mother is a Vodunsi in Lagos, and I grew up with the old practices. It is what brought me to Old London and to my Jessi.'

'Wait, there's Vodun here?' Karrion's grin grows wider.

'A little. I brought messages and fetishes to another Vodunsi. Jessi was studying our ways with her. The rest is written in the tableau of spirits.'

Jessi reaches to rest her palm on Obeajulu's cheek. The affection that passes between them causes me to look away; the moment too intimate to be witnessed by strangers. Envy sours the taste of the cake. No one has ever looked at me with such love, and I wonder if anyone ever will.

The silence goes on for a while longer before Jessi clears her throat. 'I felt there was a connection between ghosts and the wider spirit realm, and I was right. Studying with a Vodunsi allowed me to view my work with ghosts in a whole different light.'

'Why was Laene after Vodun?' I ask.

'He wanted every item of protection to have a dual purpose,' Jessi says. 'The turnip lanterns are a form of protection used in old Druid practices, but he wanted them to double as Vodun fetishes attracting good spirits to his aid. When he read about blackening his face to fool the ghost, he asked for a way of also invoking the Vodun spirits and bringing protection. Shuttering the windows facing west to keep evil spirits from entering the house should also have welcomed benign beings to watch over him. So it went. Everything he did was to safeguard him and his wife, even down to the jewellery he gave her.'

112

I recall the necklace Halen was wearing, and its mismatching colours. 'What was so special about the jewellery?'

'The gems and pearls are all designed to protect the wearer. He was very particular about the details: topaz bracelets had to be around the left wrist, and all the jewellery had to touch the skin to maximise power.'

'I understand all that,' Karrion says and sets his plate down. 'But what's the deal with burying rotting meat and bones in the front garden?'

Jessi leans towards Obeajulu, and he lays a hand on her knee.

'Rotting meat?' she asks.

'We found piles of bones and meat in holes all around the house. In some cases, the meat smelled like it had been there for at least a week.'

'The whole point of making a meat offering to the spirits is that the offering is fresh.'

'Can spirits really eat?' Karrion asks.

'Don't forget that Wishearth drinks Guinness.' I turn to Jessi and Obeajulu. 'I'm friends with a Hearth Spirit.'

'You're fortunate. Not many spirits form friendships with mortals.'

I nod, but offer nothing further about Wishearth.

'If a spirit accepted the offering, could the act of doing so cause the meat to decay at a faster rate?' I ask.

'It doesn't work like that.'

If that is the case, what rotted the offerings in Lady Bergamon's garden and at the Laene house? I leave the question unspoken, but my expression must betray something of the direction of my thoughts.

'Could it have been a spell?' Obeajulu asks.

'To what purpose? Why leave the offerings in place and spoil them?'

Obeajulu shrugs. 'It would be an easy way to interfere

with the protections in place without requiring access to the house.'

'The garden was only one layer of protection,' I say, as I think back to the crime scene. 'That said, the wreath of rosemary and rowan at the front door was torn down.'

'The sounds like the work of a mortal to me,' Jessi says.

Before I have a chance to reply, the doorbell rings. Obeajulu checks his watch and presses a kiss on Jessi's forehead.

'That's my four o'clock.'

'Have fun, sweetie.'

Obeajulu leaves, and I listen to the front door opening and closing. He leads two giggling teenagers in school uniforms to the room opposite the lounge and closes the door.

'My husband is a software developer, but he does a bit of spiritual work on the side, mostly for humans,' Jessi says.

I nod. 'Going back to what you were saying, you don't think the killer is a ghost, then?'

'No. Ghosts are no different from spirits in general, except they're weaker. Which makes sense, given that nothing feeds them. That's why they can't assume corporeal form like the stronger spirits can.'

'What about offerings to ancestors?' Karrion asks.

'That's different. Praying at the family altar wouldn't feed a recently deceased ghost who was sticking around for some gentle haunting. No, ghosts have a very limited amount of power, and everything they do saps their energy reserves. That's why a lot of what people refer to as "poltergeist activity" isn't. An average spook isn't capable of throwing wardrobes around or shattering every window in a house in one go.'

'If ghosts don't cause that stuff, what does?' Karrion asks.

'Magic, non-magical pranks, spirits. There are unseen forces in this world that aren't ghosts. Philosophy aside, I don't think an average ghost could strangle Natheniel. Whoever your killer is, Natheniel's first wife is unlikely to be responsible.'

'What about the amulet?' I ask. 'The scarab beetle inside the amber was broken.'

'That doesn't prove the presence of a ghost, only a malicious life force. A spirit could have been responsible. If your Hearth Spirit friend had attacked Natheniel, the amulet would have broken as a warning.'

'How about a killer who wasn't a spirit?' Karrion avoids looking in my direction. 'Could the amulet have reacted to a Mage or a Shaman?'

'I didn't create it, so I can't say for certain. But I don't see why not. If it detected malicious intent, it wouldn't matter whether the killer was mortal or immortal.'

'And I'm guessing that even if a very powerful ghost was behind Laene's death, it wouldn't have murdered another Mage last night?' I ask.

'No.' Jessi sets down her cup. 'When people stay on as ghosts, they have a specific reason for doing so. All their energy and thoughts are directed towards their goal. Unless the second Mage was integral to the reason the ghost cannot cross over, killing them would never occur to it.'

'The only connection we've found so far is a building project they were both involved in.'

'I don't think that's reason enough, though it would, of course, depend on the spook.'

Pushing the remaining cake crumbs around my plate, I bite my lip to keep the frustration off my face. Nothing we have done this afternoon has taken us any closer to solving either murder, and now we are at a dead end. All I can hope for is that Jamie has fresh leads for us when he gets the autopsy results.

'Sorry I couldn't be of more help,' Jessi says.

I force a smile. 'This has been most informative. We really appreciate that you agreed to see us with such short notice.'

'Much of my work involves dealing with humans. I'm always glad to help my fellow magic users.'

I ask about her fees, but she dismisses me with a wave of her hand. The door opposite the lounge opens, and Obeajulu escorts the girls out. He returns to hover in the doorway. Jessi rolls her eyes and wheels over to him.

'Did you promise them handsome husbands and many riches?'

'As handsome a husband as yours and as many riches as you have.' He presses a kiss on her forehead.

Jessi sighs. 'They've got no chance, then.'

'The spirits show what the spirits show.'

'You're a fortune teller?' Karrion asks.

Obeajulu hesitates, and Jessi nudges his side. 'Not quite. I have a family heirloom that, spirits willing, shows possible future paths.'

'Awesome!' Karrion leaps up. 'Can you do me?'

I snort, and Obeajulu chuckles even as he scowls. When Jessi nudges him again, he nods.

'Wicked. Will you do Yan as well? She could use a future with many husbands and handsome riches.'

'Thanks, Karrion.' I turn to Obeajulu. 'There's no need. You're kind to humour Karrion, though.'

'Nonsense,' Jessi says. 'It won't take long, and you won't need all the caveats he tells humans about nothing being certain and everything being open to interpretation.'

'Go on, Yan. It'll be fun.'

'You don't know that,' I mutter, but the excitement on Karrion's face crumbles my resistance. 'Fine, if it really is no trouble.'

116

'It would be my pleasure.' Obeajulu opens the door. 'Follow me.'

Along one side of the room we enter is a desk with three monitors, each showing the same photo of Obeajulu against a backdrop of azure sky and sea, Jessi in his arms. He holds her like she weighs nothing, and from their formal clothes, I assume it is a wedding photo. Is Jessi being in a wheelchair a recent development, or is he holding her so the chair was not included in the photo?

Opposite the desk, I notice a sheet of copper affixed to the wall by carved bone brackets. From the way light touches it, I realise it is heart copper and must be worth a fortune. The polished surface shines, but when I walk closer to look at it, I am surprised to see no reflection on it.

'What is this?' I ask, intrigued.

'It is a reflection of unseen things. It is what I use to catch glimpses of uncertain futures within.'

Karrion stands in front of the sheet, leaning forward in his eagerness. Obeajulu takes his place behind Karrion, and he peers at the shining surface for a long while. I fancy his eyes flicker to me and away again.

'You bear the most precious of burdens a long way, with mourning doves guarding your journey. That will be the end and the beginning of your trial.'

Karrion's teeth worry his lip piercing as he cocks his head. He looks like he wants to ask Obeajulu a question, but instead, he steps aside. When I do not move straight away, Karrion lets his fingers graze over my knuckles.

'Go on, it's fine. I didn't burst into flames, so I reckon you won't either.'

Since I cannot articulate the vague unease I feel at the prospect of having my fortune told, I allow Karrion to guide me forward. When I take my position in front of the heart copper sheet, I am surprised to see Obeajulu's reflection, but not mine. Our eyes meet, and I watch as his become orbs of blackness. I want to move, to leave the room, but I cannot will my muscles to move. Air is trapped in my lungs, and my pulse grows to a roar in my ears, until I barely hear the words Obeajulu utters.

'You are torn between your heart and your mind, and there is a dark figure ever hovering on the edge of your life. You have the courage to find your path, but in order to find peace, you must look beyond courage.'

13

FAMILY MATTERS

'What do you think?' Karrion asks as we step out of the building.

I pause and angle my face towards the pallid sun. My heart rate has returned to normal, but my muscles still carry tension that has triggered an ache in my joints. The autumn chill worms its way under my jeans, and I shiver while zipping up my coat. The cold I feel goes beyond the weather, and I long to curl up in front of a fire until my whole being is consumed by the dancing flames. Perhaps then I will find the equilibrium Obeajulu has disturbed.

'I liked Jessi. Obeajulu doesn't trust us, but I can't blame him.'

'That's not what I meant, and you know it.'

'There's not much to think,' I say with a shrug. 'What he said could be interpreted in many different ways. And that's the whole point about fortune tellers and tea leaf readers and all manner of psychics. You can never prove them wrong because you choose the light in which to view their prophecies.'

In truth, Obeajulu's words have left me unsettled. I recall Dearon from my dreams and the dark mantle of power he carries. Is he the man Obeajulu saw? Or was it Wishearth, with his hair the colour of soot and dark eyes flashing with sparks? Could Obeajulu have meant someone else entirely?

'Who do you think he meant?' Karrion asks, as if reading my mind. 'I mean, I'm pretty dark.'

'So is Lord Ellensthorne, and all the roads in Old London seem to be leading us to him.'

Karrion grimaces. 'That's a sucky future. I hope it won't come true.'

'And how interesting that yours mentioned doves, not pigeons. Obeajulu's spirit mojo must have been off.'

'It just goes to show that nothing lasts forever.'

'So you hope.'

'I don't hope, I know.'

This is not the first time I have envied the youthful certainty of his views, but I say nothing.

The scent of rainwater in the breeze draws my thoughts back to Dearon. Our lives have been connected since the day I was born, and yet I wonder whether I will ever be free of the promises our parents made. I have never asked him if he would prefer a different future; one without me. It has been easier to be angry with him, and my father, than to have a proper conversation about our future. Soon, that will have to change. The embers of anger still smoulder within me, but their burn has lessened in the past month.

Karrion's hand on my shoulder alerts me to the fact that I have been staring at a poster of a missing Feykin boy attached to an overflowing bin. I glance at my watch, conscious that we have been away from Lady Bergamon for most of the day.

'We need to return to Ivy Street. I don't want to leave Lady Bergamon unprotected if whoever broke out of her garden returns. Given how little I know about circles, I'd feel better if we both stayed close to her while she's unconscious, especially at night. Can you stop by your place and collect what you need for a few days? We may need to keep an eye on her for a while, depending on how quickly we figure this out.'

'Sure. Do you want me to meet you there?'

'Please. I have to pick up various things from home and see if Wishearth is at the Open Hearth. I want to ask him about last night.'

'I'll buy us some food. We're going to want breakfast, and it wouldn't feel right raiding Lady B's cupboards.'

'Good idea. Give my best to Aderyn.'

Karrion declines my offer of a lift and with a wave, heads home. I negotiate the busy streets through the evening traffic and park outside my flat. Upstairs, I find a bottle of brandy and a tumbler on the hearth stones next to my mattress. A memory of returning home from serving food to the homeless, cold and lonely, floats across my mind. I poured myself a glass, then another. There is something else I did, something to do with my phone, but it eludes me now; lost in the haze of fatigue and alcohol.

I pack a change of clothes and my toiletries. From the kitchen, I pick up a full foil strip of medication and what I have left of Lady Bergamon's pain relieving tea. My hand hesitates over the bottle of brandy, but I leave it on the hearth stones and slide a hunting knife into the side pocket of my bag. I check that the windows and the back gate are locked, drop my bag in the car and walk around the corner to my regular haunt, the Open Hearth.

When I open the door, a murmur of many conversations and the smell of beer welcomes me into the familiar space. Boris, Funja's Irish Wolfhound companion, is lying in his regular spot by the huge fireplace, and he barks a greeting. I crouch to pet him on my way past and his tail thumps against the worn floorboards. Funja waves at me from the far side of the bar and disappears through the door leading to his flat.

Wishearth is where I expect him to be, leaning back in the corner that is darker than the others. The dim lighting and the high collar of his coat around his face give him an air of a brooding stranger, but he no longer fools me. If his favoured spot appears shrouded in mystery, it is because he wills it so. Wishearth has a penchant for melodrama, though that is not something I would dare say out loud.

'Did you solve your case? Or are you missing me already?'

I take a seat opposite him, my back to the fire, and relish the familiar routine. It helps ground me, even as I meet Wishearth's smouldering eyes and wonder about Obeajulu's words.

'I always miss you. How could I not?'

'Sometimes I wonder. You say all the right things, but your eyes sing a different tune.'

'Are you suggesting we mortals are difficult to read? I thought we were an open book to an authority such as you.'

'Impertinence is a word that must have been invented to describe you. I never said I couldn't read both tales you tell.'

I am not certain how to respond. More than once, I have felt with Wishearth as though I am answering a question that has not been asked. Whether my response is the one he wants, I cannot tell. Wishearth may find me easy to read, but I cannot say the same about him.

Before the silence turns awkward, I clear my throat. 'I wanted to ask you about last night.'

Wishearth's expression grows bored, and he motions towards someone behind me. A waitress brings him a pint of Guinness. I am tempted by a brandy, but common sense wins, and I order a cola.

'How did you know something had happened to Lady Bergamon?' I ask.

Sipping his drink, Wishearth takes his time, until I am ready to repeat the question.

'When she goes to meet Bradán at night, Lady Bergamon is usually only gone for a few hours. When I didn't hear from her, I dropped by to make sure she was well. I found the fireplace cold and the house empty. The garden had a different feel to it. That's when I came to you.'

'Different how?'

'Mortal domains aren't my speciality, but the garden didn't feel wholly hers anymore.'

'Who does it now belong to?'

'That's up to you to figure out. I know for a fact that detecting things is your speciality. I've helped you as much as I can.'

While I am tempted to make a joke about his limitations, caution stills my tongue. The stories of old have taught me time and time again that angering spirits is foolish. As much as I consider Wishearth a friend, I am never quite sure where the boundaries lie.

'You seem troubled,' he says.

'I—'

Try as I might, I cannot find a way to describe the unease I have carried since we found Lady Bergamon in her garden. The visit to Jessi and Obeajulu did little to alleviate my discomfort.

Wishearth smiles at someone behind me, and I turn to see Funja approaching. In addition to my drink, he is carrying a black and white puppy that seems to be all paws and huge ears.

'Yannia, I want you to meet Sinta.'

I offer my hand to the puppy to sniff, which she does with a great deal of seriousness.

'Are you looking to replace Boris?'

'Never.' Funja sets the puppy down. 'Sinta needs a home.'

'Right,' I say, beginning to see where the conversation is going.

'Her coat is fluffy, so the breeders tell me she's no good. They tell me to get rid of her.'

'That's terrible. Why would anyone breed if they don't want the puppies regardless of their coat?'

Sinta is staring at me with serious brown eyes. After a while, her attention wavers and she sniffs at my shoelaces. When I reach down to run my fingers along her back, her body shivers with pleasure. I pick her up and cradle her against my chest. Her heart beats a steady rhythm against mine, and in between the beats, a connection is forged. Sinta sighs and I feel the brush of her fluffy ear against my neck as she rests her head on my shoulder.

Funja beams at us. 'This is good. Sinta, she will keep an eye on you.'

'But who'll keep an eye on her?'

'You two are perfect for each other,' Wishearth says, sparks flying from his eyes.

'Hang on. My work is unpredictable. I'd feel bad about leaving her for long periods of time. And it's not like I can take her to a crime scene or the morgue.'

'We will puppysit. Boris, he will help. Wishearth too.'

To my astonishment, Wishearth nods, no longer smiling. I am left with the impression that he wants me to say yes to this. I recall the loneliness I felt last night, and on many occasions before. Would it be so terrible to have some company? Ollie, a pointer I love, will never be a city dog, but Sinta is different. At least, I hope so.

'What breed is she?'

'Cardigan corgi,' Funja says. 'Small dog, big heart.'

Sinta yawns with a squeak and reaches to lick the side of my neck. I squirm, which only encourages her further, and laugh.

'Fine. I'll take her, at least to see how we get along. But can I delay it for a few days? I don't feel comfortable taking a puppy to Lady Bergamon's.'

'Yes. She will wait for you here.'

'I best go,' I say and pass Sinta back to Funja. 'Those murders won't solve themselves.'

'I'll see you later?' Wishearth's raised eyebrow turns the statement into a question, and I nod.

Drinking the last of my cola, I stand. Sinta watches me with confused eyes as I head out, and I am beginning to appreciate that what took place between us may have been far more than offering a cute puppy a home.

When I park on Ivy Street, I find Karrion leaning against the wrought iron fence of Lady Bergamon's house. A car driving past slows down as the driver stares at the plant pots.

'You could have gone in,' I say, and retrieve the spare key from its safe place.

'The front garden was giving me the creeps. I figured the feeling would be even stronger inside.'

After I have unlocked the front door, I remove the protection wreath and hide it behind some of the larger pots. Inside, I close the doors to the lounge and the front room, and tidy away the decaying rowan branches from the kitchen and the hall. When I open the back door, a wall of grey rain greets me. From the waterlogged pots by the steps, I am guessing it has been raining all day. I close the door without going outside.

'I'm going to check on Lady Bergamon,' I say, getting the bottle of tonic from the fridge.

'Can I tag along?'

'Of course.'

I lead the way upstairs, my thoughts turning to the circle. Is it still up? Will I know if someone or something has tried to force their way through it? Did I put enough power into the casting to provide sufficient protection to Lady Bergamon? And why did I not ask these questions and many more when I saw Wishearth?

When I step into the room, I find my fears about the circle unfounded. A current of magic brushes against my aura. It is far clearer than the echoes of Lady Bergamon's circle in the lounge. Perhaps something in the magic recognises me as its creator. Using the obsidian blade, I cut a doorway into the circle and step through.

Lady Bergamon has not moved since the morning. I give her two spoonfuls of the tonic as I study her countenance. Her breathing is even, but there is a grey tinge to her skin. Given that she has been unconscious for nearly twenty-four hours, I would have expected her to have soiled the sheets, but she has the appearance of someone who fell asleep mere minutes ago. Yet no amount of talking or gentle shaking can rouse her.

Another doorway admits me out of the circle, and I return the obsidian blade to the wooden box. Karrion has been alternating between watching me with open curiosity and staring at everything in the room. Now he steps up to the nearest cold iron symbol and runs his hand through the air. Such is my awareness of the circle that I know his hand is never closer than two inches from the barrier.

'Did you really cast this?' Karrion asks.

'Yes.'

'Is that another special Wild Folk ability?'

'No. According to Wishearth, we all have the ability to cast circles.'

'But neither of us is a Mage.'

His words mirror mine close enough that I laugh. 'That's what I said. But remember how Melissa was using the power in her blood to create illusions long after her natural magic reserves had been exhausted? We can all tap into that power.'

'Isn't that beyond stupid? Melissa nearly killed herself.'

'Yes, but we're forewarned and know the consequences of going too far.'

126

Karrion thinks for a moment, twisting to look at the ancient weapons on the wall. When he turns back to me, his expression is guarded.

'We can all cast circles? Or can we do other stuff as well?'

'While I don't think we can pick up a spell book and start learning Mage spells, I believe the ability goes beyond circles. The difficulty comes from channelling the magic. From what I know of Mage magic, the spells and the rituals are a way of focusing the magic for the specific purpose. If we tap into the power in our blood and simply fling it outward without definition, we're going to burn ourselves out quicker than you can say "Bad idea".'

Karrion nods. 'Got it, Yan.'

'We should return downstairs,' I say. 'Jamie will be here soon.'

'Right.' Karrion follows me out. 'Why do you think Lady B has old weapons on her bedroom wall?'

'I've no idea. Maybe once she wakes up, you can ask her.'

'How likely do you think it is that she'll hit me with one of the weapons instead of answering?'

'It may be a risk you'll have to take.'

We return to the kitchen, and I put the tonic away.

'Mum's been offered a promotion,' Karrion says and sets a plastic bag on the kitchen counter.

'That's wonderful.'

Karrion unpacks the groceries, and I put them in the fridge. His pleasure is evident in the way he rocks onto his toes and turns the simple act of passing me a block of cheese into a brief game of poke and tickle.

'She's the floor supervisor from next Monday. The hours are the same, but she's getting a pay rise. The Mage who was her boss quit today. Which is just as well, since

127

we both know Shamans do the Mages' share of work in Old London.'

'Will she still keep the morning shift at the Post Office?'

'I told her she shouldn't, that working one job is enough now I'm earning decent money too, but you know what she's like. She keeps telling me that I need to set money aside for my future and not worry about supporting the brood. But there're more important things than having a savings account.'

'What's stopping you from doing both? It's never a bad thing to prepare for every eventuality. You could lay off some of the dates, and maybe even stop paying a stranger to make holes in you.'

'Reinard isn't a stranger,' Karrion says and prods my shoulder. 'But you have a point. If only I could persuade Mum to see my point too.'

'Give her time to get used to the new circumstances, and she may well come to see things your way.'

'I hope so.' Karrion fills the kettle and opens a carton of teabags. 'Should we make some toast for tea? Is Jamie eating with us?'

'No and yes. I texted him when I left the Open Hearth, and he promised to bring dinner.'

'What kind of dinner?'

'Curry. I told him no chicken.'

I take three cups from the cupboard and glance at Karrion over my shoulder. 'Don't tell him about Lady Bergamon's condition.'

'I won't. But don't you think it's better he knows everything? How else is he going to be able to help us?'

'We've been through this. They're not our secrets to tell, not until we know for sure that what happened to Lady Bergamon is connected to the murders.'

'But if it is, we have to tell him, right?'

'Right.'

The kettle boils, and Karrion pours water into two of the mugs while I add milk.

'Did you find out anything new from Wishearth?'

I tell Karrion what Wishearth said. When I mention Sinta, Karrion laughs.

'You with a corgi, it sort of fits. She's going to rule you with an iron paw.'

'That's not how it's supposed to work.'

'No, but do you know anything about puppy parenting?'

'We have plenty of dogs at the conclave, and I've been involved in the training for years.'

'Yeah, but they live in a pack outside, or so you've told me. This is different. We're talking about toilet training, puppy socialisation and obedience classes.'

I shrug and burn my tongue on the tea. 'I'll just ask Funja's help. Training a corgi shouldn't be beyond a Dog Shaman.'

'He can't give the puppy a list of rules to follow and expect her to obey. Especially since she's not his dog companion.'

'Speaking of which, how come you don't have a pigeon companion?'

Karrion gives me the finger, but before he has a chance to reply, the doorbell rings. I laugh all the way to the door.

14

CREEPING DOUBT

I open the door to find Jamie staring at the flower pots.

'Someone must have a serious brown thumb to have killed all those plants. Who uses their front garden to store pots, anyway?'

'My friend is between projects,' I say, and close the door behind him.

'Where is your friend?'

'Visiting family up north.' I ignore Jamie's curious glance. 'She asked me to stay here and look after her cat.'

'Where's the cat?' Jamie asks, craning his neck to look up the stairs.

'He's shy,' I say, ushering him to the kitchen.

Jamie sets a bag of food on the table, while Karrion looks through the cupboards for plates. From the scents rising from the bag, Jamie has brought a prawn madras, a vegetable korma and a lamb biryani. My mouth waters, and I hurry to find cutlery for us and to make Jamie's tea.

'How was your afternoon?' Jamie asks and passes around takeaway containers.

With Karrion's help, I recount our conversations with Lord Ellensthorne and Jessi. By the time I finish, Jamie is mopping his plate with pieces of naan bread and Karrion has polished off the poppadums. I have half of my curry left and, after a questioning look from Karrion, I push the containers towards him.

Jamie rises to wash his hands and takes a thin wad of papers from his briefcase.

'This is a witness statement pack,' he says. 'You need to complete a summary of the statement you took from Lord Ellensthorne, add your details, and sign it. I'll send someone to visit Lord Ellensthorne and ask him to approve the statement tomorrow. He will need a leaflet about being a witness, though he may have seen one before. In any case, we need to jump through the formal hoops.'

'Hang on a minute,' Karrion says, his fork poised over the plate. 'When we agreed to consult for the Met, we didn't mean endless paperwork.'

Jamie laughs. 'You've just described my profession. Unfortunately, the paperwork is vital if we are to catch the killer and have him stand before a Herald of Justice.'

'I don't understand why people still use magic to commit murder, when the punishment is always death,' I say. 'You'd think that and the Heralds would be deterrent enough.'

'Most people think they're too smart to get caught.'

'That's because they haven't factored in me and Yan being involved.' Karrion pauses and clears his throat. 'No offence, Jamie.'

'None taken. And I agree, outside perspective can be exactly what an investigation needs.'

'At the moment, this outside perspective is a little out of ideas. I hope you have something for us.'

Jamie takes two plastic folders from his briefcase. 'If by something you mean autopsy reports, then I do.'

'Please don't cover the table in gross photos while I'm still eating,' Karrion says and shoves curry into his mouth.

'We're not in that much of a hurry, Karrion.' I stand. 'I'll make more tea.'

'This is a nice place,' Jamie says and carries his plate to the sink. 'Though I expected it to look posher inside.'

'How so?' I ask.

'This may not be where the old Mage families live, but it's still a nice area. Given how limited space in Old London is, I'm amazed any of these detached houses still remain.'

'They won't for long, if Laene's building project goes ahead,' Karrion mumbles. He swallows and leans back. 'I wish I hadn't finished your curry now.'

'No one forced you to do it.' I move the rest of the dishes to the sink.

'Mum's taught me not to waste food.'

'What does your friend think about the building project?' Jamie asks.

'I don't think it's at a stage where they would be contacting the residents. At least, she hasn't mentioned it to me.'

'I can't imagine anyone here being happy about it.'

'Surely it depends on how much the developers are willing to pay for the properties,' Karrion says.

After a glance at Jamie, I shrug. 'It's an unknown area to me.'

'At this point, we're not even sure whether the Ivy Street Project is the connection between Laene and Hailfax.' Jamie adds tea bags to our mugs.

'What else could it be?' Karrion asks. 'Have you found another connection?'

'Not as yet. What I meant is that a property developer and an architect in Old London are likely to cross paths frequently in their professional lives. For all we know, they could be good friends.'

I nod. 'We didn't ask that question of Halen Laene or Denniel Hailfax.'

'We can still do that. No doubt we'll find other things to ask them as the investigation progresses.'

Jamie and I carry the mugs to the table. Karrion had bought dessert, and he passes each of us a cookie and, as an afterthought, a plate.

'Are you sure you want dessert and autopsy photos?' Jamie asks.

Karrion bites into his cookie. 'How bad can it be?'

'Don't say I didn't warn you.' Jamie holds up the two folders. 'Laene or Hailfax first?'

'Let's do them in the same order as the crime scenes,' I say. 'What was Laene's cause of death?'

'Asphyxiation due to strangulation. Despite Mery's reservations, the ivy was the murder weapon.'

'Was the pathologist sure about that?' Karrion asks. 'Couldn't someone have draped the ivy around Laene's neck after he'd been strangled?'

'No. The marks on his neck matched the vine perfectly, down to the leaf stalks. The ivy killed him.'

I break off a piece of my cookie and dip it in my mug. Triple chocolate and tea is not a great combination. 'That means we're back to trying to figure out what kind of magic could have achieved that.'

'Yes. The lab techs swabbed the ivy, but they couldn't extract any skin cells off it.'

'It sounds like the killer wore gloves,' Karrion says.

'It's likely. So far, all the prints we've identified at the house belong to the victim, Halen or staff. There was no sign of a break-in.'

That is odd, but I keep the thought to myself. Why was the back door lock here rusted away if the killer can bypass locked doors without a trace? Unless we are looking for two different people.

'Did the pathologist find anything else about Laene's death?' I ask.

'The black substance on his face was soot. Given that he had some under his fingernails, the pathologist

133

concluded that he had covered his face with soot himself.'

'Jessi said it was to fool the ghost into thinking he was not its intended target.'

'You said a ghost wasn't involved,' says Jamie.

'No, but Laene didn't know that last night.'

'Good point.' Jamie opens a folder and thumbs through the papers it contains. 'There was one other thing.'

He sets down a photo of Laene's face. The soot has been washed off. I expect Laene's face to be dark purple, but it is no darker than his neck. Red lines overlap where the vine was, and there is a black outline around his lips. I point to it.

'What's that?'

'We're not sure. The pathologist only discovered it once he had cleaned Laene's face.'

'Could it be a consequence of the strangling?' Karrion asks. 'Maybe he was struggling for air and bruised his face.'

'It could be that, but it isn't.'

'You sound sure,' I say.

'As sure as I can be. Hold that thought, and I'll come back to it.' Jamie opens the second folder. 'Let's move on to Hailfax.'

'Cause of death?' I ask.

'Deadly nightshade poisoning.'

I cock my head, frowning. 'That doesn't make sense. Belladonna isn't that fast acting.'

'That depends on how it's administered.' Jamie holds a stack of photos to his chest. 'I hope you're done with the cookies.'

The gravity of Jamie's tone has an effect on Karrion, who gulps down the rest of his tea and takes away our plates. I don't object, even though I have barely touched my cookie. Between tiredness, the pain nagging in my joints and the talk of the autopsy, what little appetite I had earlier has disappeared.

When he deems us ready, Jamie spreads the photos on the table. Karrion's eyes skitter over them, and he turns away with a disgusted noise. This is not the first open carcass I have seen, and I am able to focus on the detail while ignoring the fact I am looking at a person cut open.

The top photo shows an autopsy in progress. Hailfax's chest has been opened to reveal his oesophagus. Within it is a belladonna plant. In the next photo, Hailfax's stomach has been cut open, revealing roots growing through the lining. Further pictures document leaves sprouting out of his mouth, and berries and blossoms littering his throat and mouth.

'Every part of the deadly nightshade is poisonous,' Jamie says. 'Hailfax ingested more than enough to kill him.'

'Death by plant,' Karrion says, his face pale. 'That's a terrible way to die.'

I leaf through the photos, trying my best to ignore the fact that twenty-four hours ago, Hailfax was alive. The sight of the internal organs and flesh spread open does not awaken the same hunger as smelling the body would, and I am grateful for that. As much as Jamie knows I'm not human, there is no need to rub his nose in it.

'According to Lord Ellensthorne's statement, there were only a few minutes between Hailfax complaining about stomach pains and the line going dead,' I say. 'That's not enough time for someone to restrain him, shove a plant down his throat, and wait for the poison to kill him.'

'Plus, what Lord Ellensthorne heard on the phone ought to have been different.' Karrion chances another glance at the photos. 'Unless he's lying.'

'Why would he lie?' Jamie asks.

It is a question Karrion and I have contemplated before. 'For him, because he can may be reason enough. Though it does seem unlikely that he would impede the investigation into his protégé's death.'

'He wasn't exactly helpful when we were looking into Gideor Braeman's murder,' Karrion says. 'Are we sure he wasn't involved in Hailfax's death?'

'I don't think we're sure about anything at this point, but I can't see what motive Lord Ellensthorne has.'

'Because he can?'

I shake my head at Karrion. 'While he could have dialled Hailfax's number before killing him, in an age when a call's location can be triangulated, a phone call is a shoddy alibi. Lord Ellensthorne may be many things, but careless is not one of them.'

Karrion crosses his arms, but from the slightest twitch of his lips, I know his accusation was not altogether serious. I flip through the photos until I find the one showing the roots of the plant.

'Take a look at this.' I tap at the photo. 'The roots grew into the lining and through it. I think the plant sprouted in his stomach.'

'Can magic do that?' Jamie asks.

I hesitate, regretting my words. But Jamie knows nothing of Lady Bergamon's powers.

'Probably. In fact, it must have been magic. How else do you grow a plant in someone's stomach? The digestive juices would destroy the roots long before the plant began growing.'

'Can Mages do it? Or Shamans?'

'Mages could probably enlarge a tiny plant, but to make one grow? I don't think so. Plant magic is more likely to be a Feykin speciality.'

'So we're looking for a Feykin?'

'Possibly,' I say, avoiding looking at Karrion.

'That narrows it down. There can't be too many Feykin in Old London.'

I know of three: Tanyella Fernlea, Eolande Pearson and the purple-eyed man we encountered while helping

136

Tim. 'Hard to say. They like to keep a low profile, for the most part, and it's not as though we keep a list. Was there anything else in those autopsy photos?'

Jamie flicks through the photos and lays one on the table. It is a close up of Hailfax's face, and straight away my attention is drawn to a black outline around his mouth.

'What's that? Is it stain from the berries?' Even as I ask the question, I see that the mark is too even to be caused by the belladonna plant.

'It's not from the berries, but beyond that, I haven't a clue. The weird thing is it wasn't there when the Paladins discovered his body.'

Karrion picks up the photo, his eyelashes touching his eyebrow piercing as he frowns. 'I have an idea, though I always thought it was an urban legend.'

'We've had several encounters with those recently. Care to share?'

'This looks like a kiss of death.'

'A what?' Jamie asks.

'I know, the name is stupid. And I've never heard of anyone witnessing one.'

My patience is wearing thin. 'Yes, but what is it?'

'Supposedly, the secret to a Mage's power leaves them at the moment of their death. And, again supposedly, it's possible for someone to steal that secret. Doing so is called giving someone the kiss of death, and it leaves a black mark around the mouth.'

'How do you give someone the kiss of death?' I ask, and roll my eyes.

'Dunno. The stories I've heard weren't that detailed. But I'm guessing there's more to it than simply snogging people on their deathbed.'

'And what does stealing the secret to a Mage's power mean?' Jamie asks, and in his eyes, I see a familiar longing. 'Would you be able to cast Mage spells?'

'You'd need magical blood, Jamie.'

His eyes flicker to me and away. 'Makes sense, I guess. But what's the point, then? Why would a Shaman or a Paladin want to access Mage magic?'

'Why would a Leech want to become the Speaker for the High Council of Mages and the First among the Light Mages?' I shrug. 'People have bizarre ambitions, and some are prepared to go to great lengths to achieve them.'

Karrion leans back in his chair and crosses his arms. 'I was going to say that the kiss of death rules out other Mages, but I don't think it does. In fact, wouldn't it make sense for a Mage to steal the secret to another school of magic? You could grow infinitely more powerful that way.' He slants a grin my way. 'That puts Lord Ellensthorne back at the top of my list of suspects.'

I smile and shake my head. 'There must be a drawback, otherwise every unscrupulous Mage in the world would be going around murdering other Mages.'

'It sounds like we need to do some research,' Jamie says.

'We can ask a Mage contact tomorrow.'

The lingering tightness caused by the autopsy photos disappears from Karrion's expression. 'Tinker Thaylor?'

'Yes.' I turn to Jamie. 'Did the SOCO teams discover anything else?'

Jamie thumbs through the file. 'The items around Laene's body were all protective in nature, though not all of them contained spells. The only recoverable prints on them belonged to Laene, which is in keeping with the rest of the crime scene.'

'I think we can safely assume the killer wore gloves,' Karrion says.

I offer no response, too busy trying to ignore an image of Lady Bergamon in velvet opera gloves.

'I also asked the SOCO team at the Laene residence to dig up the bones,' Jamie says. 'So far, the lab technicians haven't uncovered anything beyond what you told us at the crime scene.'

Karrion rises and takes our mugs to the sink. 'We've accumulated plenty of evidence about Laene being mortally afraid, but as Jessi dismissed our spook theory… where does that leave us?'

'The kiss of death confirms a link between Laene and Hailfax,' I say. 'It could be that Laene's superstitions aren't connected to his murder.'

'But doesn't it seem strange that he should die on the one night of the year when his fear is out of control?' Karrion asks, and taps his fingers on my shoulder on his way past. 'I mean, what are the odds of that?'

'Yet we have no such coincidence with Hailfax. From everything we've learned so far, Samhain was no different from any other night for him.'

'The SOCO team had no further light to shed on that,' Jamie says. 'As with Laene, all the fingerprints belonged to the two Hailfaxes, and there was no sign of forced entry.'

'How did the belladonna plant end up inside Hailfax?' I ask.

'There were a couple of belladonna seeds in the remains of his coffee. But according to the lab, the seeds were added to the coffee after it was made.'

'How could they figure that?' Karrion asks.

'Something to do with the toxicity of the liquid,' says Jamie. 'If the seeds had been brewed with the coffee, it would have caused the poison levels in the coffee to be higher. People at the lab explained it all to me.'

Karrion holds his hands up. 'I'll pass on the chemistry lesson, thanks. School wasn't that great.'

'I wish I'd had the option,' Jamie mutters.

I pour myself a glass of water. 'That, I think, narrows down the window for the poisoning.'

Jamie twists in his chair to look at me. 'How so?'

'I'm assuming Hailfax wasn't fond of cold coffee. If he drank the seeds, they must have been mixed into the coffee after it was brewed but while it was still warm.'

'But how do we know when that was?' Karrion asks.

'If the seeds were in his stomach for a long time, the digestive acids would have destroyed them. Sure, he would have ingested some of the poison in the process, but nowhere near enough to kill him. To sprout, the seeds can't have been in his stomach long. If he was working late, chances are he was drinking coffee to keep himself awake. It can't have taken that long to sprout the plant with magic. My guess is he drank the seeds either right before the phone call with Lord Ellensthorne or while they were talking.'

'I'm not sure that helps,' Karrion says. 'We already know there didn't appear to be anyone else in the flat. So how could the seeds have got into his coffee?'

'How could Hailfax's father have aged ten years in a single night?' I lean against the kitchen counter.

'Welcome to the world of ordinary police work. In my experience, killers rarely leave a handy roadmap for us to follow.' Jamie stands. 'I suggest we call it a day. Things may look clearer in the morning.'

'Thanks for the dinner and coming by, Jamie.'

'You're welcome. It may not seem like it now, but we are making progress. I'll give you a call tomorrow morning, and we can agree on the next steps for the investigation.'

We say goodnight, and I see Jamie out.

15

A MATTER OF TRUST

When I return to the kitchen, Karrion is leaning against the counter, waiting for me. He is once again frowning deeply enough for his eyebrow ring to touch his eyelashes.

'That stuff Jamie told us, it seems to me it's pointing in one direction.'

'We have no proof,' I say, and brush past him to the sink.

'A plant sprouted in someone's stomach. Isn't that exactly the sort of thing a Plant Shaman could do?'

'How do you know that?'

'I share an affinity with birds, she shares one with plants. It's what Shamans do. But beyond affinity, we also have the power to control them. I can call crows to me, just as I can send pigeons away. If Lady B wants to make a plant grow, all she has to do is give it an order.'

'That may be the case, but Lady Bergamon was in her garden, unconscious, when Hailfax was killed.'

'Didn't you say you got here gone two o'clock?'

I ignore the question and turn on the tap to fill the sink.

'You know Hailfax died earlier that night. Unless the Kelpie happened to be carrying a watch and was able to vouch for Lady B's whereabouts, saying you think she was unconscious doesn't amount to much. And don't forget, Laene was killed earlier.'

'Are you suggesting Lady Bergamon killed him too?'

'Be real, Yan. A man was strangled with a length of ivy without anyone actually gripping the vine. Sounds like plant magic to me.'

'You don't know that,' I say, dropping our cutlery into the soapy water. Splashes land on my cheek, and I bend to dry them on my shoulder.

'Can you think of a better explanation?'

'We've barely begun the investigation, and there are plenty of avenues to explore. You're quick to jump to conclusions.'

'Okay, answer me this: if the suspect was anyone other than Lady Bergamon, would you be as reluctant to entertain the possibility that they did it?'

'Don't call her that,' I whisper, scrubbing the plates with more force than necessary.

Karrion rests a hand on my shoulder, his expression softening. 'Look, I don't want Lady Bergamon to be guilty any more than you do. That would mean she'd face a death sentence. But you have to at least consider the possibility.'

I know he is right and I should concede the point. But the idea that Lady Bergamon may be behind the murders is inconceivable. She is a good person, of that I am certain. If I cannot trust my judgement of people, what have I got left?

'We aren't even sure whether she knows about the Ivy Street Project.'

Karrion sighs and allows his hand to slip off my shoulder. He picks up a tea towel hanging from a peg near the sink and dries the dishes. When I have drained the sink and wiped the surfaces with a dishcloth, he closes the bag of cookies and gets a glass of water.

'I'm guessing an early night is in order.'

'Yeah. I didn't sleep much last night.'

'Be sure to take your meds.'

142

My first instinct is to tease him about not needing a caretaker, but there is still tightness in Karrion's voice that belies his frustration. Not wishing to aggravate him further, I nod and find my medication in the pocket of my bag. I take two pills with a glass of water.

'We'll probably want to light fires upstairs,' I say as I refill my glass. 'The house is getting pretty chilly.'

'Makes sense, if it's still pissing it down out back. Do you know where Lady B stores her firewood?'

'Other than somewhere in the back garden? No idea. I don't suggest either of us goes stumbling out there in the dark. We don't know what dangers the garden holds, especially now Lady Bergamon is unconscious.'

Karrion looks like he wants to say something, but I do not give him the chance.

'I think I saw a full basket of logs in the lounge. We'll make do with them tonight and worry about the rest tomorrow morning.'

'Fine. Which door?'

I push open the door to the lounge, and Karrion steps through, his irritation forgotten for the moment. The food laid out on the black tablecloth looks no different from last night, but the smells have an edge of staleness. Karrion looks at the supper setting with wide eyes.

'Should we tidy up?' he asks.

'No. The table is within a circle.'

Perhaps it is a lingering effect of Samhain or a new-found awareness of my powers, but I can feel the circle's presence as a hum of a beehive on the edge of my consciousness.

'Right.' Karrion glances at the floor, his attention fixing to the nearest symbol. 'Why?'

'I don't know. Lady Bergamon must have her reasons. But Wishearth told me that the table is laid out to remember her family and ancestors.'

'Has she mentioned them to you? I mean, I guess her family isn't around anymore. Or does she have children of her own, or grandchildren?'

'She's never mentioned anyone. Given how old she is, my guess is that her immediate family is long gone. I had a look around the house this morning, but I found no photos anywhere. That seems to indicate no children or grandchildren.'

'Do you think she gets lonely?'

'I imagine she does. But she's not completely alone. There's Bradán. Their romance isn't recent. Wishearth is a frequent visitor. And, she has her plants.'

'Yeah, but it's still not the same. I'd go stir crazy if I had to spend the rest of my life with no one but birds to talk to.'

'Especially if they were pigeons.'

Karrion rolls his eyes, but I can see he is serious.

'You're right,' I say. 'It must be a lonely existence. Perhaps that's why she was so keen to help us find Brother Valeron.'

'You two are friends now. That must be nice for her.'

'True, though I wonder—' My attention strays back to the table and the food. 'If she's close to immortal, it must be hard for her to befriend mortals. She'll watch each of her friends grow old and die.'

I see sympathy in the curve of Karrion's lips. 'Which one is worse, losing people you care about, over and over, or spending centuries alone?'

'Perhaps that's why Lady Bergamon and Wishearth are so close. In a world where they watch their friends wither and die, it must be reassuring to have someone who stays the same. Perhaps that's also why Lady Bergamon has taken a Kelpie as a lover. The Fey do not age like we do, or so the stories claim.'

'Then again, if you live to the ripe old age of ninety,

144

that's one hell of a friendship. You still have sixty-five years to go.'

I force a smile. Even if I live that long, it will not be in Old London. Lady Bergamon has bought me precious time with her herbal medicine, but once my father dies and Dearon becomes the next Eldermen, I must return to the conclave.

Without a word, I point to the log basket by the fireplace, and Karrion appears to remember why we are in the lounge. When he picks up the basket, a rasp of paper against the bricks draws both of our attention. Karrion crouches and retrieves a piece of paper that has been crushed into a ball.

Before I have a chance to suggest that perhaps the contents of the paper are not meant for us, Karrion straightens it. When his expression darkens, I know I will not like whatever the paper says.

'She knew.'

Karrion says nothing further as he hands the paper to me.

It is a letter about the Ivy Street Project, addressed to Miss Greenslade, which must be the name Lady Bergamon goes by in Old London, and it provides a brief outline of the proposed development. The main purpose is to offer to purchase Lady Bergamon's property for what the letter claims to be an open market value. My eyebrows rise at the figure. One of the names at the bottom, signed electronically, is Natheniel Laene.

So Lady Bergamon knew about the development, and from the state of the letter, she cannot have been happy about it.

I swallow. 'This doesn't mean that she murdered anyone.'

'Her garden is out there,' Karrion gestures towards the back of the house, 'and she can't very well pick it up and move. This can't have been the first time her home has been under threat from developers. She must have defended her domain somehow.'

'But that doesn't necessarily mean murder.'

'What do you actually know about Lady Bergamon?'

I open my mouth to answer, but no words come out. Karrion notices this, but before he has time to claim a victory, I hold my hand up.

'I believe you were right when you told me she's a Plant Shaman. She's far older than she looks, and there is more to her than she has revealed so far. I know she's a healer and I know she's a good person.'

'Just because she's helped you a couple of times doesn't mean she's not capable of murder. Do you really think she's lived through the ages and kept her domain hidden from the rest of the world by being nice to people?'

'Protecting her garden doesn't make her a bad person.'

'Depends on how she does it.'

'I doubt murder is the first thing she turns to when things don't go her way.'

'But you don't know that.' Karrion rakes a hand through his hair and winces when his fingers catch on a snag. 'Okay, answer me this: are you this insistent on Lady Bergamon's innocence because you need the medicine she brews for your father?'

I take a step back, shocked by his words. 'Do you really think staying in Old London is worth letting someone get away with murder?'

Karrion meets my gaze, but in the depths of his eyes, I see regret as well as stubborn refusal to give ground. 'I don't know, you tell me.'

'My father's choice of taking the medicine and accepting the prolonged suffering is his to make,' I say, lifting my chin. 'But I would never knowingly expect others to suffer for me. If I thought Lady Bergamon was guilty, my father dying sooner than I had hoped would be the least of my worries.'

He nods, but is not willing to let the subject drop. 'And yet, you refuse to entertain the idea that Lady Bergamon might have something to do with these deaths.'

'I do. The evidence points to plant magic, I give you that much, but Lady Bergamon isn't the only person with power over plants. There could be other Plant Shamans in the city. And don't forget that the Fey and Feykin also receive their power from nature. Besides, we're friends with a Hearth Spirit. Who's to say that a Plant Spirit hasn't taken to protecting Lady Bergamon?'

'It's easier to throw out unknown suspects than to focus on the one right under our beaks.'

'The thing is, I think she is too obvious. Like Lord Ellensthorne and Jonathain Marsh when we were investigating Braeman's murder. It seems too easy.'

'Sometimes the obvious answer is the right one.'

'Not this time, I can't believe it. Besides, why would Wishearth have woken me up in the middle of the night because he was concerned about Lady Bergamon if she was busy killing Mages elsewhere in Old London?'

'Unless he's in on it.'

The suggestion is so preposterous, for a moment all I can do is stare at him. I attempt a laugh, but the noise that escapes my throat is a strangled growl.

'Anyone else you'd like to accuse of murder while you're at it? Jamie, perhaps?'

'Jamie would never—'

'But Lady Bergamon and Wishearth would? Why, because they're semi-immortal? Or because you consider them less human than us? Where do you draw the line, Karrion?'

He shifts his weight, his expression dark. The silence grows tense until the hairs on my arms stand up. Karrion is the first to look away. His attention is drawn to the log basket, to the letter I am still holding, and back to the firewood.

'You should get some sleep,' he says, words soft, while he avoids meeting my gaze. 'I'll make sure both bedrooms have enough wood.'

Karrion leaves the room, ducking his head away from me, but I see his troubled expression. As much as he regrets the argument, he is not willing to give ground. Neither am I, and I remain in the lounge, staring at the place settings on the table.

Can my instincts be this wrong about Lady Bergamon and Wishearth, or is Lady Bergamon being set up for murder? And if it is the latter, how do I prove it?

16

THE THREADS THAT BIND US

By the time I have brushed my teeth, Karrion has closed the door to the spare bedroom. I hesitate in the hallway, but the message is clear: for tonight, the discussion is over. Faced with a choice between pressing on with the argument or a night alone with my thoughts, I take the option that is likely to cause less pain and close the door of Lady Bergamon's bedroom behind me.

Lady Bergamon has not moved while Karrion was accusing her of murder, but I wonder whether she is aware of anything outside the circle. Does she know we have discovered the letter, or that the evidence seems to point to her? Is she aware that I have defended her, perhaps with more conviction than I feel?

Loneliness surges within me and threatens to spill out as tears. This is not the first time I have felt out of my depth during a case, but I have always had allies by my side. I have always had Karrion believing in me. Now, I am alone.

Or am I?

My eyes are drawn to the fireplace and the fresh stack of logs; my legs refuse to move while Karrion's voice rings in my ears. I want to dismiss his accusations, but he has sown the seeds of doubt in my mind. All I can do is hope that by being denied sustenance, the seeds will wither and die.

Forcing my limbs out of the paralysis that has crept over me, I walk to the fireplace and build a fire. When flames have crept across the wood, I choose a handful of offerings at random and feed them to the fire.

'Hearth Spirit, please guide me and help me find the truth. I don't know how to help Lady Bergamon on my own. Protect the inhabitants of this house. We give thanks for the heat you offer and for your wisdom.'

Part of me is tempted to ask Wishearth to grant Karrion wisdom to see the error of his ways, but I bite my tongue. If Karrion's suspicions are wrong, he must discover it for himself.

The night time routine to reaffirm my connection to Wishearth eases some of the loneliness. But a hint of melancholy lingers, just like it did last night when I reached for the brandy bottle instead of going to bed early.

I sit on the cushions by the fire and open my bag. Nestled between a notebook and a scuffed packet of tissues is the hunting knife. Dearon carved the bone handle himself and presented the knife to me when I came of age. Since then, it had seen regular use until I turned my back on the conclave and moved to Old London. I discovered it in a chest of my belongings during my recent trip back and brought it with me. At the time, I acted on instinct, but now I am grateful for the familiar feel of bone within my grip. I have no idea whether steel will work against the killer we are hunting, but it offers more reassurance than the ancient weapons displayed on the walls.

Having undressed, I lie down and face the fire. The knife, safe in its leather scabbard, is lying on the pillow, and I draw it to me. My thumb traces the simple decorations and the grip smoothed by years of use. I feel the ghost of Dearon's fingers over mine, turning the handle as he works the bone. They stroke the back of my hand, and a shiver runs through me. The memory of his touch stays with me until the dancing flames lull me to sleep.

I stand upon a hill of heather. Two bucks face each other in the valley below, their heads bearing proud crowns of antlers and their blood roaring with the instincts of autumn. The larger of the two keeps flashing his eyes towards me, but other never takes his eyes off his rival.

The sun is low in a sky of purple and grey, and the bucks cast elongated shadows on the opposite side of the valley. The area echoes with their deep groans and a harem of does is grazing at a safe distance. One of the bucks turns, and they pace back and forth next to each other, sizing up the competition. Their groans intensify as they face each other once more and lower their heads. The antlers come together in a clap of thunder and a murder of crows nearby takes to the skies. I watch them go, but the bucks lock their feet and fight for each centimetre of ground. With a twist of his head, the smaller buck drives his rival to his knees. Taking a step back, he raises his chin and declares his victory. The larger buck walks away, defeated but unharmed.

It is only now that the victor turns to look at me, and I dismiss him with the flick of my tail. I sense him taking a step towards me, then another, and I run. The wind howls in my ears, and the tantalising smell of heather fills my nostrils with whispers of freedom and home. The buck's longer strides reduce the gap between us until we are running side by side. In the turn of his ears and the bouncing leaps, I see his joy, and my blood sings with the shared happiness.

We come to a forest where the low hanging branches of young oaks threaten to catch the buck by his antlers. I waste no time breaking away from him and, mid-leap, I morph into a hare. The change in the vibrations through my pads tells me that he too has adopted a different form. We race through the undergrowth, tumbling over rotting logs and ducking under coils of brambles. Thorns catch my side, but I keep going; the clump of fur I leave behind is the only sign of our passing.

The change in the quality of light ahead signals the edge of the woods, and we barrel through the saplings as two wolves. Our yips and barks encourage us on, and we run along the bottom of a valley, the scent of fresh water drawing us north. The stones of a dry streambed are loose beneath my paws, and I leap onto the river bank and surge ahead. I achieve a yard or two's advantage before he is mirroring my position on the opposite bank. When I growl at him, he lets his tongue hang out in a canine grin, and inches ahead.

Changing tack, I veer left, where the rocky side of the hill reduces my speed to an awkward clamber. From the top, I see a lake ahead and I choose the quickest path towards it. By the time I reach the steep drop to the water, I am no longer alone and together we launch ourselves off the bank. I dive head first into the water and my tail kicks me back into motion.

He too has chosen sea trout as his form, and we swim through the dark waters, keeping to the edge between warm surface water and the cooler depths. I sense a current on my scales and steer towards a river draining into the lake.

When we reach the shallower waters of the stream I roll, and fur replaces scales on my body. My whiskers register movement in the murky depths and I dive deeper, eager to satisfy my curiosity. I recognise the movement as crayfish, and hunger roils in my stomach. With a quick flash of claws, I snatch a crayfish and kill it. A fish swims by, tempting me with more food, but I have my prize.

Breaking through the surface, I roll onto my back and tear into the crayfish. The meat is sweet, and I open the carapace with my claws until I have devoured every morsel. My hunger sated, I look up to see my companion on the bank. He has returned to his human form and his expression is filled with a different kind of hunger. I swim towards the shore. When my hand reaches up to grasp for purchase, it finds his hand instead. He pulls me out of the river, and we stand face to face, wet and panting. Droplets of water cling to the dusting of hair on his chest, and I draw my fingers through them. He remains still, content to watch me, and his attention is a cool spring shower on my heated skin. His dark eyes hold no flames, but they nevertheless sear through me until all of me is uncovered.

I hold out as long as I can before rising onto my tiptoes. He ducks his head to kiss me, but I lean back, keeping our lips millimetres apart. When he tries again, I duck a second time. His breath ghosts over my face as he growls and brings his hands up to tangle in my wet hair. I relent and kiss him, wild instincts urging me on. He hooks his hands behind my thighs, and I hop up to wrap my legs around his waist. Too intent upon kissing him, I am only vaguely aware we are moving until I feel the roughness of a tree against my back. I gasp, and he breaks the kiss. Our breath is short, and a flush spreads across my face. The sight of him, almost out of control, threatens to sweep me away to a place I am not ready to revisit, and I crash my lips against his. I let my actions relay the words I cannot utter, while my hands grasp his shoulders to bring him closer.

Later, we lie on the ground, my head resting on his arm. Mist rising from the river caresses my skin with the velvet touch of moth wings. There is a smear of mud across my abdomen, my knees are stained green and I have twigs in my hair. None of that bothers me, but rather stokes the embers of heat in my belly. I feel beautiful. I feel wanted.

Dearon traces a hand from my cheek down my neck, over my right breast and across my stomach to my pelvis. I shiver, and he chuckles.

'Dawn is breaking.'

As if summoned by his words, light breaches the horizon. The grass is grey with frost, and yet, I cannot feel the cold. A hint of confusion worms its way through my contentment. I cannot recall the night falling.

'Yannia, you must wake up.'

'Why?' I ask, frowning.

His side is warm, and it invites me to close my eyes and fall asleep. He will protect me, though I cannot remember what from.

'If you don't, I can't wake up.'

'What do you mean?'

'I can't wake up until you leave my dream.'

His words sever the connection between us, disrupting the magic I have woven, and I spin away from him into the awaiting darkness. I try to call out his name, but instead, I start awake with a gasp.

FRIDAY

17

COMPLICATIONS

Blinking in the grey light of the morning, I take a while to find my bearings in an unfamiliar room. My body is a mass of pain, and yet, I feel relaxed and sated as I would after a night of lovemaking.

Is that not what I just did?

When I rub my face, pain flares on my chin. A questing fingertip finds the skin there raw, and I recall the scrape of Dearon's stubble and the edge of violence in his kisses. My body bears the marks of the dream, no matter how impossible that ought to be.

Was last night the result of lingering Samhain magic, or did my loneliness manifest my power in a new and unexpected way? How could I weave a thread to bridge the gap between my dreams and his? Is that kind of power not reserved for Mages alone?

'Yan?'

Karrion's voice through the door startles me, and I sit up on my makeshift bed.

'Yeah?'

'I was just wondering... If you're up and hungry, I could make you some toast.'

Even through the door, I hear the implied apology in his voice and I imagine the worried expression.

'That would be great,' I say, and push the blanket aside. 'I'll take a quick shower and come down.'

His footsteps retreat from the door as I struggle up, my legs almost buckling from the pain that flares in my hips. Picking up my bag, I stagger to the bathroom. Under the hot spray, my hands map every twinge and ache in my body, while my memory conjures Dearon's corresponding touch, bite and move. By the time I am towelling myself dry, the heat throbbing in my veins has little to do with the temperature of the water, and I am relieved the mirror is misted over. I need not see my flushed cheeks or the predatory glint in my eyes.

While I may have been physically satisfied by the dream, the hollowness remains beneath my sternum. My encounters with Dearon offer more than just sex. That is as far as I dare to go down that rabbit hole, and I hurry out of the bathroom, still twisting my wet hair into a braid.

Lady Bergamon is worse. I stand near the circle, peering in through the barrier that manages to be transparent and opaque all at once, and I am certain her skin has taken on a sallow tone. The lines on her face appear more pronounced, and the frown between her eyebrows has deepened.

I need to find a way to help her, soon. If I cannot take her to a hospital, perhaps I can get a doctor or one of the Paladin healers to visit her here. But how will I stop them from taking her away? If the circle is vital for keeping her safe, taking it down even to admit a doctor into this room could endanger her. Damn Wishearth. Why could he not explain what this all means? Why couldn't Bradán say what we are up against? He must know more than he lets on. I am left here, watching Lady Bergamon grow weaker by the hour, with no clear idea as to how I can help her. All I have are instincts telling me that she is a victim even in the face of the mounting evidence against her.

Downstairs, I find Karrion standing in the kitchen doorway, staring at the open fridge.

'What's going on?'

Karrion turns to me, his eyes wide. 'Lady B has a bowl of frogspawn in the fridge.'

'That seems unlikely,' I say with a frown.

'See for yourself.'

I walk to the fridge, Karrion right behind me. On the top shelf is a glass bowl covered with a plate, which I ignored yesterday when putting the groceries away. At first glance, the contents do look like frogspawn. I lean closer and begin to make out round shapes within the wet mass. Chuckling, I close the fridge.

'I'm pretty sure those are white currants in some kind of liquid.'

'Oh.' Karrion's neck turns a shade of pink. 'I knew that.'

Once he has recovered from his embarrassment, Karrion is quick to butter our toast and add milk to the cups of tea he has prepared. When he opens a jar of Marmite, I make a show of gagging and reach for a packet of Gouda slices in the fridge. The closing fridge door creates a current of air in the kitchen, and my nose twitches at a musty smell.

'What's that?'

'What's what?' Karrion asks.

Following the scent, I reach for the wooden bread bin on the counter. When I lift the lid, the smell intensifies and Karrion scrunches his nose.

'The bread's gone mouldy.'

In the bread bin, a loaf of bread is covered in an even layer of green mould. The dusty smell causes me to sneeze, and I turn away from the counter.

'Bless you,' Karrion says and takes the lid from me. 'We can chuck the bread later, but for now, I'd rather not have the mould all over our stuff too. Lady B ought to check her bread bin more often.'

Out of curiosity, I open a cupboard door and set a bag of rice on the counter. Some of the grains have darkened, and the contents smell faintly of rot. Next, I retrieve the bowl of white currants from the fridge, but they seem fine. The rest of the food in there also smells fresh. Leaving spoilt food in the kitchen seems out of character for Lady Bergamon, but I am not certain what else, if anything, is going on.

'Did you sleep okay?' Karrion asks as we sit down, and a hint of uncertainty returns to his bearing.

I consider brushing off the question, but instead, I tell him about my dream and Dearon's parting words. Although I gloss over the sex, the tale takes long enough for Karrion to make himself two more slices of toast. While he chews, Karrion listens to me with unguarded awe.

'Visiting someone's dreams sounds like something a Mage might do, or maybe a Paladin. Or do you think Samhain somehow messed with Old London, and we've all swapped powers?'

I shake my head. 'That would require swapping blood. Besides, I had no trouble using my Wild Folk abilities yesterday. My guess is this was more personal. I was lonely when I went to bed and was holding a hunting knife Dearon gave me years ago. My last thoughts before falling asleep were about him. Perhaps the fact that we're in the presence of Lady Bergamon, who is undoubtedly one of the most powerful beings in Old London, coupled with the fact that she is meticulous about observing the old Samhain traditions left enough residual power in this house for me to do something unheard of. I accessed Dearon's dreams.'

'I guess you miss him.'

Stirring my tea with more focus than it requires, I shrug. 'You know it's complicated. I don't seem to be able to think about Dearon outside the context of the

160

conclave and the promises our parents made. He belongs there, and I... I'm not sure I do.'

'Why don't you just leave?' Karrion asks. 'Say that you want no part in your father's succession plans and break all ties with the conclave?'

'All that I am is the conclave's. All that the conclave has is mine. Since birth, I have been woven into its tale so that I'm not forgotten and will go on forever.'

'No offence, but that's a rubbish answer.'

Karrion's words throw me, and I laugh. This is why I love him: he is never anything but honest. Even when he risks offending me with his opinions.

'I suppose it is,' I say, still smiling.

'Is it because you're afraid?'

'Of what?' I ask.

'Losing the safety of that option.'

'I'm not sure I follow.' It is not true, but a part of me wants to hear what he has to say.

'You know exactly what's expected of you at the conclave. You may not like it, but you know what your role is and who you are. And you know Dearon. He wants you, that much is clear. As much as your life here is uncertain, your life there isn't. I don't know, I guess letting go of all that certainty for the unknown is scary.'

'I've already chosen the unknown once, when I moved to Old London,' I say, neither confirming nor denying his words.

'Yes, to a point. But you always knew you could go back. In fact, you knew you had to go back. It seems to me that gave you a safety net for your time in Old London. No matter what happened here, you could always return to the conclave. But what if you couldn't? That must be pretty scary.'

'I'd never thought of it that way, but you're probably right. And Dearon forms a part of that safety net. No matter how badly I screw up relationships here, I know he's back at the conclave, waiting for me. But I don't know if my attraction stems from knowing he'll be there or whether it goes deeper than that. And while he is tangled in the mess of the Elderman and the future of the conclave, I'm not sure I'll be able to figure it out.'

'Have you ever considered the possibility that he might be willing to leave the conclave?' Karrion asks, his voice gentle.

I laugh at the absurdity of the thought. 'And do what, move to Old London?'

'Why not? That's what you did.'

The idea of Dearon in the city, wearing his rabbit skin trousers and carrying a longbow, seems impossible. He may have visited Old London when he came to find me, but that does not mean he could, or would, stay for more than a day or two.

'It took me more than a year to decide that it was the right decision for me. Dearon... he is too wild to adapt to the city, too settled in the conclave life. While I always questioned our laws on some level, he never did.'

'Don't you think he'd be willing to make a sacrifice to be with you?'

'What right have I to ask that of him?'

'But he likes you.'

'He may have done once, but does he still? I left, remember, and even when I returned, I stayed only long enough to sleep with him once and then left again.'

'There's no harm in checking.'

'Yes, there is.' I duck my head, a rueful smile lifting the corners of my mouth. 'What right have I to ask him to leave behind the only life he knows and to give up the chance to be the Elderman?'

Karrion gets no chance to reply as my phone rings. I see Jamie's name on the screen.

'I hope your morning has been less hectic than mine,' he says after we have exchanged greetings.

'How so?'

'The killer struck again.' Jamie pauses. 'And then again.'

I push away my mug. 'There have been two more murders?'

Karrion jumps up, his chair falling back with a clatter. He looks at me, waiting for details, and I shake my head. Reaching for my plate, he clears the table.

'Two more Mages died in bizarre circumstances. Interested?'

'Where do you want us to meet you?'

'The first crime scene. I'll text you the address.'

'We'll be there as soon as we can.'

'Good. And, Yannia? This won't be a pretty sight.'

18

THE MAN WHO PLANNED

The address Jamie sends me takes us to a residential street near the Museum of London. I know which house we are looking for from the police and Paladin vehicles parked outside. As we approach it, we pass a woman who finishes a coffee and drops the cup on the pavement. In this neighbourhood, it strikes me as incongruous. She does not appear to notice my attention, and we continue on.

A Paladin is guarding the door, hand on the hilt of his sword, but upon seeing our Scotland Yard ID cards, he lets us through. We don the now familiar barrier suits.

Beyond the black door, the hallway has been painted pale blue, which contrasts with the darker wooden floor. Beneath the lemon furniture polish, I smell dog and spoilt fruit. A scene of crime officer is walking down the stairs, but he turns and indicates that we should follow.

Upstairs, a pale grey carpet muffles the sound of our footsteps. We pass several closed doors, and behind one, I can hear someone crying. The nervous glance Karrion casts my way suggests that he too heard it. At the far end of the corridor, a door opens and Jamie guides a police officer out, a hand on his shoulder. The younger man has the tense expression of someone fighting the urge to be sick. From the tightness around Jamie's eyes, I know he has also been affected by what lies beyond the door.

'Good, you're here,' Jamie says and turns to the police officer. 'Get some air and take your time.'

We step aside to let the officer pass, then we join Jamie by the door. A thrum of power tickles the hairs at the nape of my neck, fleeting enough for me to wonder if I imagined it. Without resorting to my magic, I can smell decay again, but the undertones are different here.

'The victim's name is Alfread Cullingwoed, a forty-two-year-old East Mage. The body was discovered by his husband, Colen, when he returned from a business trip earlier this morning.'

'Where's the husband now?' I ask.

'He's in one of the guest bedrooms with a vet. Their dog was with Alfread in the study last night and was injured. Considering the extent of the damage, the vet had no choice but to put the dog down.'

My head turns to look down the corridor. Jamie nods.

'Colen Cullingwoed is a Dog Shaman.'

'Are we going in?' Karrion asks.

'Yes. I just wanted to warn you that it won't be a pretty sight.' Jamie opens the door.

Even before we cross the threshold, my nose warns me of what's to come. The room smells of damp, rotting wood, bodily fluids and decomposing flesh, but above else, it smells of earthy fungus. When we step past the door, Karrion lets out a strangled cry, and even I am frozen to the spot.

'Are those mushrooms?' Karrion asks.

From behind us comes a laugh that turns into a chesty cough. 'Fuck, nobody let the city boy out of Old London. He might be scared by these creatures called trees.'

Karrion glares at Mery over his shoulder. 'Funny.'

Mery shrugs as she saunters past us to look at the body. 'Bloody hell, this one's nasty.'

165

The victim is lying on his back on a Persian rug. He is wearing black silk pyjamas and a burgundy robe. Every inch of the exposed skin is covered in destroying angels, and from the uneven shape of his limbs, I assume more mushrooms are growing under his clothes. A dark stain encircles the body, and one sniff is enough to identify its origin.

As with Hailfax, the death does not appear to have been quick. Broken picture frames and papers litter the floor around a cherry wood desk. A matching wooden chair lies on its side. There is a separate stench emanating from near the fireplace, and I sidestep around the body to a raised dog bed of red velvet. The fabric has yellow streaks on it, which smell of puss, gangrene and rotting flesh. I fight the rising tide of nausea by switching to breathing through my mouth, but my brain converts the smell into taste and I gag. While I am no stranger to the stench of decomposition, my wilder side recoils from an offering that would make me sick. Clapping a hand over my mouth, I turn and swallow repeatedly until my stomach settles.

'Even the Wild Chick is freaked.'

Ignoring Mery, I direct my words at Jamie. 'What happened to the dog?'

'That's what you want to know?' Mery laughs again. 'Not what happened to the bloke, but the dog? Jesus, talk about screwed up priorities.'

'I'll show you the carcass when we're done here,' says Jamie.

'I wouldn't let the widower hear you call his dog companion that,' Karrion says, his words low.

Jamie nods.

Mery pushes hair off her face. 'At least we've had a lesson in political correctness. All is well in the world.'

'Any active magic in the room, Mery?' Jamie asks, his expression closed. 'Any magical residue you can detect?'

166

'All right, don't get your knickers in a twist, Detective.'

I feel the unfurling of Mery's power as it extends outwards, sliding over my aura. Her green eye glows as she turns her head from side to side, her gaze unfocused. It has never occurred to me to ask a Mage how they perceive the world when they open themselves up to magic, but now curiosity overrides the lingering nausea. As much as Wild Folk have the ability to see life and death in everything natural, so do Mages have an innate understanding of power.

Mery gives no indication that our presence distracts her, but we remain still until she shakes herself out of the trance and sweeps her hair forward to cover her green eye.

'The room's warded, but you could've figured that out from the postcode. There are remnants of power still lingering on the body. Until yesterday, I'd never seen anything like it. But I picked up the same feeling at both crime scenes. Spent the rest of the day thinking up long words to explain how I hadn't the faintest idea what it was all about.'

'Could you hazard a guess as to the type of caster?' Karrion asks, but he is looking at me rather than Mery. My pulse quickens.

'It's nature magic, though I say so based on the effects rather than the spell. Beyond that, I'm really not sure. Maybe Shaman, maybe Feykin.' She turns to me. 'Hell, it could even be Wild Folk magic for all I know. Never did have a chance to sense one of you lot.'

'The opportunity may yet present itself,' Jamie says. 'Yannia, what can you tell me about the room?'

Tapping into my inner reserves, I call upon the senses of nature. Behind me, I can feel Mery's aura meeting mine, but I ignore her, just as I ignore the others in the room.

To begin with, I keep my eyes shut. The crying from the other room becomes more distinct. Amidst the jagged breaths, I hear the sound of a fist hitting a wall, followed by a gasp of pain. The smells of rot become stronger, and I separate four different sources: somewhere downstairs, the guest room we passed, the body on the floor and the dog bed. My nose tickles from the distinct tang of destroying angels, and I recall childhood lessons teaching me to identify mushrooms by their scent. Once I came into my powers, doing so became much easier. Now my instincts warn me to stay away from the mushrooms, a primal part of my brain recognising the scent of death.

Opening my eyes, I move to crouch by the body. What little skin is visible under the white caps of the mushrooms is dark from dried blood. Cullingwoed's mouth is open, and a large mushroom appears to have sprouted out of his tongue. It is likely he would not have been able to speak if he'd had the presence of mind to call for help. Even though I cannot see the rest of his expression, his eyes convey the horror of his passing. I expect he was dead long before the poison reached his internal organs.

Who could be capable of inflicting such a cruel death on someone?

Just thinking the question causes my mind to rebel, but as much as I cannot believe Lady Bergamon to be a murderer, I have to keep an open mind. Even so, beyond the cause of death, I cannot see anything here that might link her to this murder.

I move back to the dog bed and distract myself from the stench by imagining Sinta on a matching bed in my office. Will she keep me company while I work, like this dog did with the victim?

'Anything, Yannia?' Jamie asks.

168

The pain in my hips flares as I stand, but I push the discomfort aside while I try to organise my thoughts into coherent sentences.

'Destroying angels grow on rotting wood.'

'That's random,' Mery says. 'Are we doing nature facts now?'

Jamie silences her with a wave. 'What do you mean?'

'Persuading destroying angels to grow on an inhospitable surface must have taken a great deal of power. And how were they introduced to this room? Did the killer bring a single mushroom, which spread over the body, or did he introduce spores that formed a mycelium under the skin? Either way, there have to be easier ways to kill someone.'

'Can you detect any sign of an intruder within this room?'

I am tempted to point out that I cannot see the past, nor am I a bloodhound, but it does not seem worth it. Casting my senses out again, I look for anything that does not belong in the room. There is a faint trace of fingerprint powder on the desk, indicating that the SOCO team has been and gone, but nothing suggests Cullingwoed was not alone when he died.

'Nothing. Whoever the killer is, he may as well be a ghost.'

'If it makes you feel better, the residue in the room isn't Wild Folk magic,' Mery says. 'You're off the hook.'

'Thanks. Was the dog also covered in mushrooms?'

Jamie shakes his head. 'No. I don't know what happened to the dog, but I'm surprised it was still alive when we arrived here this morning. Hopefully the vet can shed some light on that. I asked him to give a statement before he leaves.'

'I'd like to talk to the victim's husband as well.'

'I assumed as much.'

Upon request, Jamie hands me a new pair of latex gloves. Careful not to step on the dark stain on the rug, I walk around the body to look at the papers. From the draft PR statements and surveyors' reports, I gather that Cullingwoed worked with property. Many of the papers contain to-do lists written in meticulous handwriting. The more I read, the more I form a picture of a man who had a plan for everything. One list even covers a plan to organise a weekend away in the Cotswolds with the steps already completed marked with neat ticks.

I am about to declare the papers irrelevant when a sheet under the desk catches my attention. When I pick it up, I close my eyes briefly. Why did I have to find it?

The page is a funding proposal for the Ivy Street Project. Judging by the handwritten comments next to the figures, this must be an early draft. But the implication is clear.

Alfread Cullingwoed is the third dead Mage connected to the project. But if Lady Bergamon is defending her domain by killing anyone involved in the redevelopment, how could she do so while lying unconscious inside a circle?

It takes me two attempts to find my voice while holding up the proposal. 'Did you see this? The victim has papers relating to the Ivy Street Project.'

Karrion's eyes widen and his expression darkens. Crossing his arms, he aims his words at me.

'How much do you want to bet the pathologist finds evidence of a kiss of death on him?'

'Kiss of death?' Mery frowns. 'Isn't that a myth?'

'We'll come back to you on that,' Jamie says. 'I wonder if it's time to take a look at the people living on Ivy Street.'

'Did the SOCO team find anything we've missed?' I hurry to ask, anxiety establishing a hold on me.

'They lifted plenty of prints, but found no sign of forced entry. Cullingwoed must have let his killer in.'

This is the third house with no sign of forced entry. Why, then, was the lock on Lady Bergamon's back door broken?

'Maybe.' I look around the room again. 'But I don't think so.'

'Why?' Jamie asks.

'What time was he killed?'

'The pathologist thought between eleven and one.'

'He's not a Shadow Mage, so it's unlikely he spent his nights working and meeting people. There's no sign of refreshments in this room, and I find it unlikely that a Mage in this area of Old London would entertain guests in his pyjamas.'

'Could he have been seeing a lover?' Karrion asks. 'His husband was away, and that might explain why he put on his pyjamas afterwards.'

I nod. 'Good point. The pathologist will be able to tell whether he had sex shortly before his death.' Turning to Jamie, I take off the gloves. 'Though there's a simple way to check. Can you show me to the master bedroom?'

Jamie takes us to the room next to study. Here, too, the colour scheme is pale blues and dark woods, and I note another dog bed next to the fireplace. From a full basket of logs, I gather the fireplace is functional, though I wonder whether the residents follow the old ways.

The king-sized bed at the far end has a cream cover and matching pillows. Ignoring Mery's question about my intentions, I uncover the pillows and bend down. Borrowing the nose of rat asleep in the basement, I inhale. On one side of the bed, the dominant scent is that of an East Mage: cinnamon, coconut and clouds heavy with rain. The other side holds the tell-tale scents of a Dog Shaman. There is overlap between the two, but I catch no trace of anyone else.

171

'If the victim was having an affair, he didn't bring the lover into the marital bed.'

'Plenty of other places for a shag, I bet,' Mery says. 'Yours is a nifty power. What other secrets can you sniff out?'

'You'd be surprised.'

Mery looks intrigued, but I choose not to elaborate.

'The bed doesn't look like anyone slept in it last night,' Karrion says. 'Maybe Cullingwoed decided he was going to do some work before going to bed, and someone murdered him instead.'

'Looks that way.'

I look around the rest of the room. A long wardrobe takes up most of the wall by the bed. Near the window, the wall has an arrangement of photos. Alfread Cullingwoed had a round face, and blond hair sticking up in every picture. Most of the photos show him with a ginger-haired man, often grinning cheek to cheek at various exotic locations. In several, one of them is holding a West Highland white terrier in their arms. Whatever the reality of their relationship, the photos document a marriage filled with love and laughter.

'We should talk to the husband,' I say, and the hesitation is clear in my voice. I have witnessed plenty of grief in the past two days and I am reluctant to relinquish the image of the happy man staring at me from the wall.

19

BROKEN

Jamie knocks on the closed door. Seconds tick by until, at last, the door opens. The man with flaming hair from the photos stands on the threshold, his eyes red and his chin covered in stubble. Dressed in a suit of fine wool, he has removed his tie and opened the top buttons of his shirt. Underneath, I can see the neckline of a white T-shirt. There are yellow streaks across the front of the suit, and the smell of decay reawakens the nausea I felt before.

While Jamie introduces us, I see a small shape covered by a white towel on the floor. My imagination replaces the Westie from the photos with Sinta, and I shudder. Colen Cullingwoed follows my gaze.

'Hamish passed away a few minutes ago,' he says, voice thick with emotion.

'I'm sorry for your losses.'

'How could this have happened? Al was a good man. He had no enemies. Who would want him dead?'

'Why don't you take a seat?' Jamie suggests, indicating the cream leather sofa.

Colen slumps on it and buries his face in his hands. I see that the knuckles of his left hand are bleeding.

'What time did you arrive home this morning?' Jamie asks, pen poised over his notebook.

'Shortly after six. I had an overnight flight from New York and took a taxi home from Heathrow.'

'You were away on business, is that right?' I ask.

'Yes. I'm a corporate lawyer, and my firm is negotiating a merger for an American client. This was my sixth trip to New York in the past three months.'

'Did many people know you were going away?'

Colen glances at me, puzzled by the question. 'Loads. I posted about it on social media both before and during the trip. And a phone call to the office would have told someone that I was out of the country.'

'Did you notice anything unusual when you came home this morning?'

'There was a weird musty smell, but I haven't had a chance to investigate where it might have come from. Normally Hamish rushes to the door as soon as he hears the lock turning. His walking has been difficult recently and we've had to carry him up and down the stairs. When he didn't appear by the time I'd taken my shoes off, I figured he and Al were still asleep. I crept upstairs to surprise them, and that's when I smelled it.'

'Smelled what?' Karrion asks.

'Hamish.' Colen looks away and wipes his eyes. 'I heard his whimpers from the study and opened the door. That's when I found... when I saw Al on the floor. I called the Paladins, and when I saw the state Hamish was in, I called our vet.'

My eyes stray to the dog's body again, but I have more questions before I am ready to see him. 'Did you notice anything about the room that seemed out of place, other than your husband's body and Hamish?'

'From the papers and pictures on the floor, it looked like there had been a struggle. But I didn't notice anything missing. I told the Paladins where the safe is located, and they said it hadn't been forced. We have valuable art downstairs, but I haven't checked whether anything is missing there.'

'We can take a look when we're done here, and you can tell us if anything has been taken,' Jamie says. 'Was it usual for your husband to be working late?'

'Yes. He suffers from insomnia, but when he is bidding for a new project, his OCD gets a little out of hand. The only respite he gets is from making lists, planning contingencies and talking through variables. When I'm at home, I can normally persuade him to come to bed at a reasonable time, but his self-care slips if I'm away.'

'Do you know if he was working on anything specific recently?'

'Yes. Some of his contacts were planning a big rede-velopment project to help meet the need for more housing in Old London. They asked Al's company to put in a bid for the construction contract, and unofficially, it was a done deal. But Al still worried and put enormous effort into the plans.'

'That wouldn't happen to be the Ivy Street Project?' I ask.

'I think so. He didn't usually like to refer to potential contracts by their name, but I'm sure he mentioned Ivy Street in passing.'

'Were you aware of any conflicts connected to the project? Was there a rival construction company that may have threatened your husband, or someone else who might have wished him harm?'

'Al never mentioned anything. He told me everything, the good and the bad. If someone was threatening him, I'm sure he would have said something.'

'Your husband was young to be running a large company,' Jamie says. 'Was there any friction within the firm?'

'No. The company is a family business, and Al worked his way up through the ranks. When his father retired earlier than expected due to ill health, he was the logical

175

replacement CEO. Not everyone liked working for a gay man, but they either adjusted their prejudices or went elsewhere. Over the years, Al has proven himself to be more than capable of running the business and following in his father's footsteps.'

'Did Samhain hold special meaning for you and your husband?' I ask.

Once again, my question takes Colen by surprise. 'No. Sometimes we'd attend a fancy-dress party, but that's it. Al used to buy sweets for the neighbours' children, but they've all grown out of trick or treating. These days, we eat the chocolates ourselves.' A flash of grief twists his features.

'What about hobbies? Did your husband like to go hiking or foraging away from London? Would he have gone mushroom picking or did he have an interest in poisonous mushrooms?'

'Mushrooms? No. Al had no interest in them. We went to the gym a couple of times a week, we attended a monthly book club around the corner, and very occasionally, Al got his saxophone out. Our shared passion was travelling, though we've been doing shorter trips recently because of Hamish's ill health.'

'Was it typical for Hamish to spend time with your husband in the study?' I ask. 'I noticed a dog bed, but I wasn't sure whether that was a permanent fixture in the room.'

'Hamish was our pale little shadow. Where we went, he went. We had a bed for him in most rooms to make sure he was comfortable. With my being away, Hamish will have followed Al from room to room and settled only when he settled. I'd have been surprised if I'd found Hamish anywhere other than the study. Whatever happened last night, Hamish defended Al with everything he had.'

'May I see Hamish?'

Colen clenches his fists, and fresh blood wells from the cuts along his knuckles. He looks away, drawing measured breaths while he battles with his emotions. When he nods, his lips are pressed together so hard that all colour has bled out of them. Despite his freckles, Colen looks pale and drawn.

'Sure.'

He rises from the sofa, staggers as if uncertain of his balance, and kneels by the body. His hands shake when he peels back the towel to reveal the remains of a portly terrier. When I see the damage, I clap a hand over my mouth. The smell of rot intensifies, but my brain translates it into the agony of the injuries.

Hamish's lips and nose have blackened and shrunk back. Where the skin has cracked, pus is still leaking out, giving his face a glistening sheen of decay. He is lying on his side, and I see that over his chest and foreleg, the fur gives way to a large oval wound. The flesh is swollen and sections have turned necrotic.

Behind me, Karrion turns away and leaves the room. I know he sees beyond the horrific injuries to the bond Colen will have had with Hamish. It has never occurred to me to ask whether a Shaman feels the pain of his companion animal, but even if Colen did not, Hamish will have been able to convey his suffering through the way animals communicate with Shamans of the corresponding power.

'He must have been a fighter to hold on until you came home,' I say, my tone soft.

Colen nods. 'He was fearless and always ready to defend us.'

'These injuries don't look recent. Did your husband mention them while you were away?'

'No, and there is no way he would have kept this from me. Al knew my love for Hamish was second only to my love for him.'

'Did the vet offer any insight as to how Hamish received the injuries?'

'He thought the wounds on Hamish's side and neck might have been caused by burns that became infected over a period of a week after being left untreated, but there's no sign of burnt hair. And he was fine when Al sent me a photo of them both snoozing on the sofa yesterday morning. To me, it looks like the hair simply fell off and the skin rotted. Same with his mouth.'

As I lean closer for a better look, doing my best to ignore the smell of the infected flesh, I see there is another hairless patch on the dog's neck.

'Do you mind if I lift him so I can see the wound on his other side?'

'Go ahead,' Colen says, but he averts his eyes.

It takes me a few minutes to figure out how to move the body without touching any of the necrotic skin, but I manage to roll Hamish onto his back long enough to see he has another large wound on the side of his neck. I am struck by how both of them are roughly the size of my hand. It looks like someone grabbed him above his forelegs, inflicting the wounds in the process.

But who could cause injuries to turn gangrenous within hours? Or what?

One thing is certain: a Plant Shaman does not have such ability. Lady Bergamon's power is rooted in the growth of plants. I pause. Or is it? Can she not control the life and death of the plants in her domain? If she can affect the death of plants, can she not do the same to other living beings?

Every step we take in trying to solve this case keeps bringing us back to Lady Bergamon.

Keeping my movements reverent, I lower Hamish's body back onto the floor and replace the towel over him. My eyes meet Colen's over the carcass.

'Whatever happened last night, Hamish must have been very brave.'

Colen ducks his head. He rises and walks to the window.

'Would you mind if we look around downstairs?' I ask. 'Just in case there are any signs of a break-in or anything that's missing?'

'You can look wherever you want,' Colen says.

Jamie and I take that as our cue to leave. At the door, I turn to look at Colen. He remains by the window, his shoulders shaking.

'I'm sorry,' I whisper.

20

A Touch of Rot

Downstairs, the smell of spoilt fruit leads me to the kitchen. A bowl on the dark granite counter contains black bananas and brown shapes that may have been apples or pears. Despite it being late autumn, flies are swarming around the rotting fruit.

'Alfread Cullingwoed must have hated healthy foods,' Jamie says, nose scrunched in distaste.

'Maybe.'

The sight has prompted a memory from earlier, when I opened Lady Bergamon's bread bin. On a hunch, I open cupboards until I find one that contains dried goods. Rice and pasta in glass containers have blackened, but the contents of the coffee tin smell fresh. I open the fridge, but all the food there – fruit included – is also fine.

'This is odd,' I say, and Karrion joins me by the fridge. 'It looks like the only foods that haven't gone off are in the fridge or the coffee tin.'

'Well, fridges are meant to keep food fresh,' Jamie says.

Karrion reaches for a biscuit tin on the counter and opens it. 'Check this out. The cake here is fine too.'

'Why would pasta in a glass jar go off, but a cake in a tin didn't? That doesn't make any sense.'

'Just like the meat and bone offerings around Laene's front garden had spoilt, even though they can't have

180

been in the ground for more than a day. Even the turnip lanterns in Laene's basement smelled off. Could that be the theme? Wherever the killer goes, organic material decays. Perhaps it's an active power, and by touching Hamish, he inflicted wounds that became gangrenous immediately.'

'But not all food decayed,' Karrion says. 'Why? And what sort of spell caster could decay flesh with a touch? Or without it, probably, in the case of the food. I doubt the killer went around poking his finger into each pasta and rice jar.'

'There's probably a Mage spell that could cause decay, though we'd have to check that point. Mery will know.'

'She went outside to smoke,' Jamie says. 'Apparently dead dogs aren't her thing.'

'We'll ask her when she gets back.'

Even though I am making plans for new avenues of investigation, part of me keeps turning back to the food and the fact that metal appears to prevent the decay. I have several pieces of a puzzle that do not yet fit together, but at least they form part of the same picture. And the picture does not depict Lady Bergamon. But there are too many unanswered questions for now, and the second crime scene may yet change everything.

We look around the rest of the downstairs rooms and see plenty of evidence of the Cullingwoeds' shared happiness. A dining room table has a pile of brochures relating to Bali, and another offering advice on bringing a puppy into a household with an older dog. There are more photos of the two men and Hamish in every room, including a series of formal wedding portraits. What we cannot find is any sign of an intruder. In truth, I expected none. From the other crime scenes, we have already learned that the killer is as untraceable as if he walked through walls.

By the time we finish, Mery has returned with a cloud of cigarette smoke. Jamie puts our question to her.

'A spell causing rot,' she repeats, pushing her hair back. 'Mages have spells that would briefly turn fingers into blades. I suppose if someone combined that with another that spreads poison, you would see a wound with accelerated growth. There are rituals that can cause disease in a localised area. Funny fact, some people think the Black Death was caused by a grumpy Mage. Anyways, the disease would still progress at a natural pace. A few students developed a spell that could spoil milk, but I can't see it being powerful enough to affect flesh. Unless someone's modified it, and I've not heard about it.'

'So it is possible,' I say.

'Well, yes, but no. A Mage might be able to create a rot effect with enough time and effort, but they sure as hell can't do weird shit like sprouting mushrooms from flesh and growing a belladonna plant in someone's stomach. That's nature magic, and way beyond Mages.'

'But I've seen Mages turn coins into flowers at One Magic Change,' Karrion says. 'Isn't that nature magic?'

Mery laughs. 'That's what we call an illusion, sweetie.'

Karrion bristles, his magic flaring in a ruffle of feathers. 'Must be nice to have the answer for everything.'

'Not everything.' She winks at Karrion. 'Just most things.'

I lay a hand on Karrion's shoulder before he thinks of a response. 'At least that narrows our suspect pool to Shamans, Feykin and Wild Folk.'

'And can your kind do spontaneous mushroom growing?' Mery asks. When I shake my head, she nods. 'Thought so. Make that Shamans and Feykin.'

'Except a Bird or Dog Shaman couldn't control plants,' Karrion says. 'But I bet a Plant Spirit could.'

'But how many of those live in Old London?' Jamie asks.

I reply for Karrion. 'None that we know of. But that doesn't mean they don't exist.'

'Perhaps there's one living on Ivy Street,' says Jamie.

Forcing a smile, I turn away before Jamie can see how close he has come to the truth. A chill creeps over my limbs while I struggle to control my thumping heart. When I told Jamie about Lady Bergamon's ability to find people, I never mentioned it was through plant magic.

'We should head over to the next crime scene,' I say over my shoulder. 'We have a lot to cover today.'

Jamie writes down an address and hands it to me. 'Mery and I will meet you there.'

On our way to the car, Karrion keeps sneaking glances at me. I pretend not to notice, knowing what he is likely to say.

He says it.

'Lady Bergamon could have done this.'

I wait until I have unlocked the car before responding. 'The murder, yes.'

'What?' Karrion catches the side of his head on the car door. 'I was expecting you to be angry again.'

'I agree that Lady Bergamon has the sort of magic to kill Cullingwoed, perhaps even to inflict the wounds on Hamish. Whether she's capable of such cruelty is another matter. But I don't think her powers could cause food to spoil.'

'But isn't mould a type of plant?'

'Not all the food was mouldy. And I cannot see her pausing to rot the meat on her way to kill Laene. Or spoil the food in her kitchen. She's served us food before, and that's been fine. It can't be that any food near her goes off.'

'Do you have an alternative explanation?'

'Not at the moment, but I'm working on something.'

'What?'

'All in good time. The next crime scene may disprove my theory.'

'By the way, why did you ask Colen about whether people knew he'd be in New York?' Karrion asks.

'It struck me as odd that in two out of three murders, there has been no one to witness the attack. And I'm not sure Denniel Hailfax was much of a witness, given that he fell into a coma around the time his son was killed. None of the victims lives alone, and yet there has been no collateral damage apart from Hamish.'

'Could our killer have a conscience?'

'Or it's easier to sneak in to kill someone when there are fewer people at home. But I do think it's strange that Laene was killed on the one night of the year when he sends his wife and the household staff away. That can't be a coincidence.'

I stop at a pedestrian crossing.

'Won't that mean the killer has been watching these Mages to learn their routines?' Karrion asks. 'They found out about Laene's superstitions and Colen being away on a business trip. Perhaps they had several targets in mind, and Laene, Hailfax and Cullingwoed were the easiest to reach.'

'You may be right. But if that's the case, then these deaths have nothing to do with the being that may have entered Old London through Lady Bergamon's garden.'

'But the wreaths were the same, as was the spoilt food.'

'I know,' I say, and change lanes. 'But how likely is it that this creature, or person, ended up in Old London and started killing at random, yet somehow managed to find victims connected to the Ivy Street Project who happened to be mostly alone? That doesn't make sense either. There's a whole subtext to this case that I'm simply not seeing.'

'Does all this throw a spanner in the works for your new theory?'

'It certainly doesn't help. I feel as though every time I'm about to make out the reflection on the surface of a pool, the wind sends ripples through the image.'

'That's deep.'

'That's my frustration talking. I don't want Jamie to start poking around Ivy Street and accidentally stumble across Lady Bergamon's secret.'

'Can't Bradán help?'

'If he could, I'm sure he would have done so by now.'

My thoughts are drawn back to the garden, and I imagine him standing in the relentless rain, waiting for a sign that his lover has recovered. Should I have gone outside to speak to him this morning, to tell him that we are not sitting idly while Lady Bergamon remains unconscious? Do the Fey need reassurance like we mortals do? Has Bradán found other diversions?

Lady Bergamon has never mentioned her lover, and my understanding of the relationship is based solely on Bradán's actions in the garden. Would he have attacked me if he felt nothing for her? On the other hand, would he have left her lying in the rain if he loved her?

My mind is filled with questions, and yet, I am not certain where to turn for answers. In trying to help Lady Bergamon and stop the killer, I may have bitten off far more than I can chew.

How can I fix this?

21

THE WOMAN WHO HID

We park by the Land Registry, opposite Lincoln's Inn Fields. The area is a relatively recent addition to Old London, having only been a part of our London for a century. It is the last area outside of the City borough to have been assimilated, and now we have to contend with the space we have carved for ourselves. Limited square footage has not prevented the richest members of our society from claiming large plots of land for themselves, to forever set themselves apart from the rest of us.

The crime scene is at Lincoln's Inn, but access to the buildings is barred by a wrought iron fence and a guard booth. I doubt our consultant IDs would allow us access. It is easier to park outside the gates and walk the rest of the way.

While we wait for Jamie and Mery just inside the gates, my attention is drawn to a woman sitting on a nearby bench, eyes glued to a phone. An older man approaches her, calling a greeting, and she rises to meet him. He hugs her. At first I assume they are related, but from the heat on the woman's cheeks when she steps back, they must be a couple. Her eyes shine as they walk away from us, close but not touching.

It has been some time since I felt the anticipation of a date, or indeed since I have been on a date. Ilana Marsh's ringing laughter rises from the confines of my memory, but I ignore it. We never dated, only slept together. But while my life is complicated as it is, part of me misses the nervous wait, the flirting and waiting to see if the night ends with a kiss.

The thought triggers a memory of last night's dream and Dearon braced over me, his lips begging to be kissed. I did so, many times, and a ghost of those kisses caresses my lips. In the privacy of my mind, I can admit that I miss the physicality of our relationship. With Dearon, I never have to worry about whether he wants me. He may not need me, but he has always wanted me. That feeling, at least, seems to be mutual.

The houses at Lincoln's Inn have been built around a central area of grass and fountains. Expensive cars line the street. The building facades are made of reddish-brown bricks, and the arches over the black front doors have been painted white. Wrought iron fences separate the houses from the pavement.

The guard at the gate lets Jamie's car through, and we follow it around the green. A Paladin guarding the door gives me a sense of déjà vu. How long will it be before I become used to going to a crime scene? While I am no stranger to death, I hope seeing a murder victim will always give me pause. Is that not what it means to be human? My kind has a reputation for being primitive savages, but we are just as capable of emotions as anyone else. Why else would the situation with Dearon and my father be so painful?

Carved pumpkin lanterns grin at us from the steps leading up to the front door, which has a skeleton garland draped across it. That appears to be the extent of the Halloween decorations. The window boxes on the ground floor contain wilted geraniums.

'The body has already been taken away,' Jamie says. 'I snapped a few photos to give you an idea of what the room looked like when the Paladins first arrived at the scene.'

'Who found the body?' I ask.

'The victim's husband, Goorge Bleckbyrne. According to his statement, he arrived home in the early hours of the morning and fell asleep on the sofa. The arrival of the housekeeper at eight thirty woke him up. He went upstairs to shower and found his wife dead on the bed. Lianne Bleckbyrne was a West Mage.'

'Only Light and Shadow left,' Karrion murmurs behind me.

Jamie takes us through tastefully decorated rooms and up the stairs. Nothing looks out of place, except an empty vase on a side table. Beads of water still cling to the lip. Perhaps it is the smell of bleach lingering in the air, but the house has a sterile feel that makes me want to conclude our investigation as quickly as possible. Even the pollution of Old London is preferable to this lifeless home.

The bedroom continues the clinical theme. Everything is white or grey and the doors to the wardrobes are wall to ceiling mirrors. I look at my reflection, and it confirms my feeling: I do not belong here.

The furniture is all minimalistic. Both the armchairs by the French windows and the seat by the dressing table look uncomfortable. The only splashes of colour come from abstract paintings on the walls. There are no photos in sight.

The bed has been stripped, leaving a bare mattress. I note a book and a lamp on the bedside table nearest to us. The matching steel table on the other side is empty.

'The Bleckbyrnes had separate bedrooms?'

'How did you know?' Jamie follows my gaze to the bedside table. 'Right. Yes. The husband slept in the next room.'

'Are they divorcing or just estranged?'

'I don't know yet. We'll have to ask the husband.'

I nod, but my attention is drawn back to the bed. With my enhanced senses, I step forward and inhale. Besides detergent and fabric softener having seeped into the mattress, I smell moss, marsh grass and stagnant water. There is a wet patch on the mattress near where the pillows should be, and when I lean over it, the scent of fetid peat intensifies.

Upon turning away from the bed, I find Mery watching me with glowing eyes. There is a new kind of curiosity in her expression, and I duck my head. Life is complicated enough without a workplace romance with an outspoken Mage.

'Show me the photos,' I say as I return to the others.

Jamie gets his phone out. The photo he calls up shows a woman in her late fifties lying on her back in the middle of the queen-sized bed. Mascara has left dark smudges under her eyes, and she has a smear of pink lipstick on her cheek. The covers are at the foot of the bed, and a single pillow rests against the headboard at the centre. The victim is dressed in a silk blouse and black nylons. Her arms are spread out, fingers reaching for the edges. Other than the pallid colour of her skin, there is no sign that she has not simply lain down for a brief rest.

After the violence of the other three murders, this crime scene feels incongruous. Yet Jamie must have a reason for saying the deaths are connected.

'How did she die?' I ask.

'She drowned.'

I blink. 'The body was arranged on the bed?'

'No. She drowned right there on the bed.'

'How do you drown on dry land?' Karrion asks.

'How do mushrooms sprout from flesh?' Jamie shrugs. 'Magic. But the pathologist was insistent that she hadn't been moved since she'd died. For one, her mouth and lungs were still filled with water.'

A spark of hope settles at the centre of my chest and grows into a dancing flame. Karrion must share my thoughts, for his frown deepens.

'I could smell peat and stagnant water on the mattress,' I say.

'Yes. The pathologist thought the water didn't come from the tap, although he will have sent a sample to be analysed to know for sure. The pillow and the sheet near the victim's head were wet, but the rest of the bed wasn't.'

'Makes sense. If you're filling someone's mouth with water, some is bound to spill.'

'Hang on,' Karrion says. 'Am I the only one who can't get their head around someone drowning in a bed? All she had to do was roll onto her side.'

'We think she was sedated. They're going to do a tox panel as part of the autopsy. The other possibility is that she was immobilised with a spell.'

Mery shakes her head. 'I couldn't find any trace of one earlier. Just that weird residue we're all beginning to know and fancy.'

'There must be another explanation.' Karrion's expression brightens. 'I've just been reading about tetrodotoxins. Maybe the killer had a blue-ringed octopus in his pocket?'

'Who doesn't?' Mery rolls her eyes. 'Here's something I don't get: our killer is bloody efficient. So why doesn't he kill more than two Mages a night? He could easily have whacked these two the night before last. Why wait?'

'Perhaps the opportunity didn't present itself,' I say. 'Alfread Cullingwoed may have been out, and Goorge Bleckbyrne home.'

'A murderer who's patient. Lovely.' Mery gets her cigarettes out and counts the contents. 'Time for another.'

'I thought you were trying to quit,' Jamie says.

'The way I see it, I deserve at least one pleasure in life. And working with you isn't it.'

Jamie laughs, and Mery leaves.

'Do you want to search the room?' Jamie asks and hands us latex gloves. 'The SOCO have already been through it, but you may spot something they missed.'

We search the dressing table, its drawers and the wardrobe. From the contents, it is clear that only Mrs Bleckbyrne occupied the room. There are no papers or keepsakes anywhere, only clothes, jewellery and toiletries.

'What did the victim do for a living?' I ask as I close the wardrobe doors.

'She was a banker organising finance for big corporate projects. Quite successful too, I understand.'

'Does she have a study?'

'The second door on the left.'

Karrion follows me out of the bedroom. A Monet print on the wall catches my attention; one side of the frame is not level with the wall. I look behind the picture. Lifting the frame, I reveal a fist-size hole in the wall. The damage looks recent. I show it to the others.

Jamie compares the hole to his fist and lets the picture cover it again.

'Too big for her fist,' he says, voice low.

'The husband?' I ask.

'Most likely.'

The study looks like it belongs to a different house. The furniture is all pine, the plush armchairs look to favour comfort over style and the rugs are decorated with bright flowers. On the wall are framed pictures from the Peter Rabbit books, close up photos of butterflies and dragonflies, and landscapes dominated by moors of heather and waterfalls cascading over dark rocks. The bookshelf is filled with contemporary romance novels, and a box of Godiva chocolates is balanced on top of a row of books. A fluffy white robe is draped over the office chair, with matching slippers set underneath.

'Yan, check this out.'

Karrion is crouching by the door, and he points to a deadbolt affixed on the inside.

'Looks like the victim wanted to make sure she wouldn't be disturbed in her office,' I say.

'There's more to it. See here?' Karrion taps at the door frame. There are slivers of wood missing near the second part of the deadbolt. 'The lock was forced and later fixed, badly.'

'Any idea when?'

'Fairly recently. I can't say anything more specific than that.'

'So the victim wanted to ensure her privacy, and someone else thought otherwise. The husband?'

'Who else could it be?' Karrion rises and turns to Jamie. 'The Bleckbyrnes don't have any kids, do they?'

'No, it was just the two of them. A housekeeper came every day, but she lived elsewhere.'

No wonder the house feels lifeless. The rooms are too large and cold for two people. A house like this needs life and laughter. Both seem to be in short supply.

Without voicing my thoughts, I cross the room to the desk. The large windows offer a view of the street. I watch as Mery crushes a cigarette butt under the heel of her boots and lights a second one. She crushes the empty pack and drops it on the ground. This feels odd, but before I have a chance to voice my surprise, the thought slips from my mind. I start going through the papers on the desk.

It soon becomes clear the victim was fond of bringing work home. The first two drawers are filled with folders relating to various funding projects. As much as I would wish otherwise, it comes as no surprise that one of them relates to the Ivy Street Project. The folder is slim, and it appears that the victim was still drafting the funding proposal and compiling a list of potential investors. Still, if the unusual cause of death was not enough of a link to the other murders, this certainly is.

I see no reason not to share my findings with the others. Karrion looks troubled.

'No question about what I'll be doing this afternoon,' Jamie says.

The bottom drawer of the desk is deeper than the others, and within it, I discover another surprise. Beneath the latest issue of Vogue are a bottle of Jack Daniels and a tumbler with a smear of pink lipstick around the rim. There is only an inch of amber liquid left in the bottle. I lift it out of the drawer.

'This could be why the victim didn't struggle more.'

'The pathologist will be able to confirm that.'

Under the bottle is a letter with the NHS logo in the top corner. It has several circular stains on it, but my eyes are drawn to the victim's date of birth.

'She was only forty-four?'

Jamie checks his notebook. 'Yes, that's right.'

'From the photo you showed me, I thought she'd be at least a decade older.'

'Enough booze can have that effect on people.'

I scan through the rest of the letter and experience a stab of pity.

'She had liver cancer. Inoperable. The doctors suggested that if she gave up alcohol, she might be able to prolong her life, but she had only months left.'

I look around and see the room in a different light. Instead of being an anomaly in a house of appearances, the study is a safe place for a woman faced with irrefutable evidence of her mortality.

'We'd better speak to the husband,' I say.

The sound of a television draws us to the lounge. After what we witnessed upstairs, I am not certain what I expected, but Goorge Bleckbyrne is not it. He is sitting on the sofa watching rugby, a beer bottle in hand. On the glass coffee table are a bacon butty and an open packet of pork scratchings. I cannot understand how he has any appetite after discovering his wife's body. The smell of old alcohol hangs heavy in the air, mixing with burnt grease and the bleach I detected earlier. He is dressed in faded jeans and a red hoodie bearing the Lions logo.

Jamie has to clear his throat twice before Bleckbyrne glances away from the television. He is slow to set his drink down and mute the sound.

'Yes?' He reaches for the bacon butty.

'We need to ask you a few questions regarding your wife's death.'

Bleckbyrne shrugs and bites into the roll. Brown sauce runs down his chin and drips onto the front of his hoodie. He uses the back of his hand to wipe his mouth and then rubs his hand on his jeans.

We are close enough that when I inhale, I catch a fleeting impression of ripening wheat, morning dew and limes. He is a West Mage, like his wife.

'Did your wife have any enemies?'

'Just about anyone who ever met her. She was a bitch.'

There is a pause while we try to figure out a suitable response. Bleckbyrne barks out a laugh, and I am struck by the unpleasantness of the sound.

'What?' he says.

'Are you aware of anyone in particular who might have wished her harm?'

'I really didn't care. She must have spread her legs a lot to get where she was in her job. How else would a woman be promoted so often? Perhaps a wife of a colleague decided enough was enough.'

'Perhaps she was simply good at her job,' I say.

'Yeah, right. A woman having natural talent for banking.'

Bleckbyrne reaches for his beer.

Jamie shifts. 'How would you characterise your marriage?'

'Frigid.' Bleckbyrne takes another bite of his butty and chews with his mouth open. He catches me staring and grins. I look away, doing my best to hide my distaste.

'Care to expand on that?'

'Not really. She was a shit lay. She enjoyed sniping me. Who the fuck was she to criticise anyone? When I returned the fire, she'd lock herself in her study and scream at me through the door.'

'If your marriage was that unhappy, why didn't you file for a divorce?' I ask.

Bleckbyrne's lips twist into a smirk. 'She couldn't afford it. I didn't bother because this lifestyle has its advantages.'

'And what happened last night? I understand you went out in the evening,' Jamie says.

'She was in a foul mood. I put up with her until we'd had our starters before taking off. I had dinner at my local, stayed there until closing time and then went clubbing, just to piss her off.'

'Can anyone verify that?'

'Plenty of people around.'

'Did you notice anything unusual when you returned home last night?' I ask. 'Did you see any sign of forced entry or anything out of place?'

'I was pissed. All I cared about was not hurling on the carpet. I sat down to watch some telly and fell asleep on the sofa.'

'How about this morning, when you woke up?'

'I went upstairs, saw that Lianne's bedroom door was open and thought I'd wake her early to piss her off. Turns out, she was beyond that. I called you lot.' A glance at Jamie. 'Well, our lot.'

Jamie turns to me. Although his expression is neutral, I see his outrage in the tightness of his posture and in the lines around his eyes. He raises an eyebrow: do I have further questions?

'I noticed the decorations outside,' I say. 'Was Samhain a special time of year for you and your wife?'

'Samhain?'

'Halloween.'

'Lianne did her thing, handing out sweets to the neighbourhood children. Liked to pretend she was everyone's best friend. Load of bollocks.'

'Were you aware of your wife's diagnosis?'

'What diagnosis? That she was a certifiable nutcase?'

'Your wife had terminal cancer. She had only months to live.'

Bleckbyrne laughs. 'Ain't karma a bitch? It must have killed her knowing that in a matter of months, all this will be mine.'

'I'd like to speak to your housekeeper next,' Jamie says.

When Bleckbyrne does not respond, Jamie thanks him for his time, the words forced, and leaves. I hesitate, wondering whether I should ask anything else. Bleckbyrne glances at me and his eyes narrow.

'Go on, keep staring. Am I not the grieving widower you expected? I've no intention of crying for your amusement, love.'

Thrown by his words, I cannot think of a response. He dismisses me with a wave.

'I have a beer to finish, so get out.'

196

At the doorway, I glance back. Bleckbyrne is sitting on the sofa, holding his beer and staring at a wedding photo on the wall. For a moment, he looks lost. Then he reaches for the remote and the feeling passes.

We find the housekeeper in the kitchen, scrubbing the stove and pausing every so often to blow her nose. She introduces herself as Irina Ivanova. Beneath the smell of cleaning products are only perfume and natural pheromones. Irina is a human. Her English is heavily-accented, but fluent.

'Mrs Lianne, she wasn't well,' Irina says and dabs her eyes with a tissue. 'She hardly ate and she was always asking me to buy her bottles of alcohol. I told her it was bad for her, but she didn't care. She said it was too late for her, that she'd finish a few things and put her affairs in order.'

'Did you know about her illness?' I ask.

'Yes. She told me. She cried for a time and then she grew angry.'

'Why was she angry?'

'Mrs Lianne said that Mr Goorge would not inherit a penny when she died. She was going to change her will and make an iron-tight case. She said Mr Goorge could not contest the will.'

'Do you know whether she executed a new will?'

'She said yes, but I never saw it. But she did burn her old one. She poured expensive brandy on it and set it alight. She was laughing and crying at the same time.'

'Did she tell her husband about the new will?' Karrion asks.

'I don't know. They were always arguing so it's possible. But she never said.'

'Was the marriage always this acrimonious?' I ask.

'Years ago, they laughed together. Mrs Lianne worked very hard to pay for everything. The harder she worked, the more they argued. Then Mr Goorge moved into the guest room.'

'Was either of them ever violent?'

'Mrs Lianne said she had proof, that she attached something to her new will. Sometimes Mr Goorge had scratch marks down his arms. And there were broken dishes. Many expensive glasses and plates broke in this household. But in front of me, they only argued. That embarrassed Mrs Lianne, but Mr Goorge didn't care. He liked insulting her in front of me. But if they had guests, they both played a doting couple. Then, later, I would hear Mrs Lianne crying in her study.'

'Did they argue last night?' Jamie asks.

'Yes. Mr Goorge left part of the way through the meal. Even though I cooked Mrs Lianne's favourite prawn dish, she didn't eat much. When I left, she had gone up to the study.'

'What time was that?'

'Just after eight.'

'You work long hours,' I say.

'The work here, it's not so hard. Mrs Lianne has been a generous employer, and my family back home need the money. My children can go to school and university.' Irina looks around, twisting the dishcloth she is holding. 'But soon, I will need to find new work.'

'When you came to work this morning, did you notice anything out of place?' I ask.

'Mr Goorge was drunk.' Irina scrunches her nose. 'He woke up and staggered upstairs. Half an hour later, he came back down and said Paladins were about to arrive. I was to take them to the master bedroom, where they would see to Mrs Lianne's body. He was smiling and wouldn't let me go up to see her. Then the Paladins came.'

Goorge Bleckbyrne's behaviour sounds odd, but I

cannot tell whether his actions are those of a man guilty of murder or simply not caring about his wife.

'What about when you first arrived? Did anything strike you as odd?'

'The flowers.'

'What about them?' I ask.

'Mrs Lianne was very specific about having fresh flowers in all the downstairs rooms. But when I arrived, the lilies in the hallway and the gerberas on the landing upstairs had died. I wondered whether Mr Goorge had put vodka in the water again, but the flowers looked like they had died several days earlier. I swear they were blooming last night, when I left.'

'How about the food in the kitchen?' Karrion asks.

My eyes are drawn to a fruit bowl filled with apples and bananas. They appear fine.

'The food?' Irina frowns. 'It was all there.'

'Was any of it spoilt?'

'No.'

I would have expected a different answer, but the kitchen is located on the far side of the dining room. If the killer entered through the front door, he may not have gone anywhere near it.

We thank Irina for her time and wish her the best of luck with job hunting. As we are heading out, Goorge Bleckbyrne barges into the kitchen, demanding more beer and a pizza for lunch. Irina disguises her sigh with a smile and turns to deal with him. I cannot help wondering how much harder her task will become if Lianne did change her will and Goorge Bleckbyrne is left with nothing.

22

DIVISION OF LABOUR

As we walk down the steps, my eyes stray to the Halloween decorations. The skeletons seem appropriate, given that someone died in the house last night. But did the grinning pumpkins protect the house from evil spirits or invite one in?

Crouching, I inspect a pumpkin. The flesh is shrivelled and the underside is white with mould. A familiar smell of rot tickles my nostrils.

I rise without a word.

'The first thing I'm going to do is check the husband's alibi,' Jamie says.

'Do you think he killed his wife?'

'I'm not sure, but I want to take a good look at him.'

'If there had been more media coverage about the murders, I might be inclined to think that he saw an easy way to get rid of his wife and direct blame elsewhere,' I say. 'But as things are, I don't think the media has made a connection between the deaths.'

'We've certainly not encouraged them.' Jamie waves Mery towards the car. 'I don't know. Bleckbyrne strikes me as a thoroughly unpleasant person, but I'm not sure he's a killer. There are too many links to the other deaths.'

'He has to be guilty of something,' Karrion mutters.

'Being obnoxious isn't illegal,' I say.

'I'll see what I can dig out on Bleckbyrne,' Jamie says. 'As soon as I hear anything on the autopsies, I'll give you a call. If Lianne Bleckbyrne was given the kiss of death, there's an irrefutable link to the others. It's a detail the media knows nothing about. Besides, if he is also a West Mage, he'd have no reason to steal the secret to magic he already possesses.'

'He is.'

The longing in Jamie's eyes intensifies. 'You checked, did you? That's a handy ability.'

'That's what makes Yan such a good PI,' Karrion says, taking a step forward.

Jamie blinks, and the look of longing recedes.

'Whether Bleckbyrne murdered his wife or not, I think it's time to learn more about the kiss of death. Karrion and I will talk to a Mage contact and see whether she can throw a light ball at it. Even if she can't, perhaps she can point us in the direction of someone else.'

'Sounds good. Whoever has news first should get in touch with the other. We can meet up later for a proper catch-up.'

I agree, and Jamie gets in his car with Mery, leaving us standing outside the house.

'Are we going to One Magic Change?' Karrion asks.

'I will,' I say, watching Jamie drive off. 'There's something else I'd like you to do, but Jamie doesn't need to know about it yet.'

'What's that, boss?'

'Find out everything you can about the Ivy Street Project. Who else is involved, how many of them are Light or Shadow Mages, who they are, everything. When you're done with that, go to the Land Registry. I want you to see what information you can obtain about Lady Bergamon's property. If Jamie starts digging into the residents, is Lady Bergamon going to stick out like a sore thumb?'

'I'm on it.' Karrion nudges my shoulder. 'But don't think I didn't notice how you picked the cooler task for yourself.'

'One of the perks of being the boss.'

Karrion's expression grows serious. 'This case confuses me. I was so sure Lady B was behind it, but she has no power over water. Unless she brought a bottle of marsh water and simply poured it into Lianne Bleckbyrne's mouth.'

I open my mouth to speak and then reconsider my words. Karrion notices this and tilts his head. I have no choice but to speak my mind.

'Bradán is a Kelpie. A water Fey.'

'So Lady B could have asked her lover to kill Lianne while she went after Cullingwoed.'

'Don't forget, she's trapped in a circle. It was intact this morning when I woke up.'

'Are you sure?' Karrion asks.

'I... I think so.' I try to recall how closely I checked the circle when I passed through it to give Lady Bergamon her tonic. 'While I'm not a hundred per cent certain, I'd like to think I would have noticed if the circle no longer existed.'

'Could she have cut a door through it, like you've been doing?'

'She has no means to do so. I keep the obsidian blade in a box by the fireplace. There's nothing inside the circle other than Lady Bergamon and the bed.'

'But if the blade is nearby, couldn't Bradán have used it to create a door?'

'I suppose that's possible, but surely we would have noticed if a huge horse had been wandering through the house.'

'Didn't you say he can take human form?'

'Yes, but when I saw him as human, he was touching a spring in the garden. The rest of the time, he was in his equine form.'

'It could have been Wishearth. He's the one who told you how to raise the circle in the first place.'

Part of me wants to ask if we are going to have the same argument again, but I bite my tongue. As much as I trust Lady Bergamon and Wishearth, this case is raising uncomfortable questions. At the very least, I should give them due consideration before dismissing them as impossible.

'Maybe,' I say, though the word feels like a betrayal. 'We need to look into it.'

Karrion looks like he wants to say more, but he nods instead. Perhaps he recognises how much the admission cost me.

I take Karrion home and drive to St Paul's. Next to the cathedral is a shopping centre of glass and steel; the largest of its kind in Old London. The residents come here to research rituals, stock up on spell ingredients and acquire magical artefacts. Tourists from New London and beyond come to gawk at the smoke billowing out of the potion shops, the illusionists entertaining the crowds with prestidigitations, and the gas lamps with flames shaped like gryphons and dragons.

This time, there is no Paladin presence at the entrances, and I pass unnoticed through a glass corridor into the heart of the shopping centre. Near the stairs, a large crowd has gathered around a young woman dressed in glittering robes. She is holding three Mason jars, and they each contain something that glows in different colours. Selecting a young boy from the front row, she offers him a choice. He picks the jar pulsing with blue colours. The Mage sets the other two jars on the ground and opens the lid. A small dragon bursts out, leaping over the people before disappearing in a shower of blue sparks. The crowd cheers and drops coins in a crystal bowl.

'Again, again,' the little boy cries.

While I too am interested to see what other illusions the Mage may conjure, I am here for a reason. I circle around the crowd and head up. The last thing I see before I reach the second floor is a group of yellow fairies flying out of another jar. What they turn into remains a mystery, but from the sound of the crowd, it is something good.

My destination is on the top floor, where the workshops are located. Here, the air is charged with residual power and smells of solder and ozone. The hairs at the back of my neck prick up, reacting to the presence of so much magic, and my thoughts are drawn back to learning to detect the circle in Lady Bergamon's lounge. Could these sensations be an extension of my ability to sense auras in others?

The question keeps me preoccupied until I push open the door to Thaylor's Tinkerings. The chimes by the door make a sound akin to a breeze in aspen leaves. Tinker Thaylor must have changed the enchantment since I was last here.

Not much has changed in the shop. All manner of devices occupy the shelves on both sides of me as well as on the shop window. The brass snake that used to hang from the ceiling has gone, replaced by a section of silvery ivy. What its magical purpose is, I can only guess. The golden dragon's head hanging on the wall now puffs out clouds of blue smoke. On the counter, a brass wren capable of flight and song remains frozen on its perch.

The bead curtain to the back room parts silently – too silently to be natural – and Thaylor steps through. She is a wizened woman with goggles that enlarge her huge eyes and a leather apron pitted with burn marks and stains. Despite her diminutive size giving her a gnomish appearance, little escapes her notice.

Thaylor adjusts her goggles and smiles. 'Yannia.'

I am surprised that she remembers me, but cover it by nodding a greeting.

'Is the spell detection device working to your satisfaction?'

With my thoughts on the current case, I take a few seconds to remember that the last time Karrion and I visited Thaylor's shop, it was to make a purchase.

'It's fine. I'm here because I was hoping you might be able to answer a question related to Mage magic.'

'I'll do my best,' Thaylor says and indicates that I should follow her into the back room.

Behind the beaded curtain, the narrow workshop is crammed full of shelves, boxes, and raw materials. Half-finished machines and animals litter the worktops, and the smell of soldering iron, metal and singed leather is stronger than in the shop. Thaylor clears two stools and offers one of them to me. We sit in a cramped space between a metal bucket of water and a bench covered in coils of wire.

'The term "kiss of death" came up in an investigation. Karrion had heard of it, but there was little he could tell me. I was hoping you might be able to fill in the blanks.'

'A kiss of death?' Thaylor shakes her head. 'It's a forbidden practice. To take another Mage's magic is akin to stealing someone's soul.'

'Do you know anyone who's done it?'

Thaylor laughs. 'I don't even know anyone who knows how to do it. As far as I know, vague stories are all that remain of that practice.'

'Okay.' I make no effort to hide my disappointment. 'That's a dead end, then.'

'Not necessarily. You could speak to the Paladins. They're the record keepers of Old London. If anyone knows why or how the kiss of death was outlawed, it'll be the Paladins.'

'Thank you. I'll do that. Can I ask you something else as well?'

205

'Go right ahead.'

'It's about circles.'

'Do you mean the predecessors of wards?'

'Yes. I understand that some spell casters still use them for protection.'

'Personally, I don't know of any, but I suppose it's possible. Wards are far more versatile.'

'How so?' I ask.

Thaylor shifts on the stool, frowns, and pulls a long pair of pliers from her back pocket. Reaching for a coil of copper wire, she begins measuring ten-inch lengths of it and arranging them in a bunch.

'With Mage magic, you can set a ward to do a great many things. Sight, smell, sound, all can be blocked. And more. A ward can protect you against one thing, or several. And if it's properly set, you can pass over the threshold without disrupting the protection.'

'Whereas with a circle, you can't.'

'Circle is essentially where warding began,' Thaylor says, coiling the wire up halfway around the lengths she has cut. 'Mages refined the process in every way. Why use a circle when you could set a ward?'

'Perhaps because anyone can cast a circle, but it takes a Mage to prepare a ward.'

'No, that's not quite true. Mages of old used circles, as did Paladins. They still employ a similar technique when summoning the Heralds of Justice. But Shamans and your kind have never been able to cast circles. Of Feykin, I can't say for sure, but then again, who can?'

I open my mouth to correct her, but I am not certain whether it is wise. Perhaps my new-found ability is a secret for me to keep.

'If someone was to cast a circle with a person inside it, could they pass through the circle without disrupting it?'

206

'Not if it was done correctly.' Thaylor spreads out the copper wires visible above the bindings. She cuts more lengths of wire and leans over to flick on a soldering iron. 'A circle will prevent anyone entering or exiting until the caster powers it down. There are ways to pass through it, cutting a doorway being one, but the only way for someone to escape a circle is if the caster is inexperienced.'

'What do you mean?'

While I watch, Thaylor attaches further wires to the base, creating an impression of tree branches. With incredible precision, she melts the surface of the tree trunk enough to hide the outline of the wires and give it an appearance of bark.

'The name is, perhaps, misleading. A circle in its simplest form is nothing but a boundary. But to prevent someone from escaping or entering, it isn't enough to just close the area around the markers. The caster must also close the top and the bottom.'

With a sinking feeling in my stomach, I clench my hands into fists to prevent them from shaking. My pulse increases to a roar in my ears.

'So instead of a circle, the caster should prepare a protective ball?'

'Yes, that's a good way of thinking about it.'

'And without doing so, anyone can escape?'

Thaylor uses more soldering line to add leaves and shorter branches to the tree. While it is beginning to take shape, I can see that finishing the piece will take several hours. I admire her patience.

'Not anyone. First of all, you'd have to know about the peculiarities of a circle. Next, you'd have to have the means to move up or down. Alternatively, if you were powerful enough, you might be able to create a bridge over the wall of the circle, but it would take a great deal of magic.'

'Who would be powerful enough to do that?'

'A Mage from the old bloodlines. Some first generation Feykin, I imagine. But not many others.'

With a few turns of her fingers and touches of the soldering iron, a length of copper wire turns into a bird, which Thaylor attaches to one of the branches. Another bit of wire becomes a nest for the bird. Thaylor even creates tiny eggs for the nest. I make a mental note to buy the finished tree for Karrion as a Christmas present.

'Thank you. This has been enlightening.'

'Anything else I can help you with?' she asks, and sets down the soldering iron.

'Not right now.' I force a smile and stand. 'But should this investigation require the help of a Tinker, I'll come back.'

Thaylor walks me to the door. 'I hope the Paladins will be able to help you with your questions about the kiss of death.'

'Me too.'

Outside the shop, I lean over the rail and stare at the levels below me. Anxiety is still coiling in my stomach as I consider the implications of Thaylor's words. Did my inexperience cause me to cast a circle that leaves Lady Bergamon in danger? Or have I unwittingly allowed a killer to roam free in Old London? Did Wishearth know that the circle I cast was incomplete? Did he mislead me so that Lady Bergamon could continue killing?

Is there anyone I can trust?

23

A History Lesson

I step into the huge entrance hall of the Brotherhood of Justice and smile a greeting to the two Paladins stationed just inside the double doors. The reception desk at the centre of the hall is my destination, and I ask a receptionist whether I could speak to Sister Alissa. Five minutes later, a familiar Paladin dressed in the grey robes of the Order strides towards me, barefoot. She smiles, but in the guardedness of her expression, I see a reminder of what took place in the Paladin General's office on the day Jonathain Marsh was executed.

'This is unexpected,' she says, once we have exchanged greetings.

'I'm hoping you might be able to help me with a history lesson, or point me in the direction of someone else.'

'What do you want to know?'

'About a Mage ability called the kiss of death.'

Sister Alissa's expression grows troubled, and she beckons me to follow. I feel a sense of déjà vu, but I match my steps to hers as she leads us away from the entrance hall. Instead of the research wing, where I expected us to go, she takes me through a maze of corridors. A heavy wooden door leads into an enclosed courtyard.

At the centre are six statues. From the elaborate swords and armour, I take them to be Paladins of old, when they still wore steel rather than Kevlar. The statues are arranged in a circle, each facing inward, and they hold their swords at arm's length with the tips just touching the ground. When I am close enough, I see that the Paladins all have the same serene expression on their bowed faces, though their features are different enough to distinguish them. Despite London's pollution, the marble gleams.

The rest of the paved courtyard is taken up by stone benches and raised boxes of flowering shrubs. Sister Alissa leads me to the nearest bench, and sits. I follow her example, wondering why we are here.

'This area is technically for Paladins only, but given the nature of your question, this feels like an appropriate place to answer it.'

'Right.'

'How much do you know about the kiss of death?'

'Not much. According to Karrion, it allows a person to steal the secret to a Mage's power and leaves a black mark around the mouth. But I don't know how it's done or what the consequences are.'

'Usually disastrous. But I cannot believe you're dealing with a kiss of death.'

'Why?'

'Because the Paladins systematically eradicated the knowledge of how to perform it.'

I lean forward. 'Perhaps you ought to tell me the whole story.'

Sister Alissa lets her attention linger on the statues and then inhales slowly. When she looks at me, there is wistful sadness in her expression.

'The kiss of death was always considered the darkest of the dark magic. The stories now claim that it transfers the secret of the magic, but it went much further than that. In reality, it consumed the victim's essence, destroying their soul and drawing their power into the other Mage. If multiple kisses of death were performed

210

by the same person and they were done in the right order, the additional magic didn't simply amplify the Mage's power, it multiplied it.'

'What do you mean by right order?'

'It wasn't to be undertaken lightly. Consume the wrong Mage and you will die instantly.'

'The wrong Mage?'

'It's all to do with the elements that underlie every Mage's source of power.'

'In what way?'

I must look as puzzled as I feel, for Alissa frowns.

'You don't know about this stuff?' she asks.

'I don't think so.'

'Sorry. I just assumed. Each type of Mage is governed by an underlying power element. Light and Shadow Mages are obvious. For the others, they are the base elements of nature: air for North Mages, earth for East Mages, fire for South Mages and water for West Mages. Does that make sense?'

'Yes.'

'Good. While Mages learn from every school of magic, those elements that are compatible with their magical blood are easier to master.'

'A West Mage will always struggle with fire spells and a North Mage with earth spells?' I suggest.

'Exactly. When it comes to absorbing power from other Mages, the elements have a far more severe impact. Should a West Mage succeed in performing a kiss of death on a South Mage, she would be instantly destroyed. Depending how powerful the two Mages were, she might take a building or two with her.'

'Wow.'

'Indeed. To absorb the power from an opposing school of magic, a Mage would need to have already performed the kiss of death on a Mage of a compatible element type.'

I cock my head while I consider this. 'So a West Mage could consume a North Mage and then a South Mage?'

'Correct. Same with everything else. If the kisses are done in the correct order, it's possible for a Mage to wield the power from all six elements. Or, at least, it was possible.'

'What happened?'

'It goes against the laws of nature for one person to have such power. That's why children born to two Mages of different types only inherit magical blood from one parent. A hybrid should never exist because the power is too much for a mortal to bear. But to give the kiss of death to five other Mages and not go mad in the process is inconceivable.'

I nod and try to keep my impatience from my expression.

'Centuries ago, there was a South Mage of moderate standing who had ambitions to become one of Charles the Second's advisors. Lacking both the influence and the education to attain the position, he decided to compensate his shortcomings with power. Over the course of several months, he proceeded to murder his fellow Mages, absorbing their essence. After the fifth murder, the Paladins managed to track him down to a bakery on Pudding Lane. Six of the most experienced Paladins of the order, including the Paladin General, entered the building to contain him and his power, concerned that he could level the entire city.'

Something about the story teases the edges of my memory, but the more I try to grasp it, the more the information eludes me.

'Paladins used their swords to separate the primal elements and draw them out of the Mage and into themselves. But we're not meant to have Mage power, and none of the Paladins survived.'

'The Paladins sacrificed themselves,' I say, and my eyes are drawn to the statues.

'Each of us has sworn an oath to protect the citizens of Old London. If that means laying down our lives for others, then so be it. And while the six Paladins undoubtedly saved the city, the Mage's selfishness had far-reaching consequences.'

My expression must convey some of the confusion I feel, for Sister Alissa points to a plaque by the nearest statue. The words are too small to read from this distance, but I can make out a year carved underneath them: 1666. Understanding dawns on me as the pieces fall in to place.

'The Great Fire.'

Sister Alissa nods. 'Fire was the last element to leave the Mage, and it started a blaze that raged for five days. Many more Paladins died trying to stop the fire from consuming all of Old London. Given the mistrust and reprisals that followed, the newly-appointed Paladin General felt it was safest to allow the King and the rest of the country to believe that the fire had been an accident at a bakery. While most of our efforts were directed towards rebuilding the city and helping those who had lost their homes, the Paladin General dispatched a group of Paladins sworn to secrecy to remove all traces of the ritual from the magical libraries in the country. Some say the Paladins travelled across the known world to eradicate it from everywhere. From there on, the knowledge of how to perform a kiss of death became a story, then an urban myth until few still remember that such a thing once existed.'

'Wait, what ritual?' I ask.

'The kiss of death.' Sister Alissa's brow creases. 'It's not just a peck on the lips, otherwise anyone could do it. The ritual takes hours to prepare and involves a protective circle, long incantations and some expensive and rare ingredients.'

'Like what?'

'I don't know. That knowledge was eradicated.'

'So if two Mages were murdered within a couple of hours of each other, performing the kiss of death on them both would be difficult?'

'Unless both rituals were set up in advance, it would be next to impossible. And that's before we consider the difficulty of a Mage absorbing two conflicting powers in quick succession.'

'Would the ritual leave evidence?'

'Almost certainly. From what I recall of the old stories, the last Mage to successfully harness the power of five others had carved a ritual circle on the basement floor. For each kiss, he filled the channels of the circle with focus materials to contain the magic.'

The process sounds fairly similar to the way I cast the circle around Lady Bergamon, and I know Mages use more components and words of power than other magic users.

'Does performing the kiss of death through the ritual leave a black mark around the lips?'

'Yes. That has always been the tell-tale sign of a successful kiss. The legend says that when an essence of a Mage is taken, Death herself leaves an imprint on the victim to mark the soul as destroyed.'

'Are you sure no one retains the old knowledge of the ritual?'

'We are keepers of peace and justice, not destroyers of knowledge, but in that instance, our actions were justifiable. The Paladins charged with the task were confident they had burnt every copy of the instructions. While that in itself may not convince you, perhaps this will: since the Great Fire, there have been no reported instances of the kiss of death being performed.'

'Do you know of another spell that would leave a similar mark on the victim?'

'Nothing springs to mind.'

I nod, everything Sister Alissa has told me swirling in my mind. This feels like another dead end, and yet, I am not certain what it means for our investigation.

'Am I right to think what I've told you complicates matters?'

Glancing up, I find her watching me with a sympathetic expression and I force a smile.

'I have two Mages who appear to have been victims of a kiss of death, and you've told me that's not possible. And there are two more potential victims. Honestly, I'm not sure what to do next.' Tapping a finger against my lips, I think. 'Is there a way to tell post-mortem if someone has had their magic stolen?'

'No. You'd have to witness the death and the theft. I believe the ritual left a distinctive magical residue.'

'That's what I thought,' I say, and bite back a sigh.

'Are you sure your killer is a Mage?'

I open my mouth to answer and then reconsider. 'What do you mean?'

'What I've just told you applies to Mages trying to increase their power.'

'Yes.' I am not certain what her point is.

'While it is my firm belief that the erased ritual is the only way for a Mage to perform the kiss of death, that doesn't mean others can't do it.'

'What do you mean?'

'Could your killer be something other than a Mage? Someone who can wrench the source of power without the aid of a ritual.'

'What sort of being could do that?'

'A powerful spirit. A Fey. Perhaps something older.'

'Older how?'

'Heralds are from another plane. So are spirits, but they are able to pass between the worlds more easily. Who's to say there aren't other creatures that have noticed our world and found a way to cross over?'

The chill of the winter worms its way under my coat. I shiver as several possibilities spring to mind. When I look up, I realise that Alissa is waiting for a reply.

'Thank you,' I say with a nod.

We speak no more as she guides me through the maze of corridors to the entrance hall, and I leave the Brotherhood. Even in the car, the cold that has settled in my bones does not lift. Why should it, when the picture emerging is far darker than I expected?

The killer has stolen the power from two Mages a night for the past two days. Unless something changes, two more will die tonight. So today I must stop him.'

24

A LEAP OF FAITH

The rain in Lady Bergamon's garden shows no sign of abating. Zipping up my coat and drawing up my hood, I step over the threshold. This time, the sense of vertigo is so strong I stumble and have to grab the rail by the steps to keep myself upright.

Whatever is happening in the garden is getting worse.

My jeans are soon soaked through, and rivulets of water run down my legs and into the wellies I picked up from home. Getting wet does not concern me, but the growing sense of dread slowing my progress does. This is not hostility I have sensed in the garden before, which I now believe relates to Bradán's dislike of people he considers intruders, but a new fear that robs strength from my limbs and crumbles away my resolve. Twice I nearly turn and flee to the safety of the house, and it is only the memory of Lady Bergamon's troubled expression I witnessed this morning that keeps me going.

Bradán said that to summon him, all I needed to do was touch water in the garden. I did not think to ask whether that meant any water or whether it had to be a spring or a brook. The rain, while water, feels too unnatural for me to assume that it will work.

When I reach the well, I spot the bucket on the ground next to it. It is filled to the brim, and I push it on its side. Once it is empty, I drop it down the well. The roar of the rain against the hood is too loud for me to hear a splash, but I estimate that the well cannot be too deep and turn the handle to bring the bucket up. When it emerges from the gloom, I see that it is half full. That should be enough for my purposes.

Resting the bucket on the edge of the well, I dip my fingers in the water.

'Bradán, I need to speak with you.'

While I wait, I become aware of the wicker man hanging nearby. Although there is no breeze, the construct turns first one way and then the other, always in motion. It has no discernible facial features, and yet I cannot shake the feeling that it is watching me. Whether it is a friend or a foe, I cannot tell.

The sound of pounding hooves yanks my gaze away from the wicker man. Bradán appears from the woods at a slow canter, dropping down to a trot and then a walk as he spots me. He stops three yards from me, ears back and eyes blazing. There is no sign of the burn Wishearth left on his forehead.

'What do you want, mortal?'

'Someone is killing Mages in Old London and stealing their power. This being leaves rot and decay in its wake, but metal negates that power. More specifically, iron and steel do.'

Bradán's ears flicker. 'Yes.'

'That being crossed over to Old London through Lady Bergamon's domain. I believe whoever attacked Lady Bergamon is responsible for the murders.'

'Yes?'

'I think it's a Fey.'

'A killer from the Unseen Lands.'

I nod, a different kind of fear sending adrenaline coursing through my blood. Could it be that my hunch is correct?

218

'Did you know?' I ask.

'I suspected.'

Balling my hands into fists inside the sleeves of my coat, I fight to keep the irritation off my face.

'Why didn't you say something before?'

'My main concern was my lady, not the intruder. I assumed that upon passing through these lands, his influence would lift and my lady would wake up.'

'But that wasn't the case.'

'I now see I was mistaken.'

'Who was it?'

'I know not,' Bradán growls.

'How could someone come through?'

'On the night of Samhain, doors that should remain locked can be wrenched open.'

At first, his words confuse me. But then I look at what is before me and see a Kelpie standing in what should be the back garden of an Old London house. Is that not impossible in itself?

'This being crossed over the same way you did,' I say.

Bradán tosses his head up and down, his heavy mane rippling with the movement. The seaweed entwined with the hair glistens in the rain. In the gloom of the winter day, his coat shines like dark water gilded by the sun. Even without seeing his red eyes and the inverted hooves, I have no illusion about him being a regular horse.

'If you don't know who crossed over, do you at least know what it was?'

'I never saw it, only sensed its decaying presence in our lands.'

'Is the creature causing the decay and the rot?'

Bradán snorts a cloud of hot air. I shiver.

'These lands are dying. Can you not feel the trees rotting and the land turning into mire?'

219

'I can sense the power of the garden being distant in a way it never was before. But if the garden dies, what happens to you and Lady Bergamon?'

'I will return to the Unseen Lands, and my lady will die. She cannot survive in your world without her garden. The era of her people has long passed.'

Another shiver runs through me. It is not just the Mages of Old London I am trying to keep safe. But with so little to go on, how can I protect Lady Bergamon?

'Can these lands still heal? Or is the decay permanent?'

'The sooner my lady recovers, the better. There is only so much I can do with this destructive rain.'

'I don't know how to find this creature,' I say, the admission tasting sour. 'With no idea of what I'm up against, I'm not sure how to help Lady Bergamon.'

The hatred in his eyes sears through the cold in my limbs, and shame heats my cheeks. Biting my lip, I fix my gaze on my boots. I am usually unafraid to admit my shortcomings. Why does doing so with Bradán sting my pride?

'If you desire to find the answers, there is only one place you can visit.'

Bradán's grudging tone draws my eyes up.

'What do you mean?'

'You must travel to the Unseen Lands.'

Terror paralyses my muscles and freezes the objection in my throat. A mortal travelling willingly to the Unseen Lands is almost unheard of. A mortal returning unharmed *is* unheard of. The Fey have snatched humans to work as slaves and act as playthings throughout the ages. The thought of spending eternity under the thrall of a Fey robs me of my breath.

Is this not what Wishearth meant when he said recently that I must choose how much I am willing to sacrifice for others? Lady Bergamon is a friend, but I also need her to remain in Old London. How much is that worth?

Forcing my jaw to unclench, I swallow. 'What would that accomplish?'

'If you want to not only know how to find a Fey, but have a chance of preventing him from killing again, it helps to know the kind you are looking for.'

'Who there is going to help me?'

'You may petition our rulers. They may see fit to offer information, or order someone else share their knowledge.'

'And if they don't?'

Bradán paws the ground, sending clumps of mud flying. Some of it splatters against the well and the bucket.

'They may accept a bargain.'

'Right.' I cough to dislodge the lump that has appeared in my throat. 'How would I get there?'

'It is a rare foolishness that allows a mortal to cross between the worlds by accident. You would need a guide.'

'A guide?' I ask, words slow. My reluctance to ask for his help puzzles me.

Curling his lips back, Bradán bares his sharp teeth at me. 'I will take you.'

I force myself to nod as my eyes stray to his wide back. A dozen stories about the treachery of Kelpies spring to my mind. Yet, I have no choice. How else am I going to find a doorway between the worlds?

'Are you frightened to sit astride a Kelpie? Are you frightened that I will drag you into the dark water and leave you there to drown?'

'No.' I lift my chin, trying to sound more confident than I feel. 'I believe your kind have been victims of old wives' tales.'

At least, I hope that is the case. Otherwise my career as a PI will be short-lived.

I take a step closer, but Bradán shakes his head. Droplets of moisture splatter my face.

'You mortals are obsessed with draping layers of garments on you. Most of them will only hinder you.'

'Why?'

'I am a Water Lord. How do you think I travel between the worlds?'

This is going to hurt. Biting back a sigh, I unzip first my coat and then my fleece. I lay them on the ground by the well, kick off the boots and remove my socks. The rain soaks through my T-shirt in a matter of moments. I shiver, and the cold triggers an ache in my bones.

Wrapping my arms around me, I turn to look towards the house. My phone is inside. I came out here to ask Bradán to confirm my theory, nothing more. It never occurred to me that I would be leaving Old London. I should go back inside, call Karrion and tell him where I am going. A text I sent when I left the Brotherhood told him I would be coming here, but I only intended to step into the garden for a little while. If I ask Bradán to wait now, will he still be willing to be my guide, or will he take the delay as a sign that I am too afraid to travel to the Unseen Lands?

If I go back inside now, will I still have the nerve to return to the hostile rain?

Bradán shifts closer to the well, and I see my reluctance reflected in his forced movements. My mind made up, I step onto the rim of the well, toes gripping the wet stones, and swing a leg over Bradán's wide back. He is warm, almost hot, despite the cool rain. The pain in my hips flares from the unfamiliar position. I lean forward and sink my hands into Bradán's mane. This is not the first time I have ridden a horse, but I am out of practice.

A brief pause is all Bradán allows me before he turns and heads for the woods. He feels tense under me, but

222

gradually his muscles relax and he moves to trot. Between his wide back and smooth gait, keeping my balance is easier than I expected. I wipe my face and squint to see in the rain, but the path Bradán has chosen is one I do not recognise.

When we reach a small lake, my fears about Kelpies resurface. The water is dark and the raindrops keep shattering and reforming the reflections of trees and the black clouds rolling across the sky. My kind has long since known that there is more to reflections on still water than meets the eye. There are times when the vista in them changes each moment. Blink, and the green leaves turn red, orange and yellow. Blink, and the branches are bare, covered with an icing of frost. Blink, and spring blossoms wreath the trees in veils of white and pink. Other times people walking along a lakeside path cannot be seen on the still surface of the water at all, even though birds and butterflies are clearly there.

Tales whisper that what we see are glimpses of other worlds, lands where magic is still strong and the wilderness pure. But even if one wanted to visit such a place, a mere touch on the revealing reflection is enough to disrupt the tantalising vision. No one knows how to access these other worlds, or even if such a feat is possible. Perhaps what we see are nothing more than memories preserved by wild magic in the bones of the world, glimpses of how things once were.

But now, as I approach the lake astride a Kelpie, I wonder if the old stories do not, yet again, contain a kernel of truth.

It is too late to object now and I lean against Bradán's neck. In his heartbeat, I hear the crashing of waves, the gurgle of a brook, the roar of a downpour. Bradán covers the last few yards in a canter and leaps off the grassy bank. I draw in a deep breath, and we plunge into the dark water.

223

25
THE UNSEEN LANDS

I am lost in the depths. The water is neither hot nor cold, and I cannot recall whether my clothes should weigh me down or buoy me up. Shafts of green light penetrate the gloom, seemingly coming from every direction. Strands of sea kelp stroke my face, gentle as a lover's touch, and I reach out, intent upon drawing them around me. The pressure in my lungs is a fleeting thought as I sink into the embrace of the water.

A hand closing around my wrist breaks the spell. All of a sudden, my desperate need for air overrides all other thoughts. The iron grip draws me away from the light, and I panic, kicking to slow my descent. Bradán has tricked me, and now I will die at the bottom of the lake. I have failed Lady Bergamon, just as I have failed Karrion, Jamie and Dearon.

We break through the surface, and my mouth opens on its own volition to take in huge gulps of air. Treading water, at first I think Bradán has been unable to take us between the worlds, but then I realise that we are in a wide river. Rushes hide the far bank from view, and I turn to see Bradán swimming towards the nearer shore. He has returned to his human form and he moves through the water with a grace that leads me to forget what I am supposed to do. When I choke on a mouthful of water, I start paddling after Bradán, my wet clothes making the movements clumsy. Upon reaching the steep bank, I take the hand Bradán offers and he pulls me onto dry land.

I rest on the grass for a few moments, catching my breath before my curiosity gets the better of me. We are in a narrow meadow that separates the river from a forest. A path weaves through the meadow, winding enough to look like a game trail. Sun is shining between grey clouds, and from the colourful leaves of the closest trees, I estimate the season to be late autumn. The air is cool, and I wring water from my hair. My T-shirt and jeans cling to me like a second skin, but there is little I can do to dry them.

At length, I become aware of my senses sharpening without needing to tap into my magic. A thrum of power runs through everything around us, stronger than in the Wild Folk lands of the north or in Lady Bergamon's garden. I can smell not only the water behind me and the grass underneath me, but the drying leaves in the forest. The air tastes clean, free of pollution, and of rain to come. I hear the steady thump of Bradán's heart, the shuffle of beetles in the grass and a squirrel leaping from branch to branch in the forest. My sight is keener than before, and the vegetation pressing against my bare feet threatens to overwhelm me with a myriad of sensations.

My magic responds to the power all around me. The weave of wildness that runs through everything is far stronger than at the conclave. It refreshes my depleted power, but each thread of the weave tempts me to explore it, to experience it in full. I appreciate the dangers of the Unseen Lands in a whole new way. All it takes is a small lapse of self-control to be lost in this place.

'We should keep going,' Bradán says.

'Where are we headed?' I ask as I struggle to stand. My muscles feel as though I have done a day of hard labour at the conclave.

'To the Courts. If I am not mistaken, the war of the Autumn Champions is about to end.'

'You fight wars here?'

Bradán looks at me. Although his pointed ears cannot move, I imagine them pulling back to lie flat along his neck.

'Every autumn. Such is the turn of our seasons.'

'I don't follow.'

He sets off along the game trail, which seems to meander alongside the river. At first my steps are tentative, but soon I realise that I need not worry about broken glass or used syringes here. It is, in some ways, like being back at the conclave.

'The year begins with the call of the Spring Heralds, followed by the law of the Summer King. Then the Autumn Champions go to war until the world falls under the lull of the Winter Queen.'

'Right. That makes sense.'

'I can feel the Winter Queen getting restless. It is in the air and in the flow of the water. Soon, the season will turn and the world will sleep.'

'Do the Fey hibernate?'

From the glare Bradán sends my way, I can tell the question was stupid. But at this point, I am not certain I could say anything he would find worthy of his attention.

'Of course not. The world sleeps, but we do not.'

The path takes us past several crab apple trees laden with red fruit. The smell of them is intoxicating, and I am not surprised to see dozens of wasps swarming around them. They pay us no heed, even when one brushes against my cheek. Beyond the trees, the river widens to a large lake. The water is dark and the surface marred by a gentle breeze.

While I watch, ripples emerge on the surface of the lake. At first, I think something is breaching the surface, but nothing follows the wake of the jets of water. Rather, I realise that the jets themselves are alive as I make out graceful limbs twisting and turning. Froth that passes for hair is thrown back as the circle of water sprites begin their dance.

There is no music I can discern, but the lake seems to pulse in time with the movements of the dancers. The small figures are both indistinct and adorned with intricate details. I watch, transfixed, while the sprites dance one way, whirl around and continue in a different direction. Soon I realise I can no longer see their feet, then their knees, as they slowly sink back into the water. Their gradual departure does nothing to detract from the graceful dance, and they continue their revelry until nothing remains but ripples on the surface of the lake.

A desire to see them again wells within me, and I come to appreciate the power the Fey have over mortals, even those who possess magic of their own. They have sway over even the strongest of minds.

'They are the Ythlaf,' Bradán says behind me. I had forgotten his presence while I watched the sprites. 'In your tongue, they are called the water relics. Memories of a time of old, when water sprites occupied all fresh water.'

'Do you know them?'

'They are to me as humans are to you. Distant relatives. Some are friends, others I merely tolerate.'

As if summoned by Bradán's words, three of the sprites rise from the water near us. They bow to Bradán, and one reaches a watery hand to caress his calf. While I watch, his posture straightens and he takes on a haughty expression; not an easy feat when standing naked and wet by a lake. The Ythlaf seem not to notice as others join the first three. Their speech resembles the gurgle of a brook, too fast for me to make out individual words. Bradán responds in the same language, and when one of

227

the Ythlaf reaches out to touch my toes, he dismisses them with a wave of his hand. The sprites sink back into the lake, leaving no ripples.

'We need to keep going,' Bradán says.

I linger by the lake a moment longer, trying to commit the Ythlaf to memory. Could I find such a sight in the deepest wilderness of the Wild Folk lands? Since I was a child, I have been convinced a deep spring is a gateway to another world. Were my childhood instincts correct? Is it possible for an Ythlaf to find its way to our land?

Bradán clearing his throat interrupts my thoughts, and I hurry after him.

The path veers away from the lake, and gradually the ground rises on both sides of us. As we steer around a black boulder, we come to the beginning of a dark holloway. Trees crowd over the path, blocking the natural light. Only a glimmer ahead indicates that the darkness does not continue forever. I step under the gloom, my balance precarious on the roots crisscrossing the path.

I have gone no further than a yard or two when something cold brushes my cheek. I reach my hand up and I feel the kiss of frost, followed by a drop of water sliding down my finger. It is snowing in the holloway. Two steps later, my foot sinks into a snowdrift and pain shoots up my leg. I hesitate, but Bradán's hand on my shoulder encourages me to continue. Strands of my hair grow stiff as they freeze in the frigid air.

Just as I am beginning to think that the cold has got the better of me, my foot lands in a puddle. The scents of fresh grass and blossoms caress my skin. Even the cool spring air feels hot after a hard winter. Birdsong fills the air, and in their melodies, I hear the joy of new life.

A tree root sends me off balance, and I land on my hands and knees in long grass. Dandelion seed heads tickle my arms, and I sneeze from the sudden onslaught of scents from trees, plants and fruit. Blackbird chicks are calling out to their parents, and grasshoppers are singing somewhere to my left. Despite the holloway being pitch black, the heat of the sun is scorching on my skin and my T-shirt is drying. I would like to pause to enjoy the summer, but again Bradán helps me up and nudges me forward.

The light ahead of us grows as the summer's warmth gives way to the damp cool of the autumn. I can smell apples, leaf mould and wet earth. A fallow buck bugles in the distance, and a pheasant takes flight in a rustle of feathers. Dry leaves crackle under my feet, and grey fog creates a veil between me and the rest of the world.

The holloway ends as abruptly as it began. I stumble out into the light, and my eyes water from the brightness of the sun. Glancing back, I see the holloway as a dark scar running through the landscape, and yet I would like to go back to experience the seasons again. It would be comforting to bask in the summer's heat and allow my senses to revel in the natural world.

Bradán has other ideas, and he steers me out of the woods and through a meadow where rosehips and blackberries glow in the sun. The smell of them causes my stomach to growl, and I struggle to recall how long it has been since I last ate. But I am not certain how safe it is to eat anything in the Unseen Lands.

'Mind your step,' Bradán says. Although his demeanour remains unfriendly, he seems a little less hostile than before.

On the ground under the shade of giant oak trees is a ring of mushrooms. Another step, and I would have ended up in it.

'Are they dangerous?'

'Not on their own. But it is never a good idea to blunder into a Fey trap. You would not enjoy bargaining for your freedom.'

Swallowing the rising dread, I walk around the circle and resolve to pay more attention to where I am going. But if I am staring at the ground, what other traps am I likely to miss?

A shuffling noise approaches in the undergrowth. At first, I think it is an over-sized hedgehog scampering towards us, but then I see the humanoid hands stroking the leaves as it walks and realise that the creature is nearly bent double. Smiling, I reach my hand towards the creature and then pause, worried about causing offence.

'What ails you, Grund Modor?' Bradán asks.

When the creature glances up, I see that it is a female with dark brown skin, shrunken limbs and hair that resembles porcupine quills. It speaks in murmurs, and I struggle to make out individual words.

'I lost it, Wæter Helm. They said it was here. But it is not. They are always saying things. They think I cannot hear, but I can.'

'The last I heard, the Blæstbearn was looking for you.'

The Fey's head whips up, her eyes narrowing as she stares at Bradán. 'When?'

'It was some time ago. Or perhaps no time at all.'

'Oh no! My hus is on fire!'

With that, she drops down to all fours and rushes off, surprisingly fast. Soon, only a few dried leaves drift in her wake.

'Is there anything I should know about dealing with the Fey?' I ask, and realise I have changed my walking style so that my toes touch the ground first.

'Here, the most important details can only be perceived from the corner of your eye.'

'Right.'

'Do not ask questions. Such impertinence will not be tolerated from a mortal.'

'I'm going to avoid the temptation to ask why.'

'Avoid striking a bargain. If you must barter, know that the Fey will do their best to outwit and trap you during the negotiation, but once you have agreed to the terms, their word is binding. So must yours be. The other way to convince a Fey to help you is to command respect. That often requires a test of strength.'

'I see.' Glancing at him, I do my best to ignore that he is naked. 'We didn't strike a bargain about you being my guide.'

'You are helping my lady. That is payment enough.'

'Thank you,' I whisper.

Bradán nods, but says nothing.

How long we walk through woodlands, meadows and shallow streams, I am not certain. Eventually, I become aware of Bradán's pace quickening and I have to hurry to keep up with him. When he stops, I nearly collide with his shoulder. Throwing me a look of exasperation, Bradán parts the gently swaying branches of a weeping willow and beckons me through.

The meadow we enter is a perfect oval and defined by a line of weeping willows. At one end, an ancient oak tree towers over the willows. Two of its gnarled branches have grown downwards, forming seats. One of them is wreathed in leaves, while on the other side, bare branches stroke the grass beneath the tree. Although the drooping branches of the willows sway in a gentle breeze, there is an unnatural calm about the meadow.

I am about to ask Bradán what the place is when the barking of many dogs shatters the silence. It reminds me of the Fey hunt I glimpsed through Lord Ellensthorne's desk, and terror leaps at my throat. The Fey were hunting humans, and I am the only mortal on this meadow. I shift back, forsaking my pride to seek shelter behind Bradán. Although I cannot hear hoof beats over the barking, I imagine terrible riders astride monstrous horses, their grim expressions betraying their bloodlust.

The willow branches at the far end of the meadow shudder, but instead of giant hounds, a pack of corgis rushes through them. The sight is so incongruous that I slap a hand over my mouth to keep from laughing out loud. Within moments, I am glad I did so for I realise that each corgi has a rider. Elaborate silver and leather bridles and saddles with leaf motifs look out of place against the sable, brindle and merle coats, and the joyful leaps of the dogs do not make them seem like the most impressive of steeds.

Bradán steps from the shadow of the tree and drops to one knee. A pointed look indicates I should follow his lead, and I kneel by his side. The barking increases when the corgis spot us, and they race across the lush grass in our direction, seemingly about to run into our laps. A couple of yards from us, they break hard enough that most end up sitting down. With ears up and tails wagging, they regard us with unbridled joy. It is easy to imagine Sinta among them.

The closest riders – a man and a woman – drop the reins and slide to the ground. As they do so, I experience a fleeting sense of vertigo akin to stepping into Lady Bergamon's garden. When my eyes regain focus, the figures tower over us. All I can do is stare.

The man is dressed head to toe in green, and his clothes look like they have been sewn from oak leaves. His features are narrow, his skin the colour of oak bark and his eyes are the deep brown of ripe acorns. Within them resides the wisdom of long summer days and warm nights, the richness of nature's offerings and the celebration of life. Out of instinct and respect, I fix my gaze to his dappled boots, but from the corner of my eye, I see a crown of sunlight and clover upon his brow. He carries no weapons, and yet I am left with the impression that he is armed and dangerous.

The woman is his polar opposite. Her skin is the white of fresh snow, her hair the moonlight of a winter's night, and her eyes the colour of sea ice. Her figure is hidden beneath a cloak of white pelts, but I catch a glimpse of a pale blue dress beneath. In her right hand, she carries a long spear tipped with a crystal head. The queen's crown is a delicate construct of snowflakes, the gloom of sunless winter days, and the deepest of shadows.

If I thought the sound of the dogs evoked terror, it is nothing compared to coming face to face with the Summer King and the Winter Queen; the rulers of the Unseen Lands and the strongest among the Fey. My knees quake even in my awkward position on the ground.

Behind the couple, other Fey dismount and change size. Half the entourage is dressed in green, bearing cloaks of lady's mantle, whereas the other half follow the white and blues of the Winter Queen.

'You have brought a mennisc bearn to our lands, Wæter Helm,' the Summer King says, and his voice booms with thunder.

'Not mennisc, my Cyning,' Bradán replies, head bowed. 'She is of the Wilde Folc.'

'Even bearns of miht are not welcome among the Aes Sídhe,' the Summer King says, but his voice softens to a rustle of leaves. His corgi steed throws himself down and rolls on the ground, all the while growling and barking.

'Yet one of the Aes Sídhe has crossed over to the lesser lands and is killing mortals.'

The King shrugs. 'As is our right.'

'The Unseelie Court will hear the Wilde Bearn.' The Winter Queen speaks for the first time, and her voice is the creeping of winter frost.

'Thank you, my Cwēn,' Bradán says.

The entourage turns to the Summer King as one. Clouds gather overhead, heralding a summer storm. The Winter Queen tilts her chin in a challenge.

My thoughts race as I shift my attention from the Summer King to the Winter Queen and back. I did not expect the Winter Queen's support and straight away wonder about her motives. Have Bradán and I stumbled into the middle of a game the rulers of the Courts are playing, and in doing so, become the Winter Queen's unwitting pawns?

'Very well,' the Summer King says in a rumble of a sudden downpour. 'The Seelie Court will also hear the Wilde Bearn.'

The Summer King and the Winter Queen turn as one, and the Fey follow. Bradán rises. I follow his example, and he motions me forward. My knees are shaking and my palms feel clammy, but I follow the Courts.

234

26

THE COURTS OF THE AES SÍDHE

The Summer King and the Winter Queen take to their thrones. I keep my gaze fixed on the ground, and from the corner of my eye, I watch as the morning sun creates a halo around the king and the winter moon cloaks the queen in deathly shadows. They are beings of indescribable beauty, and I have never been more frightened in my life.

My new perspective also allows me to see the sword strapped to the king's belt. Most of it is hidden in a leather scabbard, but the pommel stone glows with a pulsing light that multiplies my unease. Silver veins crisscross the queen's spear, although I cannot begin to guess their purpose. Yet when I concentrate on the spear, I feel its crystalline tip passing through my ribs like a kingfisher cleaves through the surface of a lake. The chill of death settles in my heart.

With the rulers seated, the meadow begins to fill with the Fey. The tallest resemble walking trees, while the smallest is no bigger than a shrew. Plenty of them have wings, but I am pleased to note that none are tiny glowing women. Tinkerbell remains nothing but a fairy tale. Instead, I see everything from mushroom sprites to bipedal cats – Cat Sìth – and from living rocks to wizened men in red caps. A cascade of water takes shape between two goat-like creatures, and I am amazed that it does not disappear into the ground. Three Kelpies arrive, dripping water, and ignore Bradán's greeting.

When the crowd parts to admit the Coin-Sìth, the black Fey hounds, I take an involuntary step towards Bradán. Even the smallest of the hounds would tower over Boris, and their sleek coats are stretched taut over muscles and sinew. I recall once more how it felt to join their dark pack and I shudder.

The nearest Cù-Sìth turns to regard me with soulless eyes.

'Have you brought us a mortal for the hunt, my Cyning, my Cwēn?' the Cù-Sìth asks, bowing to the rulers. The black claws on its front paws dig into the ground.

'One of the Wilde Folc would make a fine hound for the pack,' the Winter Queen says with the softness of fresh snow. 'But this bearn has the leave to address the Courts.'

'Who speaks for the bearn?' the Cù-Sìth asks, baring its gleaming fangs.

'I do.' Bradán steps forward.

The Cù-Sìth snorts. 'You have tarried too long in the dying lands, Wæter Helm.'

'Enough,' the Winter Queen says with a boom of sea ice cracking. 'Let the Wilde Bearn speak.'

The hounds lie down. To approach the thrones, I must either go through the pack or around them. Taking the longer route may be a sign of weakness, but my courage fails me at the thought of picking my way past huge paws and maws thirsting for my blood. I skirt around the pack, and a creature wreathed in flames lets out a hissing laugh.

When I look up, the Winter Queen is watching me, a satisfied smile playing on her lips. I am left with the impression she has just won the round, though I am not certain why. Her satisfaction derails my thoughts, and as

I reach the oak, I have to scramble to remember what I was going to say.

'Summer King, Winter Queen,' I bow, 'thank you for allowing me to speak. On the night of Samhain, one of your kind crossed over to Old London. He, or she, has been killing Mages and stealing the secret to their power. I am here seeking information about who this being is.'

'And, I imagine, how to stop them,' says the Summer King, the softness of his voice deceptive as the summer tides.

'I have little wish to see further Mages die, and this being has infected my friend with an illness that is wasting her away and rotting her domain.'

'That explains why you are here, Wæter Helm,' the Summer King says.

Bradán bows his head, but does not reply.

'One of the Hærfest Wiga has missed this season's battles,' the Winter Queen says.

I glance to Bradán for guidance.

'Autumn Champions,' he murmurs without moving his lips.

'If one of the Autumn Champions is missing, it should be easy to ascertain who has crossed over to Old London.'

'Helms of the Courts, step forth,' the Summer King says. Fey of all shapes and sizes step forward, Bradán included. 'Any of the Hærfest Wiga among you may divulge the name of your brethren to the Wilde Bearn.'

A stony silence settles over the meadow.

'It seems my kith and kin have little love for mortals.' The Summer King leans forward on his throne. 'Perhaps you would like to offer a trade to gain that which you seek?'

Bradán stands a few feet in front of me, facing the thrones. But from the stiffening of his shoulders, he expected this. I hesitate. If the Courts refuse to help me, coming here was a waste of time. If I cannot find the answers here, what can I do? How much is the information worth to me?

The memory of Lady Bergamon's deteriorating condition tells me all I need to know. I close my eyes briefly.

'Not a trade, but I offer a challenge.'

A ripple of laughter passes over the Courts, and the mocking tone stings my pride.

'And who would you have as your Wiga, Wilde Bearn? The Wæter Helm? Do you think he is a match for my Hærfest Wiga?'

'I cannot vouch for his fighting prowess, but I do know one thing: I fight my own battles.'

This time, the laughter is louder. The Summer King and the Winter Queen exchange a glance, and in their silent satisfaction, I see that challenging the Fey was no wiser than trying to bargain with them.

'Very well. You may choose your opponent.'

Eleven of the Fey remain at the centre of the meadow while the rest of the Helms retreat. It comes as no surprise that the Cù-Sìth who spoke earlier is among them. At least, I assume it is the same hound. I cannot will myself to look at the pack long enough to distinguish them. Having experienced their hunt, I know fighting a Cù-Sìth is out of the question.

Of the remaining ten, I dismiss a water Fey, a living rock and a being of flames. I have no means to hurt any of them. That leaves a large toad-like creature with moss growing on his back, a will-o'-the-wisp, a walking tree, one of the bipedal goat-like Fey, a Cat Sìth, a small man wearing a red cap with an axe on his back, and a tall and willowy warrior resembling the elves in popular culture.

Glancing at Bradán for guidance, I find his eyes fixed firmly on the roots of the oak tree. Whatever I choose, it must be my choice alone.

238

I discount the will-o'-the-wisp for the same reason as the elemental Fey, likewise the tree. The elf looks like I could take her out with a single punch, but looks must be deceiving if she has gained herself a place among the Autumn Champions. My mind recalls a story about the ferocity of the red caps, and I have no desire to discover how much truth the tales contain. I am no match for the speed of a Cat Sìth. That leaves the toad creature or the half-goat, half-man. I can only begin to imagine what their abilities are like, and the more I let my imagination run wild, the less I want to proceed with the challenge.

To gain some control over my fear, I meet the gaze of the goat man head on and nod.

'Tem, Grund Helm, you have been challenged. What say you?'

From the waist down, Tem resembles a goat, albeit one dressed in loose grey trousers. He also has the head of a goat. But his hairless torso is that of a man, and he has five-fingered hands. Tem steps forward and bows first to the Summer King and then to the Winter Queen.

'It will be my pleasure to fight for you, my Cyning,' he says, his long beard vibrating with each word.

'Combatants, step forward.'

Side by side, we do so, and the Summer King stands.

'A challenge has been issued and met. The battle need not be to death, but until one of the combatants yields.'

The implication is clear: if Tem happens to kill me in the heat of the battle, no one on this meadow is going to be concerned. I wonder if the same also applies if the roles are reversed?

Without needing a prompt from their rulers, the Courts shift back until the centre of the meadow is empty. Many of the Fey have sat down, and they are passing bowls of berries and mushrooms between them. An excited murmur fills the air, tempered by the menacing shapes of the Coin-Sìth. The spectators have arranged themselves in such a fashion as to provide the Summer King and the Winter Queen an unobstructed view of the battle.

Tem walks to the centre of the empty area and turns to face me, a smirk on his face. It takes all my willpower to keep my limbs from shaking as I join him. He looks towards the thrones, but I deem it wise not to take my eyes off him.

The Summer King claps his hand, and the dark clouds overhead respond with a rumble of thunder.

'Let the challenge begin.'

27

THE CHALLENGE

Tem makes the first move, so fast I am already flying back when I realise he has charged me. When I land on the ground, I bite my tongue and blood seeps from the wound. The crowds roar. Tem is coming after me, and I roll onto my side to dodge his kick aimed at my stomach. From the corner of my eye, I see the short edge of his hoof right before it slashes open my thigh. I keep rolling until I have put enough distance between us that I can find my feet. My leg throbs, but holds.

Reaching for the magic pulsing through the land-scape, I borrow the coat of a brown bear to shield me. Power ripples through me as my skin prickles and hairs sprout from my body, my clothes disappearing beneath the fur. But the transformation does not end there. My nose contorts and elongates into a snout, my jaw widens to accommodate larger teeth. I experience a moment of disorientation as my eyes move to the sides of my face. My hands and feet cramp and convulse while my nails harden into claws. As a final measure, my coccyx elon-gates into a short tail.

I drop to all fours.

The crowd roars again, but this time less snidely. Whatever they may know about my kind, I doubt they were expecting a full transformation. I wasn't, either.

Rage fills me: an instinct that demands I kill anyone threatening my cubs. I charge at Tem, intent upon ripping him apart, and while he jumps out of my way, my claws catch him above his hip. His grey trousers tear, and blood drips from the cuts. I turn with difficulty, my momentum off balance in my new form, and I growl. Outrage flashes in his eyes, but I am already charging again and he backpedals rapidly to keep out of the reach of my claws.

Tem changes tack and runs straight at me. I rise up to rake my claws down his torso, but at the last moment, he lowers his head. His curved horns collide with my stomach, and pain explodes along my lower ribs. I throw him off with an awkward swipe of my paws.

We circle each other, both taking stock of our wounds. My ribs throb, but do not appear to be broken, and blood is matting the fur on my left hind leg. Tem is bleeding from several scratches, but none are serious. The battle is far from over.

'A mennisc bearn is no match for a Wiga of the Aes Sídhe,' Tem says, pawing the ground. He glances around the crowd. 'I claim her as my prize. When I win, I will chain her to the ground and suck the marrow from her bones while she still lives.'

The crowd erupts in a thunderous cheer, and the Coin-Sìth leap to their feet. Saliva sprays from their mouths as they bark, and the bloodlust in their eyes resonates within me.

Having transformed fully into a bear, my vocal cords cannot form human speech. I settle for growling and charging at Tem again.

My teeth are snapping for purchase when he leaps into the air and delivers a blow to the back of my head. I land nose first on the ground, and my momentum rolls me forward onto my back. Breath escapes my lungs with a pained whoosh, and black spots swim across my vision.

Tem follows me and aims a kick at my hip as I struggle to stand. I lash out, but my claws barely make contact with the back of his legs.

Finding my feet, I see that I have made a terrible mistake. The coat of a bear offers little aid when Tem fights with hooves and horns, and my current form is too slow to react to his attacks. If I am to survive, I must choose a faster animal.

The presence of the Cat Sìth gives me an idea, and I back away from Tem as I reach for the power of the Wild for the second time. My paws widen as my claws grow narrower, sliding partly into their sheaths. My tail elongates, straight away whipping the air in an angry pattern. Even my vision changes, but my brain translates the muted shades into a full spectrum of colour.

Something is wrong. While I expect my fur to shorten, it remains the coarse coat of a bear. I also remain bipedal, despite having adopted the form of a lynx. Although my teeth sharpen into those of a feline, my head remains that of a bear.

Tem laughs. 'Having trouble, mortal?'

My attempt at a roar turns into a yowl, which only fuels my rage further. I charge at Tem and see the telltale dropping of his posture to indicate he is planning to use his horns again. Drawing on the agility of a lynx, I leap over him and rake my paws along his back. It is his turn to end up sprawled face first on the ground. He lands near a Cù-Sìth, who snaps at the air above his muzzle.

The Winter Queen rises from her throne; the Cù-Sìth lies back down, ears flat.

When he stands, brushing blades of grass from his beard, Tem chuckles. 'You have spirit, I grant you that much. But we are far from finished.'

Baring my teeth, I hiss a challenge. Tem rushes at me, head down, and I prepare to leap over him a second time.

I realise my mistake when I catch a glimpse of his smirk. By then, I am already in mid-air, and he jumps up to hit me square in the chest with his horns. I am thrown off course and roll to land at Bradán's feet. As I lie there, gasping for breath, Bradán stares at me with an impassive expression. Whatever happens, he will offer me no aid.

Tem comes at me again, and I force myself to rise, still coughing. He feigns left and aims a punch in my stomach, but I bat his arm aside and rake my paw down his face. One of my claws catches him right under his left eye and he screams. He lifts his hoof to kick me, but my back paw scores his shin. More of his blood lands on the grass, and a growl rises from the Coin-Sìth.

This time, the Winter Queen has to command the hounds twice before the pack settles.

I never see the blade coming. In truth, it doesn't occur to me that my opponent might be carrying weapons. All I know is that while I am parrying a blow from his right hand, I lose track of Tem's left. It is already in motion, and a blade sinks into my stomach, unhindered by my thick fur. I scream, and Tem twists the knife in the wound.

Wave upon wave of agony crashes over me as I struggle to comprehend what Tem has done. As if sensing my confusion, he yanks out the knife and licks the blood from the stone blade.

I will die here.

The thought paralyses me. I risked everything for Lady Bergamon, and I have lost. Tem appears to move in slow motion as he draws his hand back and adjusts the angle of the knife, aiming for my heart. No, not my heart. He is going to incapacitate me so he can eat me alive. Either way, I cannot withstand another stab.

Throwing caution to the wind, I open all of myself to the Wild. If I am to die here, I would rather give myself to the wilderness than suffer at the hands of a Fey. But I am not ready to give up just yet. Not before I have made my final attack.

As tusks grow out of my jaw and my paws harden into hooves, I realise that my will to live has chosen my third and final form. The burning pain in my stomach fades while my mind fills with bloodlust unlike any I have experienced before. I will kill this Fey even if it means dying myself.

When the knife comes at me for the second time, I throw both of my front hooves at Tem's hand. Rather than hurting or disarming him, I am content to keep the blade away from me while I yank my head down. My snout connects with Tem's stomach, and I slash my tusks up and to the side. Hot blood fills my mouth and nostrils as I tear through the skin. A coil of intestines catches on my tusk, and I pull it out, causing a cascade of guts. The blade falls while Tem scrabbles to hold the gaping hole closed.

I will kill this creature, tear him apart and trample his remains beneath my hooves. The bloodlust consumes me, and I lose myself in the simplicity of its freedom.

Snorting, I send a fine mist of gore through the air and prepare to charge Tem. Before I can do so, he falls to his knees. I paw at the ground, his throat level with my tusks and teeth. He must sense it too, for his eyes widen. Another loop of intestines slips through his fingers.

'I yield,' Tem says.

28
CONSEQUENCES

'I yield.'

Tem collapses to the ground. Disappointment begins in my belly and explodes outwards as rage. I want to charge at him, tear him to pieces for robbing me of my kill. The Coin-Sìth must sense this for they leap up, ready to stop me or aid me, I am not certain which. In their black eyes, I see my hunger reflected, and the effect is immediate. My rage dies down. I become aware of flies swarming around Tem and me, and notice grit and blades of grass clinging to his glistening guts. Nausea rises too fast to control, and I turn away to throw up. Heaving awakens the blinding agony in my side, and I fall to my knees.

At length, I become aware that I am still a misshapen mixture of boar, lynx and bear. When I try to let go of the magic, I cannot tell when the power of these lands ends and I begin. A new fear rises within me. Will I be trapped forever between these forms? Panicking does nothing to help me concentrate, and I force myself to focus on my shallow breathing and the steady dripping of blood matting my fur.

Bradán approaches, but remains a few yards away.

'One form at a time,' he murmurs, so low I struggle to catch the words.

He is right. I am aware of the power all around me as I reach inward and imagine the shape of a bear. My hands

246

and feet elongate, and the tusks disappear. Next, I try to let go of the magic so that any gifts of nature will disappear. Nothing happens. Perhaps in opening all of myself to this land, I have forged a connection that cannot be severed.

Concentrating harder, I recall what my hands look like and send power to fuel the transformation. The claws shorten into nails, and the hair recedes, while my palm softens to human skin. I repeat the process with my arms, back, torso and legs. The hardest to change is my head. As soon as I hesitate, the transformation falters. I lock an image of myself at the forefront of my mind and, at last, I am free from the bear.

When I look up, I become aware of the Courts watching me. Kneeling on the ground, clutching my side, I am an easy target should any of the Fey choose to attack me. Biting my lip against the rising tide of agony, I stand. I am lightheaded, but I lock my knees and turn to Tem.

'A name.'

Tem's eyes blaze with hatred as he regards me. He spits on the ground, and I take half a step closer.

'A name.'

'Baneacre, a Deaþ Helm, the destroyer of crops and blighter of spirits.'

'A way to stop him.'

Tem chuckles. 'Study the old lore.'

'Give me a way to stop him.'

'With a weapon of yew and cold iron, you will harm even the strongest among us.'

A ripple of outrage runs through the Courts. The Summer King stands, face twisted in anger, and lightning streaks across the sky. Tem pales and cowers in the face of his betrayal. I become aware of the Coin-Sìth creeping closer and I back away from Tem. The Winter Queen nods, and the hounds leap past me, so close I can smell rotting flesh on their breath. Tem screams as the Coin-Sìth close in on him, and a spray of hot blood lands on my cheek. I wipe it off, feeling numb, and turn away from the feasting hounds.

'Approach, Wilde Bearn,' the Winter Queen says.

There is no denying the command. I stagger forward until my legs give away. The jolt of my knees and wrist hitting the ground barely registers compared to the agony tearing through my torso. Bradán stands next to me, but offers no assistance. I cough, tasting blood.

'You are in need of healing.'

'Once I'm back in Old London, I will find a healer.'

'No, Wildeling. You will not live long enough to leave these lands. Your blood will nourish the ground, and the Coin-Sìth will feast on your carcass.'

I want to argue, but blood is dripping through my fingers and coldness is spreading into my arms and legs. The sound of wet flesh tearing and the crunch of bones behind me does little to help.

'What is the price of the healing you offer?' I ask, heedless of breaking the rules Bradán set me.

'You are in no fit state to bargain. I will accept a favour, collected when I so desire and fulfilled in such a manner as I desire.'

I don't need Bradán's warning to see the offer for the trap it is. But black spots swim across my vision, and a cough brings more blood to my lips.

'If the healing you offer allows me to return to my world and still live, I will owe you a favour. However, I will neither take nor steal a life.'

The Winter Queen nods. 'I accept the bargain.'

She leaves her throne and glides forward, so graceful I am not certain her feet touch the ground. Many hands lift me, until I kneel on the air before her. When did the Fey surround us? She bends down, eyes glittering like icicles, and presses her lips on my forehead. The crippling cold that sears through me is that of a midwinter night and it brands my soul, leaving me under no illusions about whom I belong to. Yet, when she steps back and the cold eases, I yearn for her touch. The kiss has frozen my blood, but still I want her.

At the wave of the Winter Queen's hand, the Fey set me down again and a gnarled old woman steps forward. Lichen grows in the creases of her grey skin, but her brown eyes sparkle with wisdom. I offer only a token protest when she moves the hand pressing on the wound and lifts up my T-shirt. From the many pouches on her belt, she gets out handfuls of woad, lady's mantle, puffballs and plantain, which she packs into the gaping hole. In another handful, she gives me mint, willow bark and meadowsweet to chew. The words of power she whispers over my torso send goosebumps through my body, but I can feel the damage to my internal organs mending as strength returns to my limbs. The herbs I am chewing take the edge off the pain.

The healer wraps a coarse bandage over the wound and around my torso. The fabric itches, but I refrain from scratching it while half the Courts are watching. When I stand, the world spins and settles. Bradán offers me a subtle nod, but his brow is furrowed. I, too, am beginning to regret my hasty bargain with the Winter Queen.

'The mortal will live, my Cwēn. If it pleases my Cwēn, I can see to her other wounds.'

'No need. My part of the bargain is complete,' the Winter Queen says with the softness of deep snow.

I bow. 'And I will complete my end when it pleases you.'

The Summer King steps forward and presses a kiss on the Winter Queen's knuckles. Hatred flashes through me, purer than any I have experienced before. Too pure to be a human emotion. It should be my lips touching the Winter Queen's skin, not his. The Summer King's eyes flicker up, and in the curve of his lips, I see that he knows my thoughts.

'You have shown courage beyond your kind, Wilde Bearn,' the Summer King says, his voice soft as the shiver of aspen leaves. 'I will offer you a boon without asking anything in return.'

Tamping down my hatred, I bow again. 'You honour me.'

'A Hærfest Wiga like Baneacre will have two choices in the dying lands: gain power or reduce to a shadow of a Deaþ Helm. He has chosen power, but he cannot retain the magic for long.'

'He will need a way to store it for later use,' I say, careful to keep my voice even, to ensure my words are a statement.

'He will raise a síd to begin his Court and serve as a seat of his rule. Until he has done so, he remains vulnerable. Once he has the síd, you have as much chance of defeating a winter storm as you have going against him.'

A thousand questions jump to my mind, but I utter none of them.

'It is time you left, Wilde Bearn,' the Winter Queen says. 'You have cost us a Hærfest Wiga, and from the sound of it, you will yet cost us another.'

The Summer King nods. 'You may have safe passage out of our realm, but you may not return until such time as our Cwēn summons you.'

I bow one final time and thank them both. Bradán is already striding away from the meadow, and I have to hurry to catch up with him. As we pass the hounds, I see their faces and necks are wet with blood, causing their dark coats to shine in the sunlight. I shudder. The leaves of a weeping willow caress my cheek when I push

250

through the branches, and the simple contact holds a menace I cannot define. I have outstayed my welcome in the Unseen Lands.

By my estimate, we walk nearly half a mile before Bradán slows down. When we come to a shallow brook, he leads me into the water and wades upstream until we reach a small meadow. There he leaps out of the water, landing well away from the bank, and motions for me to follow. My feet slip on the wet stones and I come close to falling in the water, but with my arms spread, I manage a reasonable jump.

'Walk in my footsteps,' Bradán says.

He is trying to throw off anyone following us. I should have realised it sooner, but my body is a mass of aches and pains, and just putting one foot in front of the other takes an enormous effort. Glancing over my shoulder, I imagine dark shapes emerging from the woods on the far side of the brook. Who else would the Summer King and the Winter Queen send after me, but their Coin-Sìth? As exhausted as I feel, I am not beyond the terror the Fey hounds evoke in me and I hurry to do as Bradán says.

We come to woods of spruce and pine, the canopies so thick that little light reaches the ground. The dropped pine needles ensure our passing is silent and no tracks remain. After a while, Bradán selects a spruce under which the lowest branches form a natural shelter.

'You can rest here for a while.'

I try to argue that I can keep going, but my legs decide for me and I sink down onto a carpet of dry needles.

'Hold out your hands.'

When I do so, he shifts them to form a cup and from his fingers comes a trickle of water. I drink in greedy gulps and hold out my hands for more once, twice, three times. Drinking settles my stomach and refreshes me.

'Do you know Baneacre?'

'No. My visits in recent seasons have been brief and I have little interest in the battles of the Autumn Champions. I serve the Summer King, while a Death Lord like Baneacre is a member of the Unseelie Court.'

'Shame. It would have been nice to know your impressions of him.'

'His title comes as no surprise given the destruction he has caused in my lady's garden. That he is a Lord and one of the Autumn Champions will make him a formidable opponent. He will be wise and cruel and cunning.'

The pine needles prickle my feet as I shift into a more comfortable position and peer through the branches.

'Do you think they've sent anyone after us?'

'The Summer King gave his word that you may leave safely. Neither he nor the Winter Queen will command a pursuit. But that does not mean there are not those among the Courts who consider it worth incurring the wrath of our rulers to hunt a mortal. Especially during a season when the King and the Queen are the arbitrators of differences rather than absolute rulers.'

'Are we heading back to the river?'

'No. Word will have spread among the Fey that we arrived there. It will be guarded. We need to find another body of water large enough for me to create a passage between the worlds.'

'I hope we find it soon. I can't fight another Autumn Champion. At this point, I'm not even sure how I'm supposed to take on Baneacre back in Old London.'

'You need not worry. By the time we return to your world, your wounds should not trouble you.'

'That's good.'

'No, it is not.' Bradán's face contorts with rage and his eyes blaze red like Tem's blood. 'You foolish mortal, there is nothing good about that. You should question every statement I make, always ask what the cost is, what the consequences are. For all you know, a day passes here, and when you step into your own world, you will wither and die because a century has gone by there.'

'I... I didn't know.'

'You must learn quicker, lest you die. I am not here for you, but for my lady.'

'There's never been any doubt in my mind about that.' I crawl out of the shelter of the branches, and stand. 'We can keep going.'

'I will change forms. We can cover more ground if you are riding.'

He makes the transformation look easy. One moment he is a man, the next a huge horse stands before me. He shifts sideways and presents me his back. Reaching to take hold of his withers, I jump, but my exhausted muscles protest. I cannot haul myself up. With a snort of derision, Bradán kneels long enough for me to swing a leg over his back. He moves straight into a trot, his hooves striking the ground with dull thuds.

'You risked everything for my lady,' Bradán says after a while. 'Thank you.'

'She's worth saving.'

The forest grows silent, and the still air takes on an oppressive quality. Bradán must sense it too, for he moves into a canter. Branches whip at my hair and bare arms, a few striking hard enough to draw blood, but all I do is lean forward until I am as close to Bradán's neck as I can get.

A hound bays in the distance.

'Oh shit.'

In any other situation, hearing Bradán utter such a human curse would amuse me. But at the sound of the terrible call, my throat constricts and tears spring to my eyes. Bradán extends his strides into a full gallop. I recall

253

the stories of old and know that the third bay of a Cù-Sìth means certain death.

'Please hurry,' I whisper against his mane.

The hound bays again, much closer.

We break through a wall of branches onto a sunlit meadow. Butterflies dance above the remaining autumn flowers, and a red doe raises its head from grazing. The details are incongruous against the backdrop of my fear. Beyond the meadow, I see the glint of water, and a tiny flutter of hope takes root in my heart. Bradán must feel it too, for he finds an extra burst of speed.

Behind us, branches snap as our pursuers close in on us. Although I sense the hounds, I dare not look back for fear of extinguishing the flame of hope. The edge of the meadow is approaching, but too slowly.

There is an intake of breath behind us. Throwing my hand back, I call upon nature to rob the breath from the hounds' chest. A gust of wind pins me against Bradán's neck as wild power flows through me and away from my outstretched fingers. The rhythm of pursuit falters, but only for a second or two. That is all the advantage we need. When the Cù-Sìth readies its third bay, Bradán's leap sends us sailing clear over the bank and into the water.

29

GATHERING RESOURCES

'Yan!'

The call is so faint beneath the drum of the rain that at first I think I imagined it. Drawing myself up on a muddy bank, I take a moment to cough pond water from my mouth. Bradán rises from the water with grace I envy, and when his feet break the surface, he loses his human form and morphs into a horse once more. He looks no different than he did in the Unseen Lands, and yet I cannot help thinking he does not belong in this grey and dreary world.

Longing for my Queen lances through my heart. Would she have been displeased if the hounds had torn me apart?

'Yan!'

This time, I am certain I heard the call. Turning my head, I try to pinpoint its location, but the rain muffles all other sounds.

'Karrion!'

I want to shout that I am over here, that he has found me, but another coughing fit overtakes the words. Since passing through the holloway, I have had little chance to think about the temperature, but now I realise how cold I am. My teeth begin to chatter.

'Yan!'

Karrion is getting closer. For a brief moment, I am overwhelmed by an irrational fear that it is not Karrion calling my name, but rather a Fey hound. That somehow they have followed us through Bradán's gateway and are here to finish the hunt. I scramble away from the pond and Karrion's voice. It is not until Karrion bursts through the branches that the fear dissipates.

'Yan!'

He stops in his tracks, out of breath, his black hair plastered to his forehead, and his eyes widen. Too late, I realise the state I am in. Although the passage between worlds and the rain will have washed off the blood, my T-shirt is torn, I have a bandage covering my torso, bruises darkening on my exposed skin, and muddy water is dripping down my arms and legs.

In three strides, he is in front of me and he pulls me into a hug. 'When you didn't answer your phone, I came. I saw your shoes by the back door and your phone on the counter, so I thought you'd stepped outside. But then I found your clothes by the well. Gods, Yan, I've been running around this forest calling your name for almost an hour.'

'I'm sorry, Karrion,' I whisper, still clinging to him. 'I never should have come out here without calling you first. It wasn't my intention to worry you.'

Karrion lets out an unsteady chuckle. 'I'd say don't do it again, but we both know how likely you are to listen.'

I try to laugh, but it sounds unfamiliar, like I have forgotten how. 'What time is it?'

'Two in the afternoon.'

'Only two.'

'Time has resumed its normal course for you, Wild Woman,' Bradán says from behind me.

Karrion seems to realise for the first time that we are not alone. His look of curiosity shifts something within me, but it cannot thaw the ice that has settled in my soul.

'You must be Bradán,' he says and holds out his hand.

Then he looks at Bradán's hooves, pulls his hand back part of the way and leaves it hanging between them.

'Correct, Bird Man. The customary greetings of your kind are not necessary.'

'Right. Sorry. Nice to meet you, I guess.'

Bradán tosses his head back and turns to me. 'Our work is not yet complete.'

'You're right. Tem said we could defeat Baneacre with yew and cold iron. I'm not sure what to do about the cold iron bit yet, but we must be able to find a yew tree here and fashion a weapon of some kind.'

'Agreed.'

'We'll need tools for that, and I wouldn't mind a coat and shoes.'

'I'll get them,' Karrion volunteers. 'Or I will, just as soon as someone tells me which way the house is. I think I got lost a while back.'

'It's quicker if we all go, otherwise we'll lose each other in the forest,' I say, and Bradán nods.

While we walk, I give Karrion an abbreviated account of my adventure, leaving out the battle and our narrow escape from the Coin-Sìth. From the bounce in his step, I can tell he has a thousand questions he wants to ask, but he is shy in Bradán's presence.

By the time we reach the house, my arms and legs have gone numb from the cold. Twice Karrion has to reach out and steady me when I stumble over a root or a depression in the ground. Bradán remains on the edge of the patio, while Karrion and I go inside. I stand on the doormat, dripping water, while Karrion fetches my towel from the bathroom. When he returns, I cast a longing look towards the kettle.

'Do you think I have time for a cup of tea?'

'I'll make you one while you find some dry clothes,' Karrion says. 'You look like you're about to keel over.'

'A hot shower would be heaven, but it'll have to wait. Ask if Bradán also wants tea.'

'How's he going to drink it? He has hooves instead of hands.'

'Maybe he can stand with one foot in a bucket. I don't even know if the Fey like tea. But it's impolite not to ask, especially given that he escorted us back here in one piece.'

'Fine,' Karrion says, but I detect a hint of reluctance in his voice. 'Go change.'

Upstairs in the bathroom, I peel off my sodden clothes and drop them in the bathtub. I am down to my last change of outfit. By the time I am dressed, a painful prickling sensation in my arms and legs heralds the return of feeling. I hobble out of the bathroom and back to the kitchen.

Karrion hands me a mug of tea. I burn my tongue, but cannot will myself to care as the hot liquid spreads more warmth through me. In between sips, I pick up my phone. I have eight missed calls, but I ignore them and find the phone number for Thaylor's shop online. She answers after six rings, and I offer her a hasty greeting.

'Does your case require a Tinker's touch after all?' she asks.

'It does. If I bring you something in a little while, will you cover it in cold iron?'

'That depends on what you're intending to bring.'

I pause. 'A wooden sword. Maybe. Or a wooden spear. Or some other wooden weapon, though my money's on a sword.'

'You need a wooden sword covered in cold iron for a case?' Thaylor asks, and I can hear the curiosity in her voice.

'Yes.'

'And your case concerns what? Sword fighting for children who don't like the Wild Folk and Feykin?'

'No, nothing like that. Can you do it?'

Thaylor clears her throat, taking her cues from my tone. 'Yes, if it isn't huge. I only have a limited supply of cold iron at the workshop. If push comes to shove, I can buy more from one of the other Tinkers, but it's not going to be cheap.'

'I'll pay, of course.'

'I expected nothing less. It takes a while to work with cold iron given that I can't heat it using natural means. The sooner you bring your wooden weapon to me, the sooner it will be finished.'

'We'll be there as soon as we can.'

I end the call and leave my mug in the sink. 'Bradán didn't want tea?'

'He looked at me like I'd morphed into a cat and then turned his backside towards me.'

'Clearly he doesn't like tea.'

'Which begs the question, what does he like? Grass?'

'He's a Kelpie, not a horse.'

'So seaweed, not grass.'

'Can you check if the coal shed near the back door has an axe or a saw in it?' I ask. The obsidian blade is in my fleece pocket, but we are going to need bigger tools if we are to fashion a weapon.

He steps out, and I get the tonic bottle from the fridge and return upstairs.

Lady Bergamon has deteriorated since this morning. Her skin is grey and her breathing so shallow I have to lay my hand on her sternum to be certain she is still alive. Most of the tonic I give her slides down the side of her mouth and soaks into her pillow, but I dare not give her more than Wishearth instructed. Concern for her overrides some of my fatigue as I hurry downstairs and put on my slightly soggy jacket and boots. By habit, I move to slip my phone in the back pocket of my jeans, but I stop myself. I have no need for a phone in Lady Bergamon's wet domain.

Karrion pokes his head in. 'I found an axe, but we could do with a big knife. Shall I raid the kitchen drawers?'

'I have a better idea,' I say and step out of my boots. 'Be right back.'

Taking the stairs two at a time, I retrieve my hunting knife from Lady Bergamon's bedroom and hurry back to the kitchen.

'This ought to do.'

'Wicked knife. Where'd you find it?'

'Every full member of the conclave receives one as a coming of age present. It's an invaluable tool in our lives.'

'And also comes in handy when you need to stop an evil Fey.'

'Something like that.'

Karrion heads out, but I hesitate at the threshold. At the sight of the relentless rain and the gloom of the winter day, fatigue washes over me. Every injury Tem dealt me flares up in a cacophony of aches and pains, despite Bradán's assurance that I would feel better by now, and I realise I'm starving. It feels like days since I last ate. Perhaps days passed in the Unseen Lands, though it felt like mere hours. My stomach growls, unwilling to settle for a mere cup of tea.

Gritting my teeth, I force myself to cross into Lady Bergamon's garden before my resolve falters. This time, the vertigo sends me off balance, and were it not for Karrion reaching out to grab me, I would have fallen. Straight away the wet and the cold worm their way through my clothes and into my bones. I want nothing more than to hurry back inside, take a hot bath and declare this case too hard.

I shake my head to dislodge the despair seeking to crush me. If I was prepared to die in the Fey Courts, I can tolerate the discomfort of wetness and fatigue. Once we

260

have fashioned the weapon, I can take a break. Until then, my willpower must suffice.

'Finally,' Bradán says.

'Hey—'

I silence Karrion with a look. 'Let's go.'

I soon find that this is easier said than done. The ground is growing increasingly water-logged and the clay in the soil turns crossing the lawn into an exercise in dexterity. Each time I slip, the pain in my legs gets a little worse until I am struggling to walk.

When we reach the well, Bradán stops next to its rim and tosses his head towards his back.

'Get on.'

'I'm fine,' I say.

'You're slowing us down. My lady has little time to waste.'

He has a point. With part reluctance, part relief, I move to climb onto the edge of the well, but Karrion stops me.

'Are you sure that's a good idea?' he asks, keeping his voice low. From the twitch of Bradán's ears, I know he has still heard every word.

'It's all right. How do you think we crossed over to the Unseen Lands?'

'If you're sure,' Karrion says, but his frown remains fixed in place.

I pat his arm and clamber onto first the well and then Bradán's back. The pain in my hips takes my breath away, but it is better than slipping in the mud and dislocating something. After a while, the heat of Bradán's skin eases some of the discomfort.

'I have a question,' Karrion says as we set off again at a more reasonable pace. 'I don't mean to offend anyone or anything, but I don't know how these things work.'

Bradán exhales a cloud of warm air. 'Go on.'

'If this Baneacre bloke needed to wait until Samhain to travel from the Fey lands to Old London, how come you could take Yannia there and back without a second thought?'

'You make dangerous assumptions, Bird Man. It cost me dearly to create the thread between my kind's shores and the dying lands. Nor can I travel between them as freely as you think. Too many journeys and I will wither like you mortals until there is nought left of me save for sea foam and fish bones. And do you think me so foolish, Child of the Sky, that I would create a gateway that anyone could access?'

Karrion is silent.

'The path I made is mine and mine alone, hidden in the deep springs and the turning of the tides, where water whispers the secrets of the earth and Kelpies sing the lullaby to the waves. None may pass without invitation, lest they be crushed by the currents and drowned in the cold darkness of the deep sea.'

I have been riding hunched forward, struggling to follow the conversation over the roar of the pain. Now, I wipe the water off my face and look at Karrion.

'It must have taken a great deal of power for Baneacre to cross to Old London,' I say.

'My lady's domain was his blessing. It exists neither here nor there, and served as a waypoint for him. Even so, the journey was costly. That is why he is changing these lands.'

'I don't follow,' Karrion says.

'Baneacre is a Death Helm, a being of decay and rot. He serves the Winter Queen in enacting the death that follows each summer. The world must die in order for it to be reborn in the spring. Baneacre derives his power from decay, and through causing this garden to wither and drown, he will gain immense power.'

Something about Bradán's words troubles me, but I cannot put my finger on what. Before I have a chance to chase after the elusive feeling, another piece of the puzzle falls into place.

'The Mages are about power.'

Karrion squints at me through the rain, forgetting to look where he is going, and stumbles on a root.

I explain what Thaylor and Sister Alissa said about the kiss of death.

'Maybe the power from decaying Lady Bergamon's garden isn't enough and he needs to steal more from other magic users. If it's possible to take not just the raw mana of a Mage, but the secret to their way of drawing power and casting spells, the latter must be a better choice.'

'It's a better choice in that he gets to kill people in the process,' Karrion says, but he nods.

'There is more to it, Wild Woman. To raise a síd in the dying lands, Baneacre needs the power of your world.'

'When he has killed six Mages, he will have more power than we can imagine. No doubt more than is required to raise ten Fey Mounds. Once he has his own síd, he'll also be able to create a gateway back to the Unseen Lands for reinforcements.'

'He will be unstoppable,' Bradán says.

Karrion swears.

'It gets worse. He's killed two Mages per night since Samhain. We need to make this weapon quickly if we're going to have any chance of going after him.'

The sounds of rain and Bradán's hooves settle over us while we consider the implications of my words.

30

A SWORD OF YEW

'There's something else I'd like to ask,' Karrion says.

'Speak, Bird Man.'

'I get that Baneacre used this garden as a stopping point to recharge his power, but why is it still raining? If he's been and gone, how come it feels like the garden is speeding towards ruin?'

'You assume he has no need to return. The assumption is false.'

I lean forward. 'Are you saying Baneacre keeps returning to the garden?'

Bradán glances at me over his shoulder. 'I expect so. There is nothing to suggest he is not somewhere within my lady's domain as we speak.'

All of a sudden, the shadows of the wet forest seem darker and longer than before. A branch snapping nearby makes me jump, as does the creak of the horse chestnut tree we pass.

'Great,' Karrion says and shifts closer to Bradán. 'Can we hurry up with the sword making?'

I think back to the broken lock on the back door. Baneacre has had no trouble gaining entrance to the Mage residences. What is different about Lady Bergamon's house? Could it be that by breaking in, Baneacre breached more than a physical door?

'But how could he return to the garden? The only way

in is through the house.'

Bradán chuckles; the sound close enough to a nicker that a ghost of a smile lifts my cold lips. 'That you know of. Besides, he was able to leave. What stops him returning the same way?'

'The fact that we've been sleeping in the house?' Karrion replies.

'What concern are you to a Death Lord?'

Neither of us has a ready response. The idea that a murderous Fey has been passing through the house while I have been asleep upstairs unnerves me. Earlier today, it would have left me in a state of terror, but the exhaustion and pain have insulated me against fear. Having faced the Coin-Sìth, I am not certain anything could evoke greater dread.

'Is there any way we could block his path?' I ask after a while.

'Yes, with a barrier of cold iron. But it is possible Baneacre could use his mortal magic to force his way past it. None of the protections used for Samhain has any effect on a Lord of the Unseelie Court.'

'In your honest opinion, Bradán, do we stand a chance against Baneacre?' Karrion asks.

Bradán is silent as we walk through a copse of birch and ash. 'Your advantage is that he is out of his element. But even then, he will be very powerful. There is hope, but not much. This, however, will help.'

We leave the dripping trees behind and enter a large meadow. The first – the only – thing I notice in the afternoon gloom is the giant oak tree. It is unlike any I have seen before, and even from a distance, I am certain Karrion and I could not reach around the trunk to touch hands. The branches cast faint shadows over half of the open space and the top of the canopy is far above the surrounding woodlands.

Even here, I see signs of decay. Yellowed leaves float down, adding to the thick carpet around the tree. With my eyes drawn down from the highest branches, I see that there is a stone bench beneath the oak and I imagine Lady Bergamon sitting on it.

'I thought we needed a yew tree,' Karrion says.

'We do,' Bradán says and tosses his head towards the far side of the meadow. There, in the shade of taller pines, stands a dark line of yews.

When we move forward again, Bradán chooses a path that takes us around the oak and its skirt of leaves. From the bending of his body towards it and the turning of his ears, I sense deep respect. There must be something special about the oak beyond its great age.

Could this be the heart of Lady Bergamon's domain?

Opening myself to the power of the garden, I allow my senses to quest out. When my awareness reaches the tree, I shudder. There is so much magic flowing through it that I wonder if its sap is pure power. Now that I am examining it with all of me, I also see that the decay is slower than elsewhere. The oak is fighting the intrusion.

Something touches the edge of my consciousness, and I jerk back; the fact that I am riding rather than standing beneath the vast canopy momentarily forgotten. I catch a glimpse of stone circles and familiar runes before the feeling passes. Bradán's ears flicker back, and I guess he must have sensed something of what just passed.

There must be yew trees elsewhere in the garden. Why did Bradán bring us here?

With my senses still cast outward, I become aware of something else. The weave of power that comes from the life and death of all things has always been there, but now I see beyond it. Trees sprout as seedlings, rush towards the sky, going through countless deaths and rebirths as their leaves fall and seeds germinate, until the weight of the ages decays the heartwood and turns their sap into dust. Birds hatch, wheel across the sky, rot on the ground. Flowers bloom and wilt. I make the mistake of glancing at Karrion, but when lines cleave through his face and muscles wither to sinew, I yank my focus away from him and break the connection with the weave.

'You okay, Yan?'

Bradán stops under the yew trees, and I lean forward, inching my leg over his back to dismount. Landing sends shooting pains up my shins, and I am grateful for Karrion's steadying grip on my elbow while I find my balance.

'Baneacre has done something to the power in this garden. Everything feels different.'

'It has nought to do with Baneacre,' Bradán says. 'Did you truly believe you could visit the Unseen Lands and return unchanged?'

'Is it permanent?'

'What did you see?' Karrion asks.

'The effect may lessen over time when you grow accustomed to it. Eventually, you will forget that you ever saw the world a different way.'

Getting used to seeing my friends wither and rot, over and over, sounds unlikely. The thought leads me to appreciate Lady Bergamon's willingness to befriend me anew. Even when we first met, she must have already known she would see me to my grave. Yet, she had the courage to not just help me, but extend an invitation of friendship. The same with Wishearth.

I hope in time, my bravery will match theirs.

'Yan?'

'It's nothing that we need to worry about right now.' I offer Karrion what I hope is a reassuring smile. 'Ask me again once we've solved this case.'

The yew trees block what little light penetrates the

rain clouds, and I squint as I look up at the branches. The green leaves glisten, and the berry-like cones seem unnaturally bright against the dark green foliage. There are several branches within reach that would work for our purposes. I point at the nearest.

'Is that okay?'

'Fine,' Bradán says. 'Cut it. There is a shallow stream nearby. We can fashion the sword there.'

Karrion steps closer, testing the weight of the axe. 'These trees won't get grumpy if I cut down a branch, will they? Or a dryad appear out of nowhere to have a go at me?'

Bradán snorts. 'There are no leaf maidens here or anywhere else in the dying lands. This forest is just a forest. You are quite safe.'

'Right.' Karrion coughs. 'Just checking.'

He grips the axe with both hands and cuts the branch with efficient blows. At Bradán's instructions, he trims off the smaller offshoots, but keeps the main branch far longer than we need. Despite my fatigue, I cannot resist a grin.

'I see all that wood chopping practice in my shed has come in handy.'

'What can I say? I'm a bird of many talents.'

'Let us go,' Bradán says and leads the way into the coniferous forest.

What Bradán described as a shallow stream has burst its banks and now flows as a small river through the waterlogged ground. On a small rise, a flat stone is leaning over the stream, and we set the branch and our tools on it. As soon as Bradán's front hooves touch the water, they contort and split into fingers. In a matter of moments, Bradán in his human form is crouching before us. The cold water does not seem to bother him, and when he stands, I am once again reminded how naked he is. I avert my eyes, and next to me, Karrion does the same.

Bradán tells Karrion to cut the branch, leaving about

five feet of the thickest section. It still seems far too long for a weapon I could wield, but I keep any objections to myself. While I use the axe to measure another length as the cross guard and Karrion goes in search of weeping willow boughs, Bradán takes my hunting knife and begins whittling away at the wood.

At length, I become aware of the acrid scent of burning flesh. Karrion, returning with a handful of branches, wrinkles his nose.

'What's that?'

'It is nothing,' Bradán says and dips his hand in the water. When he reaches for the wood, I see that his palm is scored with angry red welts that weep yellow pus. The smell grows worse.

'Bradán, your hand. What's happening to it?'

'The yew is toxic to all of my kind, not just to the likes of Baneacre.'

'Let me take over,' I say.

'No.' He shakes his head and grips the wood until his knuckles are white. 'You nearly died for my lady. The least I can do is endure some pain.'

'You what?' Karrion says and turns to me. 'What happened? Are you all right? Do you need to sit down?'

This is why I thought it would be better to leave telling him that part of the story until tomorrow.

'I'm fine. I'll fill you in on everything else later. For now, all you need to know is that my wounds have mostly healed and we have more important things to worry about.'

'You're going to struggle to convince me that anything would be more important than you nearly dying, but we'll resume this conversation later.'

'I can't wait.'

Between the efforts of the three of us, the sword soon takes shape. Bradán dips his hands in the stream at regular intervals, and I see that the water has an immediate healing effect. But by the time he reaches for the obsidian blade and carves a series of symbols along the hilt, the wounds are deep enough that he is scowling.

'What are those?' Karrion asks, leaning closer to see the symbols in the fading light. The darkness seems to be falling far sooner than it should.

'Something for luck and protection.'

As he moves his hand, I recognise the runes.

'Do you know what they mean?' I ask.

'It is forbidden knowledge. But I know these are used for protection.'

'They look familiar,' Karrion says. 'I can't for the life of me remember where I've seen them before.'

There does not seem any harm in refreshing his memory. 'The circular stone in the garden where Lady Bergamon worked the magic that located Brother Valeron.'

'Of course. Do you think they're a secret language? Maybe Viking or Greek?'

'Do they look like Viking runes? And does Lady Bergamon look like she's descended from Norse raiders?'

'Well, no, but they must have come from somewhere.'

'And that somewhere is going to have to remain a mystery, unless you can use telepathy and ask Lady Bergamon herself.'

'There, it is done.' Bradán hands me the sword and sinks both arms up to his elbows in the water. The lines on his face ease.

I test the weight of the sword. It feels light, too light to put much strength behind blows, but that will change once it has been coated in cold iron. The cross guard is attached with willow boughs and the hilt has strips of willow bark wound around it for better grip. Although the shaping has reduced the sword's length, it is still about four feet from the tip to the pommel. I swing it a few times, the movement clumsy and lacking purpose.

'Next problem: I know nothing about sword fighting.'

'Aim the pointy end at the bad guy and hit him hard,' Karrion says.

'Thank you. With such detailed advice, I'm all sorted.'

'The wood and the metal will do much of the work for you,' Bradán says. 'It should also offer you a degree of protection against Baneacre's magic.'

'I hope so. With or without added Mage mana, a Fey is going to be a formidable opponent.'

'But you must recall that as an Autumn Champion, Baneacre is no stranger to combat. If possible, catch him by surprise and hit him hard. You will need every advantage. And if you intend to change forms again in the middle of battling him, be sure you have the means to shift back.'

'Wait,' Karrion says. 'Since when have you been able to shapeshift?'

'I can't. It was a fluke in the Unseen Lands, and even then, I didn't fully change forms.'

'You did at first,' Bradán says. 'Your bear shape appeared quite complete. The other two were less so.'

Karrion appears to have forgotten all about the wet forest and my near-death experiences. 'What else did you change into? Was it a wolverine? Or a wolf? Or maybe a dragon?'

'How many dragons do you think I have encountered in the wilderness of the North Country? No, I chose a lynx and a boar.'

'Wicked.'

The memory of Tem's hot blood flooding my nostrils flashes across my mind, followed by the smell of his intestines on the ground. I grit my teeth to fight revulsion. I remember the bloodlust of my boar form, and it intermingles with the hunger of the hounds until one is inseparable from the other and I feel what the Coin-Sìth felt when they tore Tem apart.

271

'I don't know about wicked,' I say, so weary that every word is a struggle. 'Mostly I was just trying to survive.'

Karrion's grin disappears and he hugs me. 'Sorry, Yan. It must be one thing to hear about it and quite another to have experienced it for yourself.'

'Something like that.'

'Time is passing,' Bradán says. 'Here each moment matches that of your world. The sun will set soon and Baneacre will hunt.'

'You're right, we need to hurry to Thaylor to finish the sword.'

'Do you know your way back?'

I look around the growing gloom, orienting myself. 'Yes, I think I do.' I point in the direction of Lady Bergamon's house, and Bradán nods.

'In that case, we shall part ways here. The thought of Baneacre lingering in the garden troubles me. I shall see if I am able to locate him.'

'Be careful.'

Bradán snorts and steps out of the stream, shifting back into a horse. 'You need not concern yourself with my safety. I may not be a Hærfest Wiga, but I am a Wæter Helm and this is as much my domain as it is my lady's. If I locate Baneacre, he may not live long enough to pass to Old London.'

'Happy hunting.'

What passes between us is an acknowledgement of dangers faced together, a joint purpose, and a common enemy. Bradán may not like me, but for now, we are closer allies than if we were bound by blood. He tosses his head and rears in an explosion of movement. In a moment, the only sign of his presence in the woods is a fading sound of pounding hooves.

31

IVY STREET

'How did you fare after I dropped you off?' I ask. My stomach is growling, and despite the cup of tea, a pressure against my temples indicates that my blood sugar levels have dropped.

'Really good,' Karrion says, the sword resting casually on his shoulder. 'Looking at the history of Ivy Street was a breeze. All I had to do was pay some Land Registry search fees. It's been a residential street forever, and the plots are pretty big for the area. Not as big as where the posh Mages live, but decent for us mere mortals. Or at least mortals who aren't completely broke.'

'That explains why the developers are interested in the street. If the plots are large, it gives them more room to put up tower blocks.'

'That's what I figured. As for Lady B's house, I think I found out her real name. Victorria Greenslade inherited the property from her mother, Margeret Greenslade, about twenty years ago. From the history of the property, it's been in the Greenslade family for at least the past seventy years.'

'And you think Lady Bergamon is Victorria Greenslade?' I ask, doing my best to hide my smile.

'Yeah. And if her mum was alive twenty years ago, she can't be quite as old as you think she is.'

'Tell me, Karrion, if you were having to hide in plain sight in Old London for a long time, how would you do it?'

'What do you mean?' he asks and uses his free hand to push wet locks of hair from his forehead.

'Say you bought a house. How would you avoid suspicion when the owner didn't change for a hundred years?'

He nods. 'I'd fake my death and pretend to inherit it from my father. Do you think that's what Lady B is doing?'

'I do. I reckon every thirty years or so, she pays someone to fake the death of her alias. She inherits the house from a mother or an aunt, perhaps changes her appearance for a while, and carries on as before.'

'But wouldn't people grow suspicious?'

'Only if they'd lived on this street for thirty years too. I expect the residents change fairly frequently, and Lady Bergamon can easily make herself look younger or older with make-up to give the impression that she too is ageing. And if the woman who moves into her dead mother's house shares her likeness, but has brown or grey hair instead of white, who is going to question that? They are family after all.'

'That's pretty cunning,' Karrion says.

'I'm willing to bet that Ivy Street has always had houses and this plot has always been owned by a woman who is fond of plants, but keeps to herself. Who knows, there may be other entrances to her garden. If that's the case, perhaps this house stands empty for a time while the other residents forget what the woman who used to live here looked like.'

'How old do you think she really is?'

'I don't know. Older than I can imagine and I have quite the imagination.'

'I'm just thinking that the older she gets, the more hoops she has to jump through for this,' he waves at the forest around us, 'and the more it's worth protecting.'

'It's always been worth protecting, though I take your point. The longer she lives in symbiosis with the garden, the more they are dependent on one another.'

'Makes you wonder how far she'd be willing to go.'

'We'll just have to keep guessing.'

'I do think it's strange that when Baneacre started killing Mages in Old London, he happened to pick the ones intending to destroy Lady B's domain. If all he's doing is causing these lands to rot to restore his power, what does he care about whether the street is developed into tower blocks or not?'

There is it again, the feeling that I have missed something, and this time I manage to grasp the idea before it fades away.

'Here's something else that doesn't make sense. If Baneacre is a Fey of rot and decay, as Bradán said, how could he kill Mages by manipulating plants? That's a power I'd associate with the Spring Heralds or the Summer King, not someone from the Unseelie Court.'

'Maybe he made a deal with Lady B. He'd use her domain to recharge his power in return for taking care of Lady B's problem with the Ivy Street Project.'

'That's nonsense. Why would he destroying her domain be preferable to the developers doing so?'

'But remember what Bradán said: death must happen for there to be a rebirth. What if this rain is just a sign of autumn and in a couple of months, spring will come?'

Just because Bradán said Baneacre is destroying the garden does not mean he is correct or telling the truth. What if Karrion is right and Lady Bergamon did make a deal with Baneacre? Is Bradán using me to eliminate Baneacre once he has removed the Mages? But why would Lady Bergamon agree to a deal that would leave her unconscious and fading away? Or did Baneacre double cross her?

275

My headache intensifies, and I pause to rub my temples. 'I don't know. Every time I think I've got this all figured out, something else casts doubt over my conclusions. But I have to believe I can trust Lady Bergamon.'

'Why?'

'Because to be a good PI, instincts are needed. Without them, how am I going to solve cases like Marsh's?'

'I'm sorry, Yan.'

Karrion wraps an arm around my shoulder, and I lean against him, grateful for his warmth even though I am not certain what he has apologised for. I remain there until my boot catches on a low coil of brambles and my attention is diverted to remaining upright.

'What about the Ivy Street Project? Did you find out anything about it?'

'I did. A few internet searches, phone calls and a bit of legwork did the trick.'

'Tell me.'

Karrion outlines much of what we know: the project is huge and intends to make significant progress towards solving the need for more affordable housing in Old London. The whole street would be developed, aside from the pub at the opposite end of the street from Lady Bergamon's and an adjoining corner shop, which would be expanded to meet the needs of the new area. The planning permission application outlines four tower blocks replacing the existing detached and semi-detached houses.

'When you didn't answer your phone, I came over and decided to do a bit of research here. I knocked on a few doors and asked about the project. Some people said they'd provisionally accepted the offer to buy their house, while others were really cross about the plans. One man tried to persuade me to sign a petition protesting the project, but I told him I wasn't a resident. He slammed his door shut, so I guess his views were pretty clear.'

276

'Were you able to identify a Light Mage who is a likely target?'

'Yes. There were a couple, but one woman, Amitta Pandia, seems to fit the bill. When I made a few phone calls, pretending to be a reporter interested in the project's future now that some of the people connected with it have suddenly dropped dead, they directed my query to her. She's a solicitor dealing with the planning applications and other legal stuff.'

'I hope you didn't make the link between all the deaths obvious.'

'No. I was more circumspect than that and only mentioned Laene and Hailfax. We need to ask Jamie for Pandia's home address. I figured we could go over to her place and warn her about the likely attack.'

'Good plan. What about a Shadow Mage?'

Karrion hesitates and helps me over a narrow stream. 'I had less luck with that. There are no Shadow Mages connected with the project.'

'Wait, that can't be right. There must be someone. Or are we wrong about the connection?'

'I don't think we are. Everything fits. But I do have an idea.'

'Go on.'

'The project is a big deal. Ivy Street isn't the biggest or the richest street in Old London, but redeveloping the area would still displace a lot of people. As much as it needs planning permission, the High Council will also have to approve the plans. And there are three Shadow Mage seats on the Council.'

Another piece falls into place. 'Hailfax.'

'What?'

'Lord Ellensthorne said he was mentoring Hailfax who was a talented young Mage despite not having been born into the Shadow school. If Lord Ellensthorne already likes him, could that be why he was chosen as the architect for the Ivy Street Project?'

'And if Hailfax was talking to him about the project—'

I nod. 'He knew the Council would have to approve it and having Lord Ellensthorne as an ally would help.'

'If Lord Ellensthorne's connection to Hailfax is common knowledge, that would make him the most likely Shadow Mage target among the Council,' Karrion says. 'Baneacre is not making his life easy, going after the top Shadow Mage in the city.'

'He hasn't appeared too concerned with mortal security measures so far. That said, I'd hate to think we're focusing on the obvious at the exclusion of all else. We need to ask Jamie to warn the other Shadow Mages in the Council.'

'While we deal with Amitta Pandia, right?'

'Yes, we'll go to her first, then to Lord Ellensthorne.'

Karrion's expression falls. 'Why? He can take care of himself.'

'Are you certain he's a match for a Fey?'

'If his arrogance is anything to go by, yes.'

'No, Karrion,' I say and shake my head. 'I know you don't like him. Me neither. And I know you disagree on his policies. As I do. But can you live with yourself if he dies and you chose not to warn him?'

He opens his mouth to respond, but says nothing. His hand finds mine; warm despite the drizzle. 'You're right,' he says with a sigh.

'Sometimes you need to consider the sort of person you want to be as well as others. But you know all this already.'

'Maybe. But a reminder about the right path every so often can't do any harm.'

'It's your path to choose, no one else can make the decision for you.'

278

He brushes his shoulder against mine. 'That doesn't mean I can't walk it with friends.'

I am relieved to see the edge of the woods, and we hurry out of the shadows. Next to the well, the altar has been ruined by the relentless rain. A corner of the cloth has covered the skull, and the leaves have scattered across the grass. It takes me a few moments to figure out what is bothering me about the scene: the wicker man is no longer there. I look around, expecting the wind to have pulled it off the branch, but I see no sign of it. Disquiet settles in my chest, giving me a queasy feeling as I let go of Karrion's hand and veer off our intended path.

'Everything okay?' he asks, trainers squelching in the mud as he follows me.

'When you found my clothes here, was a wicker man hanging from that tree?' I point ahead of me.

'I don't think so.'

'Are you sure?' I turn to him, urgency lending an edge to my voice. 'Are you completely sure?'

'The human skull was freaky enough. Anything hanging from a tree would have scared the bejesus out of me.'

Sharpening my sight in the evening gloom, I hurry to the plum tree and inspect the branches. The bark is intact. Nothing has been hanging from this tree.

'What's so important about a wicker man?' Karrion asks.

'Perhaps nothing. But it's been giving me the creeps every time I've looked at it, and now it seems like it was never here. Makes me wonder what it was?'

'You don't think...?'

'I came within a couple of yards of the wicker man several times. It could easily have attacked me. Why didn't it?'

'Maybe it didn't consider you a threat?'

279

I think back to Bradán's words about Baneacre returning to recharge his power. A rivulet of water slides down my neck, and I recall how cold and tired I am. If we were attacked now, all I would do is lie down in the mud and wait for death. Lady Bergamon's domain is no longer a haven, but my tomb.

'Come on,' Karrion says, disrupting the darkness of my musings. 'Let's get you inside.'

His hold on my wrist is gentle as he steers me past the vegetable patch and through the orchard. I stumble behind him, blinded by despair, until the sight of Lady Bergamon's house returns a spark of hope to my heart. Hobbling up the steps, I am grateful for the meagre warmth the dark house offers. Karrion switches on the kitchen light and shakes water from his coat outside. I pick up my phone and see that I have another two missed calls from Jamie.

'Do you mind making me a sandwich for the drive? If I don't eat something soon, I'm likely to buy witch bubble tea or belladonna ice cream from One Magic Change, and neither seems like a good idea.'

'Of course.' Karrion opens the fridge.

'Thanks. I'm going to check on Lady Bergamon quickly.'

Upstairs, Lady Bergamon remains within the protective circle, but she has grown even paler. We are running out of time in more ways than one. I need to even the odds a little.

The wooden box decorated with a carving of an elder tree is still on the dressing table, and I take two of the cold iron tokens and slip them into the pocket of my jeans, ignoring the discomfort where my bare skin touches the metal. On my phone, I find a number and dial. A cool voice greets me, betraying the barest hint of curiosity.

'Fria? Hi. Remember that favour you owe me?'

32

A PLAN OF ACTION

When I return to the kitchen, I find Karrion standing next to the counter, frowning. On a plate is a stack of sandwiches.

'Has the frogspawn moved?' I ask.

'What? No. It's just... I checked the drawers in the fridge to see if Lady B had any lettuce. She didn't, but I found something else.'

'What's that?'

Instead of responding, Karrion opens the fridge and pulls out one of the vegetable drawers. It contains a selection of small bottles, each with a label of brown paper. Instead of words, the labels have drawings of plants. Calling upon lessons from my childhood, I identify them one by one.

'Lily-of-the-valley, wolf's bane, hemlock, henbane, belladonna, cuckoo-pint,' I pick up a bottle to inspect the label more closely, 'seer's sage and destroying angel.'

'I'm no herbalist, but aren't all of those poisonous?'

'Not just poisonous, but deadly. With the exception of this.' I point to the bottle containing the seer's sage. 'That's hallucinogenic. I've heard of some Wild Folk using it to access a dream stage that would allow them to connect with the collective memories of our ancestors. Regardless of whether they succeeded, the trips were intense.'

281

'Why would Lady B have seer's sage?' Karrion reaches past the bottles and shows me a clear zip lock bag. 'More importantly, why would she have these?'

The plastic bag contains dried mushrooms. I frown as I go through a mental list of edible and poisonous mushrooms found on the British Isles.

'Are those liberty caps?' I ask.

'You can use their proper name if you like, but among the youths of Old London, they're just called shrooms.'

'Magic mushrooms?'

'Yep.' Karrion grins. 'Lady B has a baggie of shrooms. How awesome is she?'

'Why would she have magic mushrooms?'

'Maybe she likes the occasional high?'

'That seems unlikely. Perhaps they're for inducing visions, like the seer's sage. Or perhaps they're not for her at all.' As soon as the words leave my mouth, I wonder at the wisdom of them.

'What do you mean?'

'People taking hallucinogens tend to be fairly mellow. Easy to handle.'

'Or easy to manipulate?' From his expression, I see that Karrion has reached the same conclusion as I have.

I nod. 'Why else would she store them with an array of poisons? I doubt we were meant to see those.'

'The bottles worry me even more than the shrooms. Why would she have so many different poisons and in those kinds of quantities?'

Pausing to run my finger along the tops of the bottles, I wonder how best to reply. 'Some of them probably have medicinal value, if administered in the right quantity. As for others, they are deadly. No two ways about it. Lady Bergamon must have her reasons for keeping a store of poisons.'

Although I choose not to voice it, I do wonder whether

the array before us has anything to do with the crumpled-up letter we found in the lounge yesterday.

'Let's put them back,' I say, and pick up the drawer. Karrion holds the fridge door open for me.

'It worries me, you know,' he says, voice soft. 'A stock of poisons makes sense for a Plant Shaman, but it seems too much of a coincidence that the drawer includes both belladonna and destroying angel.'

'You wouldn't be able to kill someone the way Hailfax and Cullingwoed were murdered using the bottles in the fridge. But I wonder if Lady Bergamon's poison collection influenced Baneacre.'

'Do you think he stopped to look in the fridge on his way through the house?' Karrion asks.

'No, but he learned about the Ivy Street Project somehow. Perhaps he discovered her stash of poisons the same way. We keep coming back to the same problem: Lady Bergamon's and Baneacre's actions don't make any sense.'

'But he's not human. Why are we trying to apply human logic to his actions? And given how old Lady B is, maybe the same goes for her.'

'We keep trying to make sense of things our way because it's the only way of thinking we can perceive. Even after my brief trip to the Unseen Lands, I can't claim to have any better understanding of the Fey and how they think. I'm not sure what it would take for a human to gain such insight, but I doubt it would be pleasant.'

My phone rings before Karrion has a chance to reply. Jamie's name flashes on the screen, and I experience a stab of guilt at not having returned his calls sooner. As far as he knows, I have dropped off the face of the earth for several hours.

'I texted him earlier to say that you were running down a lead and might be unavailable for a bit.'

'Thanks.' I answer the call as I tear off some kitchen

roll and wrap it around the sandwiches. 'Jamie, sorry for the silence.'

'Did your lead pan out?' he asks, and I can hear traffic noises in the background.

'Yes, we have a suspect.'

Before the words left my mouth, I was not certain what I was intending to tell Jamie. I have kept him in the dark more than I would have liked. It is not in my nature to be deceitful, yet that is what I have become over the past two days.

'Tell me more,' Jamie says, derailing my thoughts.

I motion for Karrion to bring the sword and head for the front door. 'We're still working on an angle, but we think the killer is a Fey who is stealing magic from Mages to raise a Fey Mound in the middle of Old London and rule as the king of rot and decay.'

There is only silence at the other end of the line as I lock the door behind us and pocket the key. A couple walking a dog has stopped by the fence to stare at the front garden. Karrion has got out a chocolate bar, which he opens and drops the wrapper on the nearest plant pots. I frown briefly, but then Jamie's voice causes me to forget what concerned me.

'You might want to back up a little. Or a lot. I'm not fussy.'

We get in to the car, and I switch the call to speaker. Karrion takes the phone and holds it between us. While I navigate the afternoon traffic towards One Magic Change, I recount my conversation with Sister Alissa and my visit to the Unseen Lands. When I have finished my part of the story, Karrion continues while I take bites of my sandwich. Jamie is particularly interested in our speculation about potential victims for tonight.

'Good work, you two. But how did the Fey know to target these specific Mages?'

'We're not completely sure,' Karrion lies. 'Maybe Baneacre killed Laene at random, perhaps drawn by all the Samhain decorations, and discovered a whole host of other Mages from reading Laene's mind.'

'Can the Fey read minds?' Jamie asks, sounding concerned.

'No idea. But if they can steal a Mage's magic, I don't think it's that much of a stretch to say they might be able to read minds too.'

While I chew, I raise an eyebrow at Karrion, who shrugs. He is a smoother liar than I expected. I must bear that in mind.

'How did you know the killer was a Fey?'

'I didn't for sure. But it was odd how the food in metal containers was fine at the Cullingwoeds' residence, when everything else had gone off. After I'd spoken to Sister Alissa, it occurred to me that perhaps the killer wasn't troubled by the wards because they were raised using heart copper foci. Things might have been different if our victims had more cold iron in their home security. And don't forget this all began on Samhain, when travel between the worlds is easier than usual.'

'And how did you make the trip to the Unseen Lands?' In Jamie's voice, I hear a familiar longing.

'I managed to find a Fey who has his own reasons for wanting to see Baneacre stopped.'

'His reasons being?'

'All to do with Fey politics.'

'I didn't know you had Fey contacts,' Jamie says.

'Bradán is not really a contact, more like a friend of a friend. Going to him for help was my last resort, and he was no keener to act as my guide.'

'I see.' Jamie coughs. 'Other than warning the Mages we think he might target, how are we going to stop this Baneacre?'

'We've been working on a weapon that should affect him, though we still need to cover it in cold iron,' I say between bites.

'What sort of a weapon? As much as you're consulting for the Met, I do need to warn you that it's illegal to carry knives and unlicensed guns.'

'What does the law say about a sword made of yew?'

'A wooden sword is hardly a weapon on its own. I suppose it depends on how the cold iron coating is going to change it.'

'I'll let you know when we find out, though in truth, I'm not sure what choice we have. Normal weapons aren't going to work on a Fey.'

'That's exactly what I didn't want to hear.'

'I'm sorry, Jamie. As much as I hate to say this, we're making this up as we go along and still learning.'

'Do you think the Paladins might have something that could work on the Fey?' he asks.

'Possibly. Their swords are part cold iron and contain some serious spell power. But would the presence of the other metals lessen the effect of the cold iron? I'm not sure. All I know is that I was told a weapon of yew and cold iron would definitely work.'

'And you're sure you can trust your source?'

I hesitate, the memory of Tem being torn apart by the hounds bringing bile to my throat. My hunger gone, I set the rest of my sandwich down.

'Yan nearly died getting the information. That should tell you something about its authenticity.'

'You what?' Jamie asks while I glare at Karrion.

'Things got a bit hairy for a while, but it wasn't that bad.' I silence Karrion's objections with another glare. 'But under the rules of the combat, I won the challenge and my opponent was honour-bound to answer my questions truthfully. This weapon should do the trick once it's finished.'

286

'If you say it will work, then I'll trust you. This is why the Met agreed to hire you as consultants: your methods are different from ours. That said, Yannia, I don't appreciate not being kept in the loop. Our agreement was that we'd share our findings and yet you've held information back since the beginning.'

My cheeks heat, and I bite my lip as I fix my eyes on the road.

'I'm sorry, Jamie.'

'You achieve a lot and I appreciate your efficiency. But trust is a two-way thing. I trust you and I hope you trust me.'

'I do trust you,' I whisper, my voice breaking.

'Time will tell.'

Rubbing my face, I try to find something to say, but no words seem adequate.

Before the silence goes on for too long, Karrion clears his throat. 'Did you receive the autopsy results on Cullingwoed and Bleckbyrne?'

'I did. At this stage, I don't think it comes as any surprise that both had been subjected to a kiss of death.'

Although it is the news I was expecting, my stomach flutters from the relief. Lady Bergamon has no need to steal the power of Mages, whereas Baneacre has. Four Mages having lost the secret to their magic tips the scales further from Lady Bergamon.

'It's what we expected, though knowing that Baneacre will have acquired that much power isn't good news.'

'I don't know,' Karrion says. 'If his magic type is taking on elements of Mage power, won't that mean the Paladins' swords are more likely to work? Heart copper to defeat the Mage within him, and cold iron to finish off the rest.'

'It's a good point. I'll ask the Paladins,' Jamie says.

I glance at Karrion. 'I don't know if combining power

types works that way, but it's worth a try. We don't have a lot to lose.'

'Except our lives.' Karrion shrugs at my look of surprise. 'I'm just saying. Baneacre is unlikely to be a nice guy. Though he ought to be less interested in us given that we're not Mages.'

Thinking back to the first time I met Eolande Pearson, I recall the curiosity with which she greeted me. If her full-blooded kin is anything like her, Baneacre may well find me intriguing. I hope not. At the very least, Karrion should be safe.

'Anything else in the autopsies?' I ask.

'Lianne Bleckbyrne's blood alcohol content was so high she never knew there was an intruder in her bedroom. The pathologist thinks she died without ever regaining consciousness.'

'It's a small mercy, I suppose. Drowning in your bed must be a terrible way to die.'

'No worse than having mushrooms sprout across your body,' Jamie says. 'The pathologist ruled Cullingwoed's cause of death as a heart attack brought on by shock.'

'A quicker way to die than organ failure from the destroying angel poisoning.'

'I think we can agree they're all terrible ways to die,' Karrion says. 'Do you think Baneacre gains extra power from causing suffering to his victims?'

'Perhaps. Or maybe he doesn't care how he kills.'

Some of the colour drains from Karrion's face, emphasising his black hair. 'Are you saying it makes no difference to him whether he kills quickly or slowly?'

'Don't forget he's a Fey. They may have a different notion of suffering compared to ours.' I find a parking spot near One Magic Change and parallel park with practised ease. 'Anything else you have for us, Jamie?'

'Not at this stage. Everything else about the autopsies

was as we speculated. Goorge Bleckbyrne's alibi appears solid, though I have people tracking down more of the regulars at his local haunt. And I haven't got anywhere with Ivy Street yet. There are too many houses and too many names to narrow it down in just a few hours.'

Perhaps that dead end will keep Jamie busy while we pursue the real killer. I shake my head to dismiss the thought. We will need his help if we are to protect the Mages.

'We need to go. Will you find out the addresses for Amitta Pandia and the Shadow Mages? Though I think we need to warn Amitta and Lord Ellensthorne in person as they are the most likely victims.'

'I'll get her address and alert the Paladins. When you're done at One Magic Change, let me know where you want to meet.'

'Thanks, Jamie.'

We end the call. Karrion shrugs off his leather jacket and wraps it around the sword. I praise him for his fore-thought. As much as it is made of wood, if we walked through One Magic Change carrying a sword, we would attract the attention of the Paladin patrols. We could probably explain our way out of the situation, but why waste time if we don't have to?

This time I spare no more than a passing glance at the illusionists entertaining the crowds. Karrion is hot on my heels as we take the stairs two at a time, climbing through the levels to the workshops. As I push open the door to Thaylor's workshop, I notice that the jade statue of a cat in the window has its eyes closed.

Inside, Thaylor is handing a parcel wrapped in brown paper to a woman in a red coat. A cursory inhale indi-cates that the customer is a human, and she clutches the parcel to her chest as if we are about to steal it. She hurries out, and the chimes by the door remain silent.

'I was beginning to wonder if you were coming at all,' Thaylor says and adjusts her goggles.

'Sorry about the delay. Fashioning a sword by hand takes time.'

'No matter, you are here now. Let's have a look.'

Karrion untangles the sword from his coat and lays it on the counter. Thaylor leans closer to examine it, going as far as smelling the wood. She looks up.

'Yew?'

I nod.

Thaylor cocks her head and blinks, the goggles giving her an insectoid appearance. 'If the old stories are anything to go by, yew is good for defeating the Fey.'

'So I've heard.'

She lets the silence continue a second or two longer than necessary before picking up the sword. 'Very well. I'll cover this in cold iron and sharpen its edges so it will become a true weapon.'

'How long will it take?' Karrion asks.

'A couple of hours, no more. I'll call you when it's finished.'

'Thanks,' I say. 'And payment?'

'Upon completion.'

'We'll see you soon, then.'

Thaylor follows us as far as the shop door. As soon as we have stepped out, I hear three locks sliding into place. The shop is closed for business. As we head for the stairs, I glance back and see that the jade cat's eyes are now open.

33

THE FEY MOUND

'What are we going to do while we wait to hear from Jamie and Thaylor?' Karrion asks as we walk out of the glass corridor of One Magic Change.

'I wouldn't mind stopping at home to take a hot shower, find dry clothes and some pain meds.'

'And you can finish your lunch.'

'That too, all the while panicking that I'm supposed to stop a Fey with a wooden sword I don't know how to use.'

'With your talents, you're one small step away from being a superhero.'

'What do you expect me to do? Stop a murderer by channelling my inner honey badger.'

'Please let me see that.'

'I'd rather you didn't have to. There must be a better way to deal with Baneacre.'

'Do you think we should try to find his Fey Mound? It must be somewhere in Old London, right?'

It begins to drizzle, and I hurry the last few steps to the car. Once inside, I push damp strands of hair off my face.

'Trying to locate the mound isn't a bad idea. I don't know if there's anything we could do to collapse it, assuming it has a physical shape, but it's worth a try.'

Karrion's magic expands like a cockerel preening his feathers. 'Great. Now how do we find it?'

'It's probably in one of the parks or private gardens.' My foot eases off the accelerator. 'What if it's in Lady Bergamon's garden?'

'Don't you think Bradán would have mentioned that?'

'Not if he and Lady Bergamon are using Baneacre to get rid of the Mages. It's possible that when he left to search for Baneacre, it was to warn him instead.'

'Then what do we do?' Karrion asks, frustration clipping each word.

'Hope that we're wrong about that. Let's assume for now that we can trust Bradán and that the Fey mound is in Old London rather than Lady Bergamon's garden. It's going to be somewhere natural, but it will take a while to check all places like that. How can we find a shortcut?'

'Could we ask the Paladins whether the patrols have noticed anything out of the ordinary in the past couple of days?'

'Great idea. Let that be your task while I try to defrost in the shower.'

'No problem, boss.'

The downstairs of my flat is cold and damp, but I hurry in just the same. The familiar smells and creak of the stairs reassure me. Upstairs, I pause by the fireplace to run my hand over the uneven bricks of the hearth. Soot stains my fingers, and I rub it deeper into the crevices of my fingers. This is real. This is home. I am safe.

Karrion's stare is what causes me to move, and I offer him a vague smile as I continue to the kitchen. After washing my hands, I take pain meds and finish my sandwich. My elbow nudges the empty foil strip of medication, and it falls off the counter. I leave it where it lands on the floor. Karrion sets the kettle to boil while I gather clothes from the wardrobe and head down-stairs.

Once I have peeled off the layers of sodden clothes, I survey the mottled map of bruises across my torso. The cut on my thigh has scabbed over. My fingers find the knife wound. Although it has been mere hours since Tem stabbed me, the jagged line on the side of my abdomen is a faded silver. As I step under the hot spray, the memory of the searing pain permeates my mind. I begin to shake, and strength leaves my legs until I slide down the wall to sit in the tub. Sobs wrack my body as the shower and my tears purge the numbness that has plagued me since I returned from the Unseen Lands. I cry until all the terror, pain and doubt have slipped down the drain, leaving me empty and exhausted.

The cooling water forces me to move, and I stand with a groan. I experience a moment of light-headedness and cling to the wall until the world settles. My hands tremble when I reach for the shower gel, and the shaking does not ease until I have dried off and dressed. The medication takes effect, and I struggle to climb the stairs.

When I push open the door leading to the lounge, I am surprised to see Karrion pacing the room and Wishearth sitting on the hearth stones in front of a blazing fire. They both turn to me.

'What's going on?'

'Sorry, Yan,' Karrion says, tugging at the row of piercings on his left ear. 'You were crying and I didn't know what to do except build a fire and ask for Wishearth's advice.'

'I didn't know you two were close,' I say and drape the towel and my wet clothes on an airer.

'There's no shame in asking for help.'

Wishearth's words draw my attention to him, and a flush creeps over my cheeks. I recall the warmth he gave me in Lady Bergamon's bedroom, and the memory makes it hard to meet his gaze. Karrion's presence only adds to the awkwardness I feel.

'We have work to do,' I say, knowing how feeble my protest sounds.

'Not right now. I'm waiting for the Paladins to call me back and you had no calls or messages while you were in the shower. You can afford a short break.'

A tremor runs through me, and Wishearth rises from his spot by the fire.

'Come.'

Out of instinct, I reach to take the offered hand. He draws me to the mattress, ignoring my hesitation.

'Sit.'

Too tired to worry about grace, I slump down. Wishearth sits behind me, and straight away a wall of warmth washes through my weary muscles and bones. When I remain stiff, he tugs me into his embrace and I allow myself to relax. Wishearth is solid against my back, and in a remote corner of my mind, I know this should surprise me. Heat penetrates my body as I rest my head on his shoulder. Gentle fingers gather my wet hair and move it out of the way. Wishearth's breath tickles the side of my neck, and I find it curious that he breathes like a mortal. The smell of wood smoke chases away the remaining tension.

'Wishearth,' I begin, but he lets me get no further.

'Just relax,' he says, and heat strokes the shell of my ear. 'You're safe.'

The creak of a floorboard causes me to open my eyes long enough to watch as Karrion turns away. His expression conveys jealousy and embarrassment in equal measures. I have no chance to consider him further before my eyes flutter closed. The last things I am aware of are Wishearth's breath caressing my cheek and his hands coming to rest over mine.

Karrion's phone blaring heavy metal startles me awake. He curses softly, and from the sound of retreating footsteps, I realise he leaves the room. I rub my eyes and push myself onto my elbow. At some point since falling asleep, I have ended up on my side on the mattress, facing the fire. Wishearth is nowhere to be seen, but his warmth lingers within me.

It feels as though I have been asleep for hours. I fumble around, trying to recall what I did with my phone, and I am still pushing myself up when Karrion returns.

'Take it easy,' he says and hurries to grab my arm.

Once I find my balance, I reassure him with a smile, and locate my phone on the kitchen counter. I see that I have only been asleep for half an hour. My stomach growls while Karrion pours me coffee.

'Here.' He hands me the mug and gets a plate of sandwiches out of the fridge. 'You need to shop more often. This was the best I could do without leaving you alone.'

'What happened to Wishearth?'

Something flashes across Karrion's face, too fast for my bleary eyes to register, and he busies himself by adding sugar to his coffee.

'I don't know. One moment he was there, the next he was gone.'

Setting down my mug untouched, I rise to my tiptoes and hug Karrion. He stiffens before wrapping his arms around me.

'Thanks for earlier. I needed that.'

'The way you were looking at the fireplace, I figured you wanted Wishearth.'

'No. I needed you both. The reason I could fall apart in the shower was that I knew I was safe here. Not just because it's my home and there's a fireplace, but because you were here.'

The tightness around Karrion's eyes lifts as he smiles. 'I'm glad. Are you okay?'

'Much better.' I take a long sip of my coffee. 'Especially now.'

'There's plenty more food and coffee.'

'What did the Paladins say?'

'That you need to eat more.' Karrion laughs, but after a glare from me, he relents. 'They have a possible spot for us, but I'm not sure it's right.'

'Why?'

'It's a construction site, not a park.'

'Odd. We'll have to take a look to know whether it's the right spot.'

I finish my sandwich and decline Karrion's offer of more coffee. While he clears the plate, I transfer the cold iron tokens to the pocket of my fleece.

The rain has increased in pace while I was asleep, and I pull up the hood of my coat as we hurry to the car. Out of habit, I glance at the upstairs windows, but they remain dark. The landlord has yet to let out Jans's old flat.

Karrion's directions take us near Farringdon Station, not far from where he lives with his mother and half-siblings. When he said we were going to a construction site, I expected to see a half-finished building buzzing with people and surrounded by lorries. Instead, we come to a gap between two buildings, where a structure has been demolished. A chain-link fence cordons off the area from the pavement, though there is a gap between two sections just wide enough for someone to squeeze through. There is no one about, but the ground is covered in rubbish, as if bin lorries have dumped it there on purpose. Street lamps cast pallid pools of light amidst the mounds of litter.

At the centre of the area are stone pillars that look to have been made from compressed rubble. Their placing strikes me as odd.

'Which way is north?'

'Shouldn't you know that sort of stuff?' Karrion asks with a grin.

'Now you're beginning to sound like Wishearth.'

He pulls a face and points the way we came.

Having found my bearings, I see two of the pillars are standing a couple of yards apart, facing east. Three others appear to mark edges of an area, while a sixth stands at the centre. My hand dips inside my coat and finds the cold iron discs. Touching them turns my stomach, but as soon as I do, my vision shifts.

The pillars mark the edges of the Fey Mound. Walls of the síd keep forming and reforming in a hypnotic pulse that increases my nausea. Instead of rubble, they are made of litter and slime moulds. Dodder and bindweed appear to thrive without a host plant. Purple toothwort adds a splash of colour that seems out of place amidst the discarded plastic and dripping fungi. Coils of ivy are choking the síd, yet I sense definite power from within.

With my altered view of the world, I notice movement beyond the síd and squeeze through the gap in the chain-link fence. Karrion calls my name, but I ignore him as I pick my way around the mounds of litter.

A figure dressed in a morning suit and a top hat is dancing the tango amidst rotting food and discarded plastic waste. The last time I saw him, I thought he was one of the Feykin. But now his copper hair blazes around his shoulders in a mantle of flames and a prehensile tail sways to the rhythm of his dance. He seems taller than before; his limbs unnaturally long.

I must make a noise for he executes a precise turn and stops. The purple eyes regarding me have slit pupils, and something about the swirling colours leads me to fix my gaze on the tip of his pointed nose.

'My, my, a little fly,' he says. 'You have travelled far today.'

'Who are you?'

'The name, little fly, is Declan Pheonix.' He speaks with an Irish accent, though I am certain he had no such accent when last we spoke. Removing his top hat with a flourish, he bows low.

'Who are you?' I ask again.

'A better question is: who are you?'

Thrown by his words, I pause. 'Yannia Wilde.'

'I think not. Perhaps you are a creature of ice and shadow. A wild hunter. Part of the pack.'

Bile rises in my throat. 'I'm mortal.'

'You assume the hounds are born, not made.'

I recoil from him, and my foot lands on a pile of crushed cans. Stumbling, I throw my arms wide to keep my balance. Pheonix smirks.

'Once upon a time, there was a Queen who needed hounds. Twice upon a land, they hunted and all cowered along their path. Thrice upon our memory, their bays strike fear into the hearts of mortals.'

The baying echoes in the confines of my memory, and I relive the moment when Tem's blood sprayed across my face. That I spilled his blood first and enjoyed it does little to ease my tripping pulse.

'You carry such fear, little fly. It makes you quite irresistible.' A forked tongue flicks out to taste the air between us.

My hand clenches around the tokens hard enough to cause sparks of pain where the edges dig into my palm. With effort, I manage to slow down my heart rate. Pheonix drops his gaze to my hand and he tuts.

'Most impolite. That's like taking a bomb vest to a pride march.'

Unwilling to apologise, I straighten my shoulders and lift my chin. 'Where is Baneacre?'

'My Cyning is not receiving at present.'

'What? Baneacre is an Autumn Champion, not the Summer King.'

'You mortals have multiple kings and the Aes Sídhe already has two Courts. Old London shall have a Cyning and our lands a new Court to rival that of the Winter Cwēn.'

'Old London already has a queen.'

'No human is a match for my Cyning.' Pheonix leans forward, eyes glittering like amethysts. 'No mortal is a match for him.'

'Not even one who takes a bomb to a pride march?'

Pheonix chuckles. 'Your little tokens can do no harm to one such as my Cyning.'

Enough of tipping my hand. 'I'd best dust off my ball gown for the coronation.'

'You shall be a guest of honour.' He laughs like a crackle of fire and bows again.

A glint of light on a stagnant puddle diverts my attention. Where is the light coming from? When I look back towards Pheonix, I find myself alone in the construction site.

299

34

THE DECAY OF OLD LONDON

Karrion is not where I left him. I spot him across the street, next to a bin. Jogging across the street, I dodge around a car as he dips his hand into the bin and pulls out a handful of litter. He appears fully absorbed in the task as he drops the cigarette packs, chocolate wrappers and pieces of paper on the ground.

'What are you doing?'

'I grew tired of waiting,' he says and reaches for another handful of litter.

'Yes, but why are you doing that?' Looking back the way I came, I see a ring of rubbish around the bin closest to the construction site.

'I grew tired of waiting.'

'Right. We should go.'

'In a minute.'

A cramp in my hand reminds me that I am still clutching the cold iron tokens. Forcing open my stiff fingers, I offer one of them to Karrion.

'Take this.'

His expression is unfocused, but he takes it with the hand not clutching a plastic bottle. As soon as he does, he blinks.

'What?'

Dropping the bottle, Karrion stares at the hand covered in mustard stains and ash before pulling a face.

After a quick search through my pockets, I hand him a tissue.

'Thanks. And also, eww.'

My eyes are drawn to the bin and my fingers twitch, but I am able to resist the urge to dive in. A shudder runs through me as I glance over my shoulder to the pillars of the Fey Mound.

'We need to go,' I say, taking a step away from the bin.

Karrion wipes the worst of the stains off and drops the tissue. He frowns, but does not move it to the bin.

'Yeah, let's go.'

As we head towards the car, a young man steps onto the road, carrying a six-pack of beer. One by one, he detaches the bottles from the cardboard packaging and smashes them on the road. A Paladin watches with a blank expression; a hand on the hilt of his sword.

It is only when we are back in the car that I can relax. A pressure against my temples I was unaware of until now eases. The air still feels charged, but less than outside.

I dig out an old bottle of hand sanitizer from the glove compartment and hand it to Karrion. He applies it liberally to both hands, balancing the cold iron disc on his knee.

'What just happened?'

'I'm not sure, but I think it has something to do with Baneacre or the Fey Mound. Possibly both.'

'Baneacre wants to make me dig around in bins?'

Tapping the token against my chin, I stare at the road. For the first time, I notice all the litter gathering against the kerbs and clogging a nearby drain cover. Yellow leaves add a splash of colour to the fast food wrappers, cans and plastic bags. It is as though all the trees in Old London have dropped their leaves in one go. Perhaps they have. But whatever Baneacre is doing, the Fey Mound is the epicentre of it.

'There's more to it than that. I think he's turning Old London into a reflection of who he is.'

'He's into rubbish?'

'He's one of the Death Lords. Decay and rot are what he's all about. It stands to reason that he wants his kingdom to reflect that.'

Karrion stares out of the window. 'We need to stop him.'

'I know.'

'No, I mean we really need to stop him. We can't live in a city like this.'

Reaching across, I lay a hand on his arm. 'Karrion, I know. If I struggled to find a place in Old London before, I won't survive in a city where the only natural life is mould and people.'

'Any word from Thaylor or Jamie?'

'No. I ought to text Jamie to see where he's at with those addresses.' I reach for my phone. I frown. 'Wait. What time is it?'

Karrion checks his phone. 'My phone thinks it's nearly eight. That can't be right.'

'That's what I thought.' I show him my phone. 'How long did I spend in that construction site?'

'Didn't you say more time passed in the Unseen Lands than here? Maybe here it works in reverse.'

'Damn. We couldn't really afford to lose those two hours. Jamie will think I've gone AWOL again.'

The screen shows that I have two missed calls and a text from Jamie. Both Thaylor and Fria have called, and I have two voicemails. Thaylor says she has finished the sword and will keep her shop open late for us to pick it up. Fria's states only that she is heading to One Magic Change.

'Can you call Thaylor and tell her we're on our way?' I ask, and hand my phone to Karrion. 'And then call Jamie to organise where we're going to meet him.'

As I navigate towards One Magic Change, the amount of rubbish on the streets gradually decreases, but never disappears altogether. I watch as several people drop litter where they stand, regardless of their proximity to the nearest bin. The realisation is slow to come, but each such instance prompts my memory of Mery and Karrion's similar behaviour. I too have done it. As much as I was aware of it on some level, the thought of cleaning up never entered my mind.

Just how powerful is Baneacre?

We park near the same spot as before and hurry through One Magic Change to the top floor. Most of the workshops are already dark, but light is spilling out of Thaylor's Tinkerings. The eyes of the jade cat are open.

As soon as we enter, Thaylor looks through the beaded curtain and nods. She withdraws from view and, after a clatter of metal, returns with a long wrapped bundle.

'All done for you.'

Thaylor sets the bundle on the counter and peels back the cloth to reveal the sword. In just a couple of hours and with the help of her magic, she has transformed a clumsy piece of wood into a weapon. Her aura is barely detectable. Working this much cold iron must have cost her a great deal of power.

'I polished the sword with yew oil,' Thaylor says, 'just on the off chance that you were going after a Fey and needed every advantage.'

'Thank you.'

My hand trembles as I reach out and grip the hilt. Although the metal ends on the far side of the arm guard, the cold iron sends my skin crawling. The magical part of me recognises the material that will null my power.

How am I supposed to wield a weapon that could just as easily be used against me?

Nausea causes me to let go of the sword and clap a hand over my mouth. Thaylor notices my desperate look.

'The toilet is at the far end of my workshop.'

The bead curtain rattles as I sweep it aside and rush past the cluttered workbenches. I have no time to take in the details of the tiny loo before I bend over the toilet and lose my lunch.

Once my heaving has ceased, I remain crouched on the floor for a few more minutes while my breathing evens out. It is easier to stare at the faded tiles on the wall than to face Thaylor and Karrion when I have just made a huge mistake.

All this time and effort wasted, and for what? My plan B is little more than an afterthought.

When my legs have gone numb, I force myself to stand and flush the toilet. A few handfuls of cold water wash the taste of vomit from my mouth, but I am shaking. Feeling returns to my legs in a tingling rush of blood, and I leave the toilet.

Karrion is hovering by the bead curtain, and his frown eases when he spots me. When I walk past him, he gives my hand a quick squeeze. I offer him a small smile in return.

'Feeling better?' Thaylor asks.

'Not really. I'm not sure the sword was a good idea.'

'That's because you gripped it with your bare hands. It takes the Paladins of Justice years to learn how to handle weapons forged partly of true silver without it impacting their power. That's why so many of those who join the Brotherhood never become Paladins.'

I bite my lip. 'I didn't know that.'

'One of the benefits of the city upbringing, I suppose.' Thaylor reaches beneath the counter and sets a pair of elbow-length leather gloves next to the sword. The material is pitted and scarred like her apron. 'Try these on.'

On the fingers and palms, the leather is dark and smooth. With some difficulty, I pull the gloves on. They are a fraction short, but it is a mild inconvenience. The wide ends flap around my elbows as I test the mobility of my hands. When everything works fine, I hesitate only briefly before gripping the sword again.

Although the proximity to cold iron causes me to shudder, the nausea remains under control. This time, I feel as though I could hold the sword for a little while. But the gloves have resolved only half of my problem.

'But what's to stop someone turning the sword on me? If they can be harmed by the cold iron, so can I.'

'By someone, I'm going to assume a Fey.' Thaylor pauses, but when I offer no response, she shrugs. 'A Fey would not be able to touch a sword of yew and cold iron.'

'Fantastic,' Karrion says with a grin.

'However,' Thaylor continues, her bushy eyebrows pressing on the top of her goggles, 'that doesn't mean they don't have other means to harm you. You must take care, Yannia.'

'I will. Thank you.'

'Fria asked me to give you something. These are all I had time to make after I finished the sword.'

Reaching under the counter a second time, Thaylor hands me a small velvet pouch. It is light, but I hear the dull clink of metal on metal from within. I count four, maybe five small shapes through the material before tucking the pouch in my pocket.

'Great.' I nod my thanks, all the while ignoring the curiosity radiating from Karrion.

'Then it's a simple matter of payment. I would like the gloves back, preferably without too much blood on them. The sword is going to cost you a great deal, but if you bring it back and I can reuse the cold iron, I will give you a partial refund.'

'Understood. If the sword isn't too broken and bloodied, I'll return it. After tonight, I'd like to think I won't have too much use for a yew sword.'

Even as the words leave my mouth, I recall the Winter Queen's icy kiss. Perhaps I am being overly optimistic.

As I grab my wallet, Thaylor says the sum and I swallow. That will use up most of my credit limit. Still, we have little choice, but I resolve to return the sword first thing tomorrow morning.

After I have paid, Thaylor wraps the sword and ties it with a length of twine. Even with the cloth between my hand and cold iron, I opt to let Karrion carry the package.

Thaylor walks us to the door and holds it open for us. 'Best of luck.'

We acknowledge the gravity of her words with a nod. By the time we have reached the top of the stairs, Thaylor's Tinkerings has gone dark.

On the final set of stairs, I am getting my phone out when I sense an aura of power brushing against mine, soft as kitten fur. Looking around, I spot Fria in the shadows of the second staircase. She steps into the light, her gaze sweeping over both Karrion and me.

'Do you mind going ahead to the car?' I ask and dig out the car keys.

'What? Why?'

'There's something I need to take care of quickly.'

Karrion follows my gaze to Fria, and his power flares in a ruffle of feathers. While his expression turns sour, I notice that his eyes linger on Fria's black leather boots, blue jeans, and black leather jacket.

'Fine,' he says with a huff. 'Just remember that we're on a deadline.'

He leaves, shoulders stiff and his free hand clenched into a fist.

'You keep interesting company,' says Fria as she approaches and leans against the railing. Unlike Karrion's, her posture is relaxed and open.

'He's my apprentice.'

'I'm aware.'

'That ought to explain why I spend so much time with him.'

Fria shrugs. 'At least you're expanding your contact list.' Her eyes flicker up.

'Thank you for recommending Thaylor. She's good at her job.'

'I know.'

Her nonchalance is at odds with my sense of urgency, and I shift. Her eyebrow twitches, but she seems content to study me.

'Do you have it?'

'I'm surprised you called in the favour. I had you down as a person whose moral code is too strict to work with the likes of me.'

'You learn something new every day,' I say, trying to keep my impatience from my voice. 'Did you get it?'

'Your request also surprised me. Again, it was at odds with the picture I had formed of you.'

'Pictures lie. Do you have it?'

Fria slips off a black rucksack that blended so well with her jacket I never noticed it. From it, she takes a small bag bearing the name Magisto: the largest artefact store in One Magic Change. She passes it to me, and I am surprised by the weight.

'Do you know how to use it?'

'I'll be fine.'

'Fair enough.'

I fold the bag around its contents and push it into my coat pocket. The weight is reassuring.

'Thank you,' I say, part turning towards the exit.

307

'We are now even.'

I nod. 'Yes, we are.'

Fria shifts half a step closer. 'Still, if you happen to need help in the future, I'm sure we can work something out.'

Ducking my head to hide a smile, I move my hand to the weight in my pocket. 'I'll bear that in mind.'

'It's settled then.'

She leaves without a goodbye. In the sway of her hips, it is easy to imagine her with a tail. Right now, it would be snaking a pattern of pleasure in her wake; pleasure I cannot quite fathom.

35

DELIVERING A WARNING

'What was that all about?' Karrion asks when I get in the car.

'I asked Fria to help me out with something.'

'Why would you need her help?'

In Karrion's voice, I hear the distrust that comes naturally to Bird Shamans when they are dealing with Cat Shamans. As much as he thinks Fria is beautiful, all of Karrion's instincts tell him she is dangerous. They are right.

'It wasn't something you and I could accomplish, or that I would want to attempt.'

'Why?'

'Because what she did was illegal and I didn't want to put you in danger of getting arrested.'

'Oh.' The lines across Karrion's forehead disappear. 'Thanks. I guess.'

'Any word from Jamie?'

'Yes, he texted you a few minutes ago,' Karrion says, and hands me back my phone. 'I figured you wouldn't mind if I read the message. He said to meet him at Amitta Pandia's home address. Apparently, she'd left her office by the time Jamie got there.'

'Fine. Where are we going?'

Amitta Pandia lives on the corner of Newman's Row and Lincoln's Inn Fields near the John Sloane Museum.

The house is not far from the Bleckbyrnes'. In the darkness and rain, Lincoln's Inn Fields looks uninviting, even to me. When we leave the car, the breeze carries the scents of rotting wood and spoilt food from the park. I rub my nose and greet Jamie, who approaches from the opposite direction.

'Did you find what you needed?' he asks.

'We did. I just hope it will be enough.'

'We'll do what we can here. The Paladins weren't sure about whether their swords would work against a Fey. They offered to look through their library for accounts of similar incidents in the past, but I said it would take too long. As a second best option, the captain of the guards promised to send Paladins to guard the houses of our potential victims.'

Jamie steps past the black wrought iron fence and strides up the steps to the black front door. On the ground floor, the facade of the house is white, and on the other three floors, the windows are surrounded by white borders against pale beige bricks. While I would expect the white parts to be kept gleaming with the aid of magic, I see rivulets of black soot marring their surface. Baneacre's influence seems to extend everywhere.

A woman in her early fifties opens the door. She is dressed in a pale green skirt and matching jacket, with a white blouse underneath. Framed in the light of the hallway, she seems to glow, and even at this hour, her black hair is carefully styled.

'Yes?' she says with a hint of an accent.

Jamie introduces himself and us, showing her his warrant card. We do the same with our ID badges, and she inspects them.

'My office called to say that a Detective Inspector of New Scotland Yard had stopped by, looking for me. Normally you would have found me there, but I had a late client meeting that overran and I came straight home.'

310

'May we come in?'

'Of course.' She steps aside and admits us in to the hallway.

After the other Mage houses we have seen in the past two days, I was expecting another home straight out of an interior design magazine. Instead, warm colours and natural woods give the hallway a cosy and inviting look. I notice that Karrion relaxes as he looks around.

'We can talk in the kitchen,' Amitta says and opens the nearest door.

The kitchen is in keeping with the hallway. A central island functions as both a food preparation area and a small table, while an Aga stands at the far end. The units are all made of polished pine and the metal finishes have a rustic look. A Weimaraner sleeps on a raised bed next to the Aga.

'Would you like some tea?' Amitta asks and pulls out chairs for us. 'The kettle just boiled.'

There is a cookbook open on the table next to a notepad, and Amitta clears them away before getting mugs from the cupboard. A lull in the conversation follows, punctuated by her checking how we take our tea. When a tea bag slips off a spoon and lands on the floor, she leaves it there. After she has set the mugs on the table, Amitta opens a box of shortbread and sits opposite Jamie.

'So how can I help you?' she asks.

Jamie sips his tea. 'It's more the other way round, actually. I'm sorry to have to come to you with news like this, but I am afraid your life may be in danger.'

Amitta was reaching for the shortbread, but she draws her hand back. 'What? That can't be right. Who would want to harm me?'

'We have reason to believe that a criminal is targeting people connected with the Ivy Street Project.'

311

'I heard about Natheniel and Hynryk, but I didn't realise the deaths were connected.'

Jamie dips a piece of shortbread in his tea. 'I'm afraid Alfread Cullingwoed and Lianne Bleckbyrne have also been killed.'

A whimper escapes Amitta's lips, and she claps a hand over her mouth. Her eyes are wide as she takes a moment to compose herself. We remain silent.

'And you think I'm next?'

'You are one of several potential victims, and we are warning them all to be extra vigilant tonight. My colleague here,' Jamie points to me, 'has some advice about keeping yourself safe, and with your permission, I would like to post a Paladin to guard you tonight. If anything should happen or anyone tries to break in, they will protect you.'

'But why me? Why us?'

'At this point, I am not at liberty to discuss details of an ongoing case. Our priority is ensuring that the culprit will not claim any more victims.'

'Isn't the easiest way of doing that catching him?'

'Yes. And while we are hot on his trail, we are also taking every precaution and warning anyone that might be a potential victim.'

'Why haven't I heard about this in the news?'

'At the present time, we have opted not to inform the media so as not to cause panic.'

Setting down a half-eaten piece of shortbread, Amitta pushes her mug aside. 'I appreciate the warning, but I'm not sure what precautions you're going to recommend. All the doors have double locks, I have an alarm system and the whole house is warded.'

'So far, our suspect appears to have bypassed regular security measures,' I say, speaking for the first time. 'Do you have any cold iron in the house?'

'Cold iron? Your suspect is Feykin?'

'We have reason to believe he carries Fey blood, yes,' Jamie says.

'I may have a trinket or two containing cold iron somewhere in my jewellery box.'

I finish my tea. 'You'll need to find those as soon as possible. Regular iron may also help. Are you familiar with circles?'

'Don't you mean wards?'

'No, I mean the protective circles of old.'

'I'm not sure I know anyone who still holds the knowledge to cast one. Didn't they go out of fashion centuries ago?'

'Fashionable or not, you are going to need one tonight. I'll show you what to do.'

'Fine. The sitting room has space for a circle, I suppose.' An edge of scepticism has crept into her voice.

'Do you want us to wait here?' Karrion asks. I nod, and Jamie, who has already half risen from his seat, settles back down with a look of disappointment.

Amitta takes me down the hall to a spacious sitting room overlooking a tiny paved garden. There is a large, ornate fireplace against the wall adjoining the kitchen. I look at the full wicker basket of logs and wonder if she follows the old ways. Once we have pushed a white sofa and a matching armchair aside, there is enough space for a circle that could protect a makeshift bed.

'You'll need to cast the circle only when you're ready to go to bed. If you step across the threshold in either direction, you'll break the circle.'

'Does that apply to anyone?'

'Just the person raising it,' I say, hoping I sound more knowledgeable than I feel. 'Do you have a candle and warding tokens?'

'Of course. Which kind?'

'Cold iron, if possible.'

Amitta frowns. 'Let me see what I can find. The candles are in the sideboard by the fireplace. Choose whichever one is the most suitable for the circle.'

When she leaves, I open the sideboard doors until I find the candles. An overwhelming mixture of vanilla, sandalwood, mango and lavender causes my eyes to water. I sneeze several times and end up having to pinch my nose shut while I root around the cupboard. Behind boxes of tea lights, I find a white taper and a box of matches.

I have time to inspect the detail of the fireplace for several minutes before Amitta returns carrying a metal box.

'I could only find one cold iron token. What happened to the others, I can't begin to guess. Perhaps I needed an uneven ward area at some point. Will another type do?'

'Heart copper would be the next best thing.'

'That's much easier to manage.'

'Good. Also, do you have a compass?' I ask.

'A compass? What would I need that for?'

'For making sure you place the tokens at the cardinal points.'

'No need for a compass. I always know where east is.'

Of course. She is a Light Mage.

I explain the set up required for the circle and how to raise one, taking care to explain that she also has to close the top and the bottom of it. As I would expect from a Mage, she quizzes me at length about the precise wording for the process. My suggestion that she use whatever words feel natural only baffles her further, and I end up giving her the phrases I used when I raised the circle around Lady Bergamon. Amitta writes them down and then questions me about the emphasis of each invocation and when exactly she should send the power into the boundary. I do my best to answer her questions, though I am left with the impression that she does not think much of me as a teacher. Given how low my power reserves are, I dare not raise a circle to demonstrate the process for fear of depleting the rest of my magic.

When Amitta appears reasonably confident with the process, I suggest we return to the kitchen. As we are about to leave the room, I point to the fireplace.

'I don't know if you follow the old ways in general, but it might be wise to ask for the protection of a Hearth Spirit tonight.'

'It's not something I've ever done. My husband used to believe in Hearth Spirits, and he would never light a fire without making an offering. I always thought it was a quaint habit, but meant very little.'

'You'd be surprised. It's only a suggestion, but in my experience, Hearth Spirits have long memories and they reward loyalty.'

'But after all this time, what will I say?'

'Speak from the heart.' I raise my hand before she can object. 'I know, I've been saying that for the past twenty minutes, but it's true. Hearth Spirits have little regard for the exact wording. They are far more interested in the intention behind the words.'

Amitta laughs and shakes her head. I must look confused for she touches my arm, still grinning. 'I'm sorry, but this is all so mad. You come to my home to tell me that a killer is after me and that the only way to defend myself is through using antiquated warding rituals and prayers to a Hearth Spirit. What next, a wooden sword?'

'Only if it's made of yew.'

It is her turn to look confused.

'I'm sorry,' I say. 'It must be a lot to take in, but I promise that everything we've talked about will help

315

keep you safe. But I wouldn't recommend you ignore your usual wards and alarms either.'

As we walk down the hall, I notice a family portrait of a younger Amitta with a man and two girls, all dressed in traditional Indian garb.

'Are your husband and children at home?' I ask.

Her eyes flicker to the photo and away. 'My husband passed away five years ago and my daughters have families of their own. It's just me and my dog, Merlin, now.'

'I'm sorry for your loss,' I say and follow her into the kitchen.

Jamie rises when we enter. 'All done?'

'Yes.' I turn to Amitta. 'I suggest you make a bed in the sitting room and raise the circle as soon as possible.'

'I will. Thank you.'

'A Paladin will arrive in the next ten minutes,' Jamie says and gets a card out of his wallet. 'Remember, if at any point you feel unsafe, she'll be there. Or, if anything happens during the night, you can give me a call. Any time.'

'Thank you, Detective.' Amitta takes the card. 'For this and for the warning.'

Jamie leads the way to the door. 'Just be safe tonight.'

We have stepped out into the drizzle when Amitta calls after us. 'Wait. What about tomorrow?'

My hand finds the cold iron disc in my pocket as I turn back to her. 'Tomorrow, this should all be over.' One way or the other.

36

RELUCTANT HOST

'That went well,' Jamie says as we descend the stairs.

'Yes, but don't expect such hospitality from Lord Ellensthorne.'

'Oh, great,' Karrion mutters. 'I'd managed to block him from my memory.'

I nudge Karrion with my shoulder. 'Isn't speaking to him the highlight of your day?'

'Sure. Absolutely. I can't wait.'

A taxi stops further down the road, and a Paladin in full armour steps out. She spots Jamie, and they exchange a few words before she knocks on Amitta's door.

'Shall I meet you there?' Jamie asks.

'If you don't need a lift, yes.'

We say our goodbyes and head in opposite directions. As he waits for me to unlock the car, Karrion glances back towards Amitta's house.

'Do you think she's going to be okay?'

'Barring encasing herself in cold iron, a circle is the best protection we can offer against Baneacre. And if luck is on our side, he'll decide to take a break from attacking Mages and we can go after him at the Fey Mound.'

'I'm not sure I'll be of much use there,' Karrion says. 'The glamour swept me away earlier without my having any idea what was happening.'

'This time you have cold iron on you. It will help keep you safe.'

We drive the rest of the way to Lord Ellensthorne's Old London residence in silence. The long day and losing my lunch has sent a weakness into my muscles. All I want is to curl up and sleep for a day or two. My brief nap in Wishearth's arms feels like a lifetime ago.

Jamie arrives only minutes after us. The lateness of the hour concerns me, and this time I bring the sword. Here the trees lining the street have retained some of their foliage, and they cast shadows across the pavement. Patches of the inky blackness seem darker than they should, and my palms grow clammy. Trying to push aside the discomfort, I jog up the steps and ring the buzzer.

Lord Ellensthorne's butler opens the door and regards us with a blank expression.

'Yes?'

'We need to speak to Lord Ellensthorne right away,' Jamie says.

'Do you have an appointment?' The lateness of our visit does not appear to trouble the butler.

'No.'

'Then I'm afraid you will have to call his secretary to schedule an appointment and return another time. Lord Ellensthorne is very busy.'

'I'm sure he'll want to see us,' Jamie says, and produces his warrant card.

The butler examines it longer than is necessary, and his gaze flickers over Karrion and me. Eventually, he nods.

'You may come in and wait in the hall while I speak to Lord Ellensthorne.'

'Thank you.'

Jamie steps past him and we follow. After the butler has closed the door, he ascends the sweeping stairs and disappears from view. While we wait, Jamie looks at the

318

dark marble floor and the paintings of stern men in suits lining the walls.

'They look like the family reunions are riotous,' he whispers, casting a guilty look at the stairs.

'Wait till you meet the Lord himself,' Karrion says, but he too keeps his voice down. 'Though that makes him sound like Jesus, and he's definitely not.'

It takes so long for the butler to return that we are all getting restless. I glance at my watch and see that it is nearly eleven. At last footsteps sound above us and the butler pauses at the halfway point on the stairs.

'Lord Ellensthorne has agreed to see you.'

We follow him upstairs and along a dark corridor. The closer to the study we get, the more slowly I walk. The memory of the wild hunt is still fresh in my mind, and I have no wish to be swept away by the power of the desk again. But I can hardly stay in the corridor.

Lord Ellensthorne is seated behind his desk, wearing a white dress shirt and a black silk robe over it. He does not stand when we enter, nor does he offer to shake Jamie's hand when Jamie introduces himself. All he does is steeple his fingers and let the silence become uncomfortable.

While Jamie explains the reason for our visit, my eyes are drawn to the figures along the edges of Lord Ellensthorne's desk. The Coin-Sìth are perfectly captured; every detail is as I remember from the Unseen Lands. As I follow the progress of the figures from right to left, I hear their growls, smell the stench of their breath and taste their hunger for the hunt. I remember what it was like to become them, just as I recall how I felt when they were hunting me.

'Ms Wilde?'

The baying of the hounds recedes to the back of my mind as I become aware of everyone in the room staring at me. I blink.

'Sorry?'

'I asked for your take on what the Detective Inspector has told me.'

In Jamie's frown, I see a mixture of confusion and irritation. He does not understand that as much as Lord Ellensthorne considers me a second-class citizen, a human ranks even lower in his eyes. I have no doubt that as the leader of Old London, Lord Ellensthorne can be diplomatic when dealing with humans, but in this instance, he has chosen a different approach.

'The threat is real. I have seen what the suspect is capable of.'

'And you are certain I'm a target.'

I hesitate, but opt for the truth. 'We believe the suspect is stealing magic from Mages. You're the most powerful Shadow Mage on our list of likely victims.'

The corners of Lord Ellensthorne's mouth lift in an arrogant smirk, and he relaxes in his chair. Jamie shifts.

'As I'm the most powerful Shadow Mage in the city, I am surprised you think I don't have the means to defend myself.'

Jamie clears his throat. 'So far, the suspect has been able to bypass all magical and mundane security systems.'

'Nevertheless, I am better prepared than the average Old London Mage.'

'I appreciate that, but on behalf of the Paladins of Justice and the Metropolitan Police, we'd prefer to take every precaution,' Jamie says.

'You may do as you wish, though I have no intention of allowing strangers to trample through my home.'

'With your permission, we would like to assign a Paladin to guard you...'

The hairs at the back of my neck prickle a warning, and the rest of Jamie's words slip past my ears unnoticed. Casting my senses out, I search for anything amiss.

320

Nothing stands out. Yet I am certain something has changed. It is an instinct of old: the sense of prey knowing that a predator is about to attack, even though nothing indicates danger.

After our last case, I said I would be smarter, plan better instead of rushing into danger. Have I been any smarter? Do a sword and Fria's package amount to a plan? Or is history repeating itself yet again?

But there is one thing I can do differently.

'Jamie,' I say, interrupting him mid-sentence, 'do you mind going downstairs and checking whether the Paladin has arrived? I want to make sure the protections are in place. I will explain the rest of our precautions to Lord Ellensthorne.'

'Sure,' Jamie replies, and I can see he is taken aback by my bluntness. 'The Paladin should have arrived by now.'

'Frankly, I'm surprised, as the Speaker of the High Council and the First among the Shadow Mages, that I don't warrant the protection of more than one Paladin.'

Ignoring Lord Ellensthorne, I draw Karrion to the side and hand him my cold iron token.

'Can you go with Jamie and check the perimeter? With the discs, you'll be able to see through Fey glamour better than a Paladin can.'

'Okay. I'll be back as soon as I can.'

'Thanks.'

Once Jamie and Karrion have left the room, I pace away from the desk and deal with Thaylor's pouch and Fria's package. Then I pull on the leather gloves and unwrap the sword. The tip drags towards the ground, and lifting the sword is a struggle. With a wooden hilt and arm guard, most of its weight is along the blade.

When I turn back, I find Lord Ellensthorne watching me.

321

'So, the danger is real.'

'What makes you say that?'

'You just sent your apprentice and the human out of harm's way.'

I swallow, thrown by his perceptiveness. Lord Ellensthorne smirks and walks around his desk to a drinks trolley. He pours himself a glass of wine; the liquid ruby red. I watch him take a sip and imagine the wine tasting of blood. My stomach rumbles.

'Are we dealing with another Leech?' Lord Ellensthorne asks.

The question takes me by surprise, and I have to think back to the earlier conversation to understand why he is asking.

'No, something different.'

'Something different, yet capable of stealing magic from Mages.'

'That's right.'

'How?'

The speculation in Lord Ellensthorne's eyes has little to do with concern for his safety.

'We're not sure.'

Lord Ellensthorne acknowledges the lie with a flicker of his right eyebrow. Turning the wineglass in his hand, he stares at me over its rim.

'Only Leeches can steal power from others. They are the ultimate enemy of magical people. Alas, even the most powerful among Mages are not immune to their thieving.'

Tilting my chin up, I meet his stare head on. 'You assume our suspect is mortal.'

'He isn't?' Lord Ellensthorne's attention drifts to the sword. 'A Fey?'

'That's what we think.'

'How could a Fey steal magic from Mages? And why?'

322

'At present, all we know for certain is that he's doing so. As for how and why, your guess is as good as mine.'

Lord Ellensthorne tuts. 'Your lying leaves a lot to be desired. But very well, keep your secrets. At least you appear to be earnest about the danger I am in.'

'I'm glad you think so. But we've wasted enough time already. I'd like to run through the safety precautions we recommend you take to keep yourself safe tonight. The Fey may never make it as far as the house, but in case he does, I'd like you to be prepared. Do you have any cold iron here? I'm especially interested in warding tokens.'

Instead of replying, Lord Ellensthorne looks towards the door, the hand holding the glass hovering a few inches above the table. A blanket of dread settles over me, insulating me from the rest of the world. I struggle to draw a breath.

'Can you feel that?' I whisper.

Lord Ellensthorne remains silent, and I see that the glass in his hand is perfectly still. The air in the room has condensed into drifts of snow. I move as if in slow motion, each step towards the desk taking so much effort, sweat breaks out across my forehead. When at last I am within touching distance of Lord Ellensthorne, I see that while he is breathing, he appears transfixed. His clothes yield under my touch when I shake him, but it elicits no response.

Turning away from Lord Ellensthorne, I call upon my magic. The first thing that strikes me is how silent the house is. It is as if Lord Ellensthorne and I are the only people here. I cannot hear a television, a radio, or any of the incidental sounds of human inhabitation: coughing, water running, opening of drawers. Perhaps Jamie asked the staff to leave. But why would he have done so without discussing it with Lord Ellensthorne? Or did I simply miss the conversation while I was distracted by the desk?

Fatigue crashes over me as the high tide, strong enough that my eyes slip closed on their own accord. There is a sofa at the far end of the room. I could take a nap there, sleep until the morning, and trust Jamie and the Paladins to finish what I started. Or perhaps I will settle on the carpet, as is proper for a loyal hound.

What was I doing again?

My consciousness is sliding into a dream, and I recall the feel of Dearon's hands over my body. What's to stop me from going to him again? It is where I belong, by his side. I have no place in Old London.

The tip of the sword taps against the side of my leg as my arm relaxes, and the brief contact sends a shaft of energy through me. My eyes snap open, and any thought of sleep evaporates with a final caress of Dearon's fingers against my lips.

How long was I out?

A sliver of ice runs down my spine, and I realise that the sweat has cooled on my forehead. When I exhale, a small cloud billows from my mouth. I can taste frost in the air, as clean and crisp as at the conclave. An unexpected stab of homesickness lances through me. I would be safe there.

Downstairs, a clock begins striking. I count the hollow echoes that permeate the house. One. Four. Seven. Ten. Twelve. My blood runs cold. Thirteen.

37

LIVE AND DIE

A startled gasp causes me to whirl around just as Lord Ellensthorne's hand jerks. The glass slips through his fingers, and a cascade of wine crests the rim. I track the droplets landing on the dark surface of the desk. Some of the wine goes over the end and lands on the cream carpet. The stain resembles blood, and I wonder if it does not portend what is about to happen.

Lord Ellensthorne stares at the stain spreading across his papers, and for the first time, his composure cracks. Shrugging off Fey glamour is like the rest of the world has gone out of sync and your body is struggling to catch up. And this is no average Feykin using their powers. I am out of my depth.

I try to ask if he is okay, but the words stick in my throat. Lord Ellensthorne's attention is fixed on the door, and I know without looking that it has opened. The scents of leaf mulch, mould and decaying flesh roll in. Dread grips my insides. Careful to keep my body between the door and the sword, I turn around.

In all the rush to get to this point, it never occurred to me to wonder what Baneacre looks like. Now the different Fey I saw in the Unseen Lands flicker through my memory, creating the image of a dark shape made up of weeping slime mould. I could never have imagined the being in the doorway.

Baneacre is tall enough that he has to stoop to enter the room. Lanky grey locks frame his face, reaching to his waist, his yellow eyes burn with plague fever, and the shade of his skin matches the colour of the destroying angels growing on Cullingwoed. He is dressed in matching shirt and trousers made of fabric that has faded to an off-grey. He is barefoot. Although skin is stretched tight over his skeletal frame, he moves with strength beyond that of his famished appearance. A silvery scar runs across his torso.

His aura spreads out, questing and assessing. Where the edge touches mine, I catch a flash of my body on the ground, rotting away while I struggle to stop the decay. There is no rebirth I can see, only death. I shrink back, shying away from him and his power.

Now he is in the room, intermingled with the scents of a Death Lord are those of autumn leaves, cinnamon, ripening wheat and sun-baked salt. And first dawn.

Amitta.

A thousand questions flit through my mind, too fast for me to consider any of them. Now is not the time nor the place, not while Lord Ellensthorne lives.

So far, Baneacre has spared me nothing more than a fleeting glance; his full attention is fixed on his intended victim. He advances towards the desk, and I marvel at the ballerina grace of each step. The edge of the desk nearest to Baneacre ripples as the hounds struggle to break free. Through the pounding of my pulse, I fancy I can make out low growling.

Keeping his eyes fixed on Baneacre, Lord Ellensthorne pulls a handkerchief from his pockets and lays it on the table. The crimson stain spreads across the white surface, and for a fleeting moment, there is no difference between the wine and Lord Ellensthorne's lifeblood. My stomach rumbles again.

'Yes, you will do fine, Shade Magus,' Baneacre says in a whisper of dead leaves.

'I hardly think so,' Lord Ellensthorne says. 'If it's Shadow magic you desire, I suggest you find yourself a less well-defended victim.'

'Mennisc magick is no concern of mine,' Baneacre says with the patience of ivy choking an oak tree.

'Don't insult me. I'm no human.'

'You will die as easily as your weaker kind.'

I step forward, bringing the sword to bear. 'No, he won't.'

Baneacre's eyes flicker towards me, and I experience a stronger version of the dread I felt when Bradán directed his unfettered hatred at me. Despair steals the air from my lungs.

'Your life is already forfeit. My Cwēn has seen to that.'

Unable to speak, I shake my head and point the tip of the sword at his chest.

My whole body erupts in agony. Pain lances through my joints and my muscles seize. I gasp, staggering back under the weight of a hundred injuries all experienced at once. Reaoul's light blisters my skin, robbing me of my sight. Lizzie shoots me with one hand while stabbing me with the other. Tem's knife finds my stomach, the blade twisting to shred my intestines. I can feel the hot breath of the Coin-Sìth all over me as they prepare to tear my body apart. Beneath all other sensations, the agony of chronic pain sets my bones on fire.

'Mortals are easy. I need no weapon against them, for they provide me with plenty.'

While I fall to my knees, Lord Ellensthorne pushes his chair away from the desk and, with a flick of his fingers, raises a ward. I feel it on the edge of my consciousness: a steady hum where before was only silence. Relaxing back in his chair, Lord Ellensthorne smirks.

The edges of my vision are fading to black. Through the roar of pain, I inch the leather glove off my left hand and grip the blade. The edge slices through my palm and fingers, slicking the sword with my blood. Nausea cuts through the agony, bringing with it blissful relief. I force my fingers to unclench, but maintain contact with the metal even as my power falters at the proximity to cold iron. Using a little of my remaining magic, I call upon the grace and stealth of a cat as I rise.

Baneacre slithers towards the ward. He finds one of the markers etched onto the floorboards and runs a finger along its edge. The hum of the ward takes on a discordant note, and Lord Ellensthorne frowns. Even through the barrier, I can feel his aura expanding as he feeds more power into the ward.

Remaining crouched, Baneacre bares his sharp teeth at Lord Ellensthorne. Their faces are level, and under different circumstances, the expression of arrogance they share would amuse me. But as I witness the rising battle of might between the Mage and the Fey, I have little reason to smile.

Lord Ellensthorne is going to lose.

As the discordant note spreads across the surface of the warded area, a change in air pressure causes the hairs at the back of my neck to stand up. The smell of crisp frost permeates the air, stronger than before. I begin to shiver as the temperature in the room plummets. Perhaps Lord Ellensthorne feels it through the barrier, for uncertainty flickers across his features.

Shadows plunge the warded area into darkness. At first I think it is Lord Ellensthorne's doing, but I see him fumbling with a bracelet of onyx beads. Every time he touches a stone, the barrier clears a little more. Mana gems. Lord Ellensthorne straightens in his chair, confident once more.

Baneacre rises in a fluid move I cannot help but envy. Pressing both palms against the ward, he leans into it as if it was a solid wall. From his vantage point, he is towering over Lord Ellensthorne, who has to crane his neck to maintain eye contact with Baneacre. My teeth chatter, and I clench my jaw shut to keep silent.

When I ease forward, I realise that my toes have gone numb. A sheen of frost is covering the floor, adding a degree of difficulty to my progress. The door frame blossoms in a pattern of icicles. A snowflake lands on my cheek, another on my hand.

Lord Ellensthorne does not appear to notice any of this; too intent upon feeding power to his ward. But I can feel the change in his aura as more and more of the magic he uses comes from the mana gems. He is growing tired. How often has he battled a being with the patience of an immortal?

A crack halts my creeping closer. Lord Ellensthorne's chair splinters; the legs encased in ice. He falls backwards, arms flailing, and lands across the boundary. The hum of the ward vanishes, replaced by the silence of the witching hour. Lord Ellensthorne's eyes widen as Baneacre leans over him.

'Your arrogance is your downfall, Shade Magus. Did you think I would only attack you one battlefront at a time?'

I feel the gathering of power as Lord Ellensthorne readies a spell. The lights grow dim while he pulls magic from the night sky and the shadows around us. As tired as he may be, he is unwilling to give up.

'Enough.' With a finger on Lord Ellensthorne's forehead, Baneacre unravels the spell. 'You fought more than your fellow mortals, but you can fight no more. You must suffer and then you must die.'

My careful steps have brought me around the desk, and I am almost within a sword's reach of Baneacre.

Testing my footing on the icy floor, I wonder whether I might be able to rush the last few feet and take him by surprise. But without ever taking his eyes off Lord Ellensthorne, Baneacre points a finger at me.

'Your turn will come.'

Agony washes over me, blinding as the noonday sun, and I slide my fingers down an inch to touch the blade. Nausea cleaves through the pain, and once more, Baneacre's glamour dissipates.

Shivers run through Lord Ellensthorne, and soon he is shaking. His pale skin takes on a blue hue as ice crystals form in his hair. If I do not act soon, he will freeze to death.

As I stare at his prone form, I recall Karrion's insistence that Lord Ellensthorne could look after himself. Karrion was wrong. But as seconds stretch to minutes, I see an opportunity to help rid Old London of Lord Ellensthorne's divisive and toxic policies. If he were to die tonight, the city could have a leader that would unite us instead of seeking to advance elitist agenda for Mages. All I have to do is leave.

But can I do that?

Lord Ellensthorne's eyes shift to me, wide with fear. Perhaps he senses some of my hesitation. As he lies helpless under Baneacre's thrall, I see him not as the arrogant leader of Old London, but as a man about to die a terrible death.

I become aware of tiny tugs on the edges of my aura. While he is lowering the temperature in the room, Baneacre is drawing together threads of Mage power. A web is stretching out from him, as clear to me as if it was made of real string. I have never felt magic this way before.

As the web spreads, I need none of my instincts to warn me against the dangers that lurk beyond the growing power. Raising the sword, I move the tip beneath the nearest thread and slice up. The magic frays and tears. There must be enough of Baneacre's own essence in the power for the cold iron to work.

The advance of the web halts as Baneacre seeks to repair the damage. Moving along with growing confidence, I slice through the threads until the edges pull apart. They sway in a breeze I cannot feel, and the spell is ruined. My feet ache from the cold, and I wiggle my toes to keep them warm.

Baneacre removes his finger from the forehead of Lord Ellensthorne, who gasps in relief. Pulling himself up to his full height, Baneacre steps past Lord Ellensthorne towards me. It is my turn to crane my neck to meet his gaze, and I am careful to keep my fingers on the cold iron.

'I had thought that you would make a fine Cù-Sìth for my Court, Wilde Bearn, but you test my patience. You need to learn obedience, mortal.'

Lord Ellensthorne struggles to rise, his movements sluggish and uncoordinated. Before he has got further than rolling to his side, ivy sprouts from the remains of the chair. The coils slither under him, around him, trapping his limbs and immobilising him. The scents of dark soil, nectar, fresh green shoots and rotting plants fill my nose; strong enough that I expect Lady Bergamon to appear in the doorway behind Baneacre.

How is he doing that?

Struggling to recall what he said, I shake my head. 'Sorry. I guess I've never been one for obedience.'

'No matter,' Baneacre says, and his voice resembles the feeding frenzy of maggots inside a carcass. 'I shall teach you.'

Behind him, Lord Ellensthorne gasps. The ivy is wrapping tighter around him, and he is struggling to breathe. Time is running out.

331

Hoping there is enough strength left in my legs for a leap, I point the sword at Baneacre's chest and launch myself forward. The jolt that follows rattles my teeth. I am rooted to the spot. The change in my momentum throws me off balance and I wave my arms in an effort to stand upright. When my left hand goes too close to the desk, black hounds strain against their wooden prison to tear at my flesh. Shying away, I manage to remain standing.

When I look down, I see that my trainers have frozen to the floor. Tapping the edge of the ice with the sword has little impact beyond sending chips flying. Baneacre chuckles; the sound akin to dead branches cleaving off a dying tree.

'You are no different from the Shade Magus. Do all mortals think in such a singular fashion?'

The web was a trap. Baneacre knew I would feel it, and he kept repairing the threads to keep me occupied while he froze me to the floor. Why didn't I see it coming?

Keeping one eye on him, I use the tip of the blade to weaken the ice around my left shoe. But as soon as cracks appear, new ice forms over them. Frustrated, I glare at Baneacre.

'You have spirit indeed, Wilde Bearn. You will make a fine hound.'

Baneacre steps closer, and his breath smells of disease, death and decay. My stomach turns. He slides close enough for his power to envelop me. It reminds me of the Winter Queen's kiss. Here I am, about to be claimed by a second Fey. Yet, I am not prepared to defy the Winter Queen's claim over me. I am hers and only hers.

Fingers brush against mine, and in his touch, I feel the rot of old age and disease. He caresses my hand like a lover would, but try as I might, I cannot pull away. His will has paralysed me. Fear shudders through me, robbing me of the last of my strength, and I do not notice what he is doing until my grasp on the sword loosens.

Baneacre's hand closes around the hilt, and his skin blisters, boils and blackens. Amidst his growl of pain, I fancy I can hear Lady Bergamon whispering words in a foreign language. Baneacre drops the sword next to me, but out of reach.

'No!'

I crouch, leaning as far to my right as I can with my shoes frozen to the floor, and reach for the sword with both hands. My fingertips almost touch the metal, but Baneacre is in the way.

'Admit defeat, my houndling. The Shade Magus will perish. When we leave this house, you will remain a loyal servant until the end of your days. You will kill for me.' Fingers stroke my hair, slowing my racing thoughts. 'I dare say you will enjoy it.'

Shifting my body further to the right, I reach for the sword again with my left hand, while my other finds the weight in my pocket. With numb fingers and hindered by the glove, I fumble to disengage the safety. When I rise, I hurl myself at Baneacre and slam my left fist into his chest. Without cold iron, I know I cannot hurt him, but that is not my intention.

'I will never serve you,' I say between gritted teeth.

The fingers that close around my wrist are gentle. He traps my hand between his and smiles. My courage falters at the sight of his sharp teeth. I would rather yield to his claim than die.

'You will.'

At this distance, I need not worry about aiming. While I open my mouth to continue arguing, I lock eyes with him. I see in his gaze that he has already won, and it spurs me on.

The gunshot sounds like a clap of thunder, leaving my ears ringing. Baneacre takes an uncertain step back as smoke rises from the hole in his stomach. He stares at the gun in disbelief. I lift the barrel and squeeze the trigger once, twice, three times. Thaylor had time to make only five bullets, and I dare not waste them all in a fit of defiant rage.

Baneacre slumps back against the desk and slides to the floor. Reaching for the sword, I pick it up in my left hand and slice through some of the ivy imprisoning Lord Ellensthorne, heedless of ruining his clothes in the process. He draws a shuddering breath, hand scrambling to push more of the coils off him. The urgency to save him that allowed me to briefly ignore the rising tide of nausea wanes, and I drop the sword.

The bullet holes on Baneacre's chest are spreading blackness across his pallid skin. He claws at them, succeeding only in prising loose chunks of necrotic flesh. A smell akin to burning rotten meat fills the room. Lord Ellensthorne gags, but I regard Baneacre with impassive eyes. He said I would enjoy killing, and in this fleeting moment, he is right.

I take aim at his head. Incandescent hatred sears through me. 'My Cwēn will have to find herself a new Hærfest Wiga. You're the second one I've killed today.'

I pull the trigger.

38

SURVIVAL

Baneacre's head explodes from the shot, and black blood splatters across Lord Ellensthorne's face and torso. Where spots of it touch my bare hand, the skin itches and burns. At first, all we can do is stare at the body between us, but then I become aware of a change in the air pressure. A storm is rising in the room, and I am certain I cannot withstand its force.

'Help me up,' Lord Ellensthorne says.

My first instinct is to remind him that I am stuck, but the edge of frost has vanished upon Baneacre's death. It takes a few attempts, but I manage to wrench myself free of the floorboards. Between us, we pull the remaining coils of ivy off his legs, and Lord Ellensthorne rises on shaky feet.

'How many Mages did he drain dry?'

'Five.'

'Fucking hell.'

The words are so uncharacteristic that all I can do is stare at him. He waves off my confusion and limps to the cupboard near the door.

'No time for that now. Can you use the sword to push him inside the ward circle? Don't touch his body unless you have to.'

'I'll try.'

My attempts to roll him onto his side are clumsy as

335

every time the sword touches him, it decays more of his flesh. The pressure in the room has grown to a point where my ears are ringing. A drop of blood lands on my sleeve, and I wipe it off.

'Hurry.'

The urgency in Lord Ellensthorne's voice sends me fumbling for Baneacre's legs. When the sword proves ineffectual, I yank on the left glove, pick his legs up and shove them inside the silvery line on the floor. Black smoke rises from the gloves. Pain sears through my palms. Whatever the substance covering Baneacre's body is, it has burnt through the leather gloves.

Lord Ellensthorne returns with six black mana gems and sets them over the warding symbols along the line. The rising pressure in the room causes my legs to give way. I slump on the floor, my fists pressed against my temples. Jagged lines run through my vision.

This time, I barely feel the ward Lord Ellensthorne raises, but the barrier eases some of my discomfort. Inside the circle, Baneacre's body blackens and shrivels while power races away from him and along the edges of the ward. A flash of light blinds me.

My awareness returns slowly. I become conscious of wet floorboards beneath my cheek, then the blood dripping from my nose. White spots cloud my vision, and no amount of blinking seems to shift them. Every part of my body aches, and all I want is to close my eyes and sleep.

A groan alerts me to the fact that I am not alone in the room. Rubbing my face, I struggle to sit up and lean against a solid surface behind me. Shapes emerge from the glaring brightness, and I realise that I am sitting in the shadow of the desk. Shrinking back, I brace myself for teeth sinking into my flesh, but the hounds seem to have settled back into their wooden prison.

The area within the ward is charred, and nothing remains of Lord Ellensthorne's chair or the ivy that grew from it. Even the warding symbols are twisted and bent, but they held on long enough to contain the explosion. Baneacre's body is gone.

Lord Ellensthorne is lying near the door. My legs are too weak to carry me, and I crawl around the circle to him, ignoring my burning hands. At first I think he is dead, but then I see the shallow rise and fall of his chest. I shrug off my bloodied coat with difficulty and use it as a pillow.

At the far end of the room, the trolley of drinks has survived unharmed. I crawl to it and pour two generous glasses of brandy. The liquid burns in my throat, and I cough, struggling to hold the tumbler upright. Where some of the brandy spills onto my hand, it sets the wounds across my palms on fire. But the alcohol also lifts some of the numbness and fatigue that is weighing down my limbs. Draining the glass, I manage to stand on shaking legs.

When I wet his lips with brandy, Lord Ellensthorne coughs and opens his eyes. When they focus on me, consternation flashes across his face, and then disappears. He sits up, rubs the back of his head and accepts the glass. I sense barely a whisper of power from him.

'Just in time.'

'Lucky us,' I croak and clear my throat. In truth, I am not certain how lucky I feel.

Silence hangs between us. Neither of us seems to know what to say, and I am relieved when I spot the gun on the floor. I shuffle over and pick it up.

'I can dispose of that quietly, if you wish,' Lord Ellensthorne says.

His expression appears genuine, but I cannot help being wary. Letting Lord Ellensthorne have an illegal gun with my fingerprints on it sounds no wiser than taking on one of the Autumn Champions. I have fought enough battles for one day.

'No, thanks. Though I suppose I'll have to explain the gun to the Paladin. I'm surprised he hasn't rushed upstairs yet.'

Lord Ellensthorne frowns. 'What are you talking about?'

'Surely the Paladin will have heard the shots.'

'Please,' Lord Ellensthorne scoffs. 'My study has the best sound warding money can buy. No one outside this room heard a thing.'

'In that case—' I pocket the gun and pick up the sword. The blade is blackened, but Thaylor should be able to salvage some of the metal. 'But won't the Paladins question the bullet holes?'

'I have enough power left to hide the evidence of your illegal activities.'

His words give me pause. To trust Lord Ellensthorne with anything he could use as leverage against me goes against all my instincts. But am I in any shape to start covering up a crime scene?

Something of my thoughts must be apparent on my face, for Lord Ellensthorne dips his chin. 'Your suspicion is a credit to your profession. But in this instance, you need not concern yourself. I owe you a debt and I am prepared to let an advantage slide in recognition of that.'

My mind made up, I exhale. 'Thank you.'

'While I cannot fault your results, you look terrible.'

His words remind me that blood is congealing on my face and my hands are covered in burns that are weeping sticky pus. The wounds smell infected. My feet are still numb from the cold.

'Do you have a first aid kit?'

'I believe the servants keep one in the top floor bathroom. Up the stairs and first door to your right.'

It is a dismissal if I have ever heard one. I nod and turn to leave. As I am about to close the door, Lord Ellensthorne's voice halts me.

'Ms Wilde, I... appreciate your aid.'

I doubt Lord Ellensthorne is capable of expressing more genuine gratitude and I nod. But I cannot resist claiming the last word.

'You're welcome. But when you are planning the future of Old London, remember that someone you consider a second-class citizen just saved your life.'

The first aid kit is where Lord Ellensthorne said, and I pour a bottle of disinfectant over my palms. My eyes water from the stinging, but I wrap bandages around the wounds and use wads of wet tissue to wipe most of the blood off my face. The narrow window offers a view over the city, and I cannot help tapping into some of my remaining power.

With my enhanced sight, I look over the Old London skyline and watch the city turn to rubble. Structures of steel and glass rust and crack, while stone crumbles to dust. New buildings rise and fall, and even Lord Ellensthorne's house collapses around me. I am left standing on a steel pillar and I alone remain unaffected in a city of ruins.

Loneliness surges through me, strong enough to leave me breathless. I understand Lady Bergamon and Wishearth a little better. Mayflies do not count the minutes of their existence, but my visit to the Unseen Lands has given me a crushing sense of time. Everywhere I look, I see evidence of the fleeting nature of our existence. Does anything have meaning when everything leads to death? I glance down at my bandaged hands. How much of that death will I cause?

But amidst the rubble and waste, I see a green shoot reaching towards the dark sky. Ants shift grains of sand.

A pigeon lands on a rusted steel rebar. A moth flutters in the flickering light of a street lamp. A ghost of a smile caresses my lips. Death is merely another beginning. The city dies and lives on, time and time again. It has stood on the banks of the Thames for millennia and will continue doing so long after my kind has faded from the memories of mortals. My fleeting existence can leave no mark upon the city that would remain. No death, little or large, will be remembered in the Londons of the future.

But will that absolve me of the guilt echoing in the corners of my mind? In the middle of the battle, I crossed a line. Will I ever find a way back to a place where I was simply mortal?

The Old London skyline has no further wisdom to offer, and I turn from the window, allowing the power to slip away. I abandon the first aid kit open on the edge of the sink and leave the house of shadows.

39

LITTLE DEATHS

When I open the front door, I find a Paladin pacing on the front step. He whirls around, hand on the hilt of his sword, and relief flickers across his face. The gems affixed to the hilt are glowing.

'Finally. I've been ringing the doorbell for the past fifteen minutes.'

'Sorry. I guess we didn't hear the bell upstairs. Lord Ellensthorne mentioned something about sound warding in the study.'

I keep the sword behind my back. The last thing I need right now is a Paladin challenging me over removing key evidence from a crime scene.

The Paladin shakes his head. 'I undid the wards on the door, but even my most powerful access spell couldn't open it.'

'We were dealing with a powerful enemy.'

'Were?' The Paladin takes half a step towards the open door. I shift sideways past him.

'Between Lord Ellensthorne and me, we defeated the intruder. Lord Ellensthorne is upstairs, recovering from the attack.'

'And the attacker?'

'The magic he had stolen from his victims imploded, taking him with it. Lord Ellensthorne was able to contain the damage within a ward.' I look around. 'Where's Jamie?'

'Detective Inspector Manning was called away on an urgent matter.'

The Paladin reaches for his radio and reports the incident. I ask him to put a call through to Jamie as well, which he does. When he heads inside, I stop him.

'Where's Karrion?'

'The Bird Shaman?'

I nod.

'He was here not long ago with a flock of birds. It was he who grew concerned when no one answered the doorbell. He tried to ring you, but the call wouldn't connect. That's when he became agitated. While I used my magic to force open the door, he said he would look elsewhere. That's the last I saw of him.'

If the Paladin says something further, I hear none of it as I rush down the steps, close enough to tripping that I have to grip the railing to remain upright. Pain shoots up my wrist.

The street is dark. All the street lights are out for fifty yards in either direction from Lord Ellensthorne's house. Leaves and litter cover the ground, and I use a little of my magic to sharpen my sight. Even so, it takes me almost a minute before the presence of a magical aura directs me to Karrion.

He is sitting in the shadow of a horse chestnut tree, his back to the house. The faint rise and fall of his shoulders show that he is breathing, but otherwise he sits stock still. When I call out to him, he gives no indication that he heard me. Dead leaves and clumps of wood surround him. A few leaves cling to his hair and the back of his leather jacket.

His aura is as familiar to me as his physical appearance, but straight away I know something is wrong. The edges of his power are frayed and shrivelled, as if something has torn through the feathers of his magic. What remains of it feels depleted, like Karrion has poured all of it into a spell and is yet to recover.

When I approach him, treading carefully to avoid slipping on wet leaves and plastic, I realise my mistake. What I thought were clumps of wood are, in fact, dead birds. Alarm spikes in my exhausted mind.

'Karrion?'

With his knees tucked against his body, he is sitting on the edge of the kerb. My first instinct is to tease him about getting his jeans wet, but the words die on my lips when I step past him. He is cradling a pigeon and a sparrow in his arms.

'I could feel them die,' Karrion whispers, his eyes staring across the road. 'They cried out to me to save them before they died in terrible agony. He plucked them from the trees and willed them to suffer. So they did, and I felt it all.'

I sit down next to him and pull him into a hug. 'It's over now, Karrion. He's never going to hurt another bird.'

His breath tickles my ear. 'But they're still dead. I can feel their deaths within me.'

'You have to let go of the birds,' I say, repeating what he once told me. 'If you don't, you'll be lost.'

Now that I am closer, I can feel the power he is pouring into the birds in his arms. Sweat drips down his temples, and his breathing grows erratic. From the weak press of his aura against mine, I know he has little magic left. A new kind of fear takes seed in my heart, spreading its roots through my body.

'You have to stop, Karrion,' I say, my lips brushing his cheek. 'No amount of magic will bring them back.'

'I have to try.'

'No, this is the natural way of things.'

'Screw nature!' Karrion shrugs out of my hold. Despite the violence of his movements, his hold on the birds

343

remains gentle. 'There's nothing natural about a Fey choosing to kill a flock of birds.'

'Not the manner of death, no. But all things must die, and none may come back from that.'

'I can change that,' he says and holds the birds to his chest. The press of his magic against their lifeless bodies intensifies. 'If you can cast circles, then I can do this.'

'You can't.' I grip his arms, uncertain how I can make him understand. 'If you keep trying, you'll burn yourself out like Melissa did. If you keep going, you could die.'

'My death is their death.'

'No, Karrion. Birds die every day, and yet Bird Shamans carry on living. Because you know, as I do, that there can be no new eggs without the older generations dying. That is the way it must be. That is why you must let them go.'

'I can't. I have to try.'

'Why?' I have never witnessed Karrion being so stubborn.

'Because it's my fault!' Tears slide down his cheeks.

'What?'

'I called the birds to me. Some were already here, but most of them I called to me. I thought maybe they'd help me spot Baneacre when he arrived. But he ripped their lives away before we were any the wiser. They all died as one.'

Ignoring his stiff posture, I draw Karrion back into my arms.

'Their deaths are on him, not you. You're a Bird Shaman. What would you be without birds? They are part of you as much as you are part of them.'

'That means their deaths are part of me too.'

'Yes.' Fear gives urgency to my words. 'Every creature that touches our lives will become part of us. Their deaths too. But that doesn't mean we must become their death.'

'But it's my fault,' Karrion repeats, his voice cracking. He shudders. 'They were here because of me and they died because of me.'

The pull of his magic sputters. Karrion's aura is nothing but a brush of a single down feather. Yet, he continues trying and I can feel the toll it is taking on him.

'Please let them go, Karrion.' A tear gets trapped in my eyelashes. 'If you don't, I'm going to lose you. And I won't survive that.'

Karrion buries his head in the crook of my neck. His sobs shake his whole body and his tears wet my neck. Witnessing his raw grief unlocks something in my mind, and my own tears fall freely. Clinging onto Karrion, I weep not just for him and the lives I took today, but for my father's suffering, the loss of my mother and for the impossible situation with Dearon. We cling to each other; the only anchor we have against the tide of our grief.

Little by little, the flow of magic from Karrion eases. My sobs return, this time as much out of relief as grief. I will not lose my best friend. I will not have to tell Aderyn her son has died. I will not have to face a life alone in Old London.

We stay in the embrace long after the swell of emotions has ebbed. I draw strength from his presence, his breath on my neck, the almost painful way he holds onto me. On a cold November night, in the middle of a dark city, Karrion is all I need. Whatever life throws at me, with him by my side, I can take it. I hope he feels the same.

Karrion is the first to pull back. His eyes are red, his face blotchy, and he wipes his nose with the back of his hand. But there is no shame or embarrassment in his eyes, only love. With soft, gentle fingers he strokes away the moisture from my cheeks and pushes a lock of hair behind my ear.

345

'Thank you,' he whispers and kisses my forehead.

The kiss is little more than a brush of a feather against my skin, and it is over almost before I have a chance to react. I understand the emotion behind it. I love him as he loves me.

I throw my arms around him again. There will come a time when we have to say goodbye, but it will not be today.

Karrion chuckles as he holds me close, pressing a kiss in my hair. 'Good to know I'm not just an annoying employee.'

I pull back enough to meet his gaze and shake my head. 'Don't.'

He swallows and nods. A blush creeps up his neck. With his eyes down, he notices my bandaged hands for the first time.

'Gods, Yan, what happened?'

Looking at my hands, I let out a watery laugh. 'I couldn't let Lord Ellensthorne's house blow up, now, could I?'

'Did we win?'

'Yes, we won.' But at what cost? I leave the question unspoken.

'It sounds as though you have a lot to tell me.'

'I do, though it may have to wait. Jamie will arrive any moment, together with a section of Paladins.'

'We'll be quite the welcoming committee.'

Karrion offers me his hand and helps me up. We lean against each other until we find our balance, but I am reluctant to leave his side. Perhaps I am not yet ready to trust that he is okay. The bird carcasses he was holding have slid off his lap without my noticing. When Karrion looks down at them, his expression crumbles into grief. I slip my hand in his, and he grips it hard enough to send agony through my palm. Yet, I cannot will myself to pull away or ask him to lessen his hold.

I may have guided him away from the edge, but he will have a long road to walk before he has laid his guilt to rest. Does the same not apply to me?

'I don't...' Karrion looks around at all the birds. 'I don't know what to do with them.'

'We should bury them.' It is the first thing that comes to my mind, but straight away I see the wisdom behind my words. 'In Lady Bergamon's garden. What better place for their spirits to roam free?'

Karrion nods, squeezing my hand. 'I'd like that.'

'Good. I think I have a couple of cardboard boxes in the car. It feels better than putting them in a plastic bag.'

'You're right. I'd hate to treat them like rubbish.'

'I'll be right back.'

When I move to slip my hand out of Karrion's, he shifts, nervous all of a sudden. 'Why don't I come with you?'

Together we retrieve the boxes and set them under the tree. One by one, we fold wings close to bodies and straighten cold necks. We treat each body with the same respect, be it a pigeon or a parakeet, a blackbird or a sparrow. When Karrion weeps silent tears onto the birds' feathers, I stand guard between him and the rest of the world; a witness to his grief.

We are covering the birds with the brightest leaves we can find when I notice Jamie's car stopping on the opposite side of the street. I step forward, putting myself between him and Karrion.

'Yannia, what happened?' Jamie asks as he jogs across the road.

The thought of having to explain everything to Jamie fills me with weariness, and I sway. Karrion is there straight away, hand supporting my elbow. I cast a grateful glance in his direction.

'We did it. Baneacre is dead and Lord Ellensthorne alive. Although,' I hesitate and regret washes over me, 'I don't think Amitta survived.'

Jamie rubs his face and nods. 'I'll call someone to check.'

'Lord Ellensthorne is upstairs. He'll tell you what happened. Do you mind if I fill you in on the rest tomorrow?'

'Sure. You look like you're dead on your feet.'

I flinch at his choice of words. 'You're not far off. Could you call us a cab? I'm in no shape to drive tonight.'

He does so. While we wait, I lock the sword in the boot of my car. When the taxi arrives, Jamie opens the door for me. Karrion gets in on the other side, placing one box between us and holding the other close to his chest. He has not said a word to Jamie.

'Call me tomorrow?' Jamie asks, and I nod. He closes the door.

I stand in Lady Bergamon's kitchen and watch as Karrion washes soil from his hands. He found me a pair of gardening gloves to wear to keep the bandages clean, but when I pull them off, I see that blood and pus have stained the fabric. Karrion also notices this and frowns.

'Maybe you ought to go to the hospital and get your hands looked at.'

'Tomorrow.' He opens his mouth to argue, but I silence him. 'I can't tonight. I just can't.'

'Fine. But first thing tomorrow. And promise you'll change the bandages before you go to bed.'

'I will. I saw some in the bathroom when I was looking for a plaster the other day.' It feels like a lifetime ago.

'Do you want me to stay here tonight?'

I consider the offer while I take in the paleness of his face and the red rims around his eyes. His mother will be shocked to see him in such a condition, but I believe he needs to be with his family tonight. I can survive a night alone.

'No. Go home. Your mum must be wondering what I've done with you.'

'Knowing her, she's hoping for honest labour and fewer piercings.'

'She's out of luck again.'

'That's nothing new.'

Despite his protests, I insist on calling him a taxi and paying for it. We wait for it together out on the street, silent but our shoulders touching. After a while, Karrion clears his throat.

'Hey, Yan?'

'Yes?'

'When you asked me to check the outside of Lord Ellensthorne's house with Jamie, did you know Baneacre was close?'

I hesitate, but truth wins out. Staring across the dark street, I nod.

'You sent me out of harm's way.'

'Yes.'

'Why? I could have helped.'

'Because even with two cold iron tokens in my hand, Pheonix's glamour still worked on me, although not completely. Baneacre was much stronger. Even with the sword, I had a hard time resisting his powers.'

'Maybe I could've created a distraction.'

'Remember a couple of weeks ago, when I told you and Jamie that I needed to be smarter about how I approach our cases, instead of rushing headfirst into danger?'

'Did you do that tonight?' Karrion asks.

'Yes and no. Do you know what the scariest part of confronting Melissa in that alley was? Knowing that there was little I could do to keep you safe.'

'Is this how it's going to be?' His voice trembles with barely concealed disappointment. 'At the first sign of danger, you'll send me away?'

'No. It means we need to have the means to defend ourselves. Had Thaylor made two swords, you would have been right there with me, taking on Baneacre.'

'Next time you start making swords with Kelpies, you better make sure you take me into account.'

I smile. 'Deal.'

When the taxi arrives, Karrion hugs me.

'Call me if you need anything,' he whispers in my ear.

'Right back at you.'

He gets in the taxi. I remain rooted to the spot long after the tail lights have disappeared around the corner. When I turn to look at the house, it no longer feels like the welcoming presence it once was, and it takes an effort to force my legs to move. As I close the door, I look back across the front garden and the dead plants filling the pots. At least the rain has stopped.

Upstairs, Lady Bergamon has not stirred. I stand just outside the circle for a long time, watching the shallow rise and fall of her chest. In the end, I allow the circle to remain. As much as I believe we have defeated Baneacre, it feels wrong to leave Lady Bergamon unprotected. I feed her the tonic, clean my hands as well as I can and get ready for bed.

As I kneel on the hearth stones, the silence of the house seems to echo the loneliness I feel, and I regret not asking Karrion to stay. Knowing that Wishearth will be looking over us through the flames does not seem enough, not tonight. I wish he would step out of the fire and hold me like he did earlier today. Karrion asked for his help and Wishearth came. But the words jam in my throat and refuse to go any further.

I light the end of the offering and say the only thing I can. 'It's over.'

SATURDAY

40

LIFE GOES ON

The pain in my hands keeps me hovering somewhere between asleep and awake. It is only in the early hours of the morning that fatigue finally drags me under and I slip into deep slumber.

Figures rise from the confines of my dreams. They take on the shapes of wolves and stoats, boars and hedgehogs, frogs and pond skaters, perch and trout, gulls and butterflies. I join them, and they lead me to a different land where cities and roads disappear and ancient woodlands creep across the fields and meadows. This is wilder country and I feel – recall – the thrum of magic in the soil, the plants, the very air.

We are not alone. Figures in blue robes gather around sacred stones. They chant, hands raised towards the sun and the stars. The trees and the winds respond to their call, while we bear silent witness. Theirs is a power we cannot fathom, and yet it comes from the same source as ours. They are allies, if not our kin.

Those that brought me here fade away, until I alone watch the figures dance round and round the stones. Were I to look closely enough, I know that the stones would bear runes I recognise, but cannot decipher.

A figure with hair the colour of freshly-tilled soil and blue eyes turns towards me. Garlands of flowers crown her head and coils of ivy run down her back. What passes

353

between us is an acknowledgement of trust and kinship that goes beyond our blood or breeding.

The voices of her companions give way to silence, and they retreat, leaving her alone on the dark clearing. A circle of wind, flame and light shimmers around her. She reaches for it with a single finger, and at the barest touch, the power fades away with the sigh of the land on a spring morning.

She is beginning to fade, her features and the flowers in her hair growing indistinct. I am drifting away, the magic that connected us severed. The last thing I see is her raising her arm in a greeting, not a goodbye.

I wake up to silence in the bedroom. The peaceful feeling the dream instilled in me lingers while I consider why the lack of sound should puzzle me. Then I realise that the subtle hum of the circle is gone, and I roll onto my side. Lady Bergamon's bed is empty, and the door to the corridor is open.

How much of the vision was a dream and how much a memory?

Rolling off the cushions, I intend to hurry downstairs, but the barest flex of my fingers awakens the fire of agony. Easing a fleece over my T-shirt is all I can manage before the pain leaves me breathless and I go downstairs barefoot.

Upon passing the lounge, I sense that a circle is no longer protecting the table. I look out the window by the front door and see that the residents of Ivy Street have converged outside, bin bags in hand as they remove the accumulated rubbish. Several are staring at the pots in front of Lady Bergamon's house. Relief washes over me at the sign that Baneacre's influence over Old London is lifting.

Habit directs me to the kitchen and the open back door. Sunlight is streaming through the windows and the steps are dry. Walking across the threshold, I brace myself for the disorientation of vertigo, but the effect is less than it has been for the past two days. I smile, and hope blossoms in my heart.

Lady Bergamon is standing on the edge of the patio, wearing a blue summer dress. Her toes are in the grass, and she is wiggling them, as if to reassure herself that the grass is still there. The table and the nearby creepers are still dripping water, but the sky above us is clear.

I need only to look around the patio to see the extent of the damage Baneacre inflicted on the garden. All the plants in the waterlogged pots are dead, and the flowerbeds along the fences on both sides of us contain nothing more than withered stalks. Even the grass is brown tufts sticking out of the mud, except around Lady Bergamon, where it has taken on the pale green appearance of spring grass.

Opening my senses to the garden, I am reminded of the first warm days after a long, cold darkness. The tide has not yet turned nor the deathly winter been defeated, but basking in the weak rays of the sun, I have every reason to be optimistic. When I look past the orchard, the wicker man is nowhere to be seen.

When I approach Lady Bergamon, I find that something of the dream remains with me. A greeting, an expression of relief, a dozen questions all die on my lips.

'We remember your kind,' I say instead, each word slow. It is as if someone is speaking through me; a memory of collective wisdom coming to life.

'What do you remember?' Lady Bergamon asks, her face angled towards the sun.

'You came to our woods, dressed in your blue robes and carrying your baskets. All hours of night and day you came, the sun and the moon and the stars guiding you, and we watched from the shadows. You only took what you needed and left no sign of your passing. Not like the humans, with their noise and stink and desire to cut things. You knew what it was like to live with things, rather than possessing them. Sometimes, you left something of your harvest for us to find and we would do the same with our kills.'

Lady Bergamon nods. 'We called you Spirit People, for you saw a world others couldn't. My mother taught me to respect your kind, but never fear you. We were kin, allies. But then the ships came, bearing foreigners with their shining armour and different language and pretence of civility. You hid and we died. The groves burned, the stones were broken, and we died.'

'The humans were always here. We always hid, for they never understood. They still don't, and although we hide less, it is easier to keep apart from the rest of the world.'

'Yet you found your way to the city and to my garden.'

I consider her statement, my head cocked. 'What has been and what is yet to be shape our paths. Sometimes a nudge from a spirit does the rest.'

Lady Bergamon chuckles, and my heart clenches. She was only unconscious for two days, and yet I have missed her wisdom and guidance.

'It appears Wishearth sent you to me as much for my benefit as yours.'

'And the rest we managed on our own,' I say with a smile.

Turning to me, she draws me into a hug. Her body holds wiry strength, but in the subtle tremor of her muscles, I feel how weak she has grown.

'Are you going to be okay?'

She steps back, and a cloud casts a shadow across her face. 'My garden will heal over time.'

The implication is clear: if the garden survives, she will too. But there are new lines etched on her face, and pain

356

simmers just beneath the surface of her eyes. I wish I could find the right combination of words and actions to heal her.

'You were brave, taking on a Fey,' Lady Bergamon says into the silence between us.

'I had no choice. He threatened us all.'

'There is always a choice. You could have decided that the fate of the city didn't concern you and returned to your kind.'

'Old London is my home. I could no more abandon it than I could abandon you.'

Her fingers stroke my cheek, rough and soft and smooth all at once. 'You risked a great deal.'

Before I have a chance to think of a reply, she continues speaking.

'I was there. Baneacre stole a part of me, and in doing so, joined a sliver of my awareness to his. I watched him kill and plot and, ultimately, die.'

'You saw that?' I recall my fear, my hesitation, my hatred, and shame heats my cheeks. My shoulders slump, and were it not for her touch anchoring me to her, I would turn away.

'Yes. I saw it all. You overcame every obstacle, external and internal.'

'I almost let him kill Lord Ellensthorne. And I even thought I'd be doing our community a favour.' Clenching my fists, I embrace the pain. 'But more than that, I killed Baneacre. He wasn't meat, I wasn't hungry, and yet I stood over him and pulled the trigger.'

'You had no choice.'

Shaking my head, I echo her words. 'There is always a choice. Several, in fact, though none of them good. And I chose to kill. I wanted to kill. Isn't that what the Winter Queen's hounds do?'

'You killed him to save lives, not to take them. That is

the difference between you and the hounds. The purpose driving you comes from protecting others rather than from the hunt. That you regret the course of action you had to take sets you further apart from the hounds.'

I incline my head to accept her words, though the memory of the Fey hunt lingers in my mind. What would it take for me to embrace the wildest parts of myself and become a creature driven by bloodlust and hunger?

But as I consider Lady Bergamon's words, something else falls into place and my breath catches.

'You said Baneacre stole a part of you. Is that why all the victims were connected to the Ivy Street Project?'

'He took my anger, determination and the darkest plans my mind could dream up, and turned them into reality. Those Mages died because of me. As much as I was determined to defend my garden, the suffering Baneacre caused was beyond anything I could have imagined. And he committed the murders using my magic.'

'It wasn't your fault,' I say, but the words sound hollow.

A single tear slides down her weathered cheek. 'Yes, it was. Without me, he would have killed others. But I singled out those Mages for him to target. That will be my burden to bear.'

I rest a hand on her upper arm, the angle awkward due to the bandages. She notices and frowns, taking my hand in hers. I gasp and shy away from her touch.

'You're injured.'

'I had to move Baneacre's body before it blew up Lord Ellensthorne's house. It burnt my hands.'

'Has anyone seen to the wounds?'

'I did my best with a first aid kit, but they feel worse this morning.'

'Come with me,' Lady Bergamon says.

At the back door, I hesitate. The outside of the lock remains a gaping hole. Lady Bergamon turns to look at me.

'Why did Baneacre break this lock?' I ask. 'In all the other houses he entered in Old London, there were no signs of forced entry.'

'Ordinary doors and locks do little more than slow down the Fey, especially an Autumn Champion like him. But this door is different. It's a barrier between realms, just like Bradán's watery gateway between my garden and the Unseen Lands. You must have realised by now that as much as my garden remains in Old London, this door is the only way to reach your version of the city. It took Baneacre a great deal more power to break through my protections than is evident upon this door.'

Lady Bergamon takes me inside and seats me at the kitchen table. Moving fast, she gathers supplies from various rooms, including a true silver bowl with familiar runes stamped around the edges. She steps outside long enough to fill a pitcher with water, setting it down on the table. Rather than sitting down next to me, she measures a small amount of white powder into a glass, adding in water and honey.

'Have you taken any medication today?' she asks.

'No.'

'Good.' She hands me the glass. 'Drink this.'

The taste of honey overpowers everything else, and the liquid slides down my throat in two long swallows. Only when I set the glass on the table do I notice a drawing of a poppy on the side of the jar Lady Bergamon left on the counter.

While I am distracted, Lady Bergamon takes my left wrist and unwraps the bandages before repeating the process with my other hand. The wounds are angry red, and the smell of decay wafting from them is strong enough that I gag. A frown appears between Lady Bergamon's eyebrows, but her face is otherwise impassive as she places my hands in the bowl and pours freezing water over them. The shocking cold eases the raging infection, and Lady Bergamon adds herbs from several jars.

'You'll need more than herbs to contain the infection. What did you do with my box of cold iron tokens?'

'It's on your dressing table. Though Karrion and I borrowed a couple of tokens, and I forgot to ask for them back last night.'

'No matter. They are easy enough to replace. Don't move.'

Lady Bergamon goes upstairs and returns with a handful of tokens and several rolls of bandages. She proceeds to soak my hands in different herbal concoctions, while the numbness of the liquid I drank separates me from the stinging of the wounds. When she smears a vile smelling salve over my hands, she whispers words in an unfamiliar language. The faintest brush of magic I sense is that of stars moving across the night sky, determining the rituals to be observed and the plants to be harvested. It startles me.

'You're not a Plant Shaman, are you?'

Lady Bergamon smiles. 'I've been called that for several centuries.'

'But you're something different?'

'Yes, though the name has been all but lost from the memories of people living on these islands.'

I open my mouth to pry further, but from the glint in her eyes, I know Lady Bergamon has revealed all she intends to. My curiosity will have to remain unsatisfied.

'You'll need to come back twice a day for me to redress the wounds,' she says and places cold iron tokens in between layers of bandages. 'And visit a doctor for a course of antibiotics. Between my magic, the tokens, and modern medicine, your wounds should heal fully.'

'Thank you.'

'I owe you a debt greater than all the healing in the world could repay.'

We share a smile, and Lady Bergamon tidies away the supplies. She pauses near the sink, the true silver bowl in hand, and cocks her head. I too catch a fleeting impression of the distant pounding of hooves. Time for me to leave.

'I guess I'll see you tonight,' I say, backing out of the kitchen.

Lady Bergamon forces her gaze from the back door and to my bandaged hands. 'Yes, indeed, my dear. Tonight.'

I turn away, smiling, as she hurries out. My imagination conjures the reunion of a woman and her lover, and part of me is tempted to follow her out so I might see it for myself. But the moment is not for me to witness. While I am able to resist the temptation, no will in the world can suppress the twinge of jealousy.

Stepping out of the Brotherhood of Justice, I angle my face towards the weak winter sun. Exhaustion weighs me down, and all the injuries I sustained yesterday add a discordant note to the background pain. After nearly two hours of giving my statement to the Paladins, I am glad to be outside. Despite all the questions, I got off easily. Lord Ellensthorne had done most of the explaining on my behalf. I never thought I would feel grateful for him.

'I'll buy you lunch,' Jamie says, as he zips up his coat. He sat with me during the interview, and his presence reassured me despite the new tightness he carries in his shoulders and along his jaw.

'Thanks.' I want to ask why, but he is already walking to his car.

We drive to the Magician's Head in silence. I watch him from the corner of my eye, but he keeps his attention fixed on the road. It is not until we walk through the pub door and receive an enthusiastic greeting from the owner that Jamie's frozen exterior thaws a little.

Given my bandaged hands, I order soup for lunch. Jamie carries our drinks to the table in a quiet corner, and without being asked, switches off the pink volcano. I offer him a smile, but it is deflected by the sadness in his eyes.

I know what I have to do. After a deep breath to steady my nerves, I launch into my story. I tell him everything I held back during the case, including the secret of Lady Bergamon's garden. The only time he speaks is when a waiter brings our food. By the time I have finished, Jamie is pushing salad around his plate and my soup is tepid.

'I'm sorry I didn't share this with you sooner,' I say when the silence has gone on too long.

He nods, but I cannot tell whether the stillness in him betrays anger or disappointment. It occurs to me that this may have been our first and last case consulting for the Met.

'What happened to Amitta?' I ask, setting my spoon down. The pain means I have little appetite.

'She was dead, just like you thought. Struck by lightning, though there was no sign of damage to anything else in the house. The Paladins found her inside the circle.'

'What about the Paladin that was guarding her?'

'Also dead. Her sword was blackened and twisted. She went down fighting.'

Would they still be alive if Karrion and I had stayed there? Or would Baneacre have attacked Lord Ellensthorne first? I will never know, just like I will never know whether the circle was ineffective, if Amitta cast it wrong, or if she didn't have time to cast it properly. In any case, Amitta and the Paladin were Baneacre's final victims. That knowledge is something else for me to carry.

'Do you know what will happen to the Ivy Street Project?'

'It's on hold while the companies find replacements for all the Mages. With new perspective, the project may be scrapped altogether. Even if it isn't, past experience indicates that it will take a long while before anything will happen. Your friend has obtained a reprieve, for now.'

I nod. Should the project ever come before the Council, I would like to think I will have some sway over Lord Ellensthorne.

'Are you done?' Jamie asks, pointing at my bowl. I nod again. 'I ought to get back to work.'

He pays and we return to the Brotherhood in silence. When we part ways, his goodbye is friendly enough, but I am left with a feeling that he has not yet decided what my revelations mean to us working together. The thought lingers in my mind, and I find myself second guessing every decision I have made over the past three days. Rather than heading to my empty house, I am in need of a friendly face and I drive to the Open Hearth instead.

I push open the door. The pub is busy, and I spot Funja carrying a tray of food from the kitchen. Everything is familiar, and yet I hesitate on the threshold, uncertain of my welcome. It is not the pub that has changed, but me. Too much guilt, pain and anger remain fresh in my mind.

A couple leaving forces me to move, and I stop by the bar to order a cola. Between Lady Bergamon's medicine and a busy morning, I am not in the mood for anything stronger.

When the bartender sets a glass next to me, I thank him and walk around the bar. Boris is lying on his bed by the fireplace, head held high in a pose rivalling the Sphinx, and Sinta is a ball of black and white fluff between his front feet. She whimpers in her sleep. Wishearth is waiting for me at his table, as I knew he would be, and we share a smile as I sit down.

'It's over,' he says and raises his pint.

I smile at his choice of words. 'Not a moment too soon.'

Wishearth's hot fingers touch the spot on my forehead where the Winter Queen kissed me, and a sliver of ice lances through me. I remember the frozen agony of her brand and I long to feel her lips on my skin again. Heat from Wishearth's touch intensifies, and the longing passes. The feeling of being the Winter Queen's pawn lifts.

'You paid a high price for protecting Lady Bergamon.'

'It wasn't just her that needed my help. The whole city would have been in trouble if a Fey had established a Court here.'

'But you didn't know that when you allowed a Kelpie to bear you into the water and beyond, did you? You didn't know that when you challenged a Fey.'

I dip my chin.

'You must know that loyalty and faith go both ways. Lady Bergamon and I have long memories.'

Something in his tone triggers a memory of the argument Karrion and I had next to a cold fireplace. Could Wishearth have heard Karrion's accusations and my jumping to his defence?

'We got there in the end.'

There is more I want to say, but a tugging by my feet draws my attention away from Wishearth. I look down to see Sinta hanging off my trouser leg, growling through her clenched teeth.

'Hey, don't do that.'

I reach down to pet Sinta, who gets distracted and lets go of my trousers. She twists around to scratch at her ear and then licks her paw.

Funja walks up to the table and rests a broad hand on my shoulder.

'It is time, *da*?'

When Sinta jumps up, I tickle her side. She rolls onto

her back, whimpering and growling, and something about the movement reminds me of the corgis I saw in the Unseen Lands. For a fleeting moment, I see her not as a puppy but as a Fey steed – my steed – and my resolve falters.

Wishearth's fingers stroke my wrist along the edge of the bandage, and the fear passes.

'She'll be good for you,' he says, flames in his eyes.

Funja picks Sinta up and places her on my lap. She wags her tail and burrows her nose in to my shirt. Without a conscious thought, I settle my hand over her back.

'I know.'

In a single afternoon, Sinta manages to turn my life upside down. She has an uncanny knack of finding everything she should not chew, peeing whenever I am not looking, and insisting on following me everywhere even though the stairs scare her and racing across my lounge is enough to tire her out. Funja gave me enough food to last a week, and I am grateful for that while I try to juggle cleaning up after Sinta, keeping the bandages dry and following Lady Bergamon's instructions.

My phone rings as I am giving Sinta her final meal of the night, and she lets out a sound that could be a bark or a howl. I shush her with a finger on her forehead and check the screen to see an unknown number.

'Hello?' I say and set Sinta's plate on the floor.

'Yannia.'

Dearon's voice sends a jolt through me, and the awkward grip I have on the phone loosens. I manage to catch it before it falls on the floor and bring it back to my ear.

'Dearon. This is unexpected.'

'You left me a message with the Shamans. I haven't visited the farms until today, which is why I didn't return your call before.'

A message? With a bit of prompting, his words trigger

a memory half-buried in a drunken haze. When I arrived home from serving food to the homeless in New London on the night of Samhain, I was feeling even lonelier than usual. Instead of going to bed, I opened a bottle of brandy. Now I recall I also rang the voicemail reserved for contacting the conclave and left a rambling message for Dearon. In hindsight, I am glad I cannot recall the precise details of it.

'Don't worry about it,' I say when I realise I have been quiet for too long. 'I've been busy with a case anyway.'

'I trust you were successful.'

His tone is formal, and I imagine the awkward way he is holding the phone. A smile lifts the corner of my mouth.

'I was. We were. Karrion was a big help, as usual.'

When he speaks, I can picture the frown on his face. 'I see.'

Lying down in front of the fire, I drape blankets over myself with my free hand. Sinta clambers onto the mattress and wiggles her way under the blankets until she is pressed against my side. Her presence next to me is comforting. I rub her belly, and her back foot beats an erratic rhythm against the mattress.

'So, how have you been?' I ask, and close my eyes. With the heat of the fire against my back and Dearon's voice in my ear, I find it easy to imagine him here with me. Under most circumstances, the thought would trigger immediate anxiety, but the loneliness within me overrides everything else. For this moment, safe in the privacy of my home, I allow myself to imagine a simpler future.

ACKNOWLEDGEMENTS

As ever, the biggest thanks go to Louise Walters and Team LWB: Jennie Rawlings, Leigh Forbes and Alison Jack. Your hard work and dedication turns my Word documents into books, and for that, I'm forever grateful.

For Andrew, who offers and receives the truth and only the truth every day. I would not be here without you. Even when the world crumbled around me, you remained my rock and my constant. Thank you.

For my family and friends, near and far, I love you and your support means the world to me. I can think of no greater encouragement than hearing my mother tell me she is proud of me.

I'm indebted to the kindness and generosity of Terry Lynn Empey, who was happy to answer endless questions about Samhain, magic and the casting of circles, and also to provide me with further avenues of research. I have taken liberties in this book and any mistakes in doing so are mine and mine alone.

In the past couple of years, I've been honoured and touched by the enthusiasm and kindness of bloggers and writers I've met on social media. I appreciate everyone who has written advance reviews, shared my posts and gushed over my characters. There are too many to mention by name, but know that I'm grateful to each and every one of you. The greatest compliment you can give to a writer is to ask what happens next.

Finally, as always, thank you to Sinta and Halla for being the wings of my heart.

FALLIBLE JUSTICE
Laura Laakso

"I am running through the wilderness and the wilderness runs through me."

IN OLD LONDON, WHERE paranormal races co-exist with ordinary humans, criminal verdicts delivered by the all-seeing Heralds of Justice are infallible. After a man is declared guilty of murder and sentenced to death, his daughter turns to private investigator Yannia Wilde to do the impossible and prove the Heralds wrong.

Yannia has escaped a restrictive life in the Wild Folk conclave where she was raised, but her origins mark her as an outsider in the city. Those origins lend her the sensory abilities of all of nature. Yet Yannia is lonely and struggling to adapt to life in the city. The case could be the break she needs. She enlists the help of her only friend, a Bird Shaman named Karrion, and